Endorsements

When the author initially invited me to read and enjoy her book and to consider endorsing it, I told her it would be an honor. That someone as kind hearted, caring and spiritually astute desired that I review her work, something that I know she had put a lot of heart and soul into…count me in. But then, I didn't need to get too far into the book when I felt honored to endorse it from a much deeper level, as it is a great read and a truly fine book. And the extent to which a story that would appeal to children, no less the kid inside of all, that is full of lessons on faith, hope and courage, is needed on the book shelf, then make space, and time, for this book.

The story also deftly handles another, no less important but less often touted virtue…acceptance. And the on-going need on any journey one embarks upon, such as life, to wisely identify what can be changed and what needs to be accepted as one goes along. The story elucidates how acceptance is not contrary to faith, hope, and courage, but rather when all working in concert, they strengthen and sharpen each other, not to mention the impact they have on he or she who wields them.

And as for love, it comes through in both the writing and the story it tells, and it provides both backdrop and active character throughout the book. I second the sentiment that Fran has shared with me on many occasions…Peace on Your Journey.
Kevin C. Elmore, MA*Psychotherapist, Masters in Clinical Psychology*

The story of Snowy and Elisha is a fascinating account of the love that a little boy has for the snowman that he has created. Many qualities that are important to always doing the right thing are emphasized throughout the book. Perseverance, forgiveness, sacrifice, kindness, love, and wisdom are but a few of the characteristics that are found in the various creatures that Elisha meets during his adventure while trying to find Snowy. The young lad ends up in a world where he is tested to the point of physical and mental exhaustion but is aided at the right time by special animal friends, who meet his needs in very unusual and special ways. Throughout the book Elisha is growing in understanding as he sees his animal friends often sacrificing for him. He reaches a point where he has to make a decision that is prompted by real love which helps him to know what he must do.

This book, <u>The Best Snowmen Have A Heart</u>, contains many well described characters that the reader will enjoy meeting. Weaved throughout the story are adventures that face Elisha and many of his animal friends. The author creates a number of characters with interesting personalities which this boy meets along the way as he struggles to find his friend. This well written fantasy is guaranteed to hold one's interest from beginning to end as it portrays the trials and triumphs of life.

Paul Palpant
Lenawee Christian School
Elementary Principal, Retired

In reading The Best Snowmen have a heart I found an enchanting and delightful adventure which spoke to my heart about a young boy and his love for his snowman. In truth, it touched my heart, and will do so for all ages who embrace laughter, rely on hope and inner healing, and celebrate love. A great read!

Cathy Jenkins
Certified Massage Therapist; Board Member of Christian Mission, Incorporated

Never give up Hope ! There's not just Light at the end of the tunnel, that Light is with you as you use Faith & Trust in God to get you through. God bless you !

THE BEST SNOWMEN HAVE A HEART

A Snowy Tale of When Hearts Speak Louder Than Words

Frances L. Sneed

Frances L. Sneed
12 - 23 -17
Philip. 4:8, Rom. 8:28

The Best Snowmen Have A Heart
A Snowy Tale of When Hearts Speak Louder Than Words
by Frances L. Sneed

Printed in the United States of America.

ISBN 9781498494038

To contact the author: www.franceslsneedauthor.com

www.xulonpress.com

Table of Contents

Dedication

To God, The Author of my faith and inspiration
To my treasured family, especially:
Christy, Nick, Zachary, Kaylynn, and Zoey, who flood my
life with joy;
Larry, who loves me still after all these years;
My cherished parents, James and Helen Vance, who provided
unconditional love and a strong Christian foundation for my
brother, Jim, and myself;
And last, but not least:
To children everywhere with hearts
Big enough—to hold love unreservedly,
Pure enough—to embrace faith, and
Sincere enough—to spark our own hearts
to once again believe and love wholeheartedly.

Preface

*W*hile working at Tecumseh Acres Elementary School, I desired to make learning dictionary skills more fun, so I wrote a Snowman Language Dictionary of silly words and phrases I imagined snowmen might use. Deciding a story about snowmen was needed to capture the students' imagination, I waited a year or so for inspiration.

After fleshing out the basic snowman story in 2013-14, I thought I was finished, but inspirations for new characters and scenes came in 2015. At the same time, I realized a new vision had replaced the simple "fun" tale. No longer was it just about a boy who has exciting adventures while looking for his snowman. While adventures still abound, the main character, without his knowing it, is being led on a path that could potentially heal his damaged emotions.

My goal, in addition to writing a highly entertaining story, became one to hopefully inspire people to let go of past disappointments and hurts. Although it had not been my original intention, my story had unexpectedly developed into healing messages for hurting souls, with a strong thread of "letting go" running throughout the story. That is why I believe that, surely, God had His hand in this writing.

2015 was spent editing with a professional editor. In 2016 I refined, tweaked and re-edited this story. God has taught me so much through this process and His hand has led me all the way. Each delay in publishing turned out to be for the best. I finally rested the timing in God's hands. My prayer is that it will be in the reader's hands at just the right time for each of them.

Introduction

*T*his is a wintry story, not of ice and cold but about the warmth and power of deep love, born in a moment, but alive for an eternity. Such love eventually wins against all odds, triumphing through sheer persistence. Giving courage when there is none, it defies the rules of time, physics and probabilities and is willing to go the extra measure of sacrifice, as happens in this story. In the story the main character, Elisha, is unwilling to accept the normal laws of the universe because the pain of reality would be too great. His deep, dogged devotion powers him through countless trials and adventures.

I wrote "The Best Snowmen Have a Heart" to delight children who, with childlike faith, dare to believe the impossible can happen. But I intended it as well for adults who have become so immersed in a painful experience, they've lost faith. I believe this fantasy illustrates that *our lives need not be bound or defined by our losses, but strengthened and deepened by them.*

Accepting the realities of life can be hard for any age. Sometimes we wish to escape hard realities, like Peter Pan did in Neverland, where children never grow up. Some dream that by believing hard enough, as Elisha did, perhaps we could stop something we love from ending. While enjoyable in a story, that kind of childish belief and refusal to let go of the past in reality stymies our ability to move on to greater joys and rewards. Such souls remain stuck in their pain.

In the real world, people do grow old and die. Things do change or end. Disappointments do come. How do those who have hardened their hearts because they fear more pain move on? I am hopeful that this story will serve to reignite faith to do so and thereby help restore lost hope.

Fantasy and fun were used to teach vulnerable children truths about life and afterlife. It is my hope that adults can use this book to guide the young ones in understanding difficult subjects of life, and thereby obtain help for themselves also.

Elisha, having built his own belief system that his snowman would last forever, is shattered in spirit when reality hits. At the end of his many adventures he is faced with making the hardest choice of his young life. At one time or another, we all face the choice of letting go. It is sometimes easier when we do it out of love for another than it is for ourselves alone.

I also find it disturbing that the world surrounding our children bombards them with mixed and inappropriate messages, often rocking them too early out of childhood innocence. Because our entertainment (television, videos, and movies) often present Evil as more exciting than Good, I've endeavored to show that Goodness and Purity are wonderful and reap great rewards, that Evil is to be shunned, and that embracing Faith empowers us to live richer, fuller, victorious lives.

Some healing truths included in a way that, hopefully, children can understand are these:

Faith is much more than just believing; it is spiritual equipment that we must use to empower us in life. It reminds us that we are never alone in our hurt, unless it is of our own choosing, for a loving God is watching over us, offering us strength in every trial.

Never meant to live defeated lives, we were created with the capacity to triumph over our losses and disappointments. To not do so, was never in God's plan. Through Faith we can overcome mountains of difficulties and see Hope shining through every darkness.

We are not just flesh and bones but also a spirit needing nurturing as much or more than our physical bodies. What we feed on, lean on and trust in makes all the difference, for good or bad.

The quality of our thought life makes a difference in our mental, emotional, and physical health. Dwelling on the past, the losses, the hurts, or the wrongs that have been done to us, causes destructive forces to set upon us and steal the joy from our lives. As instructed in Philippians 4:8, thinking on things that are noble, just, pure, lovely and of good report, is preventive medicine and should be modeled and taught to our children. It is freeing to let go, forgive, and look ahead to better things with a song in our hearts.

God created us to make choices. Like the snowmen in Snow Land, we must choose to put away the "old" and put on the "new." Whether it's letting go of hurts, former habits or lifestyles that steal our present joy or learning to love selflessly, a choice must be made. The old ways need not enslave and hold us back; our God, through Jesus Christ, will break those chains, heal and empower us to move forward to new life in Him. It is up to us, however, to believe in Him more than we hold onto our hurts or old ways. It is also my hope that parents and teachers can, by using the main character's experiences, discuss subjects including dying and eternal life, in a less scary way.

Finally, it has been my strong desire that this would be a vehicle that adults will use for "together" time. Busy adults and highly scheduled children don't get enough together time. We are also in a media age, where our devices are often supplanting talking with each other, even our children! I noticed this once in a restaurant, where I observed a mother who, though she loves her child, spent the entire meal using her phone texting, scarcely talking to the elementary age child.

Children need our undivided attention, free from texting and other diversions, where the child knows he or she is number one with that parent. Whether at bedtime or in the classroom, it is my fervent hope that both children and adults alike will find "The Best Snowmen Have a Heart" to be an unforgettable story that heals, enlightens, entertains and promotes bonds through quality time together.

Prologue

Fear in the Dark

*E*lisha took a deep breath and tried not to think of all of Owl's warnings. Whatever lay ahead, this seemed bad enough. Having always had a deep fear of the dark, here he was, not only crossing through Big, Dark Woods alone, where he could barely see right in front him, but... What was that?

His head snapped around toward the noise... it sounded like—something walking and breaking twigs! He dared not imagine what it could be, but—oh, no! He gasped as a small shaft of light revealed the dark outline of a huge body! He would just hold very still, hoping the creature wouldn't see him. Frozen, he watched it creeping ever so slowly among the trees, its size alone stunning Elisha's brain to an unthinking blob. Barely able to breathe, he watched it crouch to the ground and begin circling him in the underbrush.

Elisha suddenly felt very small and very alone. Afraid to watch, but more afraid to look away, Elisha began to turn with the beast, his heart racing at what was happening now—Stalking. That animal is stalking something, but what? Oh, God, please—don't let it be me!

Abruptly the movement stopped. Elisha held his breath, waiting for what would happen next, wishing it would go away... After a moment the sounds began anew. Quickly he realized the unknown creature was no longer circling, but was coming directly toward him!

In total panic, he wanted to run as fast and as far away as he could, but his feet were frozen in fear. Even worse, he was becoming hypnotized by the creature's yellow eyes. They blazed through the dark at him, so that he could only stand and stare back in horror.

The large predator, having left the deep shelter of the woods, now crept forward through the few trees left between them. The creature patiently closed in on his helpless prey.

Quick, Elisha, the desperate boy thought, you've got to think of something! His eyes darted wildly around looking for an escape, but there was none. No way could he run through the tangled undergrowth of the woods without tripping. Besides, if he ran at all, this outsized creature would have him in one leap.

All thoughts of escape evaporated in an instant as a low, threatening growl began. With trembling body, Elisha slowly turned towards the sound. Now that it was closer, he could see his greatest fear. Its body shape, bared teeth, long fangs and vicious snarl made it clear—this was a grey wolf—enormous in size, and apparently, hungry! As the wolf crept ever closer, the boy's fright trapped him in a vicious squeeze.

Suddenly his blue eyes burst open in astonishment when, without warning, the five-foot-long animal morphed – to one that was at least eight feet or more in length! Unable to believe what was happening and barely able to breathe, Elisha became utterly desperate. There seemed no way to save himself, but how could he just stand here without a fight?

***

Indeed, looking back to his beginnings, one could ask *how could a young boy, so loved and so sheltered from danger to this point, have ended up in such a dangerous situation, with only one obvious outcome?*

Although we begin here with a threat to his end, Elisha's beginning was years earlier in the rural countryside of Michigan...

Born to a couple who had waited many years for a child, Elisha Zachary Winters' life had been filled with joy, laughter, and much love. Christy Beth and David Winters lived in their restored farm-house, nestled snuggly between Michigan farms and fields, with a barn to play in, a creek for wading, and trees to climb.

The only thing lacking was close neighbors with children for playmates, but Elisha was a bright, imaginative boy who knew how to make the best of things, whether he had friends over or not. His parents wisely surprised him on his fifth Christmas, with a border collie puppy. Elisha named her Mollie and she seemed to fill his need for a companion, until one winter, the most incredible thing in his life happened...

Chapter One

The Best Snowman Ever

When does a snowman become "real," when built by human hands or when he is loved into existence?

*W*hat could possibly be better than a No School Day? A Snow Day! At least that's what Elisha was thinking when his mom called up the stairs to let him know. He raced to his upstairs bedroom window and looked eagerly out onto the yard below. A big grin spread across his young face.

"Oh, yeah! That's what I'm talkin' about!" he said, for everything was covered with a good five inches of snow. "Just look at that, Mollie!" The border collie lab cocked her head from side to side trying to understand, but as she picked up on his excitement, she barked in answer.

Maybe she did know that her master, Elisha Winters, the boy who was crazier about snow than any boy in Michigan, (or possibly anywhere else for that matter) was ready to go build his forever snowman with his dad.

Having waited so long for a good deep snow, Elisha could hardly wait to get started. He rushed to dress, knowing his dad would already be waiting for him, since he loved snow almost as much as Elisha did. In fact, the whole Winters family became excited every time a snowfall began. Barely finishing his last button, he yelled, "Let's go, Mollie!"

The two ran downstairs, he, yelling for his dad, and Mollie barking in excitement as Elisha finished the last few feet sliding down the old farmhouse banister. As soon as he landed, he flew through the kitchen where his dad was having coffee and headed straight into the mud room.

"Dad!" he called, "Did you see? We can finally make the best snowman ever!"

He was grabbing his warm coat and snow pants when he realized his dad hadn't answered him. "Dad? Aren't you coming? This is what we've been waiting for. Did you see outside?" Not hearing an answer, Elisha came back into the kitchen.

"Yes, I saw. I'm sorry, son. We'll have to wait till tonight. You're off school, but I have to work," he said sadly.

"Aw, Dad!" the boy groaned in disappointment.

His dad's eyes softened as he saw Elisha's crestfallen face. He remembered how Elisha had watched endlessly at the window the last two winters for snow. He also recalled how once, when he had mentioned to Elisha that he couldn't wait for enough snow for a snowball fight, the boy had answered wistfully, "Dad, I just wanna build a snowman."

"Listen, son. Why don't you go ahead and start without me? It looks like good packing snow. It should make a great snowman—"

"Really, Dad?" Elisha interrupted. "You don't mind? I'll make the best ever. You'll see!" And in a flash Elisha was ready and out the door.

His parents looked at each other and burst out laughing. "Looks like we're going to find out if he remembers how to do it himself," David said.

They had started a family tradition of building a snowman together as soon as Elisha had been old enough. Michigan's weather had usually supplied plenty of snow, but not for the last two years.

"He'll do it. You know how determined he is," Beth said with that knowing "mom" look.

"You're right. He may surprise us both. See you tonight, honey. I'll try to get home early," David said as he left.

Backing the car out of the drive, David paused to watch the son he'd waited for so long.

Elisha was already packing a ball together for the base. David sighed. Disappointed he could not join him, he still was happy for his boy. When Elisha heard Dad's goodbye honk, he stopped and waved, proudly pointing to his start of a snowman. David gave a proud thumbs up out the window and left for work, but his son's work was just beginning.

Elisha eagerly started rolling the ball in the snow. The small boy huffed and puffed as the ball grew ever larger for the base. With every roll he said, "The best... snowman... ever!... Best snowman... ever!" Eventually it was so big he couldn't move it anymore, which meant, his snowman's home would be right there in the back yard.

Before starting to roll a second, smaller ball for a nice roly-poly belly, he stopped to rest. As he did, Mollie began barking insistently for attention. Taking up the chase and running after the dog until he was out of breath, he eventually fell to the ground to rest. Instead he made a snow angel and challenged Mollie to make one, too, but she just romped around him, barking and biting at the snow. "Guess you don't feel like an angel today, huh, Mollie?"

Upon hearing her name, Mollie began barking, ready to play again. After chasing each other some more they finally stopped again for a real rest. "We sure have lots of fun, don't we, girl?" Elisha said with a happy sigh as he petted his friend. Mollie gazed at him, tongue hanging out of her mouth and brown eyes shining. She was ready to romp again, but Elisha knew he couldn't if he was ever going to finish. "You see, Mollie, I still have a lot of work if I'm going to make my snowman the best, one that will last forever," he explained, as Mollie cocked her head back and forth trying to understand.

He resumed his work and began rolling the ball for the snowman's belly. When it was just right, he tried lifting the belly ball into place, but quickly found it to be a lot heavier than he expected. "Whoa, Mr. Snowman, what have you been eating? Your belly weighs a ton!" Elisha joked. "Oh, sorry, I forgot. You can't answer until you have a head and a mouth. But before that, you need your belly."

At first try he failed to budge the belly ball. Unable to see how he could possibly lift it alone, he thought of calling his mom for help, but he wasn't ready to give up. So with one more big deep breath and a lot of groaning and grunting, he lifted the second ball into place. Elisha patted more snow around the belly to secure it, then stepped back to look. So far, so good, he decided, and began rolling the smallest ball for the head.

Elisha had just set the head in place when his mom called him in for lunch. Just like a mom would, she spotted his wet pants and insisted he take them off so she could toss them into the dryer as he ate.

"Aw, Mom!" he moaned, but he obediently removed his wet things to slip on dry sweat pants. Suddenly realizing how hungry he was, he practically inhaled his soup.

"Slow down, Elisha!" his mom told him. "That snowman's not going anywhere." Looking out the window, she added, "It looks like you're doing a fine job."

"Mom, he will be the best, ever," Elisha answered.

With lightning speed he dressed once again in his snow gear and headed for the door. Suddenly he skidded to a stop. "Oh, Mom! My snowman needs a face!"

With a smile she pointed to the counter where she had already laid out two black coat buttons for the eyes, a lighter, round one for a nose, a skinny piece of roping trim for a mouth, and his dad's old, but still handsome plaid scarf. As he admired the pieces, she added a soft knit hat with smooth, white fur trim for a hat.

"Oh, Mom! You're the best!" Elisha shouted gleefully as he gave her a hug.

She teasingly corrected him. "Oh, but I thought your snowman was the best."

With a grin and an, "Aw, Mom," he carefully deposited the items into his pocket and headed for the door with Mollie close behind him.

Elisha got back to work with only one thing in mind—to build the best snowman ever, which would be one that would last forever. That's what he'd been wishing for since he was four, when he'd first wished for a million snowmen for his birthday and was surprised not to find them. How silly to want a million snowmen, when one forever snowman would be perfect! He was sure glad he'd grown up.

After adding the face pieces and scarf, he stood back to get a good look. Grinning from ear to ear, he proudly admired the finest snowman he'd ever seen. The finishing touches had given his snowman real personality.

As he continued to stare, it seemed as if his snowman began to return his happy grin! He felt as if a special connection had kicked in between them, unlike any other snowman; of course, it was the first he had ever built by himself. Now, to think up a really good name for this new friend...

"Elisha, come in and warm up," his mom's voice called, shaking him out of such thoughts. "Coming, Mom!" he called.

Once inside, Elisha excitedly told her all about the snowman he had just finished. "He really is the best, Mom. His face looks great! I wanted to give him real snow arms and hands, but they kept falling off, so I found some little branches under the maple trees for arms and they look great. Dad's not going to believe that I did all this myself," he added proudly.

Mollie barked twice. "Yes, girl, you tried to help, too," he said, laughing and patting her affectionately on the head.

"You can show your dad when he comes home," his mom reassured him, "but right now, you need to get warm and dry and then you can rest till supper."

Still excited, Elisha bounded up the stairs to his room where he changed into warm, dry clothes, all the time thinking about what his dad was going to say. Once dressed, with Mollie on the floor beside him, he sat down by the window and looked out contentedly on his man of snow.

"This is the best day ever!" he said with a happy sigh. Feeling warm and wonderful inside, he pulled his feet up into the armchair. In no time, his eyes became heavy as his tired body grew warm and relaxed. Soon, he was curling up for a delicious nap. Just before dozing off he mumbled, "Finally... a forever snowman."

Chapter Two

Fun and Trouble

*T*he weatherman was predicting another front moving into southeast Michigan as David came home from work. Neither parent heard it as they greeted each other.

"Hi, honey. Did you see the new family member out back?" asked Beth.

"I sure did. He's a pretty good-sized one, too. Somebody must have been really tired," he commented.

"Oh, yes. He worked all day on that snowman! I think he's still napping in his room."

Anxious to praise Elisha for all his hard work, David hurried up the stairs to his room where he paused in the doorway. "Hey, buddy! There's a new sculpture out back. Know anything about that?"

"Dad!" Elisha answered, waking immediately upon hearing his father's voice. "Did you check him out yet?" he asked, stretching.

"No, I wanted to wait for you to show me. We'd better go quickly, before it gets too dark."

"Sure, Dad, let's go!" Elisha yelled, already halfway out his bedroom door, racing to the mudroom.

Barely grabbing his coat as he flew out the back door, Elisha reached the snowman first. He looked over the man of snow as he waited for his dad. Elisha filled with great pride as his dad joined him and rested a hand on his shoulder.

"He's got real personality, Elisha!"

Elisha looked at his dad and agreed softly. "Yeah, he sure does, doesn't he?" As his eyes returned to the snowman, he felt his heart warming even more toward this snow friend with personality. The snowman had a wonderful smile, but there was something poignant about him that pulled on the strings of Elisha's heart.

His dad's playful voice jolted him out of his thoughts. "So you think you make a better snowman than I, huh?" he challenged.

"No, but he is really good and strong. I think he's the best ever, don't you, Dad?" Elisha asked sincerely.

"I think this one's the best, Elisha, cause you built him yourself," Dad agreed, then added, "You built him with love, didn't you, son?"

"Sure did, Dad!" Elisha chirped proudly.

"And if you were a rooster, you'd crow, right?"

"Yep!" the young boy agreed, not sure what a rooster crowing had to do with building a snowman. But Elisha, so happy his dad was proud of him, let out a little crow anyway. Maybe he'd feel silly with anyone else, but not with his dad. Getting into the rooster spirit, his dad joined him with his own crow of pride and they ended up laughing heartily.

"Come on, Elisha. It's getting dark! I'll race you back!" his dad called, taking off towards the house. Elisha raced ahead and made a big show of reaching the porch first, pausing to taunt, "You lose, Dad!" With his dad close on his heels, Elisha bolted inside where he announced, "Here we are at Mama Mia's Pizza Place!"

David looked at Beth, teasing in his best Italian accent, "Well-a, Mama Mia! Need-a little spice-a for the pizza?" Motioning towards Elisha, he added, "I've gotta little squirt-a here-a for ya!"

"Oh, yeah? You gotta catch me first, Papa Mia!" Elisha dared, but his mom made a stop sign with her hands. "Okay, you two. No racing in the kitchen. Settle down and wash up for Mama Mia's pizza," Beth ordered good naturedly. They didn't argue, for the aroma of garlic and yeast in the kitchen was calling them loudly.

Beth smiled at her two hungry "boys" as they quickly washed their hands. They were like two peas in a pod, playfully bumping into each other at the sink. They finally finished washing and started to race to the table. "Hey, you two!" she called. Immediately halting as they remembered their manners, they settled down to walk like perfect saints to the table, where they ended the silliness with another hearty laugh as they sat down.

"Good thing you made it to the table," she said. "You two couldn't have made it much farther without losing those haloes of yours!"

Both parents joined hands with Elisha as David humbly gave thanks for God's blessings and for homemade pizza and salad. As his dad said, "Amen," Elisha quickly added, "And thanks, Lord, for enough snow to build my snowman today. Amen."

Before beginning to eat, Elisha and his dad began their weekly contest. Each took turns to see whose cheese would stretch the farthest as they picked up their pizza slices loaded with melted cheese. Elisha's stretched out several inches before breaking and, as usual, David's came up shorter. "You win again!" moaned his dad.

"Yep! I'm the King of Moz-za-rella!" Elisha proclaimed in a sing song voice before adding, "Bow down, subjects!"

His parents stifled a smile while giving an exaggerated bow of their heads towards him. Elisha accepted his royal treatment and then turned to give Mollie some attention.

After they finished eating, David turned on the radio for the weather report: "Tomorrow an unseasonably warmer front with rain will be coming in from the southwest and this accumulation of snow will be quickly gone. It could be quite a mess, with danger of flash flooding."

Out of concern for Elisha, David quickly turned off the radio. Without a word, he and Beth looked at each other, wondering if he had heard. The boy was too busy, however, to hear the message of doom for his snowman as he was finishing up his drink and talking to Mollie.

Later, his dad hung behind as Elisha took off upstairs to get ready for bed. "Honey, do you think we should say something to prepare Elisha about what will happen?"

"I don't know. It didn't bother him when his other snowmen melted," Beth said.

"But he was much, much younger. Back then it was all about our doing it together. Elisha may find it hard to lose the first snowman he made himself," David theorized, pulling from memories of his own disappointment when his first snowman melted away.

"Talk to him," Beth encouraged. "You always seem to know what to say."

David walked slowly to Elisha's room, where the boy was already snuggled in and waiting. Elisha had such a contented look on his tired face.

"Good day, huh, buddy?" his dad asked, pulling the covers up under his son's chin.

"You betcha, Dad. Are you really, really surprised I did such a good job on Snowy?" asked Elisha.

"Snowy?" asked Dad.

"Yep. Had to give him a name. He's the best, Dad, and I made him to last forever," he declared. "He can, can't he? I made him extra strong."

"What if he doesn't, Elisha? I mean, what if he doesn't last forever?"

"Oh, but, Dad, he has to last. I made him really sturdy, like you showed me. Then I packed extra snow between his bottom and his belly. He's really, I mean, really strong!" declared Elisha emphatically. "So he has to last!"

"Well, son, you know even people don't last forever. And Snowy is just made out of, well... snow." He looked at his son thoughtfully then added, "The weatherman said it's getting warmer the next few days."

Elisha lay very still as he waited for what his dad would say next. He had a funny feeling in the pit of his stomach.

"Remember what happened to our other snowmen?" his dad continued.

"Kind of," Elisha answered quietly.

"Do you remember?"

"Dad," Elisha yawned, "I'm really tired. I need some sleep."

"I can see why. You had a big day. Time to say goodnight prayers, Elisha. Dear Lord," David began, "thank You for the great day Elisha had, and most of all, thank You for the one thing we know always lasts forever... your love for us. Elisha?"

"Dear God, thank You for my mom and dad, for the super day I had and, Jesus, that You love me. And please, watch over Snowy. Oh, and Mollie, too. Amen!" Elisha ended confidently.

"Goodnight, son," David whispered as he hugged Elisha.

"Goodnight. And Dad... I *did* make Snowy super, super strong," Elisha insisted, very quietly.

"Snowy, huh?" asked Dad, referring to the name again.

"Yep. He is made out of snow, so... Snowy!" Elisha added proudly.

"Yes, that's the problem, son," Dad muttered to himself as he left the room and closed the door quietly. "He is made out of only snow."

Elisha turned over in bed, but he didn't close his eyes. Having heard his dad's last words, he stared at the wall in the dark for a long time.

Chapter Three

When Hearts, Rain, and Tears Fall, Hearts Rain Tears

*T*he next morning, the sun peeked over the horizon as if teasing whether to come up or not, but then streaked a bright pink across the sky. As David left for work, he noticed he didn't really need to fasten his coat and that thankfully, Snowy was still standing. He also noticed that the cold, crunching sound of snow was missing from his footsteps and under the tires of the car backing out. He shook his head sadly, for that was a bad sign for Elisha's snowman today.

Upstairs, outside Elisha's window, a blue jay squawked loudly, instantly awakening the young boy. As quickly as his eyes flew open, his feet hit the floor and he raced to the window to look out. Elisha strained in the early morning light to see across the yard. Then he smiled. Ah, there was his Snowy waiting quietly.

"I knew it!" he cried in great relief. "I'll be down soon, Snowy! I knew I made you strong enough! I just knew it."

Elisha barely noticed what he ate for breakfast. "Can I go out now?" he asked, swallowing his last bite of oatmeal and gulping the last of his milk.

"Make sure you've brushed your teeth first," his mom reminded him. "And… don't rush!" she called after him. He ran to the bathroom where, although he did brush, he forgot to use toothpaste. His mom called to him to make his bed and do his chores. He groaned but obeyed, doing them as quickly as possible. By the time he finished and dressed for the day, the sun was already up and beating down like in midsummer.

Hurrying back downstairs Elisha grabbed his coat and was out the kitchen door, running to the back of the yard, where he suddenly stopped. His whole morning so far had been one big rush, bringing him to this critical moment.

His brow wrinkled anxiously as he looked. There he was, his best snowman ever, staring strangely at him with cold black eyes. Snowy appeared somewhat sad. "It's okay, Snowy. I'm here," he comforted his creation as he began to pack a little more snow around the edges of where the belly met the snowman's bottom. There, that should help, but the snow didn't feel right. His gloves were already soaked.

"Oh, well," he spoke out loud to counteract the nagging feeling deep inside him. "The wetness will make your body icy and stronger. It'll be okay, Snowy," he said reassuringly.

As Snowy seemed to stare back at him, Elisha noticed the black eyes appeared to be slightly running. Though momentarily startled, Elisha shook off his concern. After all, he told himself, snowmen don't cry; they're made out of snow.

Nevertheless, he grabbed more snow to pack around the snowman's belly. As he knelt and packed, melting drops began to escape slowly from the mushy eyes of the softening white face. Like tears they fell from above, onto the back of Elisha's hands as he worked to fix the snowman. When he rose up, icy bits of sleet began to sting his face and eyes, but he thoughtlessly brushed them away.

"Come on, Mollie, let's go in!" he called, running clumsily through the slushy snow. As he lost footing and almost fell twice, Mollie romped around him barking, thinking it was all a game. "Yeah, easy for you, Mollie. You don't have these big boots on your feet!" he observed.

Although Elisha didn't understand the meaning of all these signs, as predicted it had already begun warming up to a rainy spell.

Full Clouds Rain Drops

Shortly after, the sleet changed to a steady, gentle rain. Beth looked grimly out at Snowy. Her boy was about to learn a hard lesson of life, and she feared he was not quite ready for it. Listening to him talk and watching him check all morning to see if the rain had stopped, she noted he seemed to have such an emotional connection with this snowman.

"I'm going back out, Mom, 'kay?" Elisha asked, grabbing his coat and boots.

"Not now, son. It's still raining," she said, trying to sound matter of fact about it.

"I like the rain, Mom," he said, but seeing his mom's face he sighed, "Oh, okay."

How the rain and warmer temperature might affect his snow sculpture was not what was on Elisha's mind. Rather, he was mulling over how differently he felt about this snowman. Snowy wasn't just "any" snowman to him; he was special. After all, he had made Snowy himself, with his own two hands.

After lunch the rain stopped. Elisha dashed eagerly out the door, but he found romping through the yard had become a lot harder. The snow made a sucking sound at his boots with each step, for it was more slush than snow now, but Elisha paid no attention to what that might mean.

From the kitchen window, Beth watched as Elisha and Mollie trudged toward the snowman. She shook her head slowly, knowing what they would find.

At first, getting through the slush without falling was so hard, that Elisha laughed more and more—especially at Mollie, who was also struggling. Now as the two of them neared the snowman enough to see him, his laughter drained away from the inside out. Coming to a rock solid stop, he stood still, slowly sizing up his snow friend.

At first glance, the snowman just looked very sad and alone, but then something more seemed wrong. Elisha wondered if he had grown or if Snowy was shrinking. "No," he reassured himself, as he turned and walked away, "I must be on one of those growing spurts

Mom talks about. Yep, that must be it," he repeated as he and Mollie went back inside. It had already begun to rain again.

Snowy stared blankly after the departing boy with a drooping mouth. One black eye began slipping out of place. Slowly it slid, until it dropped and splashed into the growing puddle at his feet. As the rain gently peppered down on it, the lone button eye stared up blankly—small, black and strangely out of place.

A Broken Heart Rains Tears

Inside, Elisha and Mollie were busy playing tug of war. Before he knew it, it was the end of the day and he heard the garage door opening. Excitedly he ran to meet his dad.

"Dad, you're home!" Elisha shrieked. "Let's go make Snowy a big brother, okay?"

David gave his son a serious look. "I don't know about that, son."

"But, Dad, you're home from work early and you said we'd spend time together today."

"Well, Elisha, I've got the time, but..." David searched for a gentle explanation as he hung up his hat and coat. "Remember last year, how we said the snow has to be good packing snow?"

Elisha nodded.

"Well," David ventured slowly, "this snow won't pack anymore. It's too slushy."

"Oh, it's okay, Dad. I just patted more onto Snowy this morning, you know, around his belly and sides. It'll be okay," he said, pulling on his dad's arm. By now, Elisha was leaning back on his heels as he tried to pull him towards the back door. His dad refused to move. Elisha dropped his dad's arm and looked at him quizzically, not understanding.

"Son, it won't work," his dad said sadly.

Elisha's face took on a look of panic. "Yes, it will. I'll show you!" he insisted as he grabbed his coat and ran furiously out the door. David put his coat on again and slowly followed. He watched as Elisha fought to get through the slush to his best snowman, where he came to an abrupt stop. The boy appeared very small and vulnerable to his father, who watched.

Elisha could only stare in horror as he saw his snowman was disappearing. Both of Snowy's eyes were gone. Searching quickly for them, he saw they were sunk into the puddle. Rapidly he picked them up and stuck them back in, but the snow was so wet one of the buttons pushed in too far, giving the snowman a sunken, dead-eye look. The snowman's mouth, no longer grinning, drooped down unevenly. This sad, melting man he saw didn't even look like Snowy anymore. Elisha found it hard to accept the cruel picture or its meaning.

Quietly he circled the snowman to check him out further. Snowy was missing an arm, which Elisha quickly retrieved from the snowman water and stuck back into his side. The branch stuck straight out for only a moment, then slid to a downward slant.

Elisha could see that the snowman was now definitely shorter and his chin had sort of merged into his scarf.

As Elisha continued to find more things wrong, he looked for snow to fix Snowy with but saw none. He began frantically grabbing whatever slush remained on the ground and tried to pack it onto the face. Instead of helping, the head became lopsided and quite a misshapen mess.

"Oh, no!" he cried out. The boy's breath began coming hard and fast as the growing panic welled up within him.

Hurrying over to a larger mound of slushy snow he began frantically grabbing handful after handful of dripping snow, trying to pack the sides of the once-fluffy man into his former shape. His efforts were hopeless, but he wasn't ready to accept that.

"Don't leave me, Snowy," Elisha pleaded in a hoarse whisper. He worked faster and harder, brushing his tears away with his coat sleeve as he continued.

David wished desperately that he could do something to make this easier. He touched Elisha on the shoulder and spoke gently to him. "It's no good, son. It won't work."

"Yes, it will, Dad," Elisha insisted firmly. "Remember how you always tell me to do my best and work hard? I'm going to work my hardest, and I *will* fix Snowy!"

However fiercely he continued to pat, firm and reshape his pride and joy, it was all in vain. Snowy's pieces fell out again and again, striking the boy's hand on their way to the puddle below. Elisha tried to stick them back in, but the tears now streaming from his eyes made it hard for him to see. Even so, he kept jamming the buttons in, faster and faster, but they wouldn't stick.

Mollie came up to him with a whine and tried to lick the tears on his face. Elisha pushed her away and shouted, "Stop, Mollie!" The dog stood with her head and tail drooping down and watched, unable to understand why her master was so sad.

Stubbornly, Elisha fought back the tears, willing himself to stop crying. He returned to packing snow, but it was all slush and wouldn't stick. However hard he kept trying to save Snowy, he began to slowly acknowledge that it wasn't working.

Finally he stopped. He turned to his father. With an aching lump in his throat he pleaded with difficulty, "Dad, Snowy's belly… it's sliding, and I can't stop it. Will you help?"

His dad bent down to pick up some slush with an ache in his heart. Together they tried to firm Snowy up, but David couldn't help but think how the name "Snowy" no longer fit. The once magnificent snowman was reducing to a mound of slush.

In time Elisha's frantic actions came to a halt. He simply stared at the melting man before him. The roping forming his smile drooped, barely hanging on by one end. Nothing seemed left of his snowman's wonderful personality; his efforts to save Snowy had only made him look grotesque. In despair, Elisha threw down his last handful of slush. Silently, he stood, hands hanging down limply inside soaked gloves—There was nothing more he could do.

"I'm sorry, son. Let's go inside," said his dad, returning to the house. Elisha followed slowly, turning every few steps to look back. As he did so, the sun beat down warmly upon his back. All at once, Elisha felt the heat and realized—that same warmth had melted Snowy. Angrily, he stopped walking to look up and yell at the sun, "Why did you have to come out and ruin everything!" The tears began to flow again, but as he turned to go inside, sudden bitterness welled up within him and Elisha refused to cry anymore.

As Beth watched the sad tale play out, her eyes had filled with tears. She looked at David's face as he came in the door and saw the pain in his eyes for his son. Then she looked at Elisha, who entered but turned to robotically stare out the door with shoulders slumping down.

"Here, let me help with that zipper, Elisha," she whispered, partly from gentleness, partly because the ache for her boy's pain took her breath away. Kneeling down, she unzipped his coat. Elisha remained motionless, letting it slide and fall off his limp arms onto the floor. Elisha swallowed hard, as the lump in his throat grew.

"How would you like to bake cookies this afternoon?" Beth asked as she put his coat away. "Chocolate chip," she added, as cheerily as she could muster. She knew they were a cure for many things, although she held little hope they would work this time.

"No, thanks, Mom," Elisha said in a small, flat voice. Without another word he turned and walked to the quiet stillness of his bedroom.

A Fallen Heart

Once in his room, Elisha sat on the edge of his bed, trying not to feel anything. His eyes were repeatedly drawn to the window, so he finally walked over to look outside. The sun had disappeared and rain had started anew. Elisha just stared, not really looking at anything in particular.

After a while, David came into the room to suggest a game of checkers. Elisha really didn't feel like playing, but, to please his father, the boy helped set up the game. The moves began, but Elisha couldn't concentrate. Finally he stopped and spoke with some difficulty. "Dad... Snowy was supposed to last forever."

"Well, son..." David began slowly, "snow melts."

"So that means... a snowman would melt, too," Elisha said slowly.

"Yes," his dad agreed.

"Snowy's not going to make it, is he, Dad?" Elisha said in a small voice, more as a statement of fact than a question.

"No, son, I'm afraid he isn't. Sooner or later, all snowmen melt away, not just Snowy."

"But where will he go?" Elisha asked in a muffled voice. "He won't just *disappear*, will he?"

David thought carefully, asking God for help. He couldn't lie to his son, but he couldn't bear saying the cold hard truth to him either.

"I know it's very hard to accept that. We'd rather believe that snowmen are real and go somewhere for safekeeping, until we can see them again."

"Like Heaven?"

"Well... his dad said tentatively, "People do go to Heaven, but as for snowmen..." he paused and looked Elisha in the face.

"You can tell me, Dad. I'm big now," Elisha declared in his most grown-up voice.

"It's like this... when our bodies die, our spirits live on forever... but it's *not* like that for snowmen. Snowy was just snow — with no soul." He looked sympathetically at Elisha who was staring straight ahead, at nothing. "Do you understand?"

"You're saying Snowy's gone and that's the end of him." Elisha said flatly, without emotion.

"I'm also saying, there's so much love in your heart for Snowy, I don't think your memory of him will ever die. Do you?"

Elisha didn't answer; he just stared blankly at the wall. They sat quietly for several moments. Dad waited. Finally Elisha spoke. "Then... love can't save everything."

His dad didn't know what to say. "Some things aren't meant to be saved. Some are."

Painful silence filled the room, except for the steady ticking of the clock.

"Now," said David, "it's time for you to go to sleep."

He led his son in a prayer, said goodnight and left the room. "Oh, dear Lord," he prayed as he went down the hall, "please help Elisha through this hurt. Please, I don't know what to do, but You do. I trust you to help him through this."

As the sound of his father's footsteps faded away, Elisha continued to stare into the darkness towards the ceiling. It seemed he had no power to change Snowy's end.

"I'm sorry I can't help you, Snowy," he whispered. "Please, God," his heart cried out, "don't let Snowy just disappear."

A huge crash of thunder sounded suddenly outside, startling Elisha so much his whole body jumped. A series of thunder claps followed, making the whole room seem to rumble. Elisha's little body tensed after each one. He thought of Snowy being outside, alone, in the storm, so with each loud crack, he whispered to God to care for his snowman. The thunder, however, seemed to crack louder outside as if attempting to convince him otherwise.

For quite a while, flashes of lightning continued to light up the darkened room. Finally Elisha, having had enough of it, pulled the covers over his head to block out the light and sound.

Outside in the back yard, the flashes of lightning lit up the lone, melting snowman, advertising his demise with nature's black light, but none were present to mourn.

About 2 a.m., the flashes of light and crashes of thunder ceased. With everything quiet inside and out, Elisha finally fell asleep.

The next morning, Elisha awakened slowly to the sound of an old clock ticking. The next thing he heard was not so comforting—the steady sound of rain on the roof. He got out of bed and with mounting dread, walked to the window to look out.

The dark, barren tree branches, wet from the rain, glistened in the early morning light. Down below, the white of winter was already gone and the ground smiled a forlorn smile of a sad brown with bits of green showing here and there.

Elisha looked frantically for Snowy, but he could see only a shrinking, dull white mound where Snowy's belly and head had melted into his feet. He could barely make out the snowman's scarf lying limply on the top lump of melting snow.

Elisha's heart sank deeper than he ever thought it could go.

Chapter Four

Where Have All the Snowmen Gone?

All Hope Lost

*E*lisha ate breakfast without a word. He waited all morning for the rain to stop, which finally it did. Now he could say goodbye to whatever was left of his once happy man of snow. While he hated to look, he felt he must, almost like paying respects to someone at the cemetery. He'd done that once, with his Uncle James.

As he walked towards the back of the lot, he kept his eye out for the mound that had been Snowy. It should be close to here, he was thinking, when he came across a large puddle, where he stopped short. Should he walk through it or around it? With mounting anxiety, he began to look elsewhere for some trace of the snowman. But there was no white mound. Not a sign. Nothing.

His gaze turned back to the puddle. There, sunk into the bottom, he spotted something colorful—Snowy's scarf! Once worn to keep his dad warm and then to adorn his snowman, it now lay saturated, a soggy, wet mess in the pool of sadness of the melted man.

With a deep pang in the pit of his stomach, it gradually sank in— this puddle was all that was left of his best snowman! Not only that, if it rained again, the puddle of snowman water would merge with other puddles in the yard, totally ending proof of his very existence. The impact of losing Snowy finally hit the boy.

At that same moment, the sun popped out from behind dark clouds to spread happy sunshine everywhere. But bright sunshine did not lessen Elisha's grief. Indeed, he felt angry, as if the sun mocked his loss. Doesn't that sun know my friend just... he couldn't finish the thought. "Stupid ball of fire!" Elisha muttered stormily.

Moments later, when he silently breathed the name, "Snowy," one giant tear rolled down his cheek to fall into the pool of snowman water directly before him. There it splashed, rippled and finally settled into the pool. Contained in that tear was all the love, anguish and pain of the child's broken heart.

The ripples quieted and the surface of the water smoothed, but not for long. More tears dropped silently, slowly at first, splashing one after another into the puddle, then faster, until they streamed down his distorted face. He tried to cry out loudly, "Why, God?" but only raspy air came out.

You Don't Always See Your Miracles Happen

Standing forlornly with his hope shattered, what Elisha could not see was that something amazing was happening! There was no drum roll, no swelling crescendo of an orchestra, only the quiet stillness of a flooded back yard and the poignant sob of a boy.

A single ray of light beamed out strongly to target and catch each tear as it fell, turning each into a brilliant sparkle. One by one, the drops of wet sadness fell, bounced and then settled into the shimmering pool. Grateful ripples responded to the joining of waters of puddle and tears.

Eyes that had long watched from a heavenly distance filled until a single tear spilled over and began a slow descent to land in the pool with Elisha's. The mingling of heavenly and earthly tears with the snowman water marked, not a sorrowful ending, but a new beginning.

Quietly, without fanfare, a tiny whirlpool began forming in the puddle. As the sun shone ever brighter, the whirlpool spun up into a frosty, vertically spiral mist, which rose from the pool, hovered for an instant, and then vanished. Had Elisha been watching, he'd have seen that, left behind were only lingering droplets of moisture sparkling in the still, morning air.

But of course, you don't always see your miracles happen, so he stood utterly hopeless and unmoving in the water that pooled in his yard. His despair and the still streaming tears blinded him to what was taking place right at his feet.

In his mind he could still see his best snowman, but when he brushed away his tears to look once again in the water for anything that was really left of Snowy, he was stunned to see nothing was there—not the button eyes and mouth or the round nose—even the hat and scarf were gone! Any other time such a mysterious disappearance would have caused him to go looking for Snowy's things, but today he figured it made no difference. Why should he even care? Not he, not Elisha. Right then and there he determined to never build another snowman.

He stood quietly before the puddle that had been Snowy, a small figure alone in the large yard, vowing to protect himself from ever hurting like this again. As he did so, *his heart shrank and hid behind hard walls of his own making*. His little boy heart didn't understand that, *walls, built to keep out pain, become instead, prison bars that lock out joy*.

As he turned to head back into the house, he saw something attached to one of last summer's weeds by the fence. It had once been a protective covering for a small creature, waiting for its change. Now it was just an old, gray, dried-up cocoon. He reached out to pick it off and saw that it was indeed empty. Just like he felt. Suddenly he hated the cocoon. He pinched it between his fingers and, throwing it to the ground, stomped angrily on it.

Withdrawn

In Michigan they say, "If you don't like the weather, just wait, because it will change." It did. Shortly after all the rain, a cold front came through, triggering excitement in the school children about more snow. They were more than ready to build forts, have snowball fights, go sledding, and best of all, build snowmen.

His classmates had always called Elisha "Snow Man," and for good reason. His excitement about snow and snowmen was unlike that of any of the other children. He was usually the first to spot snowflakes flying in the air, but this morning when the chorus of excitement began, Elisha refused to look.

"Look, Elisha, it's snowing!" Kaylynn, one of his two best friends whispered loudly. She always tried to be the first to call it out, but today as she waited for his response, there was none. Thinking he must not have heard, she said again, "Elisha, look! Snow!"

Elisha kept his eyes down on his paper and continued to write. Although she repeated it, he refused to look.

"Didn't you hear me, Elisha?" she asked. Confused when he still didn't answer, she returned to her work feeling very hurt. Elisha would never ignore snow, so he must be ignoring her, even though he had never done so before.

Elisha sat quietly with his thoughts as he steeled himself against any excitement. Snow just reminded him of what he didn't have anymore. After all, if the snow had lasted, Snowy would still be here. But it hadn't and even though it's snowing again now, he bitterly noted, it's too late. A whole ton of snow could not bring Snowy back, and he was not going to go through that hurt again.

At recess, the kids barreled out the door to play in the quickly mounting snow, but Elisha stood by the wall alone, kicking at the covered ground. He shut out their squeals of having fun in the snow. *They're stupid*, he thought. *They make snowmen then knock them down like bowling pins. They don't care about their snowmen like I did Snowy.*

The teacher, Miss Alexander, noted Elisha was standing alone and thought his drastic change in behavior was very strange. He seemed to have lost his zest for recess, snow and playing with others. Even if he'd outgrown his obsession with snow, that didn't answer his unhappy and withdrawn behavior the last few days.

The teacher saw Kaylynn walking cautiously up to him with her knit hat pushed back off her head. Her cheeks were warm and pink from running and her blue eyes still bright with the excitement of a chase. Untying her hat she shoved it into her pocket and tossed her head to shake out her long blonde hair. Each strand sparkled with golden highlights like gold dust in the sun. "Hi, Elisha," she said, trying to get his attention.

Elisha just kept looking off into the distance, avoiding her eyes.

"Elisha, are you ever going to play again with me, with any of us?" He continued to stare away from her.

"I thought we were friends. You won't play or even talk to me." When he didn't answer, she got into her huffy tone. "I'm getting tired of this. What's wrong?" Still he didn't answer. "Come on, Elisha. We've always been able to talk," she pleaded.

She waited for an answer, but Elisha remained silent and it finally annoyed her. "I don't understand you, Elisha Winters!"

She began to leave in a huff but after a ways, stopped abruptly to look back at him. "Well, I'm still your friend," she added, "even if you're not being a very good one anymore!" Staring at him with her flashing blue eyes, she waited for a response. Finally, she gave a tired sigh. "You know where I am when you're ready, I guess."

With that, the little girl walked off wondering at his strange behavior. She had always been a very loyal friend and Elisha had always been so kind. But now, with no explanation from him, she found it hard not to take this personally.

In reality, Elisha considered her to be his most delightful and best friend, even better than Tim. More important than her cute nose, blue eyes and adorable smile, she was smart, funny, and most endearing of all, always trying to help others. He didn't want to hurt her; he just didn't want to talk to anyone.

Miss Alexander watched Elisha furtively wipe a small tear from one eye and stare at the ground while Kaylynn went off to play. The concerned teacher slowly walked over to where he stood and casually leaned against the wall to talk to him.

"Elisha, I'm a little surprised you're not out there in the snow with the class," she said. He did not answer, so she stooped down to speak to him face to face.

"I know that Kaylynn, Tim, or any of the children would love to play with you."

Elisha still didn't answer.

"Elisha?"

With his hands in his pockets, he continued to stand staring blankly at the ground.

"Don't you feel well?" she asked.

Elisha shrugged one shoulder but kept his eyes down. "I'm okay," he answered.

"Well, maybe you're just not in the mood to play today," she said tactfully.

He looked at her, barely shook his head no and then stared at the empty field by the playground. Miss Alexander felt her heart would break for him, but she held back. Normally she would give a hurting child a hug for comfort, but she noticed he was rigid and nonresponsive as she touched his shoulder. Something was deeply troubling him.

Perplexed, she stood up again. Since school began in the fall, he had been a bright, happy, outgoing boy, always involved and playing with the others. Something was definitely wrong for such a boy to withdraw from everything. She decided to call his parents after school.

Miss Alexander looked at her watch and saw it was time for recess to end.

"Elisha, would you like to ring the bell for the class to come in?" she asked, smiling and offering the coveted bell to him. But he refused, turning his back to it. Puzzled, she gave up and rang the bell herself. Biting one side of his lip, he walked to the door.

The rosy-cheeked children ran to line up behind him, their mittens and gloves packed white with snow, voices mixing together with noisy laughter and chatter. Here and there the usual shoving occurred until the teacher called for quiet and order. Elisha stood quietly at the head of the line, looking straight ahead, his gloves and snow pants still dry.

A Heart to Heart Talk

That night the boy's grief had stolen his appetite. Sitting silently, he picked at his food, ate very little and went straight to his room after supper. After helping Beth clear the dishes, David went to Elisha's room. It was time to finish their talk.

Elisha was sitting by the window but not looking out, looking down but not really seeing anything. Mollie lay quietly at his feet, sensing that he was in no mood to play. She kept her head down on her paws, only moving her brown eyes to watch David as he came in.

"Hey, son, you haven't felt much like talking the last few nights, have you?"

Elisha just kept staring at his feet.

"Come, sit on the bed by me, Elisha," Dad said.

Elisha came over and sat on the bed, pulling his feet up beside him. He leaned his head over against his dad's chest. Having his dad's strong arms around him, usually made Elisha feel better, but it just wasn't the same tonight.

"We've made some pretty good snowmen together haven't we?" David asked.

Elisha sat quietly.

"And we had a lot of fun building them together, didn't we?"

Elisha still didn't answer, but he knew it was true. They'd had the greatest of times together in the snow, and Mom, too. It just hurt inside too much to think about it now.

"It's always more fun when you have a buddy to do things together with you. Right?"

Elisha remained silent.

David figured it was time to try to help get the hurt out. "You know, Elisha, I remember what it's like to work hard on something and have it fall apart."

He looked at the little face next to him, staring stonily straight ahead, his emotions betrayed only by the blinking back of a lone tear.

"Sometimes people stop doing what they love cause they're afraid to get hurt again. But really... you just get stuck in your hurt and still have no fun."

Dad reached over and wrapped his large hands around Elisha's small ones. "Remember when Mrs. Smith's dear little dog died? She said she'd never get another one. And, she stopped doing the things she loved to do, even baking!"

Elisha nodded, remembering it well.

"Mrs. Smith just got sadder and lonelier. One day her daughter and son, Emilee and Matthew, dropped off that cute, little pup, Ritzy, thinking it might help. Mrs. Smith wouldn't even look at it and told them to get that dog out," David continued.

David looked to see if Elisha was listening. He was looking at his dad now.

"Well, they finally just left the puppy there. Oh, Mrs. Smith fussed and complained about it, but the next thing she knew, the pup had stolen her heart. And now, she says Ritzy is the best thing that ever happened to her! But just think... she almost missed out on having Ritzy to love, cause she said she never wanted another dog."

Dad looked at his son. "Elisha, I've never seen a kid that loves snow and building snowmen any more than you do. Do you really want to miss out on that forever?"

"I don't know..." Elisha began reluctantly, his voice quiet. Finally it all came pouring out. "Gee, Dad, I just wanted Snowy to be real and last forever. I thought if I believed hard enough... he would." His voice got caught on the words and he paused. Elisha moved in closer to his dad who put his arm around him.

"Why couldn't things just stay the same!" With that, Elisha buried his face in his dad's chest and sobbed, his tears soaking quickly through his father's shirt.

Mollie sat up and looked at her master. She cocked her head from one side to the other, then whined and licked at Elisha's hand.

When Elisha's tears had slowed down and he quieted, his dad said, "Son, I know you're hurting, but you counted on something to last that was never meant to be."

David turned to look his son squarely in his eyes. "You've lost something very dear to you and it hurts," he said quietly. "But people who get stuck in hurt and anger become sad and bitter, and often end up alone, because no one wants to be around them."

Elisha raised his head and looked up at his dad again. "You mean like Mrs. Smith? She got so ornery, nobody wanted to be around her anymore, not even Mollie."

"Exactly," answered his dad.

Elisha was quiet for a moment. "I... I think... that's probably how everybody at school feels about me now," Elisha added, turning his head away.

"Why is that?"

Elisha dropped his head to stare at the floor in silence. He didn't know how to tell his dad how he had behaved with his friends.

"Have you shut others out at school, Elisha, because you've been hurt and maybe even, angry?"

Elisha nodded, thinking of how he had probably hurt Kaylynn more than any of the others.

"Elisha, you've never wanted to hurt anyone on purpose. Neither did Mrs. Smith. You have a kind heart, and just like Mrs. Smith, you'll figure out that the way to stop hurting is to love again."

Elisha thought quietly for a long minute. "But Dad, is it just *over*? Is this the *end* of Snowy?"

"I'm afraid so, son. After all, he was just... snow."

"But, Dad!" protested Elisha, "He wasn't just snow to me!"

"I know. Your love made him special. You made him, gave him a name and in your heart you adopted him, but in the end, he was only a formation of snow. But... remember how much fun you had making him? Nobody can take that great memory away from you." David paused to let as much as Elisha could handle sink in.

Still hurting, Elisha repeated, "All I wanted was the best snowman ever!" Mumbling sullenly he added, "One to last forever." Then he was silent. After a few moments, he asked in a small voice, "But is he just melted? If we go to Heaven, can't snowmen go somewhere, too?"

"It would be nice if they didn't just end up in a puddle, wouldn't it? Maybe we can talk about that tomorrow," he ended with a wink and a smile. "A-okay?"

Elisha looked at him sadly. He knew his dad was expecting his usual cheerful response, but all he could muster was a quiet, "A-okay."

After saying prayers together, his dad left. The door closed quietly and the room was silent... except for the ticking of the old clock his mom had given him. He listened to its soothing, steady tick, tick, ticking until he fell asleep. Mollie lay down on the floor beside the bed, sighed and went to sleep, too. All was blessedly quiet.

Eyes that had watched Elisha all his life, filled with compassion.

Chapter Five

A Cold Start

$\mathcal{E}$lisha woke during the night with a start. Who wouldn't be startled with Mollie barking furiously next to his bed? When he saw it was the dog, he scolded her.

"Stop, Mollie. Quiet. You'll wake Mom and Dad," he whispered loudly.

Mollie whined but obediently lay back down and Elisha turned over to go back to sleep. But something was wrong. In spite of the snug, warm covers, his face and ears were cold. He sat up to look around. That's when he saw that the wind had blown a window open causing a bitterly cold wind to tear into the room.

"Oh, great!" he said out loud. "Now I'm going to be in trouble." Elisha remembered opening the window that morning to scare off the red-tailed hawk as it waited to catch a songbird at the feeder. In spite of many reminders by his parents, he must have neglected to tighten the latch when he closed it.

Already shivering, he got out of bed to close the window. When he reached to grab the handle, he was amazed to see an unusually different winter scene below. Instead of the usual quiet back yard with falling snow, it looked like an amusement park of snowy whirlwinds blowing and swirling in different directions as he'd never seen it before. He wasn't even sure it was his back yard, but what else could it be? He only knew something strange was going on.

Leaning against the window pane, Elisha strained his eyes to see through the storm, quickly wiping the fog from his breath off the glass. He stared intensely, his eyes roving back and forth across the yard, as he tried to pinpoint what was wrong.

He could see the old pine trees in the back, but beyond them he couldn't make out the neighboring farms or anything familiar! How strange. Even in a storm, he could usually see the outline of the nearest barn and silo at the very least.

Elisha decided he would get a closer look from the kitchen door so, carefully avoiding the squeaky spots on the steps, he eased downstairs. No need to alarm Mom and Dad in the middle of the night. Besides, how would he explain where or why he was going out? He just felt he had to.

As he reached the back door, he put on his heavy coat, boots and scarf and stepped outside. What he saw captured him in amazement and awe. The moon was shining onto a vast expanse of a snow-covered landscape. It appeared as if every single snowflake that had landed was shimmering, creating a luminous glow everywhere. Although the wind had died down, it kicked up intermittently, causing magical, silvery swirls to spin over the landscape. Elisha was mesmerized by the miniature silver tornadoes as they kept appearing closer to him and then moving away in the direction of the fields. It was almost as if... as if they were inviting him to follow. But to where? He decided this was all too strange not to investigate more closely.

As he walked, he heard the wind blowing around him and the snow crunching softly beneath his feet. The silvery swirls occasionally returned and temporarily surrounded him, and every time they did, he felt a strong urge to giggle. No matter how hard he held back, one after another, giggles began escaping from him, which made him feel silly.

"Man!" he said, "What's wrong with me? I'm not a girl!" Immediately he knew his good friend would call that a cut down on girls, so he added, "Oops, sorry, Kaylynn!" Though he also knew she could not hear any of this, still he felt better to apologize. Yet, even as this giggling out loud over nothing made him feel foolish, he did it again and again!

Elisha was trying to locate the shed when he heard the sound of a rushing wind and felt its swirls envelop him. Although he let out a "Whoa!" in surprise, strangely, as the wind powered up beneath him, he wasn't afraid. In fact, he felt a joy and a keen, adventurous spirit! All the while laughing, he felt himself being lifted and transported by a power not his own.

In time the wind and its swirls dissipated, and as everything settled, Elisha could hardly believe what lay before him. This did not look like his back yard, but a vast array of wintry land he'd never seen or even imagined before. But how could this be? The bewildered boy quickly looked behind him and was even more confused when he couldn't see his house! Wait a minute. House gone, back yard, gone; what was going on? Although he didn't understand, he was strangely unafraid. He turned back to face what lay before him, drawn to go farther ahead.

All he could see for a long ways were mounds and drifts of snow. Far off to the right, he could make out hundreds of gigantic pines, all heavily laden with snow. Elisha stood still and stared, trying to take it all in. His gaze finally stopped when he looked to the left—There, looming in the far distance was a tall mountain. His jaw dropped open; a mountain had never been there before!

He advanced slowly, still gazing at everything, wondering and trying to process what in the world was going on! And what was the deal with Mollie? They were never separated, yet there was strangely no sign of her. Although he had told her to lie down at first, why hadn't she followed him when he left... but follow him where? He had no idea where he was or how he had gotten here.

Just as Elisha saw some strange white shapes moving in a distant clearing, without warning, it began to snow harder. Oh, why did that blowing snow start up making it too hard to see? He determined to get a better look. He hunched down and kept moving forward until he neared the clearing. Yes, there was indeed movement of white upon white among plump shapes grouped together. As Elisha strained his eyes to see, his brain began racing in an attempt to make sense of what was before him. These rounded shapes were moving, talking, and, yes, even laughing... almost like... snowmen? Impossible! But he was seeing something like them with his very own eyes. Elisha began to feel excited as he breathed softly in disbelief, "Snowmen. Real snowmen!" But were they really?

The white creatures did seem to be talking, so perhaps if he could hear them, he might get a clue as to who or what they were. He leaned forward and strained to hear, only to be disappointed. Oh, if only the wind would settle down!

Almost as if the wind heard his thoughts, it died down. Unfortunately, the snowmen, or whatever they were, had ceased talking and were instead playing and laughing together. As their musical laughter drifted over, it filled Elisha with the same giddy joy that the silvery swirls had aroused in him earlier.

Suddenly an urge to laugh started to overwhelm him and the harder he tried to contain it, the stronger the need to laugh grew. A big, boisterous belly laugh began rising up within him; he must stop it, for surely it would give his presence away! Quickly he began holding his breath, which only made it worse, for it seemed he would explode with wild laughter any moment. He didn't want these beings to know he was here yet. Maybe if he bit his lip, the pain would stop the laugh. He tried it. Ow! That worked. Elisha winced at the pain even as it dulled the giddy feeling.

The group's contagious laughter also subsided and with it, so did Elisha's urge to laugh. The snowmen seemed to be settling down to talk, so once again Elisha watched and listened.

Mostly seated, although a few stood, the group was gathered around what appeared to be a campfire. Or was it? As he focused on it, he saw not a normal yellow fire but white flames inside a circle of snow. Their flickering movement seemed soothing to the onlookers and, at times, the snowmen stretched their skinny stick arms towards it, as if warming themselves by a normal fire.

Elisha could actually hear the conversation beginning in earnest now. "Have you met 'the new one' yet?" the largest of them was asking.

"Yep. He's chilling out with Old Man Snow now. He has sno (*so*) much to learn about Forever Snow Land. Still kinda shaky while his new body builds up to a Forever Freeze. Sno quiet though," the practical one added.

"But sno much heart," another mused out loud.

52

"Sno much hurting heart. Misses his Builder," said a tender hearted one.

"Snoh, he'll get over it. We did, didn't we?" the practical one asked.

"Yeah, but this one... sno different," discerned the largest.

"Yep, yep, yep. Sno true!" another declared as the others nodded in hearty agreement and each one echoed, "Yep, sno different."

"Sno different, we can't help him. Hurt snow hearts take time," concluded the tender-hearted one.

"Time? Time to get back to the Lodge," said the practical one getting up to go.

"Yes, yes, Snow Lodge time," another agreed.

The snowy gathering began to break up to move away, and as they did, they turned so Elisha could see their faces clearly. Bright hope leaped within him as any doubts vanished. Faces! The moonlight clearly showed—snowmen! Five of them! The snowmen were similar, as snowmen are, yet different, each having his own personality. They all seemed fairly jovial, even when they were serious. One by one, they kicked at the snow flames, apparently to put out the "fire" before leaving.

It delighted Elisha to see, as they walked away joking and laughing heartily, snowflakes of laughter followed behind them in wavy trails. Elisha had never before actually *seen* laughter! Even as he stood amazed, snowflakes floated his way and brushed his cheeks, renewing his own laughing again. The giddy feeling soon quieted down, however, as the flakes melted. The sounds of Snowflake Laughter faded away as the snowmen slipped into the whiteness of the distance. The wind gave a giant swirl around Elisha again and when it quieted, the snowmen were completely gone from sight.

Elisha found himself excited but totally confused. "What in the world was all that about?"

Suddenly, he saw a movement out of the corner of his eye—something small and dark. He spun around to look at it, but upon seeing nothing, he shrugged and followed in the direction of the snowmen, leaving the small creature behind. He didn't get far before, without warning, the wind raged around him once more, blinding him and propelling him elsewhere. He found no joy, no urge to laugh from this trip the wind took him on.

When the whirlwind finally came to a stop, it vanished, enabling him to see clearly. Unbelievably, he was facing the back door of his house! He turned to see the same back yard he'd always played in and, looking down the road, he saw the same farms exactly as they had always been. All looked normal. No mountain in the distance, only farms, barns, and snowy fields. No swirling snow or storm. Where had it all gone? And... had he lost his chance to ever see snowmen again? He could only hope not.

Chapter Six

Snowy Conversations Bring Hope

*T*he next morning, Elisha was fuzzy about what had happened. Was that adventure in another world real or a dream? Part of him hoped it was true, but the other part told him it was ridiculous to even think something so farfetched could have happened. How could his house and a mountain appear and disappear? How could snowmen be alive? But if they were alive, did it mean Snowy might be, too? Oh, what should he believe?

His dad had said that snowmen are just snow and dad always tells the truth, unless... unless this is something he doesn't know about! Elisha briefly considered talking to his dad about it, but decided not to. He could hardly believe last night himself. How could he expect anyone else to believe it?

Elisha went about his life every day that week as before, going to school and coming home, each night looking out his window, only to see nothing more of the mysterious snowy scene. Finally, the weekend arrived. Friday night, at last!

He and his dad went bowling and had a great time. The whole time, in the back of his head, was this little hope that maybe... maybe at bedtime, there would be a repeat of his strange adventure where the snowmen live.

Now, as he got ready for bed, he remembered that tomorrow morning Tim would be coming over to play, like he always did every

Saturday morning. Somehow, he wasn't as excited as usual about anything, except possibly seeing his snowman again. But then, he would reason, all that snowman adventure had to just be a dream. It couldn't be real. Then he'd feel sad, very sad.

As long as he didn't think about Snowy, things were a little better, but Elisha wasn't the kind of kid who could easily cut off his feelings for his snow friend. His deep love for Snowy was real and forever. Questions kept nagging at him: Can snowmen become real? If so, where do they live? Was the other night showing him an answer? If so, he was sure confused as to what it might be.

When he crawled into bed, both his mom and dad tucked him in and left his room looking at each other with relief. They closed the door upon the quiet darkness of his room.

"We seem to have our boy back," Beth whispered.

"He didn't mention anything else about his snowman while we were bowling tonight. Hopefully, he's come through his disappointment," David added.

Just as with every other night, however, Elisha's last waking thought was of his dear Snowy. It still hurt in the pit of his stomach to have him gone. Although everyone around him thought he was much better, a hole remained in his heart, so empty, so deep he felt nothing could ever fill it again. Like every night, tears rolled slowly down his cheek until his pillow was wet.

The Eyes that watched, not only saw his pain, but felt it with him.

Elisha had just drifted off to sleep when, just as with the previous weekend, he woke with a shudder. Sitting up, he saw his window was open again! Still half asleep, he wondered how that could happen, knowing he had closed that window tightly – what could be wrong with it now?

As he struggled with these thoughts, a strong beam of moonlight reached through the window, stretching all the way to him. Strangely transfixed, he got out of bed and stood up. He stared at the unusual way it lit up his pajamas. The mysterious shaft of light gave him an eerie feeling, as if it could lead him to something. That possibility gave him a boldness to step into it and follow its path to the window where, once again, he had a strange feeling about tonight; something he couldn't quite pinpoint.

Now wide awake, he looked out and identified the same fantasy of snow and wind as before. Without thinking twice, he closed the window, slipped on his jeans and was into the hall. With every step down the stairs, he held his breath, hoping not to awaken anyone with a squeaky step. Finally reaching the mudroom enclosure, he quickly began dressing to go out. His mind was not on what he was doing, but where he was going.

A bit anxious and yet relieved to see the same snowy scene again, somehow he knew tonight could answer more questions and so he must hurry to get there. But every second seemed heavily laden with time. His small hands shook as he struggled with the zipper on his snow pants. He finally got them zipped, but found his jacket zipper wouldn't start. The frustrated boy stopped, took a slow, deep breath and tried again. Success! Now all fastened, zipped up, pulled on and tucked in, he was dressed for the cold outdoors.

Elisha eased the outer door open and, careful not to let it bang shut, ran out full steam ahead, but soon became confused by the wild swirling snow. Just as he began to become frustrated that he couldn't find the shed at the back of the yard or pinpoint the path he took before, the swirling wind and snow calmed so he could see, but still, nothing looked familiar.

Lost in my own back yard? Now what am I going to do, he wondered. His answer came quickly. Unlike last week when the silvery whirlwinds had led him, this time, a moonbeam like the one in his room stretched before him. He followed the path of light and as he exited out of his yard, like before, any sign of the neighbors' farms strangely disappeared. He didn't know if he could ever get used to things just appearing and disappearing! Yet while it was a bit unnerving to have things change on him, the hope, stirred in him by the snowmen he'd seen, led him on even more than the moonbeam. He was determined to do whatever he had to, if it meant he might see Snowy again.

Walking on, Elisha found the snow getting deeper and harder to get through. A drift reaching above his knees made continuing on seem impossible, but he would not give up. Determined to get through that drift, he plowed through, only to find another and another. These snow pants and boots hadn't seemed too exciting a gift at Christmas, but he was certainly grateful for them now! Elisha promised himself to sincerely thank his parents when all this was over.

Thoughts of his mom and dad gave Elisha's heart a little pang—he was not used to disobeying them, and it gave him an uneasy feeling. If they woke and checked in on him he knew they would panic, but he couldn't miss this chance to find out what he could about Snowy. Quickly asking God's forgiveness for leaving without permission, he prayed they would not wake up before he returned.

Finally, he got through the snowdrifts and the ground leveled out. Elisha stopped to catch his breath. Shielding his eyes from the blowing snow, he tried to make out what was ahead. There! There was something, maybe fifty feet before him and to the right, something moving through the blur of steadily falling snow. Now hearing noises, he followed the sound.

As he drew nearer, Elisha began to distinguish voices–voices that sounded like... like falling snowflakes! Now it seemed crazy that he could possibly know what falling snowflakes would sound like, but he did. Surely it was snowmen again. Still, they were too far away to hear clearly and so Elisha trudged through more and more snow, to get closer.

He tried to not give himself away with telltale signs in the air from huffing and puffing, but his journey through the snow had made him quite short of breath. Shortly he reached a tall pine with a huge trunk, just right to hide behind. He could recover his breath and at the same time stand close enough to catch their conversation.

Peeking round the trunk he saw these were snowmen, indeed, both younger and older. The younger ones' gentle, childish laughter bounced around, sounding more like icy snowflakes tinkling on a tin, rather than the magically mellow Snowflake Laughter of the older ones. Both delightful sounds brought joy deep within Elisha and he smiled as he strained to hear more.

Now Elisha, being a young boy, had never even considered the possibility of snowmen having their own language.* (Nor had he found it strange that he had understood the previous snowmen's conversation; he knew only that he could both hear and understand them now. Neither did he know that two laws of Snow Land had been broken: First, that humans are never allowed in, and second, that snowman language is never understood by humans. In fact, this Snowman Language was strangely being automatically translated as it reached his ears. Had he understood these matters, he would have wondered who had allowed this to happen.) The boy's ears really perked up at what he was hearing now...

"Sure is taking the new one longer than usual," reported the largest and oldest snowman with a tall black hat.

One especially well-proportioned snowman seemed to chew on a toothpick. But no, it was no toothpick, for snowmen have no teeth. Elisha saw a taller snowman break off an icicle and pop it between the black buttons of his smile. That settled it. It must be an ice pick!

The snowmen were continuing to talk so he focused on their conversation.

"Has anyone heard how his Builder, the boy, is doing?" the traditional-looking snowman asked.

"Last I heard, sno good," said one.

"Don't know," said the plump one deliberately, removing the ice pick to speak. "But I think I saw tracks out here after we met last time."

"What do you mean, tracks? What kind of tracks?" the traditional one immediately asked.

The plump one arched his stick eyebrows and in an over-enunciated fashion distinctly answered—"Boy tracks." He let the weight of his words sink in as he lazily returned the ice pick to his mouth.

After initial gasps of "Snoh, no!" the group sat silently trying to absorb what he had said. The fat one basked in the drama of his announcement as the others tried to grasp what this could mean to them and their world. As the meaning of "boy tracks" penetrated their snowy brains, each of the snowmen, aghast at such a thought, lost his smile.

"Boy tracks! You mean... you think the new one's Builder was here?" asked the shortest one, nearly breathless.

"I do," the plump one said in a very matter-of-fact way, chewing on the icicle and drooling as if it were a delicious lollipop. "In fact, I know so." Sharing information the others did not know made him feel quite important. Nodding his head he added, "They were human, boy tracks."

"Sizzling icicles!" gasped the shortest one.

"Frazzled snowflakes!" said another.

The tall, strangely gaunt snowman spoke quickly. "Boys? Sno, sno, not possible! Boys sno allowed here. Only snowmen with hearts come here from the outside."

"Perhaps," the traditional-looking snowman mused slowly, "that is precisely how the boy got here... because of his heart."

All gasped once more and then fell silent as they considered that possibility. "Do you suppose... is it possible he would be *allowed* to come here because of his heart?"

"Are you absolutely sure you saw boy tracks?" the tall snowman asked the plump one, with skepticism in his voice. "You're not just trying to make snow points with us, are you?"

"Yeah, we snow (*know*) how you are," declared another, remembering past conversations.

"I told you. The boy is here. Jefferds confirmed it!" the plump one declared.

"Jefferds?" one exclaimed. "Snoh, my!"

Sudden silence overwhelmed the whole group for a few moments. Then each began to show alarm and look furtively from one to another with big eyes.

"If Jefferds said it, then it must be true," said the practical one quietly.

Suddenly, with gasps and near whimpers, they all began to speak at once, each in a loud voice giving his input as if it were highly important, which, to the snowmen, it was. "Snoh, no! A boy? How? How did he get here?"

On and on they talked and reasoned, one after another, adding to the rising sense of urgency... "Snoh, this sno scary! Something must be done! Every snowthing we hold dear–in danger! Boys can't keep secrets! S'no way!"

"Boy means danger," said the largest.

"Yes, danger," they all repeated in agreement, "to all of us!"

Elisha's eyes opened wide. Were they referring to him? Could he, a mere boy, strike such alarm in the hearts of snowmen just by being here? And the part about... who did they say... Jefferds? Who could that be, whose words carried so much weight it stirred up fear in them? None of this made sense at all.

The more they talked, the more agitated the usually jolly men became. Walking rather haphazardly in small semi circles, they moaned again and again, "Snoh dear, snoh dear!"

Elisha felt bad to see the normally cheerful group so distressed. He was almost inclined to go reassure them that he was one boy who meant no harm, but suddenly the atmosphere made a dramatic change.

"My snow brothers, we must report this to Old Man Snow at once!" the short one cried out.

"Yes, yes!" the others said in wholehearted agreement. "We must, we must!"

"At once!" the quizzical one emphasized.

"Yes, snoh, yes! At once!" they all declared unanimously. They agreed to report to Old Man Snow the intrusion of a human boy... immediately! But strangely, rather than leaving to do so, they continued to discuss and repeat the same conclusion.

Now this puzzled Elisha immensely. Why, if this was so urgent, did they make no move to leave? It was as if their minds, as well as their bodies, were going in circles. It reminded Elisha of a car his dad had that got stuck in Neutral. He couldn't get it to move to Drive.

Poor, sweet men of snow... made only to be happy, they cannot handle being upset very long. During long periods of stress, they simply cease to exist. (Each snowman coming to Forever Snowland is taught from "Snow Way to Survive," the Snowman's Survival Book, which says: "Snow decisions made in a hurry can snowball out of control. When in trouble, talk out the problem until calm, then report to Old Man Snow.")

Of course Elisha knew none of this; besides, he was just trying to make sense of what he'd heard, when a new thought occurred to him—If he was the boy they were talking about, then the new one they referred to must be his dear Snowy. Oh, now he had to find out more! Elisha leaned in eagerly to hear every word.

A quirky looking snowman, thrown together with a bevy of household body parts, spoke up in a quick, shaky voice. "Sn'u (*You*) know, when Old Man Snow tried to give him a new Forever Snowman name, the new one cried out, 'Sno, I'm Snowy!' (*No, I'm Snowy!*)

Snowy! Elisha's heart leaped within him to hear Snowy's name. "Snowy," he breathed in excitement, "it is you after all!"

The quirky snowman continued on, "Yeah, Snowy was sno upset, Old Man Snow said, for now, he could keep his old name. Don't think he's ever done that – he says a new name helps us break from the past."

The traditional one with a top hat said, "I kept my name."

The tender hearted one spoke up quickly. "Oh, Frosty, that's just cause he knew there was no better name for you!"

They continued to talk about Old Man Snow's naming procedure. Meanwhile, when Elisha heard Snowy's name, he gave an excited little jump where he stood. When he landed, his foot hit a weak spot and fell through into an animal's burrow. Holding back a startled yell, he gasped in surprise as he lost his balance and fell sideways into the hole.

"Oh, great!" he moaned in dismay as he landed, thinking he might have broken his leg. Very carefully he pulled his leg from the burrow and wiggled it. No pain, thank goodness. Next he looked to see if any had noticed his fall. Fortunately, no one had. He somehow got himself out of the hole.

After rising back onto his feet, he looked in on the snowman group once more and saw that they continued to talk. Hopefully he'd hear more about Snowy.

Note: See Appendix in back of book for interpretation of "snow" words in Snowman Language.

Chapter Seven

A Snowman Without a Smile

"**N**ew snowman looks sno strange without a smile," the tall, gaunt one with a long stocking hat remarked sadly.

The others just as sadly shook their heads in agreement. "Sno sad," they responded.

Elisha wondered if he heard that right. No smile? Now, wait just a minute! He had given Snowy a great smile. Maybe this was not his Snowy after all!

"Yeah, must accept being here first. Who knows how long that will take?" said the fluffy one with earmuffs.

A lanker and back-woodsy looking man of snow, with pieces of bark for eyes and nose, stood leaning against a stack of snow blocks. His broken-down straw hat partially covering one eye, he contemplated the life of a snowman without a smile. His own crooked mouth of twig pieces suddenly twitched in mischief as he spoke up to make himself heard.

"What's a snowman without a smile?" he joked.

"What's a snowman without a heart?" piped up the short, quirky one.

"Just a pile of snow!" joked the woodsy snowman.

"Hee, hee, ho! A pile of snow! Which is *not* funny!" screamed the quirky one even as he held his sides laughing.

They all repeated it childishly, laughing hilariously at the joke and slapping each other on the back. "Ha, ha, ho! Just a pile of snow!"

A snowman without a heart being just a pile of snow did not seem funny at all to Elisha, but to not be funny, they surely were laughing a lot.

They continued to chant, laugh, and dance about, with some falling down occasionally to mimic a pile of snow, which would set them off again. "Ha, ha, ho! Just a pile of snow!"

As the snowmen carried on, Elisha's eyes twinkled with amusement. These snowmen sure love to laugh, he thought, but this snowman laughter sounded different from what he'd heard before. Elisha's grin stretched to a huge smile, for they definitely sounded silly!

As their laughter became wilder, it suddenly progressed into cackles and roars, which caused something unusual to take place. Elisha's eyes popped opened wide in amazement at what he was seeing. He could actually see something shooting out of their mouths! The group of snowmen turned this way and that, doubling over as each recalled their snow joke. Finally, wiping drops of icy tears from their eyes, they gradually settled down into "sniggles" (*snowman giggles*) as they began to leave.

In the distance, every once in a while, he could hear one of them sniggle, then hoot out, "Snow pile!" which would trigger more laughter. This went on for a few more minutes, their voices gradually fading away as the snowmen disappeared out of sight. Hearing their contagious Hail Laughter had left Elisha quite refreshed, and yet tired, as a good laugh will do.

As Elisha was thinking of continuing his journey, he saw that one snowman had stayed behind. The traditional and more serious snowman, a little older and more thoughtful than the rest, was well dressed, with a black top hat and a colorful striped scarf around his neck.

The snowman sat quietly, alone and unmoving, on a hardened boulder of a drift as he thought about the hard time this new snowman was having. It reminded him of how difficult his own adjustment had been...

He had felt such overwhelming emptiness after he melted and left behind his Builders, Alexis, Mya, Sydney, Chloe and Kaylynn. Now, these were exceptionally precious little girls, innocent of heart and full of love. Together they had built the snowman in great fun and laughter. When they finished, Baby Zoey clapped and squealed in delight at their wonderful snowman. As for Frosty, as they'd named him, oh, he loved them dearly.

Their happy laughter surrounded him everyday, filling him with pure joy. But, ah, then, melting time comes to every snowman. One day finding only a puddle of water left of their snowman, the little darlings had cried as if they'd never stop, begging their fathers to go and find their Frosty. But, of course, that was not possible, so their Grandpa Jim and fathers, Nick and Josh had made up a song about Frosty to console them.

Frosty smiled with great affection as he remembered their sadness, for it was their love that had saved him. This had always amazed the old snowman, to think that he now lived forever because of the little girls' pure love for him. It had all happened a very long time ago, and as Frosty recalled it all, he let out a frosty sigh.

Once again he thought of the new one and found it highly unusual Snowy couldn't adjust to Snow Land. Most snowmen gladly enter into their new Forever Life. Oh, well, it would all freeze out in time, the snowman decided, giving a tap to his hat as if to end his reflection time. With that the snowman stood up and kicked at the snow fire, as one would put out a normal campfire.

Now, although Elisha had watched the lone snowman with interest, he was still bewildered by the group's conversation. Had they been talking about his Snowy? If so, what kind of business was this, about his not having a smile until he adjusted? How could that be true, Elisha wondered indignantly, as any Builder would. And why should Snowy stay here if he was so unhappy anyway?

"Well, you won't have to when I find you, Snowy, cause I'm taking you home!" he said to comfort the absent snowman and himself. "You're mine and I'll take care of you!" he called out loudly, crossing his arms and giving a hard nod to his head for emphasis. If anyone had heard, he'd have known not to argue with the boy, for his mind was made up.

When Elisha decided to resume his journey, his ears perked up to an unfamiliar sound. He turned back and listened as he distinctly heard a "thumpity, thump, thump..." as he watched Frosty go over the fields of snow.

Chapter Eight

Encounter of the Rude Kind!

$\mathcal{E}$lisha took up his journey in search of his snowman again. He didn't know to where or to what it would lead him, but the snowy conversations he'd heard only made him more determined than ever to find his cherished snowman.

He'd been plodding through the snow for awhile, when he thought he heard a movement from a nearby pile of brush. He looked quickly in that direction, but, seeing nothing there, he convinced himself he hadn't really heard anything. He was ready to proceed again when a curt, know-it-all voice piped up right behind him "Hey, there!" The voice practically startled him out of his boots.

Elisha whipped around to respond, but all he saw was a rabbit, so he looked in another direction. "Kinda jumpy aren't you?" came the voice again. Elisha turned back to see only an impertinent looking rabbit, with a larger, fluffier tail than normal and a pair of very large front teeth. The rabbit's head tilted back to look up at Elisha, but the boy, upon seeing only a rabbit, continued searching for the source of the voice. Finding no one else, though, he thought perhaps he was hearing things. Elisha finally shrugged and thought it urgent to continue his journey.

"I s-s-suppose you are los-st!" the rabbit said with a whistling lisp.

Once more Elisha had turned around and this time saw, amazingly, the rabbit's mouth moving as he spoke! He could scarcely believe he was actually looking at a talking rabbit!

The boy backed up slightly to better observe the very cocky rabbit standing on his hind legs with both front legs folded together like arms. Elisha was speechless, and that, the rabbit thoroughly enjoyed. "Aw, don't tell me you're afraid of a little rabbit like me!" the not-so-little rabbit challenged with a wide grin, his two large front teeth gleaming in the moonlight.

"Wh-who—or wh-what—are you?" Elisha stammered.

"Well! What do I look like?" he shot back rudely; almost offended Elisha didn't know him and showing not a shred of empathy about the boy's confusion. "I'm just a mere rabbit," he began, "and yet I am no ordinary rabbit," he added proudly, as he puffed out his chest. "Mr. Jefferds is my name, and Investigatin's my game! But no need to be formal. You," he said, nodding towards Elisha, "may call me, Jefferds."

With dramatic flair the rabbit paused for effect, as if he were greatly honoring Elisha by telling him his name.

Elisha, however, was affected for a different reason than Jefferds had in mind. Think, think, think, he thought. Jefferds, Jefferds, Jefferds... where had he heard that name before? In a few seconds the answer popped into his mind. The snowmen! They had mentioned a Jefferds having seen boy tracks.

The rabbit's continuing chatter startled Elisha out of his thoughts. "Kind of far from home, aren't you?" he began interrogating with an unabashedly nosy air. "Well, aren't you?"

"I... I am not too far," Elisha hedged.

The rabbit did not answer but peered curiously at him.

Elisha shifted his weight, uncomfortable as he remembered he should never speak to strangers. Still, the rabbit said nothing but continued staring. Perhaps he didn't hear me, thought Elisha, so he repeated, "I'm... not... too far from home."

"Hmmph!" the rabbit responded, raising his head arrogantly, before adding knowingly, "You're farther than you think, boy. Farther than you think."

Jefferds' eyes narrowed as he looked the boy up and down. "Aha!" he exclaimed as if he'd solved a puzzle. "Is your name Elisha?"

Elisha was utterly tongue-tied. How strange that a rabbit would know his name. Besides, just how do you answer a demanding rabbit?

The rabbit's next words shot into his thoughts. "Well? S-s-speak up there, boy! Elisha. That is your name, isn't it?"

"Y-y-yes, but how, how did you know?" asked Elisha, flustered, indeed, to be quizzed by a rabbit who knew something so personal about him.

"Oh, that's my job to know things. Everything. I'm a very curious rabbit. Yes, yes! Very curious, indeed. My mother always s-s-s-said I'd just as s-soon investigate, as eat. And it's true! True, s-so true," he said, with one finger in the air as if to make a point.

"But," he went on, showing his large front teeth once again and making a chopping noise two times with them, "I also like to eat, so-o... I manage to do both!" He then leaned back on his large hind legs proudly and, for emphasis, he patted his belly, adding, "Yep, investigate and eat!"

This unusual rabbit's mannerisms suddenly struck Elisha as terribly funny and he began to laugh. Jefferds very abruptly turned serious and straightened up, righting himself to get back on the track of his mission. He took a step closer to the boy, peering knowingly at him. "And you are doing some investigating yourself, aren't you, boy?"

"Well... I'm not sure. I guess..." Elisha hesitated. It was now clear that a rabbit was in charge of this conversation, and somehow it didn't seem right. "Well, y-y-yes. Yes, I am investigating. I was trying to find out what those snowmen were saying," Elisha finally admitted.

"Oh, you heard what they were s-saying all right! You just find it hard to believe," scolded Jefferds, with arms crossed, head cocked to one side and frowning.

Elisha stared at him, not knowing what to say.

"You know," he continued when Elisha didn't respond, "boys never come here. S-s-snowmen are built, s-snowmen melt, and that's the end of them, except s-ssometimes... if the s-s-snowmen get a heart, they end up here. Then Good Kind King transforms them into

Forever S-s-s-snowmen, who live happily ever after, here, *without* boys!" he ended with a glare.

Within seconds, Jefferds smiled widely, sticking out his chest, immensely proud of his ability to share this information. He waited intentionally, to give the boy some time to digest his importance as an investigator and giver of information. As the rabbit waited, he idly brushed off his handsome brown coat of fur and noted how shiny it had become.

"You want to s-s-see S-s-snowy, don't you?" Jefferds asked bluntly.

"You... you know about S-s-snowy?" Elisha asked, finding himself stuttering, too.

"Kinda s-s-slow aren't you, boy? I told you, I know everything!" Jefferds answered in a most annoyed way. "That is why you're here, isn't it, to see him?"

"W-w-well, yes, if it's possible. Is it possible? Is Snowy... really here?"

The rabbit's nose twitched and his ears wiggled in sudden irritation. He was just sure the boy had never had any carrots, or he would be smarter. "Why, s-s-suffering s-s-snowflakes! Of course, he's here. What do you think I've been talking about? Really! Boys!"

He narrowed his eyes again and looked harshly at Elisha, now taking an almost contemptuous tone. "You don't know very much do you? Should've been born a rabbit! Why do you think we're always hopping around? It's not just to get around; it's to find things out! H.S.I., Hop, S-sniff, Investigate!"

Jefferds paused to take a breath and settle himself down. "At any rate, I don't know if you can s-see him. Hmmm..." The rabbit turned his head and wiggled his long ears as he pondered how giving information about Snowy could get him into trouble. He was becoming more agitated the more he thought about it,

"Now that I think about it," he began, "You, see him? You most certainly can..." He paused and turned his eyes away from Elisha before finishing "... can not see him!"

"Not! But why not, if you know where he is?" demanded Elisha as he jumped to his feet in a panic.

Now, although Jefferds was a rabbit who loved to be the giver of information, he very well knew he shouldn't. But he really did want to tell Elisha about Snowy so badly! As he fought the battle within him, he began hopping, first back and forth, then in a figure eight. He muttered repeatedly, as much to himself as to Elisha, "No, no, can't be done. No, not possible at all!" But the desire to give Elisha the information was screaming within him. Why, his very ears were burning in his eagerness to tell, even as his nose twitched rapidly back and forth.

"But, why not? Why can't you tell me?" Elisha asked again.

Jefferds continued his frantic hopping and at times paused, as if he wanted to tell the boy something, but then would think better of it and mutter again, "No, no, not possible."

His distracted hopping was very confusing to Elisha, but after a bit, the rabbit completely stopped in his tracks. He had won his inner battle and turned to briefly address Elisha.

"I must go now. Can't waste any more moonlight, you know. You'd better go home, too!" he said with finality, beginning to hop away.

"No-o-o! No, don't go! I have more questions!" shouted Elisha in alarm.

"Oh, no, can't s-stay... running out of time... out of moonlight. I s-s-still have things to do. My business is finished here," he said as he scampered away without looking back or waiting for a response.

"But, but... When will I see you... again..." His voice trailed off, falling flat and thin into the night air. The rabbit was gone with no response to his pleas.

Everything suddenly seemed cold, unfriendly and frightening as only silence answered the boy. No answers. No leads to Snowy. How would he ever find him without help? What's the use, he asked himself, as he turned to head toward what he thought was home. Abruptly, he stopped.

"No, wait! What's the matter with me?" he asked out loud. "I've come this far. I must find out what happened to my Snowy. If he's here, I will find him and take him home, no matter what!"

Following that defiant declaration, he turned with a determined set to his chin. As his mother knew well, once Elisha made up his mind, it took a lot to change it.

Chapter Nine

Cold Tracks and Two Trails Meet

So, he started out again, a small boy travelling alone in a strange land. With no instructions, no map, and no one to help, he had only his will and heart to carry him on. He didn't know or care he was in territory unknown to any human; he only knew one thing — he had to find the Snowy they were talking about.

His small bit of Boy Scout knowledge told him he could be in trouble. Without a compass or sun shining to establish his direction, he could end up going in circles, or worse, end up far away from his goal with no help to get home. He could even fail and not find Snowy... No! He stopped such a thought and charged forward.

With chattering teeth he trudged on through the snow, sometimes falling into drifts but always getting back up and walking against the wind. Soon he began to feel very cold, colder than he'd ever felt before.

After a bit, he started to panic over which way to go. The left, the right, it all looked the same: a huge whiteness with a few trees here and there. A feeling of helplessness rose slowly within him until he once again remembered the reason for his quest.

But after walking a while longer and seeing nothing but white snow, Elisha's frustration began to build. He felt a growing anger — at the rabbit, at the weather, at this whole situation — but he knew he couldn't stop. "I'm not giving up. I'll just keep marching. Eventually, I'll have to end up somewhere, unless I get lost and freeze to death!"

Almost as if his spoken words triggered more cold, he began shivering hard. He hoped with a shudder that he wouldn't end up where there were any – wolves! As little bits of fear crept into his heart, Elisha glanced around him just to be sure there were none, before going on. Ever since he was little, he'd had a fear of wolves. But surely he wouldn't have gotten this far just to be devoured by such creatures.

Wearily, the boy looked ahead. Whiteness everywhere. He looked behind. Everything was just as white and overwhelming. Elisha shook his head helplessly as he realized, he couldn't turn back now if he wanted to, for he didn't know which way was home!

Feeling quite disheartened, he hoped he was not going in circles. The snow closed in, leaving a wall of white behind him. As he walked away, the wind whistled a lonely, plaintiff moan across the snowy landscape. It no longer felt magical, just bitterly cold and a little frightening.

His body appeared to grow smaller and smaller as he walked on into the blizzard-like distance, until soon he faded and couldn't be seen at all. Nevertheless, there were Eyes that watched him everywhere he went, discerning and evaluating his every move and response.

$$***$$

Jefferds was a busy rabbit with many things to do and many places to go and little time to do them in. He looked hopefully at the night sky but saw no sign of light. If the moon was there, it was hidden by clouds. He rushed ahead, wary that it was not good to be out when there was no moon for tracking.

"Oh, s-s-s-snow pebbles!" he sputtered. "Why does everything have to be as hard as melting an icicle in an ice storm!"

Just then the moon popped out from behind the clouds sending down generous beams to light up the white terrain once again. His large teeth glistened in the moonlight as Jefferds smiled with pleasure. Now he'd be able to see better to do his moon light business.

"Well, thank you, Mr. Moon!" he said, saluting the luminary lantern of the night sky. He continued to grin as he walked along until something disturbing appeared at his feet causing his cheerful smile to vanish instantly. Boy tracks! Immediately he was vexed. The only boy tracks he could possibly be seeing were Elisha's. This meant only one thing – the boy had not gone back home.

"Oh, grrr-reat! This is just great! He's still here. Now I s-suppose I'll have to check on him and s-see what he's up to. I don't s-s-suppose he's looking for S-snowy," he muttered sarcastically. Then he answered himself, with great drama. "But of course, he is! I've heard how boys are. Just what I need–*more trouble!*" Jefferds sighed deeply to show his aggravation.

So it was that, somewhat begrudgingly, Jefferds set aside his own agenda of moonlight business and, marching against the wind, followed the boy's footsteps.

"Here I go," he muttered as he went, "looking for a boy I don't even want around! Should have kept my raving mouth shut, but, no, I had to boast about knowing the snowman's whereabouts. Well, this is what I get... and is there anyone else around to be the hero and save the boy? Oh, no. It falls upon me alone to do what I don't want to do!" he said aloud, making his case, apparently to the wind. "Of all the inhabitants of Snow Land, why must I be the one to get these thankless jobs?" he cried out. Only the wind answered, moaning and whistling around him as he pressed on with this unwanted task.

***

Meanwhile, Elisha, who was struggling through the extreme cold, was finding it harder and harder to move as fatigue and numbness of body and mind were setting in. His teeth had stopped chattering and his body had ceased shivering long ago, and now, his lips were so cracked and stiff he could scarcely move them.

He had no idea of how long he'd been in the harsh temperatures or, for that matter, where he was. The storm had kicked in again, blinding Elisha to the sky and the moon. Unable to see, he lost his footing and fell. At first he just lay there... But then he knew he must keep going.

Slowly, with great effort, he stood up in the drift where he had fallen, pursed his lips in determination and willed his legs to pick up and go on. "March, march, march," he said again and again, forcing himself to keep moving. As the danger of freezing hovered over Elisha, it energized him to move. "Got to keep going," he mumbled with barely moving lips. Finally, though, he dropped heavily to the frozen ground. He lay there, unmoving and unfeeling.

It was not surprising, given the circumstances, that all he wanted was to remain lying down and resting, but Elisha had heard to never give in to sleep, and so he fought mentally to push on. One more time, he rose to continue, his body so numb with cold and his thinking unclear, he wasn't even sure if he was still walking or not.

Eventually the boy could take no more and slumped down into a snowdrift, oblivious to all around him. As he lay there, he surrendered to a merciful slumber, one that had snuffed out the lives of other intruders in this land. As snow began to blow and pile up on his body, his face, eyelashes and eyebrows quickly turned white with snow. If the wind kept blowing snow like this, there would soon be no trace of him.

***

With the worsening weather, Jefferds found it increasingly difficult to follow Elisha's tracks. Finally the wind stilled and once more moonlight lit up the snow, but of course the wind had erased all tracks of any kind. Jefferds, however, was not a rabbit to give up. As he looked ahead, he noticed that the glittering snow crystals had become like millions of teeny lamps! They were marking a path, each urgently pointing the way, so he began hopping quickly, looking all around him for the boy.

When Jefferds reached a small rise he stopped briefly. He needed to rest and surveyed the landscape before him, one of which he never tired. He prized Forever Snow Land's unending beauty, her secrets and intrigue and the creatures that inhabited her. And, too, he loved that there was always something new to discover here in the land protected by Good Kind King.

Sometimes the rabbit felt pity for poor human creatures, with their bare skin and no fur, unable to survive in such harsh weather. Jefferds took great pride and care of his warm fur coat and was especially proud of his large hopping feet. His whiskers twitched in satisfaction as he looked behind him, admiring his tracks, when the mental image of a small boy with a bare, naked face against the fierce wind, jarred him out of such thoughts.

With renewed urgency, he decided to thump an S.O.S. to his rabbit cousins. With their help he could find Elisha in a fraction of the time it would take him searching alone. In this suddenly frigid weather, he knew he had precious little time left if he was to find the boy alive.

At that very moment, the rabbit's foot hit something under a mound of snow. "What in the blizzards is that?" he wondered aloud. Carefully, he began brushing snow off of the heap to see what was underneath. Soon he realized what the heap was. "Oh, no! Not the boy!" Jefferds gasped as he began furiously clearing snow off Elisha's body. He worked frantically, saving his irritated muttering about the trouble that boys bring for later. Was it already too late? The grim reality was that in Snow Land a frozen slumber comes quickly with little hope of revival.

Upon seeing the boy's face, he dug feverishly to dig his body out. He couldn't tell if Elisha was still breathing, but in hopes that he could be revived, he decided to get him to a warm place. Jefferds paused to reach into his backpack for his handy collapsible sled, a gift from Old Man Snow. Pressing a button was all he needed for the sled to pop out into a useable tool, one he often used to haul treasured finds to his home. With great effort, he loaded the boy onto it, strapped him in and, putting the harness on his own shoulders, he began the laborious trek home.

Chapter Ten

Strange Warning of the Underground Flames

*T*hankfully, Jefferds' home wasn't far and with a strong wind blowing against his back, he arrived there quickly. That a mere rabbit was able to pull the dead weight of Elisha's body through the snow and down into his burrow, was in itself a part of the mystery of this unusual land. (Of course, Jefferds was no ordinary rabbit, either, as he often announced to whoever would listen.)

With a few extra grunts and one final heave, rabbit and boy were inside Jefferds' cozy home. There, the somewhat winded rabbit laid the boy down and carefully covered Elisha's cold body with a warm, downy blanket. He quickly stirred the embers to get the fire going. It roared up sending out welcome heat to warm the pair before gradually settling into comforting, crackling flames. Shadows of the flames flickered on the underground earthen walls.

Now all the rabbit could do was wait to see if Elisha would come around. Exhausted, he welcomed the rest and sank down into the down-covered cushion of his twig chair. Within minutes, the cozy warmth of the fire relaxed Jefferds enough that he dozed off muttering about what trouble boys are.

The hours passed quietly until he was disturbed by the movement of his large ears rotating to sounds from the nearby bed. Now wide awake, he jumped up to take a look.

Elisha was indeed stirring slightly and dreamily opened his eyes only to see an exasperated rabbit demanding an answer. "Just what did you think you were doing, going on into a land where you aren't s-s-s-supposed to be?!"

Elisha looked at Jefferds in bewilderment. In his dazed state he was asking himself pretty much the same question. Where on earth was he and why was he here?

He looked around the room, a strange, earthy home of some kind. It was warm and comfortable and for that, the boy was grateful.

Drawn to the source of the warmth, he started to gaze at the fire. Its glow gave the drab earthen walls the coziness of home, but the eerie shadows on them spoke otherwise. As the fire flared up, Elisha was astonished to see shadows, not only leaping wildly on the walls, but singing a hypnotic melody, "Dark Song of the Underground Flames." He drew back even as the strange song came with a warning and an underlying driving beat, to his ears:

> *In the midnight dark of underground*
> *We, the flames of light, are found,*
> *Dancing, leaping, with crackling noise,*
> *"This is not a place for boys!"*
> *If in this dark you dare intrude,*
> *Better change your attitude.*
> *Go back home to dog and toys,*
> *For this is not a place for boys!*

The flame shadows leaped higher, dancing even more wildly as the song hissed, continuing on to its end:

> *But if you choose to stay down here,*
> *Let us make this one thing clear;*
> *We give this warning in flaming voice:*
> *"This is not a place for boys-s-s!"*

By now Elisha was hypnotized by the shadows' dance and song. The final hiss lingered before fading away, leaving only the quiet crackling sound to fill the silence of the room. The flames continued to turn and twist even after their song disappeared. Mesmerized by the flame shadows' dance and warning song, Elisha struggled to become alert. Though the song had ended, the warnings continued to repeat over and over in his head, although he had no idea what they were about.

Jefferds, who apparently hadn't heard the song, finally got Elisha's attention. "Boy! What are you doing here? You were supposed to go home." He tapped his big hind foot impatiently, waiting for an answer, an explanation as to why his evening had been ruined.

The boy didn't answer, for the flames, and the song as well, had roared up again, distracting him from the rabbit's persistent questions.

"Boy! I say, Boy! Don't you think I deserve an answer?" insisted the rabbit as he continued to tap his foot while the flames' song continued to menace.

All the sounds mercilessly bombarded Elisha's ears... tapping, crackling, singing, tapping... until it all suddenly became unbearable. The poor boy closed his eyes tightly shut and covered his ears. He wished it all would stop. If only they'd just be quiet!

But the rude rabbit pressed impatiently, with a sharp tap, tap, tap, of his foot. "Well?" he repeated again and again, raising his voice more and more in agitation. "You do see what your stubbornness has done, don't you?" The tapping now changed to thumping on the earthen floor. "Well, what do you have to say?" he demanded, his large foot thumping even louder.

Jefferds paused for his answer, but, hearing none, huffed loudly in impatience, "Come on! Speak, Boy!"

It all continued, Jefferds demanding and thumping, the fire crackling and warning... Elisha, suddenly flooded with more than he could bear, cried out, "Stop! I don't know where I am or what's going on! I don't understand any of this!"

Next, Elisha began to do something he rarely did; he began to cry, not just a whimper, but all-out sobbing. The mounting frustration on top of the painful loss that had been bottled up within him for so long came pouring out. Embarrassed, he buried his face into the pillow to muffle what quickly became wailing.

Now, Jefferds could not handle this at all. No, no; not crying! He became agitated and upset, not knowing what to do, pacing this way and that, stealing frantic, sideways glances at the boy. Finally he stopped and stood with paws on his hips as he tried to think how to get him to stop. As the crying continued, once again the rabbit paced, paws locked behind his back, the boy's desperate emotions just too much for him.

In fact, if the truth were known, for Jefferds it was easier to be rude than chance getting lost in emotion. He never cried, not since he was a wee little hopper when his mother had died in a green, far-away place where they'd lived. She'd gone out to gather lettuce from Farmer Payne's garden, where he had been lying in wait for her and cruelly ended her life. Jefferds had secretly followed her and watched the whole tragedy play out before him in uncomprehending horror.

Momentarily stunned and hiding in the bushes, he waited for her to come to him. When the farmer left, he called her name repeatedly, "Mom! Mom?" She never got up, so the young rabbit had high-tailed it back to the burrow in fear. Being the runt and youngest of his brothers and sisters, who had already left for lives of their own, he waited alone in the dark burrow, trembling and fearful, but afraid to cry. He waited, afraid even to breathe, wondering if the farmer would find him, too.

When Jefferds' mother didn't return home, he hid in a corner of the dark burrow for days, nibbling on his mother's store of carrots until they ran out. None of his relatives or neighbors ever came to help him. Hunger eventually forced him to venture out, but what he'd witnessed stayed with him, deeply reinforcing in him the need to be alert at all times.

It was not until he had already learned how to survive that he met up with his family again. By then, he had learned enough on his own to only need a bit of mentoring by his Uncle Peter. Having lost his father before he was born, and then his mother, Jefferds had never recovered from his loss. The scars that lay deep within had caused Jefferds to make up his mind – he would never show his feelings or allow himself to need anyone ever again. Although deep within he did have affection for his uncle, he would make his own way in the world.

And so he did. The rabbit's spunky determination had kept him going. In spite of many difficulties that would have done other rabbits in, he survived and ended up creating quite a life for himself. The knowledge gained from his busybody ways had made him quite valuable to everyone in Snow Valley. But to boys? No way, and good grief, a crying boy? That, he couldn't take.

As for the moment, Jefferds finally sensed he must address Elisha's tears, but he ended up only grasping at things to say. "Now, now, we'll figure out s-s-something, boy. Don't fret," he said, awkwardly reaching out to pat the crying Elisha on the shoulder. "It's not like the end of moonlight, you know!" he added, trying to lighten things up a bit.

"I just want to find my Snowy, and I'm going to! And *no one* can stop me!" Elisha said, stubbornly defiant but then breaking down again, wailing even louder.

This unexpected outburst caught Jefferds by surprise, and he jumped back in response.

"There, there! Let's not have a meltdown in S-s-snow Land, boy!" reassured the rabbit quickly, more to soothe his own panic than to comfort the boy. His mind scrambled to think of what to do.

"Uh, let's s-s-see now… think, think, think!" Jefferds said, tapping his forehead. (Elisha couldn't help but notice that he often did the same thing to help himself think.)

Suddenly Jefferds brightened. "Tea! Why, of course, tea!" Turning to Elisha he asked cheerfully, "Boy, how about a warm cup of tea?"

"Tea!?" exclaimed Elisha incredulously in mid-sob. He looked up, distracted from his tears by the unexpected offer and was tempted to laugh at the idea of a rabbit offering him tea. "Whoever heard of a rabbit making tea?" he asked, sniffing back his runny nose.

"Whoever heard of a boy coming to Forever S-s-snow Land!" declared the rabbit with corresponding disbelief.

Jefferds was not about to entertain such a ridiculous discussion. He simply did what he knew to do; he picked up a rabbit-sized cup fashioned from a large snail shell, poured a steaming cup of parsnip tea and offered the aromatic refreshment to Elisha. The thought crossed Jefferds' mind that he could add a carrot cookie... but he decided to hold off to see if the tea did the trick. (He had much more tea than cookies and, after all, a rabbit does need a bite of comfort at the end of a hard hopping day.)

Elisha hesitated, but since he was still cold, he accepted the tea though he'd much rather have had hot chocolate.

"I s-s-suppose you'd rather have hot chocolate," Jefferds said.

"How do you know about hot chocolate, rabbit?" Elisha asked.

"I told you, it's my job to know about things that are none of my business! It's what I do," the rabbit explained, somewhat exasperated that the boy didn't yet have this straight. "And, my name is Jefferds," he added.

"Then you can tell me, Jefferds, something I need to know," said Elisha, taking a sip of tea and finding it not half bad as it warmed his insides.

"I am the one to ask, of course, if you need to know s-s-something," admitted Jefferds without a shred of humility as he took a sip of his own cup of tea.

"Okay, then tell me — Where is Snowy and how can I see him?"

First Jefferds' eyes popped open wide, and then he coughed and choked on his tea. He sputtered a bit before answering gruffly, "That, boy, is two questions, both of which you are not to know the answers!"

"But you do know the answers, right?" asked Elisha, like a hound on the trail of a... well... a rabbit.

"Of course, I know. Of course! But it's not an answer you need to know," Jefferds said emphatically and with some satisfaction, knowing that he held the answers Elisha so desperately wanted. To give in to that power though, however tempting, would be dangerous, therefore he abruptly began shaking his head in his most convincing manner and muttering, to himself more than the boy.

"But, Jefferds, you *do* know the answer! You must tell me!" Elisha pressed.

"No, no, must not. Can't do that at all," Jefferds defended.

Elisha felt an unusual anger rising up within him and he was ready to take on this rabbit's stubborn refusal to help. "Yes, you can, Jefferds. You just won't!" Elisha declared with righteous indignation.

Jefferds, unused to being so strongly confronted, increased his mumbling, all the while trying not to look at Elisha for fear his resolve would weaken. A wee bit of him sensed the boy's loss and emptiness. He identified with that and began to feel swayed to give him the information he desired... maybe, maybe just this once...

No, move, move, move and don't talk, Jefferds told himself as he started hopping around in a very agitated manner. He weighed it out—his desire to impress Elisha, against the unwritten rule to never give Snow Land information to outsiders. Why, no one had ever broken it before, and Jefferds wasn't about to be the first. The idea! To go down in Snow Land history as the first one who had helped a human! Yet, the boy was so persistent... Jefferds didn't know how much more pressure he could handle.

As Elisha watched him going in circles, he could not figure out Jefferds' strange, agitated behavior, alternately waving and wringing his hands, until he was quite distraught. Suddenly, the rabbit stopped. Elisha now gave undivided attention to him. Perhaps the rabbit had finally decided to tell him what he needed to know.

Finally, without another word or look at Elisha, he promptly hopped out the door.

"Wh-where are you going?" Elisha finally stammered, then, after a minute he called out, "Jefferds?"

Elisha listened for an answer but heard only the now familiar silence and the wind outside. It finally sank in that the rabbit had indeed left. Suddenly the boy became indignant – abandoned again!

"Have you no heart at all?" he shouted out the empty doorway.

Still no answer and no returning rabbit. The boy sat in silence. Alone in the near darkness with the fire dying out, the questions finally came rolling out.

"Why?" he moaned. "Why did you leave me again and why won't you tell me where Snowy is, if you know? Oh, Jefferds, why won't you help me?" His questions fell in the burrow as dead as the silence filling the room.

This whole night was like a bad dream. Maybe it is a dream, he thought gloomily.

Now, feeling very frustrated, Elisha plopped down in a chair. Not made for the weight of a boy, however, it promptly broke and dumped him into the floor. As he looked at the pieces of the broken chair, it reminded him of his mission—all falling apart. Once again he started asking himself why he was even here at all.

As he waited, the barely flickering flames weakly took up the refrain again: "This is not a place for boys-s-s; this is not a place for boys-s-s..."

Elisha was not one to give up easily. But as he listened to the song's message, it no longer seemed a warning but the truth. This was no place for him. He needed to leave.

"Snowy, you're out there, somewhere. I must be getting closer to finding you, so here I come!"

Feeling more resolved, he bundled up and without delay exited the cozy little burrow. As he stepped outside and the stinging cold struck him in the face, he immediately missed the warmth but forged ahead, totally unaware of what was waiting for him.

Chapter Eleven

Pensive Thought at Ponderous Pond

A "Sly" Direction

*E*lisha shivered and lowered his head into the wind. Even the scary shadows and Jefferds' scolding were better than this frigid cold. Soon his teeth were chattering and his back muscles were tense and sore from shivering.

Elisha became so engrossed in his battle with the cold, he didn't notice dawn had come and gone. Just when he thought he couldn't take any more, the sun burst out with brilliant sunshine. Elisha stopped, closed his eyes, and gratefully basked in the warm rays at the top of a steep hill. He did not recall how angry he had once been with the sun; instead, he marveled at how the sun could be so far away and yet so warming on a cold day. His mom would say that's just one of the wonders of God's creation. A tug came at his heart with the thought of his mom.

Without warning, a gust of wind burst forth powerfully from behind, hitting him so hard he lost his balance and pitched forward. The force of his fall sent him flying down the steep hill flat on his belly, totally out of control. Faster and faster he careened, with white powdery spray flying into his eyes.

"Oh-h-h!" he cried out, half in fear and half in excitement. Eventually he hit a bump, flipped into a ball and rolled the rest of the way, coming to a stop before an icy pond. Dazed, he lay still on his back, wondering how all that had happened so fast. As he lay there with closed eyes, Elisha gradually became aware of warm air moving on his face, almost like something... breathing!

In a panic his eyes snapped open to behold two bright, shiny black eyes staring him in the face. "Whoah!" he cried, quickly covering his head with his arm. The boy waited breathlessly, keeping his head protected. Nothing happened. Everything sounded very quiet except for a crow cawing in the distance. Dreading what he might see, yet knowing he must look, he tentatively lowered his arm. Why, there was nothing, nothing but an ice-covered pond. Elisha sat up and glanced around. To his right were only a few snowy bushes, but when he turned to his left, there, something caught his eye.

A large, furry ball, surely some kind of animal, lay unmoving on the snow. Whatever this is, it must be sleeping, Elisha reasoned to himself, but... don't animals sleep in caves or something, not out in the open, unless... whatever it is might just be "playing possum?"

Taking a few steps at a time, he ventured closer and closer until he reached the sleeping animal. He did not know why he felt he must look at this unknown creature. Normally he would've run the other way, but instead, he bent down to get a better look. Just then the animal sprang onto all four feet to face him.

The startled boy fell backwards and landed on his bottom. Quickly he scrambled to his feet. Now he could clearly see that the creature was a beautiful red fox with long, silky fur that swayed with his movements. Elisha had never come face to face with a fox before and didn't know what to expect.

The animal stood up on his hind legs and looked him over. "Well! Now that we've given each other a scare, might I introduce myself? I am Sly, so named because I'm a cunning creature. Not conceited, just cunning, and I know it." With a grin Sly watched for Elisha's reaction, but saw only a blank look on the boy's face. The fox's joke seemed to have not been understood.

"Heh, heh," the fox laughed, repeating, "not conceited, just cunning and I know it."

Elisha simply stared at the strange red fox staring back at him.

"You do know what cunning is, don't you?" Sly asked.

"No, but I know what conceited is. It means you think you're the most important."

"But we're talking about cunning." Then, giving a curt, dismissive wave with his hand, he went on. "On second thought, you're kind of young, so maybe not. Cunning means, I'm clever."

"Like smart?"

"Ahh, more than smart. Cunning, or clever, means I can figure out most anything. I am not easily fooled, but I could easily fool you if I had to. You could never 'outfox' me!" the fox declared. "No bragging. Just the truth."

He proudly held up his head, which showed off his face and a fluffy white chest above a handsome "suit" of fiery red. The lustrous hair of his red mane, longer than normal for a red fox, also swung gently as he moved his head. Elisha noticed that Sly had black markings on his legs and ear tips, as well as having black eyes, nose, and whiskers. He was, Elisha concluded, the most beautiful animal he'd ever seen.

The impressive looking fox now walked on all fours around Elisha, slowly looking him up and down. The boy became very uncomfortable, but not knowing what to say or do, he simply stood still, following the fox with his eyes.

Finally Elisha spoke up. "Uh... if you don't mind, would you please stop going around me in circles?"

Having already sized the boy up, Sly nodded affirmative and stopped. "And, if you don't mind, might I ask your name?" he asked in a smooth, intelligent sounding voice.

"I'm Elisha and I... I think I'm glad to meet you, Mr. Sly," he answered. "Are, are you the one who was staring me in the face before?"

"Yes, that was me, trying to see what in Snow Land came barreling down the hill into my territory!" the fox explained. "Do you always go down hills belly first like that?"

"No, Mr. Sly, I'd prefer to go on both feet!" Elisha said with a grin.

"Yes. But, of course, the danger of having only two feet would make one quite awkward, especially on hills," Sly added with a sympathetic smile.

"No, it wasn't my feet. It was the hard wind that made me lose my balance." Elisha smiled back, realizing the fox had no clue what it would be like to walk well all the time on two feet.

Sly, though, was busy trying to figure out what business the boy had here. "Well, well, well," he added, making a clicking sound with his mouth. "It seems the next question would be—why are you in Snow Land?"

"I'm looking for my snowman," Elisha explained. "Maybe you can help me."

"I'm not in the habit of helping boys, but, what do you need?" Sly responded as politely as possible.

"Have you seen a snowman around here?"

"A snowman is not what you need now," said Sly.

"Oh, but I do! I need him very much," Elisha said most sincerely.

"Hmm. I know that's what you *think* you need, but you need something more," the fox replied with a toss of his long, silky mane.

Elisha, perplexed at what the fox could possibly mean, took a deep breath before going on. "Sir," he said, "not to be rude, but I don't think you know what you're talking about. I do know what I need... my very special snowman, Snowy. He is –"

"Yes, yes, I know," interrupted the fox in a very weary tone. "He's gone and you want to find him. I assume he melted and came here."

"Well, I don't know that for sure. I did hear the snowmen talking about a Snowy, so I started looking for him and almost froze to death. If you tell me where to look, who knows? You might save my life!" he said trying to convince the fox to help him. "I sure would love to find him and get him home," he added wistfully.

Sly gave him a knowing look. He sighed and spoke with practiced, but wearied patience, "My dear boy, it's a matter of fact that what you need is to visit the pond first."

Elisha, quite puzzled at such advice, looked first at the fox and then at the pond. "You mean this pond?"

Sly nodded. "But of course, Ponderous Pond."

"That's a very funny name for a pond," said Elisha.

"Quite an appropriate name, however. This pond is one of a kind. Made for thinking and pondering," Sly said.

"Why do I need to go to a pond to think? Ponds are for fishing," Elisha said with a frown. It seemed that the fox was trying to complicate matters for him.

"This pond is for thinking and finding Truth. Just look in the pond and see for yourself," Sly said.

"Look in a pond? That seems kinda silly," replied the boy, now becoming annoyed at the fox's insistence.

"Ponderous Pond is the place to think and sort things out before doing something important. It's also where you find out if you have what it takes to get you where you're going. If you're wise, you'll do some pondering at the pond. Nice meeting you, Elisha," he said, and with a courteous nod, he trotted off.

Elisha wondered what on earth Sly could have meant. Although the boy had already made up his mind to just go on, he nevertheless thought through everything the fox had said, item by item. First, he didn't need to sort things out and think. Second, he already knew he was tough enough to find his snowman! Look at what he'd already gone through. He shook his head. It just didn't make sense. The only important thing I have to do, he concluded, is to find my snowman, not waste time sitting by some thinking pond.

"Wait a minute. What am I thinking?" he burst out, with a laugh. "I don't have to do what a fox tells me to do."

Elisha looked to see where Sly had gone. He spotted a red blur moving quickly up the slope, too far away for Elisha to catch up with. Upon reaching the top of the hill, however, the fox stopped and turned around to give the boy one last piece of advice.

"Trust me, Elisha," he called, looking down. "Look in the pond. Your success and survival depend on it, but... it is your decision." With that Sly dropped out of sight over the top of the hill.

He did want to succeed, so Elisha decided to take a minute to check it out, though he couldn't imagine what might be so special about some old pond.

The nearest side of the pond was open except for an old tree that had grown up at its edge. To the left of the tree a large, flat-topped rock jutted out over the pond's short bank. Elisha grabbed a low hanging limb for balance as he walked out and carefully sat down to peer into the pond directly before him. He sat and he looked. Nothing happened.

Although he looked from every angle he could think of, he decided it was pretty boring, kind of like staring at a bucket of solid ice. The only thing he found himself pondering was how this would sound to his class at school–"What I Did on My Weekend: I sat and stared at the ice in a pond. Why? Because a fox told me to!"

After a few minutes, Elisha became impatient and prepared to leave. He didn't have time to waste and surely the fox was mistaken. There was no help here.

As he rose to his feet something hovering under the tree sparkled and caught his eye. He heard a faint silvery laugh. What now?

An Iridescent Direction

Elisha drew closer for a better look. Unbelievably, the sound was coming from the most unusual, beautiful snowflake he'd ever seen. Dainty, but larger than the usual snowflake, a shimmer of light swirled and sparkled around its symmetrical form. It dipped and twirled before hovering before him, much like a hummingbird would do.

"Whoa, is that ever beautiful!" Elisha said, barely breathing.

"Why, thank you!" the snowflake said, laughing in a musical way.

"What?" Elisha exclaimed. "A talking snowflake? Unbelieveable!"

As he continued to gaze in bewilderment, he was even more astonished to see a lovely face in the center of the snowflake which floated before him.

"Now, I really don't believe it!" Elisha said emphatically.

"Oh, but belief is what I'm about, my little friend," the snowflake responded with another silvery laugh.

"Are you what Sly meant that I should come to see?" asked Elisha.

"Oh, no, no, no," laughed the snowflake, "although you did come to the right place."

"I'm confused," said Elisha.

"You're confused? Well, I'm Iridescence. Iridescence Snowflake," she said introducing herself.

"You're... Oh, I see. Your name is Ir... Ir-si-dense?" he said, stumbling with the unfamiliar word.

"Ir-i-des-cence, cause I sparkle, sometimes in colors. You can call me Iri, though," she added.

"Iri Snowflake. That is much better," Elisha said, relieved to get that settled. "So, if you're not what I'm supposed to see, then why was I told to come here?"

"Hmmm. Let me give this some snowflake thought," she said and swirled around in place for a moment. Coming to a stop, she answered, "It's obvious you must be on a mission. That means you need to sit by the pond and gaze into it."

"But that's what I don't understand. It's just a bunch of ice in a frozen pond," Elisha replied. "I can see that from standing here."

"Just a pond? Ah, but it can be so much more, if one needs it to be."

"No offense, but I need to get going. Everybody keeps trying to tell me what I need. What I need to do is find my snowman and stop wasting time here! No offense, Iri," he added.

"No offense taken, but it is not a waste of time to stop, think and look inside yourself. Why are you on this mission?"

"Because I need to find my snowman."

"Why?"

"Because I miss him and love him with all my heart."

"Ah, the heart. A curious thing. Sometimes it can bring you to the wrong place, and... sometimes your heart alone is not enough. Try Ponderous Pond and you will see," she said and, giving a shimmering spin in the air, she began to float away.

"See what? Wait! What do you mean?"

"Just look in and believe. You'll see," she said, her voice sounding smaller as she floated farther away.

"Look, where? Believe what?" Elisha sighed as she was already gone. "This Snow Land life is so frustrating!"

He walked back onto the rock and stood on its edge. As he stared into the pond, all he could make out were bird tracks in the light snow that blanketed the ice. He sighed again, more mightily this time. It looked like any other pond to Elisha, but he figured if a fox and a snowflake had both said the same thing to him, maybe he should try it.

A Mirrored Truth

So... Elisha sat down and began staring into the ice. He waited and waited. "This isn't working," he muttered impatiently. Iri had said to believe, but believe what?

"I just don't get it, but I guess I should keep trying," he mumbled. Closing his eyes tightly, he began repeating, "I believe, I believe..." But saying you believe without knowing what you believe, doesn't make sense. Okay, Elisha, he asked himself, what do I believe? There was only one thing he knew for sure– that he wanted to find Snowy. But could he? Somehow he had to believe he would be able to.

Oh, all this thinking was too much! Elisha put his head in his hands and slumped down wearily into "cucumber mode" – the position he takes when his brain is too weary to think anymore!

Meanwhile, something startling began to happen. The snow began to blow away from a particular spot on the ice and into his face. Raising his head to look, Elisha saw a clear oval shape forming in the ice right before him! Very curious to see what was happening, he stood up to get a better look.

The oval shape had begun to ebb and glow brightly. Elisha watched as a swirl formed directly above it and began to spin. The swirl spun faster and faster, until the ice became as finely polished as a mirror. Shortly the swirl stopped and vanished. All that remained was a bright, shining mirror.

Still amazed at what he'd just seen happen before his own eyes, Elisha looked into the oval mirror. First he saw the reflection of his own face, but then it blurred and was replaced by another glowing face, different from his own!

This startled poor Elisha so much that he fell backwards onto the ground, landing on his elbows. He frantically pulled himself farther away, afraid to look at a face appearing in the ice out of nowhere. Once he had composed himself though, his curiosity drew him back to the rock's edge.

Slowly, cautiously, he peeked into the ice mirror again. It was still there—the strange, glowing face. It was not just a normal face one would describe with eyes, nose and mouth; no, somehow it was more, and he knew it was the kindest, most loving face he'd ever seen.

"Don't be afraid, Elisha," spoke a voice ever so gently. "I will not harm you."

A definite calm settled over the surprised boy as his fear left him, and he waited, wondering what this strange apparition could all mean.

"So! You finally decided to try thinking before you go any further."

Elisha didn't know how or what to answer. Finally he said, "I don't know what I'm doing here."

"You need to find Truth."

"Huh?" Elisha certainly didn't think he was looking for Truth; he thought he was looking for his snowman. "Who are you?" he asked. "All I can see is your face."

"I am the Face of the Mirror of Truth."

"Truth of what?" Elisha asked.

"Truth of things as they really are. Things you can't see with your eye."

That statement, like so many other things in Snow Land, made no sense at all to Elisha, but the Face went on. "Do you believe, child?"

"Uh… some things, but I don't know about any of this."

"Well, what do you believe?"

Elisha sighed in exasperation and threw up his hands. "Hey, I don't know. I'm just a kid! I believe this is all confusing."

"It's okay," assured the Face. "You're still learning. Just think. What do you believe?"

"I believe what Mom or Dad tell me," he said. "Some things I figure out on my own."

"Like what you decided to believe about your snowman?"

"What? What do you mean?"

"Well, are there not certain things you believed about your snowman just because you wanted them to be true?"

"Uh… yes, I… I guess so."

"Like thinking Snowy would be a forever snowman?"

"How do you know about that?"

"Oh, I've known about you for a long time, Elisha," said the Face. "You wanted your snowman to live forever, correct?"

"Well, yeah, doesn't everybody?"

"You, more than most, I'd say," said the Face.

"What's wrong with that?" Elisha asked. "I wanted a Forever Snowman and so I believed with all my heart!"

"I know, but just believing is not enough. You need Truth."

"Oh," Elisha moaned. He felt weary, for all this thinking stuff was really hard.

"Once you find Truth, Faith will get you through. You'll see," explained the Face with a warm smile.

Elisha responded with a helpless little grin for he really did not understand. After pausing to think a bit more, however, his face lit up. "It's easier just to believe and understand later."

"Yes, yes!" exclaimed the Face, extremely pleased. "That's Faith. I believe you're ready to look deep into my mirror. Well, go ahead — look," the Face instructed.

After hesitating, Elisha looked casually down into the mirror.

"No, no. You must believe you'll find Truth when you look," the Face chided gently.

Without understanding, he tried to believe and look for Truth in the mirror. At first he saw only the Face, but as he believed, suddenly the image glowed brighter and brighter until he thought its radiance would surely blind him. Instinctively he covered his eyes until he no longer sensed the bright light.

"What was all that?" he asked, uncovering his eyes. "Some kind of X-Ray?"

The Face ignored his question, instead giving further instructions. "Let's try one more time, Elisha. This time, ignore the light. Just relax but think deeply as you believe."

As Elisha tried harder, the image in the mirror blurred again and this time when it cleared, had he not been looking with his own eyes, he would not have recognized himself. His own eyes, nose and mouth appeared faintly but were oddly covered by a mixture of muddy looking smears, which gave his face a strange and confusing appearance. Thinking his face was dirty, he tried rubbing the smears off, but they did not disappear. This somewhat alarmed him.

"What's wrong with my face? Why won't this stuff come off?" he asked as he continued to rub.

"You can't rub those off, Elisha."

Elisha touched the smears again. "Where did this mud come from?"

"It is not mud. Some smears are hurt that took over your life. Hurt so bad, you couldn't let go of it. The other streaks are fear. Fear that you may hurt again. Fear from what might happen.... that kind of thing."

Elisha thought this a very strange explanation. Only the Mirror understood these were dark traces of fear and hurt that had crept into his heart and shaken his faith. What Elisha did with them would determine his success in Snow Land. In spite of all this, the Mirror also saw the boy's image shined with strong love and determination. The Mirror was greatly relieved to see no selfishness or evil in the boy.

"This is one crazy mirror," Elisha said. He had never seen anything like this before. Really! Mud, that wasn't mud? As he stared in puzzlement at his strange reflection, his own face abruptly disappeared and a swirling glow rose to hover in the air above. There, the kind Face reappeared and its voice spoke again.

"I've seen what I needed to see, Elisha, and so have you. You may go on and look for your snowman now."

"Are you kind of like, giving me permission?"

"Yes, but more of a blessing. I warn you, child, it will not be easy, not even if you were a grown up. You will be tested and in danger many times. It may all seem more than you can handle, but if you keep on believing, Faith and Love will help you make it."

Elisha didn't have time to focus on what the Face said about dangers. Instead, a warmth filled him from the top of his head to the tip of his toes. He smiled in response and watched the swirl enclose the Face and begin to leave.

"Will I find my Snowy?" he called out hurriedly.

"Will you believe?" the Face called in a fading voice.

"I..." he began but stopped, for the swirl had now disappeared.

"Wow!" Elisha exclaimed in wonder at what had happened.

He looked at the empty ice before him. Snow had already covered the oval mirror. A few birds had landed on the other end of the pond making new tracks. It was almost as if nothing had happened; it looked like any other pond. As he glanced around, standing completely alone, his sense of awe began to ebb. "Well, once again I don't know where I'm going or why all this happened. I hope... no," he corrected himself, "I believe I got what I came here for."

At that he heard a little silvery laugh, "Yes, now that you believe, you'll have Help when you need it, Elisha."

Instantly recognizing Iri's voice, Elisha turned to greet his snowflake friend. His mouth dropped open in awe to see Iridescence appearing in more dazzling, iridescent colors than before.

"What happened to you, Iri? You're so... so colorful!"

Her laugh now cascaded out like a tiny musical waterfall, which seemed to enfold and wrap around him. She went on to explain, "My happy colors always happen when Faith to Believe is present! Do you remember I'm all about believing?"

"Oh, yes, you did say that, but I had no idea..." Elisha's voice trailed off as he stood transfixed by her beauty. It had tripled a thousand times and all because he believed? There must be a lot more power in this believing stuff than he realized. "I've never seen a snowflake like you before," he said.

Iridescence swirled joyfully around in a display of pinks, blues, lavenders and greens before swooping down to say, "Goodbye... only Believe." Then she rose again to hover high above. There, spikes of light flashed out to trigger a shower of shimmering frost. It fell gently and as it landed on him, a great encouragement filled him. "Guess this kind of believing makes you feel better, too!" he said.

At that moment Elisha decided that *what* he believed could in no way be something he made up in his head. It had to be Real Truth. He only had to find it.

Chapter Twelve

'Hailarious' Danger

*A*t least the sun was shining now, but he wished he had sunglasses with him. The blinding reflection of the sun on the snow made it difficult for him to see his way. To protect his eyes, he lowered his head and walked on, hoping that surely something would turn up that could point him to Snowy.

Gradually, as Elisha's eyes adjusted, he began to discern the area around him. As he did, he noticed that strange, dark clouds were rapidly rolling in, beginning to cover the sun. The wind started to kick up as well. "Here we go again," he muttered. This seemed to be a land of constantly changing weather excepting the cold — that never seemed to change.

Soon, Elisha sensed that something large was looming just ahead of him. He looked up to see a snowy mountain standing majestically, its top disappearing into not dark, but fluffy, white clouds. They hung in the sky like mounds of cotton candy floating in a sea of blue. This must be the mountain he had seen from his yard. Unaware of what happens to trespassers on this mountain, he simply appreciated the beautiful view for a moment.

His appreciation was short-lived, however, for as he neared the base of the mountain, the wind took on a surprising fierceness. It blew so hard against him it was almost impossible to stand. For a brief moment when he could look around, he saw it was blowing nowhere else, only at him!

He doggedly began his climb and that's when a sudden intensity of the wind felt as if it were deliberately whipping him and only him. He was confused as to why the wind should single him out. Was he a target? If so, why?

While he didn't understand, the wind's seeming attack on him just made Elisha more determined. The harder it blew, the more resolved he became... I believe. I believe I'll find Snowy. With head down, he leaned into the wind and pushed himself harder, struggling to climb and often stumbling over rocks he couldn't see for the wind in his eyes. He was so in hopes that he might find snowmen on this very mountain, so in spite of the wind beating relentlessly against his body, he kept climbing upward.

"You're not going to stop me!" he cried out. Then, suddenly, the wind just stopped. How could it be that wind, blowing so fiercely, would suddenly stop blowing, as if someone had turned off a switch?

The tired boy, panting and sore from fighting the wind, was grateful to rest. I do believe I'll find Snowy, he thought. With everything so quiet and still, he heard the distant sound of wonderful, magical laughter.

"Snowmen!" he cried out hopefully. Could it be? Newly energized by that hope, he hurried on, a wide grin spreading across his young face. If only he could talk to the snowmen, perhaps they would tell him about Snowy... or better yet, maybe Snowy would be right there with them and this would all be over!

Halfway up the mountain, he came upon a flattened area, slightly above him but still a good distance away. The sound of laughter grew stronger as he approached. What he saw next on the plateau, however, stopped him in his tracks.

At last, there they were, happy snowmen of various kinds and sizes, dancing and frolicking in the snow, which was spraying in all directions from their activity. What a wonderful sight! Elisha, for now keeping a distance, eagerly began twisting and turning, trying to get a better view. Oh, please, please let me see Snowy, he prayed. He checked out each snowman, one by one. His face was filled with hope and excitement each time he looked at another snowman, only to be disappointed.

Eventually the last snowman turned around and Elisha could see a happy snowman throwing snowballs... But, alas, it was not Snowy. His smile drooped sadly as his spirit fell within him. Despair now began to creep over the boy, but before it overwhelmed him, the snowmen's Snowflake Laughter started to flood the air. Enchanted by this beautifully carefree sound, he soon found the laughter so contagious, that, not only did he feel like giggling, he was totally unable to stop himself. He watched as dancing snowflakes settled on his jacket, causing Elisha to giggle right out loud.

He couldn't know that each exposure to the snowmen's laughter caused his control to lessen. The first time, he was able to somewhat withstand their laughter, but now, the harder he tried to stop, the more laughter swelled within him. The small giggles rapidly grew into hearty ones.

How was he going to keep from giving himself away to the snowmen? Just the idea of being unable to stop giggling triggered outright laughter. Concentrating hard he tried to laugh as quietly as possible. It soon became clear, though, that he couldn't even do that. Still, there was no need for him to worry. The snowmen were making too much noise themselves to hear him.

As their laughing grew wilder... that's when "it" began. One of them had rolled onto his back trying to make a snow angel, but he looked so ridiculous, clumsily flapping his arms and legs, that it caused the others to hoot and holler loudly. The downed snowman joined in on the hilarity. As he laughed, he rolled in the snow with all fours waving goofily in the air.

Elisha, observing all this comedy, burst out laughing also, thinking the snowman looked more like a beached whale. Then, amazingly, something began spewing from the snowman's mouth and shooting high into the air like a geyser. This was like what he saw before.

"What in the world is that?" Elisha cried out as it cascaded high up into the air and dropped down nearby. Could a snowman shoot water out like that? Quickly he ran over and crouched down to check it out. Expecting a puddle of water, instead, he saw pieces of something. It looked like... Could it be – hail? Picking up some pieces, he realized the laughter shooting out of the snowmen's mouths was, indeed, hail! At this, Elisha also began laughing hilariously. (Since it was hail and it was hilarious, that is why Snow Landers named this phenomenon, Hailarious Laughter, or Hail Laughter, for short.)

"This is s-s-stronger than Sn-sn-snowflake La-la-laughter!" he stammered between hoots. Soon the laughing effect grew into an epidemic as one by one, all the snowmen fell down shooting hail everywhere. With ten snowmen on their backs, the hail sprayed in arches from one snowman to another.

Each arch of hail pieces, shining in the sunlight, became rainbows of sparkling color. Upon seeing the rainbows they were creating, the snowmen laughed so hard icy tears ran down from their eyes.

"Sno funny! We snoot (*shoot*) rainbows!" one cried out.

"Snoh, no," *(Oh, no)* another argued, "not rainbows—snowbows!" He laughed uncontrollably as he opened his mouth wide to shoot another snowbow at a tall snowman near him.

"I snoot you back!" the tall one shouted between his own spurts of laughter.

"Good snoot!" judged another as the tall one's shot hit the first squarely on his carrot nose.

Snowbows were now shooting back and forth rapidly between snowmen, the icy rainbows crossing and crashing into one another, sending brilliant sparks of color into the air.

Elisha watched the spectacle in delight amid the white snow and sunshine. "It's a fireworks show!" he exclaimed. "No, it's a *snoworks* show," he laughingly corrected himself as he adopted the snowman way with language.

Elisha was laughing so hard by now, he nearly lost his breath– hard belly laughs that made his sides ache. It was strange… he no longer even wanted to stop.

Meanwhile, as the snowmen's Hail Laughter continued, some of the misfired snowbows landed farther up on the mountainside. A slight rumbling sound began to grow on Snow Mountain above them, but Elisha and the snowmen paid no attention as they continued their merry laughter. Little did they guess, their snowbows had triggered Hailarious Danger.

Totally caught up in the joyous chaos, Elisha slowly became aware of a familiar voice shouting at him, "Boy! What are you trying to do, get yourself killed? Stop that laughing! You must get out of here!"

Still giddy with laughter, Elisha turned aside to see the very angry but frightened Jefferds reaching out a paw to him. This made the rabbit look ridiculous to Elisha and it set him off even more. "It's… it's okay, J-J-Jefferds!" he said as he doubled over in hilarity.

"No, it is *not* okay! You foolish boy, you're in danger!" scolded Jefferds, not only alarmed but strongly offended that the boy wasn't showing him respect by listening. He continued to reach out to Elisha, who was suffering from the worst case of Hail Laughter Jefferds had ever seen. The angry rabbit shouted loudly, "Come with me, *now!*"

Practically screaming in laughter by now, Elisha not only couldn't stop; he did not want to. He was finding the whole experience strangely exhilarating.

Elisha tried to get the rabbit to look at the funny snowmen. "Come on, lighten up and look, Jefferds!" the boy urged. "They're so funny!" Jefferds, however, wanted no part of it. Hail Laughter has no effect on common-sense rabbits. Instead, he was growing so alarmed he grabbed again for the boy, but Elisha struggled away, assuring the rabbit that he was just fine.

Suddenly the rumbling noise, which had been growing louder by the second, seemed to be moving towards them. This got Elisha's attention and he looked toward the mountainside above. Seeing nothing, however, he gladly returned to his laughter.

"Come on, Boy! No time to waste!" Jefferds warned as he seized the boy's jacket.

"Stop! Stop it!" cried Elisha. "I'm having fun! You – you," he said gasping for breath, "you should try laughing, too!" With that Elisha pulled away, but when he paused to catch his breath, he realized he was laughing alone. He suddenly was overcome by a weirdly uncomfortable feeling, as if something was very wrong. Even the snowmen had gone silent. He turned around to look at them.

Not only had their Hail Laughter stopped, but every snowman stood as if frozen in silence, staring at the mountain above. As they came to their snow senses, an alarmed cry began to swell from them all, "Snoh, no-o-o-o!" There was not one chuckle or sniggle left in any of them. With snowman snorts and pitiful cries they scrambled to run helter-skelter down the mountainside in their usual, clumsy way, waving arms and rocking back and forth, all unable to keep their balance—some half falling, some in a gallop, and others just sliding wildly whether on bottoms, sideway or on their bellies. Any other time, they would have appeared hilarious, but this was no laughing matter. The snowmen knew, even if Elisha didn't, that the snowbows and loud laughter had gravely disturbed the mountainside. An avalanche was coming and coming fast! They were all in Hailarious Danger. Everything and everyone on the mountain were running for their lives—except for Elisha!

The rumbling had become steadily louder, growing in force and intensity. Small clumps of snow rolled down towards Jefferds and Elisha, becoming larger every millisecond. Turning away from the snowmen, Elisha looked back up the mountain in time to see a monstrous blur of white headed right for them!

"Suffering snowflakes! Are you crazy, Boy? Stop staring!" cried out Jefferds. He tried jumping to safety pulling Elisha with him, but Elisha stood unmovable as he stared in horror at the snow slide that was almost upon them.

"You're going to get us both kill—" Jefferds screamed, his words cut off by the snow as it roared over them. In the same instant, he gave the mightiest pull possible and dove under the edge of a huge sheltering rock, pulling the speechless boy under with him.

A deafening sound thundered over the two as the avalanche traveled on with the force and might of a freight train. The sliding mass of snow instantly buried them and their rock, leaving them in complete darkness. The boy and the rabbit listened as the avalanche continued to roar down the mountain. Gradually the roar faded away and they were left in dead silence.

The pair lay unmoving, in the still, dark quiet of their prison of snow.

Chapter Thirteen

Buried Alive!

*T*hanks to the heroic efforts of the rabbit, the two had been saved from the fast fury and weight of the avalanche. But they were buried alive! Alive for the moment, but how long could they last? These were the thoughts occupying Jefferds. How on earth could they ever get out... if they could at all?

A pocket of air surrounded their heads and Jefferds' upper body. Unfortunately, there was only enough air to last for a brief time. If they'd landed a foot lower, there would've been no air pocket at all. The slope of the mountainside meeting the underside of the huge flat rock had created their safe haven. This same rock, jutting out from the side of the mountain, prepared and placed there thousands of years before, had saved the pair from being utterly crushed.

Stunned, both of them lay still in the dark, neither speaking nor moving for a long while. The stifling silence was eerie. Finally Elisha tried to move his arms and legs, but to his dismay, he couldn't. Grunting, he tried harder, but the weight of the snow covering him from his chest down was too much. That was frightening enough, but the dark was blacker than any he'd ever known. Elisha didn't know which was worse, the feeling of being completely trapped or the total darkness. Either was too scary to handle alone; at least he had Jefferds with him. Or did he? He couldn't see and he hadn't heard him at all.

Jefferds, as the smaller of the two was safer, having crawled closer to the underside crevice of the rock, leaving only his feet and hind legs weighed down with snow. Ever thinking, he had set to work trying to figure how to get out of this impossible mess.

"Jefferds?" Elisha said in a small voice, hoping against hope the rabbit would answer and that he wasn't harmed.

Finally Jefferds spoke with a warning. "Be still," he cautioned. "At least we have air around our heads, so we can breathe... for a time."

"But... but... how will we get out of here?" asked a very frightened Elisha, before adding timidly, "*Will* we get out?"

Jefferds remained silent as he contemplated about what to tell the boy. Certainly not known for being tactful, he had to think carefully to keep from blurting out an answer that would further frighten the child. After all, Jefferds knew what it was like to be small and afraid.

And Elisha, very afraid, cried out in the darkness again, "Jefferds?"

Quickly Jefferds tried to think what to say. He couldn't tell the boy they might never get out alive, so perhaps it would be kinder to get the boy's mind on something else. His silence as he thought, however, only made Elisha even more panicked.

"Jefferds? Jefferds! Answer me. I can't see! Are you still alive?" the boy cried out in fear.

"S-sufferin' s-snowflakes! Of course, I'm alive, you s-s-silly human! Why I ever came up here looking for you, I'll never know. Boys! Nothing but trouble! If I'd gone on my way, I wouldn't be in this mess, but then you'd be here alone without enough s-sense to come in out of the avalanche," grumbled the rabbit, intentionally trying to keep the boy from thinking about their being buried alive. "Barely even got you saved."

"Yeah, you're still alive all right!" Elisha muttered, quite hurt by Jefferds' words. Then, adding louder, "Just as ornery as ever, too."

"Ornery! Look at the mess we're in and whose fault it is! Don't you think I have reason to be ornery?" the rabbit yelled as his own words stirred up his true feelings.

Elisha remained silent for a few moments before speaking. "You are right, rabbit. It is my fault, but I didn't mean to hurt anyone. I was only looking for my snowman friend."

"You never mean to get into all the trouble you manage to get into, but it still happens, and it always means trouble for others. Perhaps you'll learn to stay where you're supposed to and take no for an answer."

"If you mean going home and not looking for Snowy, that'll never happen!" Elisha cried out defiantly.

"Has anyone ever told you before, you're stubborn?" Jefferds asked accusingly.

"Yes, they have! Has anyone ever told you, you're a nosy rabbit?" Elisha fired back.

"Yes! Remember, I investigate?"

"And where has that gotten you?" muttered Elisha.

"Stuck here with an ungrateful boy," Jefferds first mumbled but then raising his voice a bit, he added, "I did save your life and nearly lost my own!" With that, Jefferds gave a huff and lapsed into silence.

Elisha was quiet as well. He found it strange to have his eyes wide open and see absolutely nothing but blackness. The darkness along with the silence seemed to have swallowed him up. Eventually the continued quiet became so deafening, Elisha could stand it no longer.

"Rabbit?"

"What!" Jefferds answered begrudgingly, in his very grumpiest voice.

"I'm sorry."

Elisha waited for a response. There was none. The rabbit was totally focused on how they might get out of this disaster while the boy was occupied with their argument.

"Will you forgive me?" Elisha asked simply.

"I am not into forgiveness," said the rabbit coldly, as if making an announcement.

"My parents say forgiveness is important," Elisha offered. "Without forgiveness we just get more... ornery. Besides... Mom says God forgives us, so we should forgive others." Elisha waited, but Jefferds didn't answer. He waited and waited.

There he goes again, thought Jefferds with sad irritation, stirring up things within me, talking about his mom, reminding me what my mother would've taught me had she lived. He knew he would need his energy to figure a way out and didn't want to waste it on emotion, but he struggled with ignoring the boy's attempt to make things right. Eventually Jefferds spoke, ever so quietly, the closest he would come to a partial apology. "I cannot say I forgive yet, but I do realize you cannot help it that you're a boy and you're nothing but trouble to me."

Elisha was so relieved to hear the impertinent rodent speak again, he ignored the half insult. All was quiet again for a long moment.

"Rabbit, how are we going to get out of here?" Elisha asked, with trembling voice.

"S-sufferin' s-snowflakes, there you go again! How am I s-s-s-supposed to know that?"

"You said investigating and knowing everything is what you do!" Elisha shot back.

"Well, I've never been inside an avalanche before. I do know that if it weren't for you, we'd both be s-safe!" Jefferds carried on accusingly. "You were told to not come on S-s-snow Mountain, but you came anyway. Do you ever do what you're told to do?"

"I did what I had to do! I couldn't just give up on Snowy! I don't give up on the ones I love! **Ev-er**!" he shouted as he turned his head, staring in the dark in the direction of the rabbit's voice. Had there been light, the rabbit would have seen the boy's eyes blazing and his face reflecting an even hotter temper.

As for Jefferds, he was so angry he was tempted to give the boy a good thumping with his large thumpers... If only he could in this dark, cramped place.

Elisha, coming back to his normal tenderhearted way, repented quickly of his anger and softened his tone.

"Well, there's no sense in blaming each other, but... what are we going to do?" he asked.

"Do? You're not going to do anything. You've done quite enough already! Besides, you're s-stuck. I, on the other hand have a plan, as I have a little wiggling room here." Jefferds began digging snow away from his lower body. "If I can just..." he grunted, "get my hind feet... out!" Out popped one foot, so he dug even harder with his front paws, only stopping to pull repeatedly at the other. "There!" he said as his other hind foot finally came out from under the snow. It hurt a bit but at least both feet were free.

"These magnificent feet of mine can be digging machines, snow shoes, thumpers... whatever I need them for," he said, wiggling them in pride. "Now, let's see them get to work. I do have the best thumpers in Snow Valley!" he boasted.

Grateful to be partially free he set to work, though wincing in pain from a strained tendon. First he tried to tunnel out, but the snow was packed too tightly. "Eh, I was afraid of that," he murmured. "But... if I can just carefully push some s-snow up into the end of this air pocket, without making more snow fall in on us, maybe I could clear enough area to thump for s-some help."

"You don't really know what to do, do you, Rabbit?" asked a discouraged Elisha.

"Boy! I am doing something, and my name is Jefferds, not Rabbit!" he huffed, in his most offended manner.

"And my name's Elisha, not Boy!" shot back Elisha, equally offended.

"Hmm-ph!" the rabbit commented grumpily.

"Hmm-ph to you, too!" returned Elisha, just as grumpily.

Now with the boy silent, Jefferds began working with his large hind feet to gradually widen the area below him but still underneath the rock. The weight of the snow prevented his pushing it down farther than the air pocket. He would have to try to move some of the snow from below into the top of his air pocket. He had no other choice; he had to create thumping room for his feet. Finally, huffing and puffing, Jefferds stopped to rest, lying back and pitifully gasping for air.

"Oh, Jefferds, I should be helping," said Elisha sympathetically, feeling sorry for the tired, winded rabbit.

Jefferds lay still, trying to regain his strength and breath. Finally, still tired and irritated, he spoke. "And how could you possibly help? You're s-stuck under an avalanche of s-snow!" he shouted. Sensing the boy's distress, he softened as he added, "At least we're able to breathe!"

"Breathing is good," joked Elisha lamely.

"That's usually my choice also, when given the choice of to breathe or not," answered Jefferds with a small grin, appreciating Elisha's brave attempt at humor.

"I suppose breathing and not killing each other are both good," Elisha responded. Although they could not see each other, they both grinned weakly before turning more serious. As Jefferds returned to his digging Elisha spoke up again.

"Jefferds?"

"Yes?"

"Will a search party come?"

"A... search party?" questioned Jefferds.

"Yeah, where rescuers come after an avalanche to... you know, to save us," Elisha said.

"Nope. Don't have 'em," said Jefferds without emotion, remaining focused on his work of enlarging his area. "There," he said, "now I think I have thumping room."

"What do you mean, thumping room?" asked Elisha, completely puzzled.

"I mean this..." the rabbit said beginning a gentle, tentative thumping.

"Oh," said Elisha as he listened. "That sounds like a code. Who are you sending it to?"

"Well, we can hope that it will carry down the mountain to my cousins. S-sometimes, we rabbits talk in secret to each other by thumping the ground in rabbit code. Then we wait. It is hard to be heard from under s-so much s-snow, but the thumping sound travels underground. Hopefully one of my cousins will have his ear to the ground after this avalanche."

Jefferds felt around, poking carefully here and there into the snow. He stopped and became very serious as he thought out his plan.

"I must not thump too hard, though. It could cause more snow to cave in on us or... start another avalanche. On the other hand, I must thump hard enough to be heard. Hmmm. Quite a dilemma. I'll just have to... play it by ear," he decided. Then, sensing Elisha's worry, he added, "And I do have the ears for it, don't you think?"

Elisha snickered at that. "Yeah, you've got the feet for it, too, Jefferds!"

Knowing that to be true, Jefferds started to thump, determined to try hard in spite of the pain. If they made it through this, he hoped Elisha would not remember him as a wimp because of a hurt leg.

Jefferds knew they didn't have a lot of time left. The air was already getting pretty thin from his activity and their arguing.

The boy waited helplessly from his pinned state as the rabbit thumped rhythmically, listening for any signs of disturbance. Of course, if there were any, there would be nothing Jefferds could do about it, besides stop thumping... and then it could be too late. It was a very tense waiting time for them both.

"Jefferds?"

"Yes, what is it?" he responded, not really wanting to be disturbed.

"What are your thumps saying?"

Jefferds paused to answer, "Uh... Help."

"Of course," Elisha giggled, "but how will they know where we are? Are you telling them?"

"Well, a thoughtful question," said Jefferds. "You see, our rabbit ears can tell us a lot. We hear a thump and we can just about tell the distance and direction it's coming from. Hopefully my cousins will hear and figure out where we are in time."

"In time?"

"Yes," said the rabbit quietly. Whether help could come before they ran out of air was very doubtful, but Elisha didn't need to know that. Jefferds also knew that at any second a thump could set off another snow slide. Still, it was their only chance for rescue, so he kept rhythmically thumping the rabbit code for S.O.S. Once, they did hear an alarming movement of the snow, but it quieted and Jefferds returned to thumping.

After a time Elisha spoke the unspoken thought that hung between them. "It's... it's getting harder to breathe."

"I know," Jefferds said quietly. "Getting harder to thump, too. Save your breath," he cautioned.

"What if no one comes?"

Jefferds became still. He did not answer. In silence he renewed his efforts, weakly thumping his rabbit S.O.S. and listening.

After a while, Jefferds noticed things had been quiet for too long. "Boy! Are you awake?" he called. "I say, Boy! Wake up!"

Elisha's eyes fluttered, trying to open. "Tired," he barely mumbled. Then he roused a little more adding, "Name... Elisha... not Boy."

Now Jefferds was alarmed. Elisha's voice sounded much weaker. He left his digging and began shaking him and smacking his face to rouse him up.

"Mmm... hurts," Elisha moaned slightly.

"Hey, Elisha! Do you know how to pray?"

The boy mumbled, "Mm-hmm."

"Well, then... this would be a good time for us to do it," suggested the rabbit.

"You pray?" Elisha asked weakly in surprise.

"Of course, I pray! We rabbits always remember Who made us and how short our lives are. We don't get so busy with unimportant things like you humans do. Always being one breath away from meeting our Creator, keeps our lives 'real.' Could go any day, any time," he concluded philosophically, then explained in his very matter of fact voice, "Predators, you know. Or maybe, when it happens, it's just that our time is up."

Elisha could not understand how the rabbit could talk so easily about his own possible death, but he didn't have the energy left to say so. He remembered hearing his parents talk about people living like they're never going to die and face their Maker. They said you have to live right and be ready. And know Jesus. Elisha had accepted Jesus into his heart at five. He didn't hate anyone and he loved God, so he knew he was ready. Elisha wondered if this is what dying is like. It was getting harder to think. He thought he could hear Jefferds calling his name.

"Elisha?" The rabbit began to panic but kept trying to keep Elisha alert. "Boy! You awake? If you are, it's time to start praying!" He patted the child's cold cheeks hard again, urgently saying, "Pray, boy!"

"God," Elisha began weakly, "Not... afraid... cuz You're... with me..." Elisha's voice faded off, but Jefferds kept rousing him regularly, until he himself became too tired.

Then Jefferds prayed, "Oh, Creator... I'm just a little rabbit, but... this boy is made like You. He's pesky to me, as I probably am to You..." Jefferds' lips barely moved as he whispered, "but You've... let him come here... for a reason. Please... ss-send us help. Amen."

Elisha roused himself enough to barely mumble, "Sorry, Mom... Dad..." Elisha began to drift again, when the picture of his shoving

Mollie away came to his mind. He stirred to say, "Sorry... girl." As his voice trailed away, he whispered, "Snowy-y..."

Jefferds faintly heard the boy's last word. He felt a prick in his conscience that he had not helped him find his beloved snowman. Having raised himself, Jefferds hadn't experienced love like that from anyone. Except... his mother! Oh, how fondly he remembered his mother! And now, it looked as if he would meet her again soon.

Though he had been a very small hopper, he could still remember her cautioning him, "Always remember your Creator, Jeffie. We rabbits have very short lives, so make every hop count, live your bunny best every day, and never run out of carrot cookies and tea to share."

As Jefferds remembered these things, he smiled. He hoped she would be proud of how he'd managed his life. He had shared his tea with Elisha; she would have liked that. As for the cookies... well...

As he continued to think about his mother Jefferds determined that, if by some miracle he lived through this, he would smile more. And... maybe even laugh out loud sometimes. Maybe he would even share more cookies. At the last, his thoughts turned towards the boy, who, he had to admit, had a lot of spunk.

"Elisha... I forgive," Jefferds breathed softly, but Elisha did not hear.

Seconds steadily ticked away. As they finally surrendered to rest, they drifted off to that darkness that sometimes comes to those who trespass on Snow Mountain.

Chapter Fourteen

Rescue from Snow Mountain

*T*he two companions, strangely forced into friendship by events beyond their control, now lay in a deep sleep, unaware of the disturbance above them. Neither did they know when a sudden ray of light burst through for a moment, but then was blocked. A small rabbit's head had popped into the opening of a tunnel the rabbits had dug beside the air pocket. The rabbit wondered if he had calculated correctly as he peered down into the darkness.

"Cousin! Cousin Jefferds!" he called. "Are you there?" He listened for a response, but heard and saw nothing. Again the rabbit called and listened, but heard nothing.

"Hmm," he wondered, puzzled. Being the best thumper locater in Snow Valley, he was sure this was where the thumping had come from, so he dug furiously to widen the opening. He couldn't bear the thought that he might be too late!

"Cousin! Please answer if you hear me. A word, a thump, anything!"

The little rabbit had succeeded in opening the air pocket enough that fresh air began to pour in, causing Jefferds' nostrils to twitch and take in the oxygen. As Jefferds began to revive, his legs jerked slightly and he opened his eyes. Opening his mouth wide he breathed in deeply. Soon he faintly heard his cousin's voice calling to him, "Cousin, please, answer me, if you're there!"

"Yes, I'm here," Jefferds answered, weakly at first, then a bit stronger. "I'm here!"

The littlest cousin stopped and perked his ears up to listen. "Cousin Jefferds, is that you?"

"Yes, yes, it is. Can we get out?"

"Yes, yes! We're coming!" answered the little rabbit. Gratified to hear his cousin's voice, he signaled to the rabbits behind him to dig faster.

Soon Jefferds began to feel stronger. Air to breathe wasn't the only thing he felt. Help had come! The Creator had answered their prayers. As relief flooded throughout his being he felt a thankful tear start to roll down his cheek. He self-consciously wiped the tear away and shook himself to wake up his more familiar, grumpy side. "It's about time you found us!" he called out hoarsely. He had tried to sound annoyed, but a choking sound betrayed his emotion.

As the rabbits continued to dig and light entered their hiding space, Jefferds looked over at Elisha, who appeared lifeless. Once again, the rabbit was filled with alarm. "Hurry!" he called.

"In a few minutes, the snowmen will be here to help us get you out," his little cousin called out.

"A few more minutes might be too late," said Jefferds, glancing anxiously at the boy. He crawled over to Elisha's side. "Elisha! Boy! Are you all right? Wake up!" Jefferds said, shaking Elisha and patting his face. There was no response, causing the rabbit to shake the motionless boy harder.

"You must wake up, boy!" he cried out fervently. Jefferds had not allowed himself to feel such deep emotions since his mother died. "Boy, please, please wake up," he moaned.

By now the snowmen had joined the rabbits and all dug frantically to make a larger tunnel beside the smaller one the littlest rabbit had made to verify the location. As they enlarged it, the rabbits carried snow up from the area where the two had been trapped. Soon there was a clearing around the two leading over to the escape tunnel. Jefferds' littlest rabbit cousin called to Jefferds again. "Sorry to take so long. You are alone, right?"

"No, I'm not. I have a boy here with me, but he's not talking anymore," the rabbit said, his voice filled with worry and tears filling his eyes.

"A... boy!" the littlest cousin repeated, so astounded that he stopped digging.

"Yes, a boy, and he's not doing well," Jefferds fretted and then put his ear on the boy's chest.

"Littlest Cousin, come quick! Come down and listen for the boy's heartbeat. Maybe your excellent thump-locating ear can pick it up better than mine."

The littlest cousin left the digging crew, dropped down the tunnel and hopped over tentatively, looking curiously at the boy.

"What an ugly creature. Awfully pale and bare-looking, isn't he?"

"That's how they all look, cousin. Just put your ear to his chest and tell me what you hear, please?" asked Jefferds, then adding softly, "He's... he's my friend."

"Okay," said the small rabbit. He came close and bent over, placing his ear to Elisha's chest. He listened with a frown. After a minute he lifted his head and shook it from side to side.

"Well?" asked Jefferds. "What do you hear?"

The rabbit held up his paw to quiet Jefferds and placed his other ear on Elisha's chest. "It's very, very faint, but I can hear a heartbeat," he told his frightened cousin.

Jefferds spoke quickly in response. "Littlest cousin, could you administer a Thumping?"

"Just what I was going to say," he answered.

The small, wiry rabbit climbed onto the boy's chest and began a rhythmic thumping with his hind foot. He kept at it for a few minutes before hopping down to listen. He frowned again and climbed back up to repeat the process. Once again he hopped down to listen and this time his smile spread as wide as his whiskers.

"There it is," he said with delight. "And, it's getting stronger!"

"Thank the Creator for answering prayer! And thank you, cousin," Jefferds cried in relief.

"I tried my bunny best," the little rabbit said modestly. "At first, it was hard to know when he was doing better, since his normal heartbeat is so much slower than ours. Then I remembered my Thumping training that our hearts beat five times faster than a big animal's."

"As you said, Littlest Cousin, you did your bunny best, and that was just what was needed!"

As the snowmen, Jefferds and the littlest cousin worked together, even more fresh air poured in to Elisha who began moving, ever so slightly.

The snowmen, upon discovering a boy was present, began to quickly leave. "Sno sorry snowmen make trouble," they first apologized for causing the avalanche. The last one was gone by the time Elisha opened his eyes to see a tired, but relieved rabbit.

"Oh, Elisha! Our prayers have been answered!" said Jefferds.

"Oh-h-h," Elisha groaned. "Has help come? Thank You, God!" he sighed weakly. Quickly he realized he was still trapped. "Help!" he cried, struggling to move his arms and legs. "I'm still stuck."

Jefferds and the littlest cousin quickly hopped over to remove the remaining snow. "There. You're not stuck anymore! Now you can get up," he encouraged.

Elisha felt so cold and stiff, he felt he couldn't move, but gradually with some help, he was on all fours and began to crawl forward.

"There you go!" Jefferds cheered. "Now let's get out of here!"

With much effort, the weakened and half-frozen Elisha made it to a part of the tunnel high enough for him to stand. It felt good to stretch. They all began climbing out with the littlest rabbit cousin leading the way.

At the top, Elisha struggled to exit the tight tunnel opening last. Although he held his breath and tried to pull himself up with all his strength, it was just too tight. "I think this opening was made for rabbit size!" he diagnosed in his still weak voice.

"It was," said the littlest cousin sheepishly.

"Should've been born a rabbit," Jefferds added, flashing an impish look at Elisha with a grin.

Elisha returned the grin before grabbing onto an exposed tree root. The boy pulled with all his might, but in his weakened state, he could not thrust himself out. As the others saw him struggling, they quickly hopped over to help. Together they widened the opening and then gave one mighty yank. That did the trick; he landed safely outside, leading everyone to cheer. Mission Freedom was completed!

Jefferds heard the sounds of happy snowmen also cheering in the distance, so he began giving instructions right away to distract Elisha. Jefferds certainly did not want the boy's mind to become stuck on snowmen again. He hoped Elisha would give up and return home without causing further trouble.

"Elisha, don't be making any quick moves. We are out but not safe yet. The mountainside is still quite unstable," warned the rabbit. Elisha readily agreed and began walking cautiously. It felt so good to be out in the sun and moving, even though he was very weak.

The other cousins and snowmen had already left the mountainside, so Jefferds led the way, limping a bit from his injury. Soon they could see their journey's end at the bottom of the mountain.

The trio traveled quietly, each absorbed in his own thoughts. Soon this ordeal would finally be over. Elisha never, ever wanted to come on Snow Mountain again. Jefferds decided he was done with helping boys. The rabbit cousin was just glad he had an exciting story to tell the other cousins. He could just picture them sitting in a line before him, with all their little rabbit ears perked up like a row of corn, grabbing his every word.

By the time they reached the bottom of the mountain, Elisha was dragging quite far behind the rabbits. When he caught up with everyone, all he wanted to do was rest. As they paused to catch their breath, Jefferds had something to say. "Well, Elisha, we've been through a lot." Elisha smiled and nodded in agreement.

The rabbit continued, "But s-s-sufferin' s-s-snowflakes! You need to go home before you get us all killed!"

"But I told you, I have to find Snowy first!" Elisha said, raising his voice. "And, and, you could've stayed and helped me, instead of leaving me all the time!"

"And I told you before–this land is not for humans! Only trouble has come from your being here —"

"If you want to get rid of me, then tell me where Snowy is!" Elisha interrupted, in a most challenging way.

Jefferds was too upset to notice Elisha was a little wobbly and not looking well.

About that time, the other rabbit cousins, at least thirty, came running ahead of Uncle Peter to join them. They excitedly surrounded Jefferds, who happily greeted them all. In a moment, they made way for the elder rabbit who arrived without noticing Elisha. Uncle Peter motioned for quiet and began to speak in his aging voice as Jefferds and all the little rabbits looked at him respectfully.

"I'm surprised at you, Jefferds. You know how dangerous it is to go onto Snow Mountain during the snowmen's silly game time, so why were you even there?" Uncle Peter scolded.

As Uncle Peter waited for an explanation, all thirty little rabbits turned to Jefferds, looking and waiting, too.

Feeling quite guilty that Jefferds was getting chewed out for saving him, Elisha stepped forward unsteadily and cleared his throat. All the rabbits turned their heads in unison back to Elisha.

"Ahem. Excuse me, Mr....?" Elisha began.

"Cottontail. Peter Cottontail's the name," he volunteered, standing taller and giving an unconscious wiggle to his fluffy cottontail. The little rabbits all giggled, their own cottontails shaking also.

Elisha grinned feebly at that. "Yes, I see, Mr. Cottontail, sir. Please don't blame Mr. Jefferds. It was my fault. He found my tracks and came to save my life!"

Elisha turned gratefully to Jefferds. "Thank you, Jefferds, for saving me twice now."

As Jefferds tried to look appropriately humble, it was the elder rabbit who looked sharply at Elisha, cleared his throat and spoke. "A boy! Well, that explains a good bit. Boys do get into a lot of trouble." Then he turned to Jefferds. "I suppose, nephew, you did what you felt you had to do. Your mother would've been very proud."

Jefferds' mouth fell open, then slowly closed. He was totally unprepared for any compliment from the scolding older rabbit, much less this one concerning his mother. He felt a tear coming into his eye, but no, no, he couldn't show tears in front of all these cousins.

Before anyone could notice Jefferds' emotion, Elisha appeared to lose his balance and stumbled forward a bit. Jefferds quickly grabbed his arm to steady him and Uncle Peter hopped closer to peer into the boy's face. "Boy! Are you okay?" He saw that Elisha, looking worse by the second, was weaving unsteadily. "No, I see you're not."

Touching Elisha's body, he immediately exclaimed, "Why, the boy is half frozen! Little cousins, come at once! This boy needs immediate warming. Let's get to work!"

By now Elisha had slumped to the ground and was too woozy to know what was happening as all thirty-one rabbits and Uncle Peter gathered closely around him. Uncle Peter wisely realized Elisha needed first aid, and fast. He speedily gave the rabbits their directions, including, for the tiniest rabbits to thump on Elisha's half-frozen limbs and chest to help get his blood moving.

This was becoming an historic day for everyone, as Elisha was the first human about to experience Cottontail Warming! Some of the rabbits blocked the cold from reaching him; others turned their fluffy tails to his face, so rapidly shaking them on Elisha's frozen cheeks that their tails became a blur. A few larger rabbit cousins vibrated their larger fluffy tails on the rest of his body to warm it as well. Some of the smallest lay down on top of him to speed things up with their own body warmth.

Gradually the rabbits' efforts took effect; color returned to his cheeks and Elisha began to feel much better. Although he was a bit flabbergasted at the whole process, he knew he owed his life to rabbits now in more ways than one.

Peering into his face again, Uncle Peter reassured him, "You'll be hopping around in no time now, boy. Our work here is done."

"Thank you, so much, little rabbit cousins!" Elisha said.

But his thank you was drowned out, for the troop of rabbits had all begun talking at once, gathering around their hero cousin to hear every detail of the avalanche.

A rabbit cousin took each side of a smiling Jefferds to help bear some of his weight and ease his pain. They all turned to begin walking back to Snow Valley.

Elisha watched. Were they really leaving? Just like that? All of them? "No, Jefferds! Please don't leave," he called out. As the rabbits kept on walking and talking, he became more frantic. "Wait, wait! Oh, won't anybody help me?" he wailed.

This caught the rabbits' attention. Turning to stare at him they began whispering excitedly to one another, but Uncle Peter shook his head, no, and motioned for them to resume walking. One by one, they shrugged and obediently followed, except for the littlest cousin, who started to return to Elisha. The others grabbed him quickly and dragged him back.

"But somebody needs to tell him!" the littlest one cried out loudly.

"Not you!" they all shouted in unison, their volume causing him to cringe. The littlest cousin wiped a tear, gave one last apologetic look and regretfully followed the others. All their excited voices quickly faded away as they disappeared over the next hill.

Suddenly Elisha found himself standing alone, again. Questions to which he had no answers flooded his mind. He only knew one thing for sure – He couldn't count on rabbits for help.

Feeling quite downhearted, he looked up to see a black, angry-looking cloud, travelling rapidly towards him from the mountain.

"Oh, no! Not again!" he cried. He ran as fast as he could, but the gale roared in quickly, hitting him full force. Fighting to stand, he grabbed at bushes, weeds, branches, anything to keep from being blown away by this hateful wind. In no time at all, his hands were cut and burning from hanging on to the rough branches.

The wind continued to blow relentlessly against him. Feeling as if he'd been chased down by the wind, he called out angrily, "Go away and leave me alone!"

Seemingly in answer, the gale knocked him face first to the ground. As he rose up, Elisha rubbed his smarting face and saw his hands were bleeding. No matter if they hurt. For now, all he could do was cling to the branches in hopes of not getting blown away.

Sheltering his eyes, he looked ahead and saw the wind had swept the ground ahead bare of snow. It seemed an easier way to crawl to the pines ahead for protection, rather than trying to stand and walk. So he dropped to the ground and began to crawl.

Slowly, the boy made his way into a grove of tall pines surrounded thickly by bushes. Thankfully, this lower growing vegetation knocked off some of the wind. Exhausted and breathless, Elisha leaned against a tree inside the grove. He was too tired to give anymore thought as to why the black cloud and wind had come directly at him.

After a while he felt rested enough to leave his shelter although the wind continued to rage. Undaunted, he steeled himself against the cold, not realizing that, once again he was putting himself in danger of the elements.

"I will find you, Snowy!" he called out, but the cruel wind snatched the words right out of his mouth. But for Elisha, there was no turning back.

For a while longer, the wind howled and then it just stopped, as quickly as it had begun.

Chapter Fifteen

Tired and Trapped

*H*ow long he had walked, he didn't know, but it felt like forever to Elisha. In fact, this whole ordeal felt like forever. He was tired and he was tired of the cold. Even more than that, he was so terribly tired of everything going wrong and not getting any closer to finding his Snowy. In fact, his faith to find Snowy, truth, or anything else seemed frozen.

Upon coming across a large flat rock where the sun had melted the snow, he decided to rest. But he plopped down so hard it hurt. That only added to his discontent. In his frustration he started to dwell on all his misfortunes. The more he thought about it, the ornerier he felt. Soon he was grumbling out loud.

"I should have never started this. Nothing ever works out. Everything's against me," he began. Hmm. That felt kind of good just to vent and get it out, so he continued. "I'm just a dumb kid anyway, who doesn't know what he's doing." At that moment, all that had gone wrong grew bigger than anything else in his mind, so his gripes grew stronger.

The more he talked, the more convinced he became that his mission was hopeless. The first round of grumbling had seemed to make him feel better. Now the more he complained, the worse he felt, but the more he wanted to continue. "Prob'ly never will find Snowy anyway. Prob'ly never get out of here alive!"

All at once an unbearably loud, whining howl interrupted Elisha's complaining.

"Me-ow, yeow, yee-owww!"

"What in the world is that?" he exclaimed.

The intense, sharp howling continued on and on, causing Elisha to cover his ears. He quickly traced the plaintive wailing to a tall, narrow, grey shack made of wide, weather-beaten boards nailed helter-skelter over one another. The pitiful looking structure was topped with a steeply slanted roof of weathered and crumbling shingles. There, before it, standing on his hind legs and leaning against the rickety looking shack, was a large, skinny brown cat with oddly placed black spots. Elisha had never seen anything like it. And the sound? Well, it actually hurt his ears.

"Oh, this is great, just great! Just what I need, a screeching cat in my ears! It'll probably make me lose my hearing," he complained, feeling no compassion at all for this weird-behaving cat.

Elisha decided he wanted nothing to do with such a strange, wailing creature. He would walk away and act as if he had not seen him or his falling-down shack. Just as he turned, the creature's sharp wailing grew stronger and louder, stopping Elisha in his tracks. He quickly covered his hurting ears and hurried on pretending he'd not seen or heard him.

"Meowww, yeow, yeow! Don't ignore me!"

Of course I'm ignoring you, he thought, but then he began to feel guilty, so with a sigh Elisha politely turned around. He returned, ever so reluctantly, to the area of the shack and the determined cat.

"Were you talking to me?" he asked wearily.

"To whoever will listen," the cat answered in a strangely sad voice.

"Why were you howling so loud?"

"For someone to hear me. I have no choice. I must."

"I would think," Elisha replied with certainty, "that you could stop howling, if you really wanted to."

"Me-oww, yeow-ow. Perhaps I would, if I could, but I can't."

Elisha gazed at the cat with a quizzical look for that was one of the most confusing things he'd ever heard!

"Listen, I've got more important things to do than listen to you howl. I'm cold, I'm tired, and I'm lost," Elisha retorted bitterly. "The cold, the wind and clouds, even an avalanche tried to kill me. Nobody will help me find Snowy. He could be in the next mile, but there'll probably be another wind or snowstorm and I'll miss my only chance to find—"

"Yee-ee-owww!" the cat began to howl even more pitifully. Elisha didn't care. He had had enough so he walked away. The howling continued on and on. Elisha was so deeply absorbed in griping, however, that he failed to notice that the more he grumbled, the grouchier he became. Finally, he became so outraged by the cat's intense howling, he launched into a loud rant to drown out the repulsive racquet.

Just then, out of nowhere – which seemed to happen a lot in this strange place—a startling sight appeared. In stark contrast to the snow, a beautiful path, as lush and green as if in the height of summer, led through a group of snowy trees.

Elisha blinked his eyes in disbelief. "Whoah!" he breathed in surprise and wonder. At once entranced and refreshed by its green beauty, Elisha knew he must explore it. Looking in, a clear path weaving through the trees seemed to invite him to enter. Since it was well worn Elisha assumed that surely it would lead him somewhere, instead of wandering around blindly as he had been.

With Elisha's first step onto the path, a strange excitement stirred within him. The cat must have been excited, too, for he let out the most horrific howl ever. At least I'll get away from that cat, Elisha thought. After just a few steps more, however, Elisha's excitement was replaced by doubt. With every step he took, he began feeling worse.

"This is just dumb. Something terrible could happen," he said out loud. "Why am I doing any of this anyway? I'll probably get more lost either way I go and still not find my snowman." But, not knowing what else to do, he walked several feet further down the path, his complaints and the howling cat's screech both growing louder. The yowling strangely seemed to follow him although the cat was not in sight. "I can't even grumble in peace," he complained, and suddenly, his anger came bursting out of him.

"Stop it, you stupid, annoying cat!" he shouted.

No sooner had he said this when, as if on command, the lush greenery surrounding him transformed into an ugly mass of long, tangled vines reaching toward him. Shocked by the sight, he stepped back to run away but found the tendrils had already reached him and were beginning to wrap around his legs.

"Wh-what's going on?" he cried out in astonishment.

Quickly he reached down to untangle them, but instead they came after his hands. Jerking his hands back, he thrashed his arms and legs about, trying to fight off the vines, but to no avail; smaller creeping vines were entwining themselves around his feet, even as the larger ones reached for the rest of his body. Frantically, he tried to untangle the vines, but it was impossible, for as soon as he untangled one, alas, another would immediately take its place. Even worse, more skinny stems and tendrils, writhing and hissing as if they were snakes, reached for him. "

"Ahhh! Get off!" he cried out.

Even as the tiny vines hissed, the thickness of the other vines choked out the light. The once beautiful green path had now become a darkened tunnel to trap him.

Barely able to see now, Elisha felt a large vine snaking its way around his waist and tightening its grip. "Stop, stop! Get off me!" he screamed. With all his might he tried pulling it off, but he couldn't budge it. "Help! Somebody, please help me!"

But instead of someone coming to rescue him, Elisha felt a third smaller limb threading itself around both of his ankles and gripping them tightly together. Now he couldn't walk. It became clear to the boy that he was imprisoned in the tangle and a wave of fear swept over him.

"Help!" he cried once again, but he was on this journey alone, with no one to help. "How can I ever save Snowy if there's no one to save me?" Elisha cried.

Suddenly the vine around his waist snapped apart and for a fleeting second he thought that would help. But it did not, for he fell backwards into the reaching tangle of vines on the ground. There a new maze of growth slithered toward him. It came from every direction and covered his body. In horror he fought to stand but, with his ankles tied together, he could only sit up, screaming for help every breath. "Help, help!"

"Hang on! I'm trying to help you, boy!" he thought he heard from behind him. Elisha thought at first he was just imagining it, but then he seemed to hear a chopping sound. Suddenly he felt a pull at his waist as hands gripped him from behind, trying to pull him out of the thick growth. The vines, though, continued reattaching themselves to him as quickly as the hands untangled them.

"You must help me, boy!" said a voice.

"How can I help you? I'm all tangled up!" Elisha cried out.

"Change your thinking—fast!"

"Change my thinking? I can't think at all!" Elisha cried out, even more terrified, as a vine attempted to seal his mouth. He began thrashing his head back and forth trying to avoid the vine.

In the midst of this terror, a musical voice spoke calmly into Elisha's ear, "Elisha, you've complained yourself into a tangle."

Out of the corner of his eye, Elisha spotted Iridescence, the Snowflake, giving him an encouraging smile but speaking hastily, "Fight the bad with good words of faith!"

"How? I'm about to choke to death," he gasped as another tendril wrapped itself around his throat.

"Quickly, repeat after me and believe!"

"I believe I'm being killed, Iri!"

"No, no, believe in good. Say... I believe—"

"I... I... oh, Iri, it's too hard..."

"Elisha, you must! Quickly, or it will be too late! Repeat—I believe in a Plan of Good..."

Elisha began repeating the words Iri whispered into his ear, but paused as he saw more vines reaching for him. "Elisha, don't look at the mess you're in! Only believe," she warned. "Keep saying 'I believe'."

Obediently, Elisha closed his eyes. "I believe... I believe in a Plan of Good!" he mumbled behind the coil of vines wrapping his mouth.

"That's it, Elisha. But you must truly believe!"

"I believe. I believe, I believe in Good..." Suddenly, Elisha felt a righteous anger as well as faith rising within him. "Oh, I do, Iri, I believe it! Yes, I do! Yes, I believe... not in what I see, but in a Plan of Good..." Amazingly he felt faith growing, strong enough to overwhelm the bad. "I believe that no vine or anything else can stop me!"

As Elisha spoke, his mouth and hands became freed. Encouraged, he continued his chant of belief even more fervently. The small vines' hold onto him seemed to be snapping off and the larger ones loosening. That charged him to fight even harder, with his words and his hands, as the vines snapped off, one by one.

Hearing one last chop behind him, the last thick vine snapped and slithered away. Iri immediately declared happily, "There! You're free!"

Elisha opened his eyes to see that, not only was he completely free, but—the tangled growth in the path had completely disappeared! The boy was utterly astonished. "Wh-wh-where did it all go?" he asked as he turned and looked all around him. There remained only a corridor of beautiful green plants and trees, with no tangled growth at all. "How can all this be?" he cried. Fearing the vines' return, he ran out of the path into the snow.

When he turned to look back at the path's entrance, his eyes were drawn to see what he had missed before—a broken-down sign with faded letters saying, "Grumble Weed Path." He had never heard of Grumble Weeds; he only knew this path didn't look so inviting any more.

"Thank you, Iri," he said quietly, looking gratefully around, but she was gone. When he looked for his rescuer, he saw only a panting raccoon holding an axe, waiting in the snow outside the green path.

"Guess you didn't see the sign," said the raccoon with a sad little smile.

"No, I didn't. Are you the one who just saved me?" Elisha asked.

"No, not by myself, couldn't do it myself; you had to help. You do know how you got trapped in there, don't you?"

"No, no, I don't. How?"

"You did it. Every one of those vines that entrapped you, were planted by your mouth."

"Are you kidding?"

"No, I'm not."

"But..." began Elisha, struggling to understand, "how can a person plant vines with his mouth? I thought you plant with seeds."

"Yes, you do. The seeds you planted were complaints, grumbles, and thinking the worst. You planted those words and got Grumble Weeds. Then they got you!" The raccoon paused to let that sink in.

"Do you remember how grumbling made you feel better at first and then not?"

"Y-y-yes."

"It's all a trick. You grumble cause you're upset. It feels good, so you do it more." The raccoon grabbed a piece of twig and chewed on it. "Did you notice the green path you took seemed beautiful at first?"

"Yeah. It was so nice, but then it changed into a nightmare!" Elisha remembered. "And it happened super-fast, too!"

"Oh, yes, indeed!" agreed the raccoon. "You grumbled – the seeds sprouted. You kept grumbling – they grew into something you couldn't get out of. Had you not stopped when you did, I'd never have been able to save you. My axe could only do so much to free you."

"Why didn't you get trapped?" asked Elisha.

"I wasn't griping. Only complainers get trapped," answered the raccoon, "and you were doing plenty!"

"Yes... yes, I guess I was. Thank you, Mr...?"

"I'm Rack. Rack Raccoon at your service. Don't thank me. Thank Good, Kind King."

"Who? What did he do to help?"

"Not much," Rack grinned. "He just sent Iridescence and me to stir up your faith ..."

"Oh," Elisha breathed softly, "I see. But how did he know I needed help?"

"You see that old dark cat over there? You heard him yowling?"

"Yes, he's kind of annoying, isn't he?"

"Yes, definitely. He's meant to be," Rack said with a grin. "Come, I'll introduce you."

"Oh, no, no, you don't have to. I've already met him," Elisha said, wanting nothing to do with the unpleasant animal with the dreadful howl.

"Oh, but you need to meet him. Really," Rack insisted, his black eyes twinkling in his black mask with mischief and a knowing look.

Elisha felt he'd already heard enough from the strange cat, but he owed something to Rack, so to please him he agreed. "Oh, okay," sighed Elisha.

Rack led him over to the shack where the tall cat stood, looking a little sheepish.

"Hello, Yowler," said Rack.

Yowler looked quite embarrassed and only responded with a slight wave of his paw.

"Don't have much to say now, do you, Yowler?" Rack asked.

The cat looked down and shook his head. Rack gave Yowler a compassionate pat and smile.

"You see," Rack said, turning back to Elisha, "this cat is not so terrible as you think. Once known as the Cat Hatter in the Kingdom of Goodness, he made and sold wonderful hats in the town. Everyone bought his creations all the time, but there was one thing everyone hated... In spite of his success, he was so-o-o pessimistic!

"First, he complained about not selling enough, but whenever he got orders, he complained he had too many. Nothing was ever good enough. From morning to night, he did nothing but complain."

"I bet that was hard to listen to," said Elisha.

"Oh, yes, it was, and soon it began to affect everyone in the Kingdom. Some caught the complaining like a sickness and began complaining, too. Others would come into the shop happy, but after hearing his complaints, would leave upset, never to return. Then the Cat Hatter complained about having no friends."

Elisha noticed that Yowler was looking sort of miserable, but Rack continued his story.

"Finally all the grumbling noise of the people grew so loud, it hurt the ears of the King. The King had warned the Cat Hatter many times, but, it seemed he just couldn't stop. Finally Good Kind King could take no more. He banished him from the town and sent him here to be the Official Yowler of Snow Valley."

"So what does the Official Yowler do?" Elisha asked.

"He howls, so people know how their complaints sound to the King. But when they hear the awful howling, most people stop. Most in Snow Valley want to say good things to please the King. The longer someone complains, the louder and longer he howls."

"So it was my complaining that set you off, Yowler?" asked Elisha.

The cat nodded miserably.

"I'm so sorry," Elisha said most sincerely. "And here I was upset because you were so noisy, when it was my fault you howled. Sounds like I made a mess of things with my mouth today."

"You're not the first. Be thankful that Yowler continued to howl. That let Good Kind King know you needed help," explained Rack.

"Is howling all Yowler is allowed to do?" asked Elisha, feeling very sorry for the cat.

"Well, you notice he is quiet, now that all is well?"

Elisha saw that the cat was very quiet and apologetic. "Poor thing. Yes, I do."

"He's quiet because he is not in pain right now, only when he hears complaining. It reminds him of what he lost," Rack said.

"Will he always live like this?" asked Elisha.

"Only as long as he wishes. He has learned his lesson and is free to go home to the Kingdom of Goodness. Instead, he stays to warn others. He's so thankful the king helped him, this is his way of paying back."

Elisha looked at the cat with new eyes. "That's what you meant when you said, 'I would if I could, but I can't.' You meant you couldn't stop, because you had to help people."

Yowler nodded sadly. "I can only try," he said.

Elisha found his feelings towards the cat had totally changed. Instead of being disgusted, Elisha now admired Yowler. He wasn't just living for himself anymore but was giving up his life to help others. "You have become quite a wonderful cat, Yowler. I'm glad to meet you and thank you for trying to help me."

Yowler grinned a wide cat grin, his green eyes gleaming with pleasure. "You are welcome. I only want to save others from taking the path of grumbling." The gleam in his eyes disappeared as he added sadly, "So many won't listen. I know what that's like."

"Just like me. I wouldn't listen either. Do very many people go down Grumble Path, Yowler?"

"More do than don't," he answered. His green cat eyes opened very large as he added, "Too many get swallowed up in the tangle of Grumble Weeds... and stay trapped forever! It's as if, who they are just..." The cat leaned in closer to whisper, "... disappears."

"What?" Elisha gasped, falling back a few steps, staggered at what might have happened.

"Oh, yes. Habits are very, very strong, Elisha, just like those Grumble Weeds," explained Rack. "Not until you had Faith, could even I chop you out."

"Are you kind of saying, I caused the weeds so I had to stop them?"

"Exactly," agreed Rack. "You gotta sprinkle Faith to keep the grumbles away, boy! Sometimes a body just has to stir Faith up, to get it out!"

"I'm glad Iri helped me stir it up. Thank you both so much and to Good Kind King also, for saving me," said Elisha. "I would sure like to meet this king, but I must get on with my search."

With an exchange of goodbyes, Elisha left Rack and Yowler behind and began his journey with a new appreciation for looking for the good in life. He would not go down Grumble Path again!

Chapter Sixteen

Unprepared

*A*s he journeyed on, Elisha came upon a huge wooded area stretching out before him in both directions as far as he could see. There seemed no way to go forward other than go through it. And yet, as he looked in, it was very dark. He groaned within. Dark, again!

That much darkness within the woods, however, seemed very strange since, it being winter, there should be no tree leaves to block out the light. His eyes traveled upwards to the tree tops, tipping his head way back. Yes, many tree tops were bare, but the oak trees' dry, brown leaves still clung stubbornly to the branches. Still... it was so very dark in there.

Cautiously he stepped forward and looked again into the darkness of the woods. Everything within him said, don't go in. He felt like he used to, when he stood at the top of his grandma's basement steps, looking down into the darkness. Humph! That dark, scary basement would be comforting now, compared to this! To go into these woods, Elisha would have to dig deep down inside himself to find something stronger than his fear – That would be his deep love for Snowy and his need to find him.

As he was thinking these things over, a nearby voice interrupted his thoughts, startling him.

"Who, who? Who are you and where do you go?"

As Elisha looked around, he saw no one. His brow furrowed into a worried frown. It was a bit frightening to know someone was near, but not know where or what it might be.

The voice came again, this time louder and as more of an order. "Who, who? Whoever you are, identify yourself and your intentions!"

"I'm, I'm Elisha," he answered hesitantly, "and I guess I'm going into these, these... dark woods."

"Are you prepared?"

"I... I don't know. What do I have to prepare for?"

"What do you have to prepare for?" the voice asked with scorn. "Don't you think it rather silly and foolish to enter Big, Dark Woods without knowing that?"

"Don't you think it's rather silly to talk to someone you can't see?" Elisha mumbled. He felt uncomfortable and small before the towering trees, so he decided he should make himself sound bigger than he felt. He called out in as big of a voice as he could, "Who and where are you? I like to see who I'm talking to!"

"Look up, Elisha," said the voice.

Elisha tipped his head back and looked high up into the giant tree before him. "All I see is an owl," he said. "A very, very big owl."

"That, my un-feathered friend, would be me, Ominous Owl," said a much larger than normal owl, perched on a branch of an old oak tree.

"W-w-wow! You're really big," said Elisha.

The Great Horned Owl gazed down upon Elisha with large, luminous round eyes. He felt the eyes were looking right through him, in kind of a scary way. It was quite unsettling to a small boy. He began to twist and turn uncomfortably.

"Must you keep looking at me that way?" he asked.

"I am, after all, Ominous Owl and my looks are not meant to make you feel comfortable. And, although a boy has never come this way before, I discern that you are a boy. The question is, are you a fool?"

"A fool?" Elisha gave an offended huff. "Why in the world do you ask that?"

"Because, only fools enter Big, Dark Woods unprepared," the owl stated bluntly.

"How do you know I'm unprepared?"

"I told you, I discern things. Are you prepared?"

"Prepared, for what?"

"If you don't know for what, then you are certain to be unprepared," the owl answered without a blink of his voluminous eyes. That remark caused Elisha to begin to feel foolish after all.

"Well, what do I need?" asked Elisha innocently.

"First you need a heart of courage. Do you have one?" asked the sentry.

"Well, a-a-although I do sometimes get scared," Elisha said hesitantly, "Y-y-yes, yes, I think I do."

"Think? You can't think you do. You must know," insisted the bird.

"Well, then, I do," Elisha decided quickly. "I've already had things try to scare me away, and it hasn't worked. I've shown courage. What else do I need?"

"That is a good start, but it's extremely dark and dangerous in Big, Dark Woods. There are places where a bird can't see his wing in front of his beak. Do you have eyes like I do?" The owl stretched his neck downward looking at him closer. "No, you don't. They're very small and squinty. How did you plan to find your way in the dark?" the owl asked.

"I... I don't know. I hadn't planned because I didn't know I would end up here. Usually I don't go into dark places, but I'm looking for someone and I'm not going to let a few old trees stop me."

"There is much more here than these trees. There are other dangers."

"Other... *dangers*?" asked Elisha, quivering a little as he glanced nervously around.

"Yes, there are other dangers in Big, Dark Woods. Why do you think I said you must have a heart of courage?"

Elisha wavered a bit at the thoughts of dangers in the dark.

The owl pressed on relentlessly. "What weapons have you? Show them," he demanded.

Elisha first pulled out his empty pockets, then held out his empty hands. "I, I have none. I didn't know I'd need any," Elisha explained timidly.

"Only fools enter Big, Dark Woods with no weapons!" the owl boomed with near contempt. "You do not appear to be a true fool, but you're as unprepared as one. You may not go in," informed the owl.

"What? Who's going to stop me?" the boy challenged.

"If I didn't, which I can and will, there are plenty more in the woods to do it!"

"But I have to find my Snowy. I have to!" Elisha pleaded.

"Oh, so you're the one, the boy who built Snowy. Hmmm," he paused thoughtfully, tapping his beak with the tip of his wing. "I hear you're very determined, but that's only half the battle. You can't go in unprepared–you'd be devoured. You're only a small boy."

"*Devoured*?" Elisha asked, with a slight tremor in his voice. "Like in… eaten?"

"Yes, devoured or ripped apart, whichever, unless you can get a weapon. Only then might you have a chance."

"Where is a boy like me going to get a weapon in a land where no one will help me? I'll just go in and take my chances. I'm not going home without Snowy!" he said adamantly.

With that announcement of intention, Elisha began heading into the woods. Suddenly, without warning Ominous Owl swooped down to knock him clear out of the trees with a tip of his large wing span. Elisha landed on the ground before the woods with a loud thud. The bird then circled back up and landed on his branch, where he sat calmly staring straight ahead.

"What did you do that for? I thought you were friendly!" shouted Elisha, partially angry that he was being stopped and partially just plain frightened. Defiantly he stood back up, brushed himself off and stared up indignantly at the bird. "That hurt! You're just plain mean!"

"That, my friend, is the friendliest encounter you'll have in these woods. Besides, you forget. I said I am *Ominous* Owl, not your friendly barn owl. I am sentry of these woods. No one enters or exits unless it is cleared with me or the King. I descend swiftly, silently, and without warning," stated the owl flatly without emotion. "However, if you noticed, I did spare you my powerfully sharp talons."

"Thanks, I guess, for that," said Elisha still smarting from his hard landing. He thought for a moment. "Since you're, like, the soldier bird, can you help me with a weapon?"

The owl took his time and preened his wing a bit. "I can, if I'm so inclined," he stated.

"Well?" asked Elisha. "Will you?"

The owl stopped preening and stared down at the boy so long and so hard with those large yellow eyes that Elisha's confidence withered. He began to back up, but then thought better of it and stepped forward again assertively. "I'm going in with or without your help!" he declared with more pluck than he felt.

"Hmmm. You are small but determined, and you do have a heart of courage. But there is one more stringent requirement. Tell me, why do you wish to find your friend again?"

"Why do you want to know?" Elisha asked.

"Like I said, there's one more requirement. What drives you to find this snowman?"

"He's mine! I made him. He disappeared and I'm getting him back," Elisha said even more indignantly.

"So to you, he is simply something you own. Hmm. Well, you have not passed the crucial test. Entrance denied," decreed the owl and closed his eyes as if going to sleep.

"No, wait!" Elisha panicked. "You don't understand! Snowy disappeared and somehow, I got here. I know he's alive, 'cause the snowmen were talking about him. He, he's mine, and I have a right to get my own snowman back again!" he added a bit defensively.

Elisha waited for a response.

The owl remained unmoved and unresponsive. He simply sat with closed eyes.

"Oh, how could an owl possibly understand!" Elisha cried out in frustration.

Ominous Owl opened his eyes and without a blink, stared at him coldly. "Oh, but I do understand." He lowered his neck down, looking harshly at the boy. "You are selfish and that is not what it takes to conquer what is within Big, Dark Woods. Final decision: Entrance denied!" he declared with a shake of his head before settling to close his eyes again.

"No, no! Don't say that. You don't understand. I have to see Snowy. I heard he's not happy and I can't stand that. He's probably sad because he misses me, too!"

Elisha could see his panicked explanations had not helped. The owl remained unmoved.

"Oh, don't you see? I *can't* stop looking for him. I love him, and I can't leave without knowing he's okay," Elisha pleaded, his eyes brimming with unshed tears.

He dropped to his knees as streaming tears covered his cheeks. The owl recognized them as the same life-giving tears of love needed to bring children's snowmen to Forever Snow Land.

The owl's eyes softened. He began dropping a few of his soft, downy under covering feathers. As they floated down, he called to the boy, "Here, have one and dry your eyes. It is decided. You have met the last requirement after all."

"Wh-wh-what?" asked a stunned Elisha as he looked up, with cheeks wet from his tears. He saw the feathers floating down.

"Well, go on. Grab one and dry your eyes," said the owl.

"You m-mean, y-y-you'll help me?" Elisha stuttered as he took a feather and dried his eyes.

"Well, somebody needs to help you, before you get yourself killed," said Owl.

"Oh, thank you, Om, Omiss… aw, could I just call you Mr. O.?" he asked.

Ominous Owl blinked and nodded, yes.

"Good! Mr. O, then, thank you, so much," he said in relief. "By the way, what was the last test?"

"The most important of all—that those who enter must be driven by a heart of pure love, the kind that gives one the power to Triple O—Overcome Overwhelming Odds. I discern now that you have met two out of three tests. You have also convinced me to help you with the third requirement of preparedness," explained the owl.

Mr. O saw the boy didn't understand preparedness. "You need a weapon," he explained.

"Oh, thank you, Mr. O! Thank you so much," Elisha said gratefully.

"You are most welcome. Now, take ten steps to your left to that ancient tree missing a massive branch. Go on, go on. Do as I say," instructed the owl.

"Okay. I don't understand about exploring right now, but if you say so, I'll do it. Besides," he said with a grin and a sideways glance, "I really don't want to get smacked down again!"

Owl showed no outward response to Elisha's attempt at humor, but inside he smiled at the boy's joke. The owl watched as the boy counted off ten steps, then stopped before an ancient tree deeply rutted with aged bark. "There, where the tree lost its branch over a hundred years ago, you'll see a vertically oblong oval."

"Vertically? Oblong?"

"Shaped like an egg standing up."

"Oh." A few feet up, Elisha found the oval, though if the owl hadn't mentioned it, he'd not have noticed it. "Now, what?" Elisha asked.

"I've shown you where. If you truly believe and seek, you'll find what you need," said the owl, and with a lunge into the air, he flew away.

"Wait! What do I do next?" Elisha called out, but the owl had already gone, leaving him even more perplexed than before.

Elisha gave an irritated sigh. "Just when I think I've found a friend, they disappear," he said somewhat bitterly. As he thought about the situation, however, his logic quickly kicked in. "Wait. He said I needed a weapon and he pointed me to this roundish spot on the tree, so I just need to figure this out."

He looked at the oval. Perhaps it might be a door. Elisha could see right away, there was no handle, so how could he get inside? He felt carefully on the trunk, over and over, as he searched for a spot to push on, something that would allow him to enter, but nothing worked.

"Now what am I going to do, if I must have a weapon but can't even find it?" he asked totally frustrated. He continued to search for a way to open the oval. Eventually, feeling totally overwhelmed, the weary child buried his face in his arms against the trunk. Iri, as well as the owl, had said to believe, but Elisha was finding it hard, very hard.

"You're leaving out something important," said a tiny, squeaky voice followed by a series of hiccups.

Elisha raised his head and looked around, seeing no one until his eyes dropped to the ground where the sound had come from. Something small scampered up the trunk to the gnarl in the tree before him. Elisha half laughed in surprise, for there, looking directly into his eyes, sat a very tiny mouse with her tail curled around her feet.

"Don't tell me a little, tiny mouse is going to help me now!" he said in dismay.

"Oh, but I will tell you that (*hiccup*). Size is not what counts; it's what (*hiccup*) and who you know," squeaked the mouse again.

"Okay, and who are you?" he asked.

"My name (*hiccup*) is unimportant (*hiccup*) to your dilemma at hand. You appear to be trying to gain entrance into this tree."

Elisha noted that the mouse's shiny black eyes were just as friendly as her voice. That inspired him to talk further to her.

"Yes, I need a weapon for protection to go through Big, Dark Woods," he explained.

"Oh. Are you sure, very sure, you want to go in there?" she asked, looking into the shadowy woods, then back at him with raised eyebrows.

Elisha answered, "Yes."

"It is very dark," she pointed out.

"Yes, very dark," Elisha grimly agreed.

"And scary," she added, looking him over.

Elisha pulled himself up to stand straighter. "Sometimes, you just have to do the hard things and not think about the scary part. But first, I need to find the weapon. It must be in this tree somewhere."

"I saw you pushing and getting nowhere. You left out the most important part of all," said the mouse.

"What is that?" asked Elisha.

"Why, the name, of course. You didn't say the name," the mouse stated with surprise that she even had to explain.

"You mean, *my* name?" asked Elisha.

The tiny mouse began laughing as if Elisha had made a big joke. As she quieted down, her hiccups stopped and she noticed Elisha was not laughing. That's when she realized he was serious.

"Of course not your name, but the one that authorizes entrance. Sounds to me like you don't even know that name," she observed with disdain.

"Listen up, Miss... Mouse, whoever you are, I don't know what name you're talking about!" said Elisha in exasperation.

"Then you don't deserve entrance! You don't have authority without the name," she insisted.

"*How can I use it, if I don't know it?*" he asked, the pitch of his voice rising as he threw up his hands in extreme frustration.

"Exactly!" said the mouse as she promptly scampered back down the tree.

"Exactly, what?" he asked.

"You don't know the name," she called as she kept running.

"Wait. Wait just one minute! Don't you go taking off, now. At least tell me, what kind of place is this and where am I?"

She abruptly stopped her run and turned to face him again.

"Ha! Everyone knows this is Big, Dark Woods, south of the Kingdom of Goodness. Or... maybe you don't know. You must not be from Snow Valley."

"No, I'm from far away. Is Snow Valley far from here?" he asked.

"Oh, no, it's next to here, to the northwest," she said. "I must go now. Too bad you don't know where you are and what you're doing. So sad," she added, shaking her head and beginning to leave again.

"Wait. You said kingdom. Whose kingdom is this?" called Elisha.

"Oh," the mouse said smiling, as she stopped again. "That would be Good, Kind King, the most beloved and revered monarch of any kingdom." She sighed in pure satisfaction.

"Oh, I've heard of him. He sounds very nice, but I really need to get into this tree," Elisha insisted, as he continued to look for an entrance.

"Tell me, who told you about this tree?" asked the mouse curiously, pausing for his answer.

"Mr. O, the owl, told me."

"Oh, I see," said the mouse, nodding her head. "Well, that means he must've thought you'd be smart enough to figure things out. However, if you're not..." The mouse ended with a shrug.

"Not what?" Elisha asked.

"If you're not smart enough, then you're not ready to go into the dark...." The mouse's voice trailed off as she ran off before Elisha could ask another thing.

Elisha huffed for a moment in exasperation. Staring after her, he thought over what she had said about the Kingdom of Goodness and Good, Kind King. The mouse said he must use a name. That gave the boy an idea. "What more important name could there be around here than the king of the kingdom? Well, it's worth a try..." He stood and addressed the tree, "Open, in the name of Good, Kind King."

Suddenly the earth beneath him shook. Elisha jumped back but then looked at the ground to see what was happening. The movement stopped and he heard a strained, creaking sound coming from the tree. There, before his eyes, the oval had transformed into a door and swung slowly open.

Looking in eagerly he saw, not a sharp, shiny weapon, but an old, gnarled walking stick. At least that's what it appeared to be. Surely that could not be the weapon, but then... it was the only thing in there. Had he been tricked?

His heart sank. Just a stick. How was a stick supposed to protect him from danger?

Elisha decided it was time to trust the owl. He reached into the opening, but no matter how hard he tried, the stick wouldn't budge. It seemed that this stick was not for just anybody; it would have to be someone who had the power to withdraw it.

Elisha was stumped momentarily, then he remembered what Mr. O had said, to just believe and he'd find it. That had worked, so now, how to get it into his hands?

He thought it all over: Heart of courage. Believe. Power of pure love to Triple O—Overcome Overwhelming Odds. He had all that. Iri had said to believe. Rack said to have Faith. Hmmm. The door had opened using the king's name... then, suddenly, he knew.

He believed and spoke firmly, "In the name of Good, Kind King, come into my hands!"

The stick released immediately from the tree into his hand. That was truly amazing, but as he began to examine it, the stick still seemed so very ordinary. It was hard to believe it could be of help to him so he raised it to toss it away. Elisha then decided it had been too hard to get, to just get rid of it. If nothing more, it could at least be a walking stick.

Sensing something above him, he raised his eyes to see the owl landing silently again. "So, you found it," the owl observed with satisfaction.

"Yes, but what is it?" Elisha asked as he turned it over and over in his hands looking at it.

"Remember, you're in a land where things are not always as they seem. You spoke to a tree and it opened. You used the name to receive your weapon. Now, you must believe – believe that this stick is more than it appears to be. At the right time, it will bring what is needed. But now, this last warning..."

The owl dropped to a lower branch and looked keenly into his eyes to emphasize the warning. "The power of the King is already in your weapon, *but its release depends upon you.*"

A quizzical look came to Elisha's face as he thought, what a strange thing to say. Elisha watched the owl lunge from his branch and fly away. Seeing the size and breadth of Mr. O's impressive wing span, he drew in his breath and thought what a formidable enemy that owl could be. Maybe that's why he's called Ominous Owl.

"Goodbye," he called after the soldier bird.

"May Snowflake Blessings fall on you, who-who!" called the bird from a distance, and surprisingly, snowflakes began falling, but only on Elisha! With great delight he laid his head back and laughed as he watched them falling down, flakes of all kinds—big fluffy ones that floated lazily down, sparkling swirling ones, ones that danced and bounced off his coat. As they gradually stopped he stood quietly a moment in reflection about these last events.

The owl was so big and the mouse was so small, yet each had helped him. Mouse must be right—it's not size, it's what and who you know that counts. And, as Elisha had just learned, how you use what you know!

Chapter Seventeen

Fearful in Big Dark Woods

ow that he was prepared, Elisha readied himself to go deeper into Big, Dark Woods. With only trees as far as he could see in either direction, he understood why it was called Big. When he peered deep into the trees but saw only blackness ahead, then he understood Dark! Deeply dreading actually stepping into such unknown territory, Elisha took a deep breath and decided to lighten the scariness by calling it BDW, short for Big, Dark Woods. There, that seemed better.

After stepping nervously into BDW, he realized he was standing in a woods of towering, old oak trees, with some huge spruce trees sprinkled in. He looked high above to see that the ancient oaks were still hanging onto their dry brown leaves, creating such a canopy above, it was if a curtain had been drawn against the sunlight. As he walked on, Elisha could feel the darkness closing in behind him. As bad as being unable to see, was not knowing what might be hiding in that dark or where he would end up. Somehow a dim patch of light here and there helped him fight his fear and keep going.

As he ventured deeper into the darkness, he walked into an area of old spruce trees. Huge masses of something long and stringy began hitting him in the face and wrapping around him. Terrified, he began swinging and clawing desperately at it. "Get off me!" he screamed, trying to untangle himself.

He would just become free from one tangle of stringy stuff, only to be hit by another and another. He did find that he could eventually loosen each one, but it was annoying as well as frightening to not know what it was or when it would hit you. He began to think of the stuff as sinister hands of the trees reaching down to grab him. That made him more fearful.

Elisha's spirit drooped as he felt Faith leaving him. If only he could get through this. Then, he remembered his stick. He could use it to help part the way! He began swinging it back and forth to clear a path, but the despised clinging continued. How much longer? Just as he was despairing of ever getting out, he remembered Faith. Could this stick help more than he thought? The owl had said Believe. But did he have enough Faith to get light in this darkness?

He held the stick up high before him and spoke as he tried to believe. "Light my way." Nothing happened. His faith wavered, but then he remembered the Name. "Light my way, in the name of the King!"

Instantly the stick illuminated, revealing enormous masses of moss hanging thickly down from the branches, like row after row of stringy curtains. "Moss!" he exclaimed in surprise. "Just annoying moss." Now that he knew what he was fighting, he felt a bit better.

The slight boy walked guardedly on, using his stick to help part the hanging moss until he got through it all. "Glad to be out of that mess," he said in relief, using the stick to help him walk again.

He had found it was truly hard to be brave in the darkness, but a small amount of faith had made all the difference. Being young and inexperienced, he didn't think about what more help he might have had, with more Faith.

Neither did Elisha wonder at why those branches were thick with living, green moss in the dead of winter. In fact, as he left the hanging moss behind, if he had looked back, he would have seen a change; no longer was the moss behind him living and green, but frozen and brownish-white.

******

The farther into the woods he went, the more difficult seeing his way became. The stick did give him some security as a walking stick, but perhaps it could do more. Cheered with that thought, he playfully commanded, "In the name of Good, Kind King... Stick, do your stuff!" Hardly expecting a response at all, he was pleasantly surprised when the stick began to glow in the dark. That brought a smile to his face and saved him from stumbling over many exposed tree roots. He decided Good, Kind King must like Light.

In spite of that encouragement, he soon grew weary of this ordeal. He wished his strong dad and Mollie were here by his side. Oh, how that would change everything. "But," he said with a sigh, "they aren't here." So, as he fought back tears, Elisha decided to use his heart of courage, even if he had to fake his bravery.

"I know what I'll do!" he whispered loudly as an idea came to him. To fight his fear, he would pretend these dark trees were the enemy. With growing excitement over his game, he imagined himself a hero with super powers. Yes, and leading the way before him, a nine-foot soldier angel, with the king's army following behind! He began to feel bravery rising within him. Waving his weapon, he charged forward, shouting, "Elisha never surrenders!" Elisha thus showed true courage, doing what he must, while afraid.

Although that helped for a while, he soon tired and slowed to a quiet walk. The deep darkness, the unknown in the shadows, and the sounds of many woodland creatures combined to fuel his imagination of something scary hiding behind every tree. How he wished he could find the end of these towering, ancient trees, because in spite of his game, Elisha wanted out of this creepy dark. He wished for his warm, safe bed at home with Mollie on the floor beside him... how good that all sounded.

"Come on, Elisha, buck up! Stop being a baby," he scolded himself.

Although BDW was still dark and shadowy, Elisha began to come upon occasional faint patches of light here and there with breaks in the canopy above. Several squirrels, chasing each other and chattering, darted in front of him. Upon seeing him, they split and scattered quickly into the woods, tails twitching as they went. Other than that, he seemed quite alone in the woods, which, considering what he could run into, suited him just fine. He gave an involuntary shudder at the thought of bears or wolves. Either of those would be just too scary.

Soon he came to a stop. Something seemed different. As he listened, he was no longer hearing any birds or seeing any squirrels. The cold wind through the trees began a low, moaning sound, making him feel even more alone. But he didn't feel that way for long—an eerie feeling came over him that he was being watched. He hoped he was just imagining things. Shortly, however, he became sure, for he heard a very slow, quietly creeping movement nearby.

Instantly his body froze and he jerked his head in the direction of the sound from deep within the trees. Although he saw nothing, he could tell by the sounds of breaking twigs, that when he moved, whatever it was moved as well.

He barely breathed. The hair stood on the back of his neck, his body tensed, and his heart began to race. The boy impulsively picked up a couple rocks and threw one hard in the direction of the next sound, yelling, "Go away!"

In answer, Elisha heard a slow, deep growl. He looked to see the form of a creature, dark and threatening, moving between the trees. Elisha looked around desperately. Where could he go? He saw no escape! His own eyes became glued to the glowing eyes watching him out of the darkness. They narrowed and seemed to hypnotize him, so that he forgot all about his stick.

Elisha could see a huge body crouching close to the ground as it moved stealthily through the underbrush. Elisha knew enough about animals to know that this one was stalking. That would mean this is a predator. He began to tremble for he knew what would come next! A predator stalks, then pounces and... Elisha shook himself, stopping his mind from racing ahead. The real question was – who or what was the wolf stalking? Elisha cried out silently to God, "Oh, please, don't let it be me!"

Elisha caught his breath as he heard the creature stop circling and change directions – but not away – it was coming right at him! Ever so patiently, the beast bore slowly and steadily down upon him, with those wicked yellow eyes putting him under a spell.

If there had been a chance to escape, it was too late, for Elisha's fear had frozen him to his spot. He now knew—this predator was truly coming for him. To make matters worse, he could see the creature clearly now. Elisha trembled in fright as he faced his worst fear, not just a grey wolf, but a gigantic one, ready to attack!

What happened next was so unbelievable he would never be able to explain it to anyone. Elisha watched the animal grow instantly and incredibly—from five to eight feet in length! He could scarcely believe what he was seeing; the animal had morphed into a monstrous size before his very eyes.

A terrifying, sustained growl erupted from the wolf as he showed his red gums and bared his teeth. This was a signal that, in the next seconds, the wolf would make his final leap and go for Elisha's throat. But just as the ferocious animal leapt into the air at him, Elisha finally remembered his weapon. Swiftly, he raised the stick in his hand, pointed at the wolf in mid-air and loudly called out, "In the name of the King of Goodness, stop!"

In an instant, the stick transformed into a flaming sword. Emboldened by this weapon, Elisha swung it mightily into the air with both hands. "Arrgh!" he growled back at the wolf. The blade flashed and shone brightly, momentarily blinding and striking terror into the wolf! For good measure Elisha threw a rock at the beast, then turned and ran with all his might. Behind him he heard a whimper as the rock hit the animal squarely in the face. He did not stop to wonder that a small rock would hurt such a large animal.

What Elisha couldn't see was that the creature began shrinking as it ran away, changing back to its true state of a small weasel. The evil manifestation had been overcome by a very small boy's faith and brave use of his weapon. Since Elisha knew nothing of the wolf's transformation, he continued running over the fallen branches and exposed roots of the woods' floor. His flaming sword lit the way and, at times, literally lifted and carried him over the treacherous spots.

Too scared to look behind him, Elisha ran on and on until he fell to the ground breathless, sure he could go on no longer. But with a loud crack of a branch breaking beside him, he sprang to his feet again. He did not stop to find out if it was the wolf! He just raced on as hard as he could.

Finally the trees began to thin, showing light ahead, giving Elisha hope that he would soon get out of here. He paused long enough to glance behind him, but saw nothing but trees and the broken path he'd made running. All seemed clear. Good. Deciding the wolf had finally given up the chase, he came gratefully to a stop. He bent over, his hands on his knees, huffing and puffing, as he tried to catch his breath. It hurt to breathe for a couple minutes.

So, this is why Owl had warned him to be prepared. Was he ever grateful to the soldier bird that he had not let him come unarmed.

Then he remembered—The weapon. Elisha looked at the sword with new respect. It had been hard to believe it could be anything other than the stick it had looked like. But together with believing and using the king's name, he had held power in his hands without knowing it.

Realizing he couldn't have made it through on his own, he paused. "Thank you for the weapon and your name, Good, Kind King!"

With a deep breath he sighed and relaxed. He was glad for a chance to truly rest.

Suddenly something blocked out the light; as he looked ahead, he saw something gigantic rising up before him. He couldn't tell what it was, but already he trembled at the huge size. His eyes traveled upward, dreading what this new challenge might be.

A sudden roar exploded in his ears, rattling his very insides. Jarred and stunned, he fell backwards onto the ground, dropping his weapon. There was no time to grab it, for this new threat claimed all his attention.

What Elisha now faced, darker and much larger than the first, stood directly before him on its hind legs. The shaggy head of a monstrous bear, darkly outlined against the light, rose high into the trees above him. To Elisha, it seemed twelve feet tall. And indeed, it was!

Quickly, Elisha wasted no time reaching for the sword he'd dropped. But, where was it? All he could see was sticks. "Oh, no!" he groaned as he instantly realized what had happened. Of all things— it had transformed back into a stick, looking like all the others on the ground!

"Oh-hh!" he groaned again. What was he to do now, dwarfed by such a monster, without a weapon? Elisha scrambled to think, but the next deafening roar scattered his thoughts and shook the ground beneath him.

The weapon, Elisha thought desperately, I've got to find the weapon! Finally spying the only stick free of snow, he reached out to grab it, but as he did so, the bear's mighty paw crashed down, pinning his hand to the ground!

"Arrgh!" he cried as he strained to reach the stick with his other hand, but no matter how hard he tried, he could not.

The bear threw back his head for another roar before lowering his head to shake his long teeth at him. The boy's entire body vibrated with every roar. As the monstrous head shook at him, long streams of saliva strung down from his massive jaws, swinging saliva from side to side. Just then the bear's other giant paw came reaching down to grab him. Next would come the clamp of vise-like jaws onto the trapped boy's body.

Meanwhile Elisha had wriggled, stretched and twisted, trying desperately to reach the stick with his free hand, only to find he'd lost track again of which one it was! And now he would be trapped by this monster's giant paw. A sudden burst of righteous anger filled the trapped boy with a bravery he had not felt before. He decided that this evil bear would not end his mission; not this day, not this way!

With new boldness, he pointed his finger at the beast and spoke forcefully, "In the name of the King of Goodness, be gone now, you puny wimp!"

Instantly the sword rocketed from the ground into his free hand and flamed into action, swishing back and forth before the bear. Elisha was astonished to hear the roar turn into a whimper. As he wondered about that, what Elisha saw next was the most unbelievable of all. Immediately the monster began to shrink and transform into a small rat, squeaking as it retreated into the darkness.

"A rat!" he exclaimed in shock. Looking at the ground where it ran away, he was utterly amazed to see that the only footprints in the snow were his own and—rat tracks—not one bear track! Wait a minute. Did that mean he'd been fighting a rat all the time? Quite dazed at these happenings, after a moment he began to think... What was it Owl had said, that things are not always what they seem to be? Is it possible the wolf hadn't been real either? But then, if this was all a trick... who was behind it?

Whatever, he thought. He just knew that he was getting out of BDW as quickly as possible when he heard a tiny hiccup nearby. "I see you made it," the little mouse squeaked, ending with another *hiccup*.

"Yes, and I see you got your hiccups back," said Elisha sympathetically. "Do you get them often?"

"Only when I face something (*hiccup*) frightening or much bigger than I," confessed the mouse. "But remember, it's not size that's important, it's—"

"It's what and who you know," Elisha finished for her with a laugh. "But let me tell you, that bear scared the hiccups out of me!"

"Ha!" said the mouse, "he scared them back into me!" (*hiccup, hiccup!*)

They both began laughing in relief. It felt so good to share a hearty laugh together, and that, also, soothed the mouse's hiccups away.

Elisha was saying goodbye to the mouse when Ominous Owl flew down, landing silently in the nearest tree. "Well done, Elisha. You may now leave the woods and enter the meadow."

The owl finished speaking and flew away.

"Thanks, but what about this weapon?" Elisha called after him. "Seems I shouldn't just leave it lying here." The owl did not respond but continued his flight. "Talking to myself again," he muttered. Shortly, he happened to see a tree just like the one where he'd found his weapon. Could it be he was supposed to leave the sword here? Surely he wouldn't need it in the sunny meadow, he reasoned.

Elisha figured that seemed the most logical place to leave it, so he walked to the tree and opened an oval door as he had before, using the king's name. As he watched the tree accept the sword and close up again, Elisha decided that meant he didn't need it anymore.

Gladly he turned to face the meadow. It seemed as if he'd just finished a marathon of bad dreams. Surely all the dangers were behind him now.

Chapter Eighteen

Moment of Spunk and Serenity

*S*tepping out of the dark woods, Elisha found the sun on the snow-covered meadow was so bright he had to shade his eyes in order to see. At one time the meadow must have been green and growing, considering all the grass and plants that lay under the blanket of snow. Elisha was amusing himself, by imagining the seed pods to be ladies of the meadow, peeking their heads out from under their scarves of snow. Suddenly something startled him out of his whimsical imageries.

"Ah, it is nice to relax and get your breath after a difficult ordeal," said a voice speaking in soothing tones.

Having no idea what to expect after his last encounters, Elisha turned cautiously toward the speaker. This time it wasn't yet another scary creature, but rather a doe of grace and beauty looking at him with liquid, brown eyes. The deer smiled reassuringly and took a few steps toward him out of the shelter of the woods.

"Well, hello," said Elisha, pleasantly surprised.

The graceful doe nodded in return.

"Did you see what happened in there?" he asked, motioning towards the dark woods.

"I heard and came," she said. "You handled yourself well."

"Thank you, but I didn't really know what I was doing. What's your name?" he asked.

"I am Serena," she said oh, so serenely in a silky smooth voice. In total contrast, an excited, young voice piped up abruptly. "Hey, what about me? What about me?"

Elisha looked to the woods where a spunky young deer bounced out into the light, impatient to be introduced also. Serena turned and gave her fawn a serious look. "I didn't call you out yet, Spunky!" she chided.

"Yes, Mother," the young deer said lowering his head contritely, but seconds later he brightened up to ask excitedly, "But now that I'm out, may I meet this funny looking animal with only two legs and a bald face? Makes him look kind of weird, if you ask me," he added, spouting forth all his thoughts.

"Spunky. I didn't ask you. Now, mind your manners." In response the young deer dropped his head again with a "Sorry."

Serena turned back to Elisha. "This is my son, Spunky, who keeps me on the tip of my hooves every moment."

"But at least you never get bored, right, Mom?" the young one asked brightly.

Serena smiled and conceded, "No, son, I certainly never get bored with you around."

"Me either! He-hee," Spunky giggled and pranced around some more. It was clear that this young deer enjoyed every moment possible.

Elisha smiled as he listened to the two. He found them a refreshing change from all the trials he'd been through.

Serena turned to a nearby tree and, pulling delicately on a small piece of bark, began to chew. Spunky pranced over to Elisha, once again bright and excited. "Hey! Bet you wonder why I'm called Spunky! I've got lottsa energy — lots more than Mom. I'm lottsa fun, too, and wouldn't you like me to keep you company? And hey, who are you anyway?" the young deer asked practically in one breath as he continued to bounce around.

"Spunky!" Serena said, looking quite embarrassed. "It is impolite to invite yourself to his journey."

Spunky twisted his mouth into a tortured smile. "There I go again, right, Mom?"

"It's okay, Serena. I'm Elisha, and I'd be glad for you both to come with me. I've been alone enough in this land."

150

"You're very fortunate to have survived. Only the purest and bravest visitors survive Big, Dark Woods. Most are faithless and are consumed by their fears," she added wisely.

"I can see why. BDW—that's Big, Dark Woods—oh, it is a very scary place!" said Elisha. "Without Mr. O's help and my sword, I couldn't have made it. It would be nice to have a couple of friends go with me."

Serena explained that they would join him for a bit but couldn't be in the open for too long. Just before they left the woods, she had a question. "You seem to be a very smart boy," said the mother deer, "but I watched you put your weapon away. Forgive me, but I wonder if it is wise to enter the meadow without it."

Elisha hadn't thought of that. "Owl told me I'd need it in BDW, but I didn't think I'd need it in the sun," Elisha explained.

"Some of my worst life experiences have been in the sunshine," the deer offered politely.

"Oh, not me, Serena! I'll take sunshine any day. Most of my scary stuff has been in the dark. Oh, do I ever hate it!" he said most emphatically.

"Perhaps the dark is where your fears are strongest," Serena offered.

Elisha thought that was a no-brainer. "I'm just glad all that is over," he said in relief.

And so, the three of them began walking peacefully into the meadow, with Spunky stopping to sniff curiously at the tall weeds only to be poked in the nose by burrs. After a few more pokes, his smarting nose discouraged further investigation of the prickly plants. Rejoining his mom and Elisha, he continued to frolic and bound around them in circles as they talked.

Eventually, Elisha's thoughts turned to Snowy. "By the way, would you know where I could find snowmen?" he asked hopefully.

"No," she answered. "Deer don't mix with snowmen. I haven't even seen any." She paused, glancing around to check for safety. They had already covered about one third of the meadow. "We must return to the woods immediately. Come, Spunky," she called with quiet urgency. "May Snowflake Blessings fall upon you, young friend," she said, and then rounded up her young one to head for the camouflage of the woods.

"Thanks for being my friends. Bye," Elisha called after them wistfully.

"Bye!" called Spunky. "I'll bet you'll remember me!" he added confidently with a giggle, his white tail wagging.

"I sure will, Spunky," Elisha agreed.

"Hope you grow your other two legs!" the fawn shouted before bouncing into the woods with his mother.

Elisha chuckled quietly to himself that Sly and Spunky had both seemed so concerned that he only had two legs. A brief picture came to his mind of himself with four legs. How confusing—how would you decide which foot to put forward first? He was just glad he didn't have to figure that out.

With a happy sigh, he focused again on his mission and looked beyond the open meadow. Lots more trees, larger than BDW, and way too far to go around, but where to enter? His eyes slowly followed the forest's edge from the end of the meadow, until he saw a strange and intriguing structure just inside the forest. He almost missed it, for it oddly blended in with the snow as well as the mixture of spruce and pines. The building looked humble yet truly massive. This land seemed to be a place of constant contradictions!

What could this unusual looking building be and would it help him find Snowy?

Chapter Nineteen

Sno Scary

*E*lisha set out again with quite a ways to go to reach the other end of the meadow. He was determined to reach the forest and check out that building, but after the harrowing ordeal he'd just been through in BDW, he just relaxed and walked at a leisurely pace. Since his mind was drifting along as well, he was at first oblivious to the growing noise of crows squawking in the trees. The raucous chorus grew louder and louder, but then... very oddly, the noise abruptly stopped.

The sudden absence of noise snapped Elisha to full attention. He listened. The silence seemed eerie, almost spooky. Looking around slowly, then back and forth, he saw nothing out of the ordinary until he looked to the tops of the trees of BDW. No longer bare, the tree tops were filled with something black.

As he wondered what could be so thick and dark, suddenly the silence was replaced by a stunningly loud sound of fluttering and beating wings. Elisha watched as hundreds of large, very black birds, rose from the tree tops. Why in the world would they leave their perches all at once? And where are they going?

Their dark mass formed rapidly into a solid black triangle shape moving swiftly, like an arrow flying to its target. Funny, it seemed as if they were coming at him. Surely that could not be true. He had just decided they were probably going to pass over him, when he realized—they were flying low and were, indeed, headed straight for him! That set his feet to running at super speed. Of all the things he'd imagined in the dark woods, he hadn't expected to be attacked by birds in the open sunshine!

He needed to do something, quick. Certainly he didn't want to go back to the woods, so he began trying to run across the meadow toward the structure; perhaps he could take shelter there. With the birds close behind, his legs and arms were pumping as hard as they could, but he was unable to pick up speed running through the clumps of tall weeds. The flock of birds quickly closed in on him.

Everything darkened around him as the huge flock of birds blocked out the sun. Elisha was scared to death now. Birds had never frightened him before, but this was completely different. The sound of hundreds of beating wings, as well as the loud squawking and the dark... these all overwhelmed him with fright. That all was nothing, however, compared to the attack.

The birds began to surround him, closing in to beat at his head with their wings. Elisha threw his arms over his head to protect himself as best he could. Some landed on his back and began pecking on his hands and head. "Ow-w-w-w!" he cried in pain.

What could he do now? Greatly outnumbered and unable to see, the boy had lost his direction, so to protect himself he fell to the ground, hunched over and covered his head. But now he'd become an easy target as the birds dive bombed at him to peck his back and hands. With nothing but his voice to fight them off, Elisha cried out, "Stop! Stop!" Then he blurted out, "Stop, in the name of Good, Kind King!"

Within seconds the air began to clear, giving Elisha a chance to jump up and run as fast as he could. Although the birds had ceased attacking as before, they continued to fly alarmingly low, just above his head.

Tired of being a target, he stopped to shout out at them, "I will not be wiped out by a bunch of evil, feather brained birds. You're not part of Goodness, so in the Name of Good, Kind King, be gone!"

Catching a glimpse of the lodge ahead, he hurtled himself toward it with a renewed burst of energy. Within moments, though, just as suddenly as the birds had appeared, they disappeared! Slowing to a stop, he stood cautiously a moment, looking around, only to be amazed. There was nothing—not a sound, not a trace of birds any- where—nothing except a loose, black feather floating here and there! He stood bewildered in the silence. Where had they gone?

Although he didn't understand the attack, it was over. He finally exhaled in relief, "Whew!" Looking aimlessly around, he spied one of the blue-black feathers and picked it up. Elisha looked at it briefly and then pocketed it to remember his escape by, not that he thought he'd ever forget this strange and scary trial. "Why did they attack me? I never did anything to them!" he fumed indignantly.

Whatever had caused them to begin or to abandon their attack, the boy couldn't imagine. Could it have anything to do with what was inside that building? Could it be the angry birds were delivering a warning, to not go on with Mission: Find Snowy? On the other hand, perhaps it was an actual attempt to keep him from going inside the building. Then the thought came to him that, maybe his snowman truly was inside. If he wasn't supposed to be in this land, maybe something did not want him to go inside and find his snowman.

Elisha had stopped about thirty feet away, studying the strange structure. The building had an odd appearance, a mixture of snow and old wood. It didn't look like any house he'd ever seen lived in by a… human. He dared not think of what else might live there; Elisha cautioned himself to rein in his wild imagination.

Now, as he began walking toward it, Elisha was startled by unusual sounds coming from somewhere behind him. It was snorting. Something was snorting at him! He turned around slowly to see no creatures; nothing but a snowy meadow. Each time he advanced, however, the strange sounds began anew. Whenever he stopped, there was silence. Was this another attempt to scare him away from this unusual building? The snorting grew louder.

Elisha had experienced so many scary things he couldn't imagine what these snorting beings could be. He suddenly felt tired of all the constant hindrances to finding Snowy. "Hey, I'm just a kid! Why can't somebody just tell me what to do, instead of all these warnings I can't figure out!" he yelled in exasperation.

The strange, intimidating noises stopped while he talked, as if the "they" were listening. But then they began again with every move forward, unnerving him further. Something did not want him to go into that building! But, why? The wolf, the bear, the birds, and now this... what else could there be? Regardless, Elisha was not going to let these strange happenings stop him, and he was *not* going back into BDW! Absolutely not. No way!

As Elisha began moving forward again, the warning snorts changed into muffled voices with a distinctly childish quality. If these were meant to sound threatening, they surely were not. As the voices grew louder, Elisha was able to tell that the sounds were coming at him from different directions. Now he saw several large mounds of snow surrounding him ten to fifteen feet away. Oddly enough, he hadn't noticed those mounds before.

He began walking towards the structure again, but each time he looked back, the snow mounds seemed to follow him. That does it, he thought. I'm going to find out what's going on! But as he moved cautiously towards them, a chorus of voices shouted, "Boy, go 'way! S'no come here. Leave. S'no welcome here. Go, go! Back, back!" These voices began repeating the last phrases over and over.

That childish sounding voices would be threatening him, caused Elisha to snicker. What kind of animals would snort and talk like children, he asked himself, but then he recalled all the unbelievable talking creatures he'd already met.

Thump! Something hit the back of Elisha's head. He raised his arm to feel his head and... wham! Something struck his arm, then his shoulder. Quickly now, he felt himself being pelted all over. Guarding his eyes with his hands and arms, he peered out to discover that he was being slammed with snowballs. They didn't really hurt, but they delivered a deliberate warning... go away!

Before another flurry of snowballs began, Elisha decided to meet his attackers head-on. Letting out his fiercest cry, "Ahrrr-gh!" he steam-rolled himself toward them, waving his arms wildly and yelling in his scariest way possible. As he did so, a sudden burst of blowing snow made a blinding wall before him, so that he ran guided only by the noises. Once again the wind seemed against him.

Unable to see or stand very well in the swirling wind, Elisha reached out to grab for anything to hang onto. Finally he grasped a handful of something, but it kept moving so he hung on for dear life.

Having no idea what it was, nevertheless, he clung to it. He wasn't about to let it get away!

In moments he heard creatures in retreat, seemingly whimpering. Had he grabbed one of their own? Elisha certainly didn't feel sorry for a gang of attackers; he only wanted to know — just what was he holding prisoner in his hands? Since it had stopped moving, it was time to find out. Giving a hard tug onto what he held, it unwound like a top. The snow swirling around him stopped blowing just as it quit unwinding. Now he could see clearly. Much to his astonishment, Elisha held in his hand nothing but a long, fuzzy scarf.

Slowly he raised his eyes from the scarf to see what its owner might be. This "dangerous" creature was nothing more than a large, very fluffy snowman staggering as he tried to recover from his dizziness. Elisha burst into laughter both in relief and at the comical sight of a dizzy snowman. When the tubby man of snow stopped, he wobbled back and forth as if he would fall over.

Just as the snowman's rocking stopped, his hat fell off. "Snoh, no!" he cried in great alarm. The plump, flustered snowman began struggling greatly to retrieve his hat. Elisha laughed even harder. The snowman stopped his efforts to look straight at Elisha, quite hurt and offended that Elisha found his dilemma so amusing.

"You s'no laugh! S'my hat!" he exclaimed, trying again to pick it up.

Elisha could not take his eyes off the snowman's increasingly humorous performance. Repeatedly he bent over, but was totally unable to reach past his large belly to pick up his hat. The snowman's grunts grew increasingly louder until finally, the agile boy bent down and retrieved it for him.

"Here you go," Elisha said, handing the hat over.

Surprised and confused by the kind gesture, the fluffy snowman hesitatingly accepted his hat. "My thank you, sno much," (*I thank you so much*) he muttered in an embarrassed, childish voice.

Elisha wondered at the snowman's childish talk. This big, amusing snowman doesn't look like a baby, he thought, but he sure sounds like one!

The snowman awkwardly plopped his hat back onto his head. As he tried to process this unexpected kindness, little puffs of snow began flying out of his head for a moment. When he finished his snowy thinking, he stood before Elisha looking quite sheepish. Now quite embarrassed to have attacked the kind boy, the poor snowman offered a sincere apology. He simply stated, "Sno sorry." Then, with a look of genuine concern, he held out his hands questioningly, palm side up to ask, "Sn'u all right?"

Elisha was intrigued by this white, obviously soft hearted creature. "Yes, I'm okay, but why were you snowmen throwing snowballs at me?"

The snowman squirmed a little in place before speaking. "S'no harm. My scare boy – snu go 'way." With this he gave a single, short motion, as if he were attempting to shoo Elisha away like a fly.

Elisha chuckled at that. He felt a growing affection for this snowman. "You don't look very scary to me."

The snowman had no argument there. "Boy leave," the snowman said soberly, looking down, obviously not wanting to deliver his warning or make eye contact.

"Why? I can't leave. I'm looking for Snowy, my friend. Can you help me find him?"

The snowman's eyes widened as Elisha said "Snowy." He slowly pointed to Elisha and asked, "Snowy! S'nu... builder?"

"Builder? What do you mean?" asked Elisha.

The snowman pointed to Elisha. "S'nu! S'nu make snowman? Snowy?" *(You make Snowy?)*

"Yes," said Elisha proudly, "all by myself."

"Good. Snowman, good," repeated the tubby, white creature.

"Well, who are you? Who made you?" Elisha asked.

That question affected the simple snowman deeply. Tears quickly filled the corners of his button eyes and began to trickle out. As drops of sadness rolled down his round cheeks, they froze, making an icy ping as each hit the ground. As more tears formed he recalled, "Austin, Gavin, Colton make me... call me, Chilly Man."

"Where are they now?" asked Elisha.

Chilly shook his head. "Builders no here! S'no boys! Sn'u, go," said Chilly sadly, giving one more pitiful attempt to shoo him away. The snowman turned halfway around covering his eyes and paused.

When he turned back around, he peeked between his hands to see if Elisha was still there.

As the snowman peeked, Elisha couldn't resist saying a playful, "Boo!"

The poor snowman's arms flew wildly into the air. He appeared ready to run but wobbled too much to do so. He wobbled to the left, he wobbled to the right, then back and forth in a total Snowman Wobble. Although the snowman finally regained his balance, Elisha couldn't help giggling at the snowman's comical reaction to his "boo." His giggles travelled from the meadow to the woods, returning an echo.

Chilly looked pitifully at the boy and just said, "Boo, s'no bad." (*Boo is so bad.*)

Elisha sobered immediately and apologized to the silly man. "I'm sorry," said Elisha. "I thought you were playing peek-a-boo."

Chilly smiled a crooked smile back. "Sno—just peeking."

Elisha smiled back for a moment before turning serious. "If you know Snowy, please, Chilly Man, tell me where I can find him. If you cared for your Builders, then you must know how I feel," he pleaded.

Chilly Man stood very still before finally lifting one solid arm and pointing to the building at the clearing's edge. "There," he said simply.

"Really? The building?"

"Snowman Lodge," Chilly answered and left.

Elisha's heart leapt within him. "Oh, thank you, Chilly!" he called.

Could this be the end of his search? Elisha began walking toward the rugged wooden door. What a strange place this Snow Land is, Elisha thought, with childish snowmen for guards and rabbits that talk and make tea!

Chapter Twenty

Does Evil Have a Face?

*M*assive and heavy, the door was constructed with strong log halves crisscrossing it to bar unwanted visitors from breaking in. It didn't look too inviting, but Elisha needed to find out what was on the other side. Perhaps he should knock, but who or what would answer?

Before knocking, Elisha turned to call goodbye to Chilly, but he was already gone. A twinge of sadness came upon him as he realized he was going to miss that fluffy snowman.

Once again he faced the door. He reached his hand out to knock, when he heard the faint voice of someone calling him from far, far away. Maybe Chilly was returning! Pleased at the thought of seeing him again, Elisha turned around with a smile.

Instead, Elisha gasped back in fright, pushing the small of his back against the door with arms spread out. Something dark was breathing right into his face! But, what? All he could see was a black robe with a hood!

"What in the world? What are you and where did you come from?" Elisha demanded with all the bravery he could muster. Elisha's mind raced at lightning speed. He wasn't here, and then he was. How could something calling from so far away appear so quickly? And what could this be, with no face?

The boy was flattened against the door, unable to escape, while a foul odor reeked from beneath the hood. He recoiled in disgust, but the rotten egg smell had already turned his stomach. Realizing it was the being's breath, Elisha turned his face away and demanded again to know who this was.

"Oh," said an old man's voice, cracking and sounding quite pitiful, "I'm just... just an old man..." he paused to cough, "... concerned about a small boy alone out here."

"I asked who you are. What is your name? And, and, *back off!*" Elisha insisted as disgust and irritation replaced his fear.

The hooded figure bowed his head deferentially and stepped back quietly a few steps.

Elisha, now breathing fresh air, gained some space to step forward, away from the door.

"Now what's your name?" the boy boldly asked.

The old man avoided Elisha's eyes and answered quietly and humbly. "Why, it's Mose D. Seat. You can call me, Mose, of course, but enough about me. I am more concerned about you." Then he asked sympathetically, "You are alone, aren't you?"

"Why do you want to know?" Elisha replied uneasily.

"Oh, well! You look so alone and frightened, poor child. I thought perhaps I could help," he said, loosening his hood and peering intently at the boy. "You are lost, aren't you?" he asked cagily.

"No, I'm *not* lost," Elisha insisted as he looked the old man over.

From what little Elisha could see under the shading hood, although the old man was a sickly, pale color, he had a dark feeling about him. Something about the old man's instantaneous arrival, as well as his creepy appearance, made Elisha feel as if he had a rock in the pit of his stomach. Although the man sounded pitiful and harmless enough, he didn't seem trustworthy, and he was a stranger. (His parents had drilled into him, when alone, to never trust strangers.)

The old man kept bending slightly with each weakly cough, while giving quick, furtive glances toward Elisha.

"Why don't you show your face?" asked Elisha suspiciously.

"Others... don't like to look at me," he said. "I can't help how I look, but it frightens some. Maybe... you're different," he seemed to challenge. He slowly loosened his hood to slightly push it back.

The boy withheld a gasp as he cringed inside at a hideous looking face with a long, crooked nose. Quite strange and broken looking, the nose hung out and over his mouth, nearly reaching his chin. Elisha was aghast to see, the nose flopping loosely when the head moved!

As a little more light hit the face, Elisha saw skin with a sickening, yellowish green cast. His eyes were half closed slits until he looked right at Elisha; then his eyeballs bulged, large and intruding, as if they were fishing around for everything about him. Elisha felt invaded but he didn't know what to do. What could he do? He instinctively drew his head back as far as he could. The old man's eyes returned to his normal slits and the shaken boy breathed a little easier.

The old man coughed even more pitifully.

"Are you... sick?" Elisha asked, more out of curiosity than concern.

"Oh, no, I'm not sick. I'm merely a harmless, bent-over man with a nagging cough. Nothing for you to worry about, you poor child. More importantly..." he paused, showing his brownish, yellow teeth in a careful smile, "what can I do for you?"

Elisha couldn't help but think there was something amiss in this whiney, nasal voice, dripping with exaggerated kindness.

"Uh, nothing, I'm fine," Elisha answered, shifting uncomfortably. "I'm just looking for someone."

"Oh, but a small boy— out here all alone? You must be lost," the old man insisted, raising his head to look furtively around. "Allow this poor old man to be of help to you. I like to look out for small, lost boys... *and snowmen*, you know," he added, raising his eyebrows and looking sideways at Elisha to see his reaction.

"I told you, I'm *not* lost and... wait. Did you say snowmen?"

"Yes, yes," the old man said very nonchalantly. "I help lost boys and sometimes poor, lonely snowmen. Yes, yes, indeed, I just try to be a helpful person, but you don't seem to want any help."

He began to walk away with a slow, halting gait, dragging one foot behind him.

"Wait," Elisha said. His mom always said not to judge someone by his looks or clothes. And, as gross as the old man was, maybe he had helpful information. "Wait, Mister... Mose. Maybe you can help me."

The old man paused with a satisfied grin before he turned around to give Elisha a serious yet pitiful look. "Yes, my boy. What can I do for you?" He reached out his gnarled hand and rested it on the boy's back as if to comfort him.

Immediately Elisha felt repelled by his creepy touch but instead steeled himself to stand still to try to get more information. "Did you say you help snowmen?"

"Oh, yes, whoever happens along and needs me," he reassured.

"Have you seen any lone snowmen lately?"

"Oh," the old man continued casually, "there was one, the other day—I forget which day it was. Bad memory, you know," he added, beginning to walk away again.

"Wait, Mr. Mose! For real? You saw a snowman? What was he like? Did he have a name?"

"Oh, I'm getting tired—I need to go sit down." Knowing he had the boy's interest, he lifted a hand to his forehead, appearing quite unsteady. "Let's go to my little cabin where I can rest and I'll tell you all about him."

"What cabin?" Elisha asked, stunned. He hadn't seen a cabin anywhere.

The old man had already moved along so Elisha felt like he must follow. Mose didn't stop or slow down until he almost reached the door of a very tiny, small cabin in the edge of the forest.

Elisha was very puzzled. He had looked carefully along the whole forest's edge before, so how could he have missed it? He was sure there had been no cabin here, but he was seeing one now with his own eyes, so he must have missed it before. "Oh, I've overtaxed myself. Perhaps you could let me lean on you a bit just to help me into the cabin. I..." he said weakly with a hand to his forehead and wobbling slightly, "... I don't know if I can make it on my own."

Elisha chided himself for his suspicion and hurried to the old man's side. Putting his arm around him, he let the old man lean on him. Elisha was repulsed by the feel of the scrawny, bony frame leaning against him. Yet, he was ashamed of his feelings towards such a pitiful man.

"Do you know where my snowman is now?" asked Elisha as they finally reached the cabin door.

"Yes, I might," he began in a very faint voice, so that Elisha had to put an ear near the man's mouth to hear, "but first, I must know you better. We don't give out information like that to strangers in Snow Valley. I must protect helpless snowmen as well as help lost boys." He paused as if to get his breath. "I am feeling better, but I must rest. Come on in, my boy, and we'll sit and talk." the old man said as he stepped inside the dark cabin, holding the door open and waiting for him.

Elisha hesitated. "You do know my snowman?" he asked.

"Well, if you mean Snowy, I do," the old man, said emphasizing Snowy's name.

"Snowy!" Elisha exclaimed in amazement. "You... you really do know my snowman then!"

"Oh, yes, yes. Fine snowman, that Snowy. Come in and have a seat," he said, motioning in the darkness to a straight backed, wooden chair.

"Uh, I can't even see the seat... don't you have a light switch?" Elisha asked.

"No, no. I just use candles. Come on in while I get one," he said.

Still, Elisha hesitated. In addition to his distrust of the old man was his extreme fear of very dark places and yet this old man seemed to know about Snowy. He decided he would just go in, get his information and leave right away. Besides, it seemed rude to refuse.

The old man continued to hold the door open for him, motioning toward the room and chair. "Have a seat, boy, and we can talk all about where your poor Snowy was this morning."

"This morning? I thought you said it was the other day."

The old man's eyes shifted away from Elisha. "Oh, yes. I saw him, uh, both times, but it was this morning that was so... disturbing." He began shaking his head sadly before going on. "Poor snowman, in that handsome scarf. He seemed so terribly distressed."

"Scarf? It had to be Snowy! But did you say distressed?"

The old man nodded yes. "Oh, no! What was wrong?" Elisha asked anxiously. Forgetting his qualms about the man and the dark, he stepped inside and waited for his eyes to adjust to the darkened room. Even with the door open, the room was still dark.

"Go ahead and have a seat," the old man urged. "Poor boy, you must be so tired and cold. Perhaps I could start a fire."

Now that Elisha thought about it, he did feel tired and cold. He would sit for a bit and get warm...

Having just taken a few steps toward where the old man was pointing, he felt an unexpected, hard shove into his back. Caught totally off guard, the force sent him flying into the center of the room against a straight backed chair. With arms flailing, he grabbed for the back of the chair, but he could not stop himself. Instead, tumbling over it headfirst, he landed flat on his back.

"Ow-w!" he yelled, his body smarting from his hard landing. Then he scrambled to his feet shouting angrily, "Hey! That was rude! What do you think you're doing?"

He was more than ready to face the old man, but to his dismay, he saw Mose slipping out through the doorway. Before Elisha could make another move, the door slammed shut, closing him into darkness. For a second he was stunned, unable to understand what was happening; in the next instant the darkness sent him running with a loud cry of, "No-o-o-o!" all the way to the door.

Just as he reached for the handle, he heard the latch on the lock drop down. The terrified boy shook the handle. It was locked. "Hey! What are you doing? Open this door and let me out of here!" he screamed.

A crackling, old voice cried out in glee, "That was easy! I shall return, my boy. I have plans for you!" A cackling laugh followed, loudly at first, then fading away. "He-hee, he-hee-e-ee!" Loud or soft, the sound was of pure evil.

Elisha stepped back as reality set in. The old man had intentionally lured him inside and trapped him! Once again, he shook the handle hard, but to no avail. With pounding heart, he backed away from the door, dumbfounded how the old man had played him. The dreaded darkness settling around him let him know that things had just gotten worse, much worse.

Still in shock at the sudden turn of events, Elisha found himself standing small and alone in a depth of darkness like he'd never known. It was not just darkness from no light, but from the evil that had done this to him. It felt unbearable.

"Let me out of here!" he screamed. As only silence answered him, he shook himself into action. In desperation, once again he tried the handle, which was, of course, locked and wouldn't budge.

He scrambled to make sense of this. What kind of place could this be? Elisha couldn't tell by looking for, with no window, the only light was a small crack from underneath the door, not enough to light the room. He felt on each side of the door for a light switch. Nothing. He felt further. The wall was made of rough, wooden boards and all he gained was a splinter in his finger that really, really hurt.

"Here I am, stuck in the dark, again! Why does this keep happening?" he cried out.

Elisha decided to continue feeling his way around the room, hoping to discover another way out. As he did so, soft, sticky things began clinging to his face. "Augh!" he cried out and tried to brush them away, but they stuck to his hands. Unable to shake them off, he remembered the same thing happening once in the attic at home. Then he realized what they were.

"Cobwebs! Ugh! I hate cobwebs!" Giving a shudder he tore them away.

Elisha continued investigating and soon determined that the chair he had fallen over was the only furniture, nothing else. No bed, no table, no cabinets, no sink, and worst of all... no way out. How strange. What kind of room could this be? What possible use could it have?

It seemed to be a tiny one-room cabin, not big enough to live in, just big enough to... big enough to *keep* someone locked in! And not just someone, me!

More terrified of his dark imprisonment than ever, Elisha wished for his flaming sword, but it was in the tree and he was here, defenseless and locked in the dark. With that realization, Elisha felt the darkness seem to intensify by the moment. He began to knock on the door, but it was totally solid. Not a chance he could break a hole in it with the chair. There's no way out, he thought.... no way out.... no way out...

Feeling hopelessly frightened and trapped, Elisha remembered the words he'd spoken to the ancient tree. Could it work again?

Within himself, he only scrounged up a timid answer—maybe. So he fearfully, desperately addressed this door, "Oh, please, please, in the name of Good, Kind King of the Kingdom of Goodness, open!"

Maybe that would work. He stared at the door, waiting for it to open. Nothing happened. But why? He had used the same name as before. Maybe he didn't say it right. He tried again, using his finger this time to point at it as he had to the bear. No good. Why didn't it work here? He had a terrible thought. Is this place so bad, that the king's power isn't strong enough here?

The small prisoner kept feeling on the walls, looking for a latch, a secret door, a window, anything, but again, nothing. Nothing, that is, but more cobwebs. (He knew he would never like grand daddy long legs again.)

Unwilling to give up without a fight, he began pounding on the door, but it was so thick it sounded more like pecking. "Help! Someone help me!" he yelled, hoping someone would eventually hear him. Just how long he'd spent pounding on the door and calling for help, he didn't know, but no one came. His voice became hoarse from shouting and his hands hurt, so he finally felt his way back to the chair and sat down to think.

Now, confusion, as strong as the darkness, swirled in, filling his mind with questions...Why did that old man pretend to be so nice, like he wanted to help me? Why did he lock me up and leave? And how did he know Snowy's name? He knew about Snowy's scarf, so he must've seen him... But he wouldn't tell me what he knows. He didn't care about my Snowy. He only wanted to trap me, but why? On and on, all kinds of questions whirled around in his mind at a dizzying speed, over and over, with no answers.

Finally, as he thought of the old man's last words and evil laugh, worry set in. What possible plans would an old man have for a little boy? He said he was coming back. What was he going to do when he returned? Elisha didn't even want to think about that—he couldn't think of any good reasons that would involve locking someone up. This kind of thinking was getting him nowhere and so he returned to the door, the only thing standing between him and freedom. Elisha pounded and yelled repeatedly at the door. Still, no one came.

After a good long time, Elisha slumped utterly exhausted to the floor, feeling hopeless. Despair filled him as he stared into almost complete darkness.

He could almost hear that laugh again, as if it were from a wicked witch. "Oh," he wailed, "what have I gotten myself into this time? For all I know, that creepy old man could be having me for dinner!"

Having me for dinner... He had said those last words thoughtlessly, but hearing himself say them, he cringed in horror. "O-oh!" he wailed again. "Where did that come from?"

Elisha took a slow, deep breath. He knew that he must think clearly. What's the matter with you, Elisha? Nobody does things like that... except in Hansel and Gretel! But that was just a fairy tale. Although he tried to shake off the thought, it stuck in his head of that ugly, old troll with weird skin and grossly yellow teeth and what he might do! No, no! He couldn't stand such creepy thinking, and yet, as he sat in the dark, such thoughts ran over and over in his head, filling him with horror.

His thoughts then turned wistfully to his parents... I wish Dad was here—he'd know what to do—and Mom, too. They'll both be so worried. What will they think when they find I'm gone? They know I'd never run away. They might think I've been kidnapped. Then the police would come! Oh-h-h, he inwardly moaned, there's no way anybody would ever be able to find me here in this secret world. Even worse, if that old creep does what I thought, no one would ever find anything left of me... except maybe just... bones.

He shuddered in horror again. These morbid thoughts were too much for him, so he jumped back up onto his feet. Okay, where's the door, he wondered as he stood in the darkness. The thin crack of light under the door gave him his bearings again, but then Elisha began to reason the situation out. Why bother? Who would hear? The last person he had seen was Chilly Man. Even if the snowman heard, he would be too easily scared to be of help. So why waste his time banging on this door or yelling?

He deliberated for a moment and then Elisha declared out loud, "What else do I have to do? I can't do anything from in here, except become someone's supper, and I'm not going to let that happen!"

With renewed determination, he began pounding, rattling the door handle and yelling until exhaustion overtook him. With bruised and swollen hands, he finally gave up and slid to the floor once again. There, in the dark, in a hopeless heap at the only exit out, he fell asleep.

Chapter Twenty One

Feathered or Furry, Friends
Always Help

Frantic Flight

*E*arlier, Ominous Owl had returned to his perch on the far west side of the woods by Snow Valley. After a while he determined that all seemed as it should be there, so he soared up high and winged his way back to the east side of the woods by the Meadow, to take up his post as sentry there. He scanned every bit of the meadow, watching for anything unusual.

Fortunately, as his keen eyes crossed the Meadow and searched the edge of Deep, Dark Forest, something seemed out of place. His head bobbed forward and he quickly zeroed in on the tiny log cabin. Immediately alarmed, his entire sentry body came to alert. The sight of that cabin meant no good. It appeared only now and then when Mose D. Seat, the master of deceit, came from Deep, Dark Forest to Snow Valley, where he watched for tired or lost wanderers. They were usually easy targets for his traps.

The owl knew Elisha had gone in the meadow toward Deep, Dark Forest. Surely the boy had not fallen for one of D. Seat's tricks, the owl reasoned. But then, being just a small, inexperienced boy, he was a perfect target for one of his traps. Ominous Owl's head began circling, as owls do, to listen intently. After a moment, he stopped. Something didn't sound right.

A sinking feeling deep inside caused Ominous Owl to give a mighty lunge off his perch. He rose easily into the air, to fly swiftly across the meadow and swoop down past the front of the cabin. Oh, no! The pounding and weakened cries he heard signaled his worst fears were true.

With a burst of speed, he turned to rocket across the meadow back to Deep, Dark Woods. No time to talk to the boy now. Besides, with that kind of pounding, he'd be worn out in no time and probably fall asleep. Having seen this happen before, Owl wasn't about to let D. Seat hurt that boy, and there was no time to waste. He quickly returned to the woods where he began hooting and calling to his smallest friend.

In seconds, Minute Mouse, so named because of her tiny size and speed, (as small and quick as a minute), crawled out onto the ledge in front of her house. With hands on her hips, she looked about, then up, as Ominous Owl flew by and in one swoop deftly landed on a nearby branch.

"Quick, Minute! I need your help. The boy is trapped in Mose D. Seat's cabin."

"I'm coming!" she called, her voice showing great concern. She paused only to grab her shawl and throw it around her shoulders.

The owl flew down, barely hesitating to tip a wing down to her as he swooped by. As quick as a minute, the mouse hopped aboard and ran up his back. Her wiry fingers grasped the feathers at the base of Owl's neck and she hung on for dear life. "Ready!" she squeaked loudly.

The timing was perfection, for they'd done this drill before. As Minute Mouse clung to a handful of down beneath the outer feathers, Owl burst into turbo speed and flew swiftly across the meadow to the cabin. There he dropped her as gently as he could before the cabin door.

"Hurry!" she squeaked as she watched him fly away. "There's not much time left."

"Don't worry. I'm not about to lose another one to that vermin!" the owl called.

Minute crawled under the door into the cabin. Used to working in the dark, she quickly found the boy's body in a heap on the floor. The mouse weighed out whether she should awaken him, but decided to let him sleep until Owl returned. She only hoped Owl could find help and return before D. Seat did. Ah, yes, it was all in the timing, whether the boy could be saved or not.

Owl flew swiftly to Snow River's Big Beaver Dam, the engineering marvel of Snow Valley. The beavers took great pride in their mammoth success of building a dam to hold back the waters of the river. Snow Valley, once the river bed, was now a home for many animals. Oftentimes the older ones proudly brought their young to visit Big Beaver Dam. It taught them the good that comes from everyone working together to make Snow Valley a good place to live.

As the official sentry serving the King, Ominous Owl did not live an ordinary owl's life. The King supplied his needs so he could devote all his time to looking out for any evil. His job was to take care of intruders himself or alert the inhabitants of Snow Valley. Owl would call for the soldiers' help if needed. Therefore, Owl had an important part in keeping the valley and meadow safe.

After first scanning the entire area for safety, Owl flew in and landed at the beavers' dwelling. Now that he had arrived, he faced his next dilemma. Since beavers usually stay inside the lodge for winter, he needed a plan to get the largest senior beaver to come out. Perhaps, if the beavers felt their storage of food was being threatened... yes, that might work!

Owl looked for and found a bulge of sticks poking up through the top of the lodge. Below that would be where the beavers stored their food; Ominous Owl began tapping on them with his beak. There, that should bring someone out. Owl continued to tap until Big Slap, a burly, sixty-five-pound beaver appeared, irritated that he had been disturbed from a nap. His rolls of winter fat rippled as he walked and took position.

Big Slap called out to the intruder with the typical whistling between his long bottom teeth as he spoke. "S-s-stop that incess-sant banging! I s-say, s-stop that racquet and s-state your business-s-s!"

Owl came forward a few more steps.

"Who goes-s there?" the senior beaver demanded with a warning growl. Big Slap had to rely on his keener senses of smell and hearing since beavers have such poor eyesight. "Who is it?" he demanded again quickly.

"Who, indeed?" hooted Owl.

"Ah, is that you, Ominous-s Owl?" he asked with near certainty.

"Yes, Slap, it is me," he said.

Slap, relaxing as he recognized Owl's voice, gave his big, toothy grin and called, "Well, hello, Owl! What brings you here on s-such a cold winter night?"

"I need your help quickly. That insidious Mose D. Seat is back, living up to his name and his legend."

"Oh, no!" Big Slap moaned.

"Oh, yes! He has a poor child—a boy—locked in his cabin. I need help getting him out before the old man returns to do his evil. Can you come?"

Big Slap wanted to help but he had a concern. "Where is-s it, friend?"

"It's over past Big Dark Woods, beyond the meadow at the edge of Deep, Dark Forest."

"Oh," the burly beaver explained, shaking his head, "past Big Dark Woods? That's-s much too far for beavers-s to travel in this-s weather! I'm already freezing out here, Owl. Als-so, there's wolves-s and bears-s in those woods-s. It would not be safe! No, I'm afraid I can't. That journey in winter is simply too long and hard," Slap apologized with a hard shiver that caused his winter fat to shake again. "Be-sides-s, we were jus-st getting ready to have a nice, ta-s-sty meal of as-s-spen and birch bark. Won't you join us-s?"

"No, Slap, I must get help. Perhaps you didn't hear me. The boy's life is in danger! Time is of the essence," said Owl urgently.

"Well, if time is-s important, as-s you know, we beavers-s are s-slow at covering land. The fact that it'd take s-so long in this frigid air, plus-s being exposed to my enemies in the woods-s, would be too much danger," the beaver said, explaining his reluctance. "I do have my family to think about, you know."

Time was slipping quickly away with no solution in sight. Now Owl began to feel more than urgent. He stepped quickly back and forth, from one foot to the other. "I must find someone to help!"

Owl began pacing as he thought. He felt desperate. But he remembered that as Sentry of the woods, the King had given him special wisdom. He encouraged himself that he could figure this out. As he thought, an idea began to form in the owl's mind.

"Don't you have a young one smaller than you? Someone I could carry? A flight would get us there faster," said Owl.

The beaver thought carefully for a moment. "The only one would be Benjy, my two year old. He's-s not proven yet, though, at how fas-st he can cut. For what you're talking about, you'd need additional adult beaver help."

"Please listen, Big Slap! I have an idea that just might work, but we must leave right now, please! The old man will be returning soon."

The owl spoke with such urgency the beaver could no longer resist. "The thought of that ins-sidious old man winning over a s-smaller creature is enough to make me want to be part of s-stopping him."

Having decided to help, Big Slap jumped down and slapped his fifteen-inch tail hard on the icy water. Owl couldn't believe how hard and loudly the big slap hit, which explained how the beaver got his name.

They didn't have to wait long for a response to the warning signal. In less than a minute, the youngster, Benjy appeared. The young beaver was bristling and ready to defend against whatever. "What's wrong, Dad? Where's the danger?"

"The danger's not here, s-son. You need to go with Owl to res-s-cue a boy."

"A boy! A human? Haven't you told me to watch out for humans?" said the confused young beaver. "Why help a boy?"

"No time to waste, Benjy. Owl will explain on the way. Quickly, hop on his back and hang on! Owl will follow your directions to the s-stream not far from Big Meadow," Slap quickly told his boy, enlivening his instructions with his many whistles. "S-stop there at my brother, Big Chopper's Lodge. Tell them Big S-s-slap s-sent you, then round up his fas-stest chopping men to go with you for the res-s-cue. We owe Owl many times over. This-s is the least we can do. And...

we owe that wicked old man in a different way, if you remember how we've lost many of our beaver brothers. We all have reason to s-s-settle up with D. S-seat. Now, go!" Big Slap urged.

"Okay, whatever you say, Dad. I'm ready. Let's go!" said Benjy turning to the owl.

The large bird rose into the air, made a circle, then leaned in. "Hop on!" he said and Benjy hopped aboard as he flew by slowly. Benjy's landing seemed to nearly stop Owl in his flight and he struggled to rise back up. After fluttering and much pumping of his wings, Owl finally overcame the extra weight and they were on their way. "Be careful!" Slap called out. Already shivering from the cold, he braced himself and dove into the icy water. As he came back up inside his lodge, he heard Mrs. Slap calling his name. First Big Slap shook off the water. Then he gave an extra quiver, but it was not from the cold. The frigid cold was nothing compared to telling Benjy's mother where her youngest had gone.

****

As Owl frantically flew back to the meadow, he hoped with every pump of his wings it wasn't too late. He explained the situation to Benjy, who was more than ready to take on a rescue. The young beaver, hanging on tightly, also thought the ride atop the back of an owl was a most thrilling adventure. He could hardly wait to tell his brothers about it later. Owl listened closely to Benjy's directions and soon found Big Chopper's lodge, where he dropped off young Benjy with a plea to hurry.

Carrying Benjy had really been too much weight for Owl. Winded and hurting, he flew on to the cabin to wait. As he arrived he scanned the area for the old man first; all seemed clear. After landing, Owl staggered and stumbled a bit from the painful strain on his wings and body. Pausing only to catch his breath, he tapped lightly with his beak on the door. Minute Mouse popped out promptly.

"What took you so long?" Mouse first asked, then taking one look at Owl, became concerned. "Owl, my friend, are you all right?"

"I will be, in time. I just dropped off Big Slap's youngster at Big Chopper's. He's rounding up a crew to help. Hopefully many beavers will speed Elisha's rescue."

Mouse gasped. "You, what? You carried him? All the way from Snowy River? But, Owl, an adult beaver is a good fifty pounds! Even though Benjy is not full grown, he is more than even a strong bird like you should attempt."

"No matter. We need help and this was the only way. Every cousin, uncle, friend or otherwise that Benjy can round up will be here shortly. I just pray the old man doesn't return first. I doubt I could successfully take him on right now. How's the boy?"

"Still asleep. He exhausted himself before I arrived trying to get out," she said sympathetically. "It's best he rest for whatever is ahead."

"You'd better check on him. Don't want him to panic if he awakes. I'll wait for the Beaver Rescue Brigade," said Owl, already looking over the meadow for them. "Beavers can't travel too fast and when they do get here, they'll have a big job. I do hope they can get it done in time!"

Quite concerned for her friend, Mouse gave her wisest mousely advice, "Please, Owl, you must rest and heal."

"Yes, I hate to admit it, but I think I must," he agreed.

Satisfied with his answer, she promptly crawled back inside and settled down in the dark to wait with a nervous hiccup. That one was followed by more. She covered her mouth trying to muffle the sound, but it didn't work.

Soon Elisha began to stir. Opening his eyes and seeing only darkness, he was gripped once again by fear. Thankfully, he was distracted by something small and familiar sounding. Is that, could it be... hiccups?

"M-m-mouse?" he asked hesitantly.

"Yes, it is I, Minute Mouse. We are friends now so, please, you may call me Minute," she answered.

"Minute Mouse—That fits you. Am I ever glad to at least hear someone else's voice! I'm so glad it's you, Minute. How did you get here from Big Dark Woods?"

"It's a long story," she said.

"I think I have time. At least, I hope I do."

Just as she began her story, they both heard a gnawing, chiseling sound at the door.

"What's that?" Elisha gasped. "Is that old man already back?"

"No, it's your rescue!" Mouse told him.

"My, what? What do you mean?"

Elisha sat back down to listen as she filled him in. He felt great relief that perhaps this frightening chapter in his life could end well after all.

The Beaver Brigade Begins Under Sky Guards' Cover

Outside, several big burly beavers and a few smaller ones had returned with Benjy. Owl was relieved to see them and gave a quick greeting.

"Welcome, Big Chopper, and thank you all in the Beaver Brigade for making this journey at such a bad time of the year for you. The time to accomplish your mission is growing short so I'll let you get right to it!"

The most senior beaver, Big Chopper, took one look at the log cabin door and sized it up. He gave quite a long whistle and exclaimed, "Logs crisscrossing logs!" but added confidently, "We should be able to chew through that wall, and the door if need be, in no time at all. Let's get chopping, boys! If we can cut down trees — and we can — then we can chisel through these logs."

The Beaver Brigade gave a mighty shout and a series of whistles in agreement with the foreman of this daunting task; daunting, that is, except to a crew united in vengeance towards D. Seat.

It was an amazing thing to watch the teamwork of the hard-working beavers. Each knew his job and did it speedily. They turned it into a serious contest to see who could break through first. They showed how quickly 1/8 inch grooves can add up using their strong, long bottom teeth like chiseling machines. The more they chiseled, the sharper their teeth became. When a beaver needed a break, he'd lean back on his big flat tail to rest as another would take over. Two at a time worked on the wall about a foot apart as two others gnawed at the logs on the door.

All Ominous Owl could do was rest and watch. Owl remained tense and on guard, however, during this race against time. Not up to attacks himself, Owl did not know how he could handle it if D. Seat returned. His large eyes grew troubled at the prospect.

About that time, Owl's keen eye was caught by the shadows of something circling up above. He raised himself up to stand as tall as he could and called into the sky, "Who-who? Who goes there?" As he heard the answers, he recognized his old friends.

"Me, Hawkeye!" called Red Tailed Hawk.

"And me, Spotter. We heard you were hurt, so we're here to patrol for you," said Spotter, the sharpest-eyed Peregrine Falcon in the kingdom.

"Yeah," said Hawkeye gruffly, "if that weasel, D. Seat shows up, we'll gladly take care of him."

Owl, deeply humbled by their concern and willingness to help, was still somewhat embarrassed. "I... I don't think I will be much help, though."

"Don't worry," said Spotter. "We owe you big time and trust me, I will relish poking some holes in that wicked hide!"

"Yes," added Hawkeye, "We'll be only too glad to take over. Our plan together is deadly; with Spotter's eyes and speed and my ability to attack, you won't have to lift a feather against him!"

"Not a feather!" agreed Spotter.

"I am humbled and I thank you, old friends. Vigilance, now!" said Owl, much encouraged.

Even as they had talked with Owl, they had taken turns to keep watch and now they returned Owl's battle cry, "Vigilance!" Both birds took off to be the Sky Guard, soaring high to look out for trouble and guard, from many thousands of feet in the sky.

Owl felt some relief, knowing that he wouldn't need to worry about his old enemy sneaking up on them. The raptors' vendetta against D. Seat dated back to the day he'd shot some of their off-spring. Now, they were all only too happy to spoil his plans.

With Spotter's vision and speed, D. Seat would not sneak back in easily. As the falcon and hawk began systematic circling over the meadow, forest, and woods, Owl was greatly reassured they would be warned in time. But then, what? They held the advantage of a surprise attack and with Hawkeyes' razor-like beak, they could do damage... unless D. Seat had his gun. Owl winced at that possibility. The thought of his friends being harmed gave him pain. They simply must get done and clear out in time!

Owl returned his attention to the chiseling contest where they were making some headway. Occasionally, an extra hard knot in the wood slowed down their work, frustrating a beaver and causing the animal to let off a loud, blowing sound. Big Chopper would give a few words' pep talk that would set them to chewing harder and faster. Benjy and the younger beavers kept the work area cleared for the mature working beavers.

Minute slipped out under the door to check the progress. Quickly avoiding being stepped on by the busy working beavers, she ran over to speak to Owl.

"Owl, do you think they can get Elisha out?" she squeaked quietly.

"Oh, as good as these beavers are, I'm sure they can get him out," said Owl. "The question is—can they do it to rescue the boy in time?" As impressed as he was with their speed, Owl worried that if they could not clear out before D. Seat returned, everyone would be in danger, not just Elisha.

Minute said nothing; she just gave a hiccup and with a nervous twitch of her tail, she ran back inside to be with Elisha.

Chapter Twenty Two

Fighting Fear in the Dark

The young boy was becoming quite restless; it seemed to Elisha that he had been trapped in the dark forever. Unable to see what was happening, he could only sit and listen to the sound of the beavers working. Although he knew what these noises were, in the dark the continual chiseling, chipping, and gnawing sounded strange and frightening to him. He began to wish the sounds would stop, and yet, he knew they must continue. The darkness and weird noises began to discourage him.

"Do you really think they can get me out of here?" he asked Minute Mouse as she returned.

"Of course, they can. You're not the first one they've helped save," she said knowingly. "That's why the old man hates beavers so much and traps all he can. Anytime Good, Kind King hears D. Seat is back, he sends his foot soldiers out to clear him from this area. The only way he can enter is through the big woods and the forest. It's from those dark places he watches for his prey."

"You mean I was his prey?"

"Yes, you were, but D. Seat does not stalk like a wolf. Old D. Seat tricks his victims into believing he has something they want or need," explained Minute.

"Yeah, he sure did that!" Elisha was thoughtful for a moment. "Minute, can I ask you something?"

"Certainly, you can. Whether I'll know the answer or not is another matter entirely, but go ahead," she replied in her common sense way.

"How come when I used the King's name in the woods, the tree doors opened, but in here, it didn't work on this door?"

"Hmm. Let me think," Minute said with arms crossed and a finger resting aside her cheek. After a moment, she spoke.

"Elisha, did you feel you were supposed to come into this cabin?"

"No way! I didn't want to come in here, or anywhere, with him!"

"Why not?" she asked.

"Are you kidding? I didn't trust him. Too creepy!" he remembered with a shudder.

Minute gave a puzzled frown. "Then why did you come in?"

"Because I thought I could just get the clues I needed about Snowy and get out of here."

"Ah. He could see you'd never trust him, so he offered you something you wanted. That meant you ignored your bad feelings about him, right?"

"Yeah..." Elisha replied slowly as he thought about it. "Yeah! That's exactly what happened. I see it now, but I didn't then!"

"That's how D. Seat works," she explained. "Deceit is his favorite weapon..."

"Deceit? What's that? Deceit sounds just like his name."

"Because that's who he is and what he does. Deceit is, well, sort of like, tricking—he makes something seem like something it isn't. He pretended he would help you, but he really wanted to trap you."

"Oh... I see. Deceit is bad."

"Oh, yes. D. Seat, the man, is evil and so is the deceit he uses. And why did you not have your weapon with you?" she asked simply.

Elisha looked startled. "What do you mean? I thought the weapon was just to use in the dark woods."

"Did anyone tell you that?" she pressed.

"No."

"Oh, that's so sad," said Minute. "You saw what the sword did for you in the dark of the woods, but you didn't bring it with you."

"Well, yeah, I guess," admitted Elisha. "But if I had taken it, then the next person who needed it wouldn't have had it."

"You didn't think that the King would have helped someone else in need, just like he did you?" she asked sadly.

"I... I guess I didn't think of that. Besides, when I got into the sun, I thought I'd be okay."

"And did that work?"

"Uh, not really," Elisha said sheepishly.

"Elisha... The weapon was yours to use for as long as you needed it."

"But, but," he stammered, "I thought just using the King's name would work, like before, and that would be all I'd need."

"What you really needed, was Faith. Without the sword to help you fight your fear of the dark, your fear grew stronger than your faith."

The boy was quiet for a few moments. "I guess I blew it, didn't I?"

"You're not the first to be tricked by D. Seat. Unfortunately, you won't be the last," Minute said. She saw how quiet Elisha remained and her heart tendered toward him.

"Even grown men have been deceived," she said quietly, "and become a prisoner of Fear. When you're locked in a dark place, it's natural to be afraid. But when Faith comes in, Fear runs out!"

"Faith must be strong!"

"In the sunny meadow, it was easier to have faith in the Name. You ordered the birds to leave, and they left. But, when you became locked in here, in the dark, Fear weakened your faith and stopped you from believing the door would open. D. Seat tricked you to enter, but your fear sealed you into your own prison. If it hadn't been this cabin, it would have been something else."

Elisha was stunned, not even knowing what to think.

"But I'm just a kid. How was I to know?" he asked in frustration.

Minute Mouse walked closer to him and laid her tiny paw on his arm.

"At your age you couldn't know. Journeying alone in this land, unprepared, has made this a painful time for you. But someday, Elisha, this experience will help you in a harder place than this."

Right now, he could not think of a harder place in life than the one he was in. Elisha knew he'd have to think this through later, if and when he got out of this mess.

"This is a hard lesson," Elisha said sadly, "and it's not even over yet!"

"Just remember—the King will come through for us, as long as we have Faith."

"You mean, like the King sending you, the owl, and the beavers to help me?"

"Certainly."

Elisha's spirits brightened up a bit. "So, Minute, you think they'll get us out of here?"

"Yes, I do. Good Kind King's plan is always to deliver us. He never wants his people trapped or in misery," she replied.

At that very moment, a shaft of light burst through the cabin with the brightest, happiest ray of light Elisha had ever seen! Smiling from ear to ear, his heart leapt within him to see dust floating in the light. "Look, Minute! Dust! I can see the dust!"

"Yes, Elisha," she agreed, laughing. "Even a speck of dust can be a welcome sight after so long in the darkness."

The first breakthrough in the door was followed by loud whistles and cheers from the beavers outside. "Hip, hip, hooray! Hip, hip, hooray!"

Their small success urged the long-toothed workers on to create an opening large enough for Elisha. The boy was excited and amused to watch the chopping teeth break through. At first only the teeth showed, but as the opening enlarged, the beaver's nose appeared, followed by the snappy black eyes, and eventually the entire face. The victorious beaver peered through the hole before stepping back and giving a mighty whistle. The whole Beaver Brigade began cheering.

"Elisha!" Mr. O hooted. "See if you can get through. This may be it!"

"You can do it," squeaked Mouse with a tiny hiccup.

Elisha tried putting his head through the opening, but his shoulders were too wide, so he pulled his head back inside. "Not yet," he called.

"Here, let me at that," said Big Chopper. Being the most senior beaver and the largest, at a good seventy pounds, he prepared to take over.

The others stepped back a distance to watch Chopper at work, but as they did so, their attention was caught by a shocking sight. As they pointed and whispered, Big Chopper turned to ask, "What's-s-s going on? What is all the fuss-ss about?"

His eyes following theirs, he stepped back to look up high above the door. As he recognized what they saw, Big Chopper stiffened with hostility and anger.

There, stretched above the door, hung a small beaver hide, an obvious trophy of Mose D. Seat's revenge against the beavers. The furry rodents, standing sadly with flat tails hanging down, became silent as they remembered their dear, missing cousin. They watched as Big Chopper was grief stricken, but enraged as well, to see his nephew's hide. It was clearly hung up to give D. Seat's message to all beavers: "This is what happens when you spoil my plans!"

Finally Big Chopper looked toward the others and motioned to them. Without a word the largest beaver came over to the wall and bent down on all fours. The younger beavers climbed onto his back to form a pyramid. Next they placed Benjy on the top where he was able to gently remove the hide and then climb down. The young beaver, ever so respectfully and carefully, folded the hide and handed it quietly to Big Chopper.

No one moved or made a sound for a few moments. The whole group, including Owl and Mouse, waited in silence.

Big Chopper looked much older as he accepted the neatly folded hide and stood quietly, staring glumly down at it. "Oh, Bucky," he moaned softly.

Finally the elder beaver regained his composure. He wiped a tear and cleared his throat to speak.

"Well, at least now... we know what happened to you, little nephew. We won't have to wonder and worry anymore." Looking up at the others he gave a coughing sound, then continued on somewhat hoarsely. "Pure evil cut off his life and there will be a payment some day for that kind of wickedness! For now... we'll finish our job, to save the life of another of D. Seat's victims." With that, he handed the dear hide to the others for safe keeping.

***

From inside Elisha had heard only muffled sounds followed by a long, strange silence. Minute had slipped out to find out what was happening, but hadn't returned. Beginning to worry, he called out, "Hey! What's going on?" Owl came to the opening and briefly explained what had happened.

"That's so awful," the boy responded. "Will they be all right?"

"Yes, in time," answered Owl, but he was interrupted by Big Chopper who came to the opening and spoke in a restrained voice.

"Excuse me, Owl. I have a job to finish."

Elisha could see through the hole that Big Chopper's eyes were blazing mad. Owl stepped aside to let the old beaver work, which he did with a vengeance, taking over the main opening himself.

All the beavers took up a chant, "Chop, chop, chop!" until in a short time he completed widening the hole. A cheer went up from all as Elisha eagerly climbed through.

He inhaled deeply, enjoying the fresh air. It felt so good to be free and see the openness of the outdoors again. As the rays of sunlight fell upon him, he was grateful. He had never been so glad to see sunshine in his life.

Dirty Cobwebs of Deceit

Elisha looked at each one in the circle and was overwhelmed with what they had done. He spoke to the beavers. "I'm so sorry, my beaver friends, for how hard this has turned out for you. You only came to help me, and you found sadness."

"Yes, we came to help you, but through it, we have been helped. It happened as it was supposed to," assured Big Chopper.

"How can I thank you?" Elisha asked, brimming over with gratitude. He began choking up a little as the group lined up before him, all grinning proudly, their long teeth gleaming in the sun, bashful but happy with what they'd done.

"Just don't fall for any more tricks. Remember, things are not always what they seem," Big Chopper said, referring to the old man. "That's why he is so insidious. Mose D. Seat certainly has the *most deceit* of anyone in Snow Valley!"

"Indeed!" agreed another larger beaver.

"I know that now," said Elisha. "Trust me, next time I get that awful feeling that something's not right, I'll pay attention. Thank you all, beavers, Owl, and Mouse for your help."

Looking over at Owl, Elisha saw him standing in a peculiar way. Nor was he used to seeing Owl on the ground this long either. Elisha stepped forward to have a closer look. "Are you all right, Mr. O?" he asked in concern.

Owl didn't want Elisha to know the trip carrying the beaver had strained him. "All is well, now that you're safe," he said. "Now you are free to continue on, boy, with your search."

The others gave a wave and began walking away. Elisha felt like running away from the cabin, but instead he turned to inspect the door and the chiseled opening the team of chopping beavers had created. He thought of what Mouse had shared and made a mental note of what he had learned—to be armed and on guard all the time and, he smiled to himself, to use Faith to open locked doors.

Elisha was just leaving when he heard something fall. Turning and looking behind him, he noticed something lying on the ground before the door. When he picked it up he found it to be an irregularly shaped, weather-beaten piece of wood with dark knots. Benjy must have loosened it when he retrieved the beaver hide.

Something that had been scratched on it caught his eye. He rubbed the dirt and cobwebs away, but it still took him a moment to make it out. He read aloud, "Property of Mose D. Seat." Underneath it was something else -"Place of Answered Wishes." Well, that was deceitful, Elisha thought. He wondered why he hadn't noticed it before he went in, but then he remembered that his attention had been only on the old man and finding Snowy.

Owl had intentionally waited for Elisha to leave before beginning his painful walk across the meadow with Mouse on his back. Benjy and the other beavers waited in the meadow for him, knowing it would be safer for Owl to walk with them in his condition.

Owl spoke to Minute. "We can send now for the King's guards to get this band of beavers safely home," he told her. "They'll all need protection when old Mose discovers what we've done. He will, however, be no match for the King's Snow Soldiers."

"You go rest, Owl. I'll put out the call for the soldiers," said Minute, hopping down and running ahead to spread the word through her woodland friends.

Owl called out a thank you followed by a tired sigh. It was a job well done, and he did not regret any of it. As for himself, he knew he would heal in time. His King always made sure of that. Finally Owl reached Big Dark Woods and, with extra effort, flew up to his perch to settle in and let the healing begin.

Back at the cabin, Elisha shuddered at a brief thought of the old man. Had it not been for friends coming to his rescue, it could have been a different ending – his own. He had found he had family, even in this unfamiliar kingdom, who would fight for him.

After a brief walk away, the boy seemed compelled to turn back to give one last look at the cabin. When he did, he was totally shocked.

"What? I don't believe it!" he gasped. The cabin. It was gone, totally gone!

Elisha shook his head in utter disbelief. For whatever reason it had disappeared, he was glad. This was just another demonstration of the hard-to-understand things that happen in Snow Land. Greatly relieved that another in this incredible chain of events had ended, he once again turned his focus to the Lodge where the snowman had directed him. He was back on track with Mission: Find Snowy.

Chapter Twenty Three

Echo in a Black Cap

*E*lisha stood before the door and with a sigh he reached for the knocker. Curiously, it was not there. But how could it have disappeared? Wait... that door wasn't that big before. With a shake of his head, he laughed at himself. That's silly; doors don't grow, but... as he stared at the door and then looked upward, he gasped and stepped back, for... this one had! The knocker was now way out of his reach. How could that have happened?

Was this yet another attempt to drive him away, he wondered. But, who would be doing all this? "Well, I'm not scared!" Elisha announced loudly to convince himself and whoever else might be listening. Instead, he heard his statement echoing through the meadow behind him and fading into the woods, a seeming mockery of his brave words...

"I'm... I'm... I'm... not... not... not... scared... scared... scared..."

The echo kept repeating for a bit. Elisha had heard echoes before, but nothing that kept on going this long. Finally it faded and stopped.

"Whoa, that was weird! Is someone trying to scare me with my own words?"

Quite surprisingly a tiny chickadee landed on the door knocker and with quick, short movements looked Elisha over, cocking his head from one side to the other, as if trying to figure him out.

"Chirp, chirp! Maybe you should be scared, scared-scared."

Elisha burst into a sunny grin at the perky little bird speaking to him. The black-capped bird went on.

"Sometimes being scared saves you from getting yourself into a nest you shouldn't be in, in-in!" said the white faced chickadee staring at Elisha with bright, black eyes below a black cap. "At least, that's how it works for me, me-me."

"Well, hello there, little friend," Elisha said with a smile. Then, remembering that things here are not always what they seem, he questioned seriously, "You *are* a friend, aren't you?"

The chickadee continued to cock his head from side to side. "Are you, you-you?" the bird repeated.

"Sure, I can be your friend, if you'd like," Elisha said with a smile.

"I'd like you to be, be-be," the chickadee repeated.

Elisha couldn't help but wonder why this cute little bird kept repeating himself, like an echo.

"What is your name?" asked Elisha.

"Chirp, chirp. I'm Echo, co-co," the Chickadee answered. "You must be Elisha. Yes, siree, ree-ree. You're the only boy I've ever seen, seen-seen."

"How do you know my name?" Elisha asked.

"Most everyone in Snow Land does by now. Are you going in here, here-here?" he asked, pointing his beak at the lodge. "You said you aren't scared."

"Well," Elisha whispered, "sometimes I say I'm not when I really am. It helps me do what I have to do."

"Helps you do what you have to do. So, is going in what you have to do, do-do?"

The chickadee's constant repetition amused Elisha, and although he felt like giggling, he tried to answer seriously.

"I have to, to look for Snowy…" Elisha paused for a moment to worry as he looked at the strange building, "even though I don't know… what's in there." He felt something barely brush by his face and he absent-mindedly waved his hand at it while continuing on nervously. "It might be dark in there. Bad things happen in the dark, you know. Something terrible could be hiding in there. Something more terrible than anything I've seen... I'm not sure I'm—"

Whoosh! He was interrupted by a sudden movement of a shadow crossing before him, but it was not a shadow from something blocking sunlight. Whoosh! As it swiftly flew past him a second time, he instinctively put his arm up to protect himself, but when the boy looked around, it was nowhere to be found, almost as if it hadn't been there at all.

"Now, what was that?" he asked.

"What?" asked Echo.

"Oh, nothing, I guess," Elisha said nervously.

"You were saying... about going in..." reminded Echo.

"What? Me go into that strange place? Inside? No way! Who knows what might be in there? I need to get out of here. Oh, what am I saying? I must go in, but... but, I can't..."

Instead of making sense, Elisha began arguing with himself, pacing on the porch, worrying and wringing his hands. He suddenly felt very anxious, which was strange for him. He was normally a very confident, happy boy. "Something's wrong with me," he said. Yes, something was definitely happening, for his stomach began to tighten and he felt very shaky and jittery, inside and out. He continued to worry as he spoke to Echo.

"Oh, what am I going to do? I have to find out if Snowy's in there or if anyone has seen him, but, but... so many scary things have happened. I-I, I'm afraid," he added looking frantically at the door. With that he began to bite nervously at his lip.

"Then don't go in," Echo said simply.

"But, I must, I'm just afra—" Whoosh! There went that same shadow again, but larger, darker and closer this time. "There! Did you see that? Something dark?" asked Elisha, rising back up after ducking. "Surely you saw it this time!" he said as he looked furtively around for where it had gone.

"Oh, no! The Worry Shadow! Don't let it get to you," warned Echo, as he looked around as well.

"What do you mean, don't let it get to me? It keeps coming at me!" Elisha began looking around more frantically than ever. "And I suddenly feel awful. I'm afraid... afraid of what's going to happen."

The Shadow flew by again. "Echo, what is that, that... thing?" Elisha asked, wrapping his arms around himself protectively. Beginning to shake, the once brave little boy felt like a lump of human jello!

The Shadow returned, this time trying to land on him. Now Elisha was totally spooked. He tried to push it away to protect himself. "Stop! Stop it! Echo, what *is* that?"

Echo, alarmed to see that Elisha's hands were trembling violently, landed on his shoulder. "Oh, no, Elisha! I know what's happening! You're under attack. Listen to me."

The Shadow flew even closer, brushing Elisha's face and circling him once.

"Oh, I don't like this! Echo, how do I stop this creepy thing?" Elisha cried out, flailing his arms and hands at it. The Shadow flew away briefly.

Echo firmly tapped Elisha's shoulder with his beak. The uncomfortable tapping got the shaking boy's attention.

"Listen to me," Echo explained. "That's the Worry Shadow. He'll be back. Whatever you do, *do not give in* to worry, Elisha." He emphasized the words with a tapping of his beak on Elisha's shoulder. "If you give in, it will land and attach itself to you."

"Attach! Attach to me? Then, what? Will it *kill* me?" the boy said, looking around wild-eyed and scared. If Elisha's parents could see him now, they wouldn't recognize him. The usually calmer Elisha was becoming more worried with every passing moment. Continuing to look frantically about, he wrung his hands harder than before. "I feel sick. I think I'm going to throw up."

The Shadow buzzed around him, coming at his face, closer and closer. Elisha waved his hands and arms wildly about, trying to stop it. "Stop! Get away! Leave me alone!"

Echo shouted into his ear. "It's trying to take over. The only way to stop it is to block it out, by thinking *good* things."

"*How can I think of good things when bad things are happening?*" he moaned.

Elisha batted at it, recoiling sharply as The Shadow continued to come at him. "Oh, great! I'm going to die. I just know it. I can't stop it!"

"Elisha, you can stop it! Instead of thinking of the worst that can happen, have faith that good will happen!" shouted Echo. Normally the bird would never shout, but being so small, he had to be heard over Elisha's mounting cries of terror.

The Shadow hovered oppressively around Elisha as it bombarded him with its darkness. Now thoroughly panic stricken, Elisha screamed, "It's going right through my hands at my face!"

"Your hands cannot stop it," Echo warned. "Only good thoughts can."

The poor boy moaned even more as The Shadow swooped up and hovered over his head.

"It's getting stronger," Echo warned. The little bird decided he'd better attack the Shadow himself. He could not make the Shadow leave, but he could certainly annoy and weaken him with his happiness. So Echo began chirping a happy song at his very loudest, while flying around the shadow. Although The Worry Shadow owned no face itself, oddly, a frown appeared and the dark shadow began flinching at the bird's happy notes as if in pain.

"I can't think! Help me, Echo," Elisha begged. "I can barely see anything! Echo, where are you?" Elisha cried out.

Echo flew into the air and hovered like a hummingbird before Elisha's face. "I'm here! Say what you believe now!"

"Okay, I'll try!" said Elisha.

"No, don't just try—*do* it!" Echo shouted. "Believe and speak good things!"

It was hard to think good with worry in your brain, but Elisha concentrated by thinking of his parents. The Shadow barely wavered. "Echo, it's not working. I'm worried I may never see Mom and Dad again!" The Shadow tightened its hold on him.

Echo fluttered before Elisha's eyes and chirped loudly. "Elisha... Stop worrying! Say the strongest thing you believe until you're shouting it. Now!"

"But I don't feel strong enough!"

"Don't go by how you *feel!* Go by what is *true*," Echo urged.

Immediately Echo threw his happiest song at the Worry Shadow. The bird began singing "His Eye Is on the Sparrow." The happy notes flew like arrows through the air, striking at the darkness of the Shadow... "I sing because I'm happy. I sing because I'm free. His eye is on the sparrow, and I know He watches me... " Each strike weakened the Shadow's grip.

The happy message of the song also reminded the boy of what he believed and encouraged him. He closed his eyes and began to speak. "I don't need to worry. God watches over me. He loves me. He's always with me. He makes me strong. I don't need to worry." Elisha felt himself calming. "I trust in Him."

The Shadow began to flinch as Echo's notes and Elisha's words of Trust struck its center. Elisha felt the Shadow's hold on him loosening, so he continued. "God takes care of me, so I don't need to worry! He is all I need."

Elisha still felt sick, but he had heard that laughter is good medicine, so he decided to laugh as loudly as possible. Even though it was a forced laugh, amazingly, his stomach settled. That encouraged him, so he laughed some more until he realized that, although its grip was weaker, The Shadow was still on his head!

Elisha closed his eyes again and thought as hard as he could. Things his parents had taught to him began flooding his mind. "I know that Good is stronger than Evil and— "

"Keep on," shouted Echo. "It's working!"

"I believe in Good. His Goodness is all around me. He is greater than anything that can come against me. God's love never fails..."

As Elisha repeated truths he'd been taught, he felt the vise-like grip loosening more. Good! It was getting weaker. Elated, he shouted, "It's leaving. I can feel it!"

"Great, but you must take charge. Order The Shadow to leave. in the name of the King."

"Oh, yeah!" said Elisha. He began to laugh more as he thought upon the other times the name had saved him. He felt no fear or worry any longer.

"Are you ready, -dy-dy?" asked Echo optimistically.

"Ready!" Elisha commanded confidently, "In the name of Good, Kind King of the Kingdom of Goodness... Shadow of Worry—leave!"

With a loud pop, The Worry Shadow detached and floated a short distance away but still hovered in the air.

"The Shadow is waiting for you to worry again. Let's sing him out of here, Elisha!" chirped Echo.

As the two sang happy songs, they watched the Shadow grow smaller and begin to fade away. As Elisha began to dance for joy, it gave a weakened shriek — as if it could stand no more — and disappeared.

Elisha looked to where he had last seen The Shadow. "Guess it didn't like our music," he gloated and yet he watched to see if it might return. Finally satisfied it was truly gone, he asked Echo, "Where did that awful thing come from?"

Echo just shook his head from side to side. "First worries float into your mind. If you don't replace them with Faith, the Worry Shadow will come. The Shadow usually attaches so softly and slowly, you don't notice at first, but the longer it stays, the harder it is to get rid of. Next thing you know, worrying is all you do!"

"Why didn't the Shadow bother you?" Elisha asked curiously.

"He hates my happy songs. Happy is like a dagger of light to the darkness of The Shadow," answered Echo.

"Hard to understand why anyone would not like being happy."

"The Shadow can't live on Happiness, only on peoples' worries," said the bird simply.

"He needs my worries to live? Then I won't help him out with that anymore! Thank you so much, Echo. If you hadn't been here, I'd have been swallowed up in the Shadow's darkness, for sure!"

"Sometimes Good Kind King does test us, but he would not have allowed you to be destroyed. He cares about you for some reason," said Echo.

"I don't know the reason either," said Elisha nodding. "By the way, Echo, you have not been echoing for a while. How come?"

"Oh, that's only when I'm hap, hap-happy, like now, now-now!" he chirped and sang. "Birds don't worry, we sing! So just keep sing, sing-singing. Goodbye!"

"Good bye, Echo!" Elisha smiled, thankful for another helpful friend and another rescue. In Big Dark Woods, he had learned much, but this new and valuable lesson would also stay with him for life... Don't worry. Just trust and sing, like a bird.

Chapter Twenty Four

Contradictions Grow

*H*appily, Elisha returned his attention to the strange wood-and-snow building. Once again he found himself in shock. The door! It was again its normal size and the knocker within his reach! That settles it; this winter world has some spooky stuff in it... Doors change sizes, mountains and cabins appear and disappear, green paths appear in snow... He didn't understand all these changes, but this one made knocking easier.

Standing on his tiptoes to look, he saw two traditional fixtures of a snowman on the metal door knocker. The knocker itself was shaped like a snowman's smoking pipe. Underneath it lay a metal piece shaped like a black top hat, tipped as if greeting someone. Could that mean a snowman might live here?

Elisha gingerly grasped the knocker and rapped twice, softly at first, and waited. No response. Perhaps no one heard, so he rapped a little harder. Again he waited with no response at all. A third time he knocked loudly, then again, each time more insistently.

Determined not to give up, he put his hands on his hips and raised himself to his full height. "You might as well open the door. I'm not leaving!" he cried out, raising his voice to whoever or whatever waited on the other side. He had decided he'd act brave even if he didn't feel like it. Boldly he reached to knock again, but his hand stopped in midair when the door swung open slowly, with a very loud cr-r-r-reak — much like a scary movie.

Tentatively poking his head inside, he saw no one around. That's strange; who could have opened the door? What he saw appeared to be a very old, very large, very dark place. "Oh no," he moaned with mounting dread, "not dark, again!"

Did he dare go in? Thinking of what had just happened in the other dark places, he definitely did not want to. But one thought of Snowy renewed his resolve. "I can do this!" he said bravely to steel himself. After one hard swallow the boy slowly put one foot in the doorway. "Okay, here goes," he said under his breath.

Ever so quietly, he stepped over the threshold and waited as his eyes adjusted to the darkness. With his first step, the old floor boards creaked, betraying his presence to whoever might be ahead, but he did not let it stop him; here or elsewhere, he had to find Snowy!

Looking around, he began to make out the shadows of an ancient lodge with high ceilings, a dark hallway and an unusual atmosphere. Elisha couldn't imagine what kind of place this could be; he only knew he felt uncomfortable. Oh, if only this was over and he could already be home with Snowy.

A shaft of light shined dimly through a window in the top of the door. The window's glass panes, geometrically cut into a simple snowflake design, seemed to have a magical effect, for amazingly, he saw shimmering snowflakes floating in the shaft of light. As the light stretched across the hall, it seemed as if it were actually snowing within the light ray. "Awesome!" Elisha exclaimed. It was pretty clear that somebody here likes snow. Maybe, he thought cautiously, that's a good thing?

He took one step in the entryway and was instantly jarred by the loud thud of the front door slamming shut behind him. Elisha spun around in fright, thinking perhaps the owner had returned home. Looking first at the door, then to either side, he saw no one there or anywhere else for that matter. Elisha was relieved but still his heart was pounding. With no wind outside and no one around inside, what had closed that door?

The impact of the slamming door had sent dust flying with some settling on the boy's hand. Elisha observed it was not ordinary dust;

it was more a dry, powdery frost. How strange, but he'd think about that later; for now he needed to go exploring.

Here he was, once again, in a strange, dark place that seemed to be totally silent and empty. But, as he stood still, he heard faint noises coming from a distant part of the building. He decided to explore to find out what the noises were and who... or what... lived here.

A long dark hallway dimly lit by burning torches on the wall here and there stretched before him. Briefly he wished it was more like that path of moonlight in his room that had led him at first. A quick look at one of the torches found it was no ordinary fire. Although a flame was burning, it was white with no heat. Even as he wondered how that could be, he knew he needed to see, so he lifted the strange torch from its place. That did the trick.

"Ready or not, here I come," he muttered, but somehow he didn't feel as confident as when he played that game with friends at home.

Elisha walked hesitantly down the long hall, watching for what might appear in front of him, as well as on either side. It went on and on, every step dark and scary. The flickering torch cast large, mysterious moving shadows on the wall, which unnerved him further. "I... I will not be a scaredy-cat," he told himself, in an attempt to build his courage.

Barely breathing, Elisha continued to walk cautiously down the hall. The farther he walked, the lighter and warmer the air became. Even so, Elisha's breath still came out in frosty puffs. He'd never seen that happen indoors where it was warm. What kind of place could this be?

By now he began to hear laughter and muffled voices. Knowing that laughter doesn't always mean friendly, Elisha became more and more anxious as he neared the source of the noise. Would this lead him closer to answers or to more danger? He swallowed hard. Since Chilly had directed him here, Elisha's hopes of finding Snowy were high, but, on the other hand, he was trespassing, and that made him nervous indeed. What would this house's owner think of his being here?

It was easy to find the right room by following the sound of laughter. It sure sounded as if someone was having a good time! Upon reaching the room with apparent partying in it, he first flattened his back against the hall wall and carefully peeked around the corner. He saw right away he wouldn't need the torch for light. After hanging it up, Elisha slipped just inside the door. As he stood quietly he looked to the right side of the room where the noise had been coming from. All partying stopped and sudden silence filled the room—whatever had been laughing had stopped to look at him.

Now he could see clearly that they were snowmen! While Elisha was exhilarated about this, the snowmen were startled to see a human. Chaos ensued as the slow moving creatures awkwardly scrambled and attempted to run from the room tripping over each other and falling. Calls of "whoa!" and "snoh, no!" in half comical, almost monotone voices filled the room.

Some of the snowmen who fell sat momentarily stunned on the floor until they caught sight of the boy again. That renewing their panic, they fought to get up. Those standing tried to help the others but, in their clumsiness, they lost their balance and also landed on the floor. Such upset caused several to begin choking in their panic and cough up small puffballs of snow, more resembling a cat's fur balls. Elisha didn't know whether to laugh or feel sorry for them.

"Snoh! My got idea!" cried one. As he tried his new method, the others copied him. They first balanced the front of their bodies on their stick arms and tried to rise up. Alas, they only found themselves stuck with their snow hinds (*behinds*) in the air. "Oh-hhh!" they moaned as one. "Now what we do?" Unable to stand, they were stuck with bottoms up, waiting for help.

Finally one collapsed to the floor, triggering the "snow domino effect" of one falling against another, causing all the others to fall like dominoes. The simple-minded snowmen simply couldn't remain standing! They lay there, moaning in misery until they spied him again, then all the confused scrambling began again.

Elisha couldn't help a giggle or two. Were these the same snowmen who had tried to scare him in the meadow? No wonder they had camouflaged themselves as mounds of snow. Once seen, they couldn't scare anyone! Thinking about this Elisha couldn't hold it in any longer and he began laughing loudly.

With much grasping, grunting, huffing and puffing, the snowmen finally stabilized. Cries of, "Snoh, no!" and, "Snoh, dear!" were heard as they all began leaving the room. Elisha calmed himself enough to check each face as they left. Alas, none of them was his beloved Snowy. But maybe he was getting closer!

Finally the last one skedaddled out of the room, skidding and sliding round the corner as he left. Elisha thought to follow them, but didn't want to panic the poor, silly snowmen again!

With the room empty, Elisha was free to slowly scan the other side of the area. It seemed to be a type of study, with a huge desk, fireplace and shelves of floor-to-ceiling books. His eyes were drawn to the fireplace, where something white stretched out on a rug before it. He moved closer to see what it was.

Why, it appeared to be a white sleeping dog. Elisha, wondering if it was real, quietly drew closer to get a better look. Its white "fur" had the appearance of thick, curly wool and yet, as he gingerly reached out and lightly touched it, he found the strange creature was as much snow as were the snowmen. Wow, a snow dog! Wait till the kids at school hear about this! Aw, what was he thinking? No one would believe any of this except, maybe Kaylynn.

The dog snored gently, unaware that a stranger was here. Boy, he's not a very good watch dog, Elisha thought, when just then it stirred, making a "snowoofle," a muffled woof sound. Instantly the boy jumped back, but the dog continued to sleep. He had no idea if, once awakened, this would be a friendly dog or a creature of terror and he didn't want to chance finding out.

Although the room had a cozy fire, Elisha did not find it welcoming. The study that had seemed bright and happy filled with snowmen, now, lit by only the light of the fire, was quiet and shadowy.

Elisha began to look up and around. A massive stone wall surrounded the large fireplace with a heavy wooden mantle stretching across it. Above the mantle hung an intriguing painting of a girl and a boy on either side of a snowman. As he looked, it touched something within Elisha and he felt a connection with that boy and girl. They were gazing in wonder at a light glowing around the snowman. It was easy to see they were happy with their creation, but to Elisha, it seemed something more than that.

Elisha sensed there was a meaning to the picture, although he didn't quite understand. At the picture's bottom, he noticed a small brass rectangle with writing on it, so he rose on his tiptoes to read its title. "Becoming Real." What does that mean? He thought upon that for a minute. Does it mean a snowman can become real? But then, what does "real" mean? He shook his head; he just didn't get it. But somehow the picture seemed to be perfect for this space.

Elisha thought more about it as he began to walk away. Hmmm... Becoming real.... Suddenly his eyes lit up. Is that what happened to Snowy after he built him? He spun around to look back at the picture. The children's faces were filled with wonder, but it was more. It was... love.

Next he noticed the glowing snowman. Was he glowing because he had become real? As in, alive? If so, his Snowy must be alive – just like these other snowmen—because he sure had loved him! The thought made his heart jump with hope.

His eyes happened to drop down to the fireplace and he saw that, just like the other fires in Snow Land, this was no ordinary fire. In fact, nothing was actually burning, although the fire itself appeared to have the movement of "flames."

He stopped to think further about the camp fire, the torch flames, and now this fire... Why would snowmen need them? Also, the room itself felt warmer, brighter when the snowmen were in here. With the fire still going, shouldn't it feel the same? None of it seemed to make sense.

Moving on around the room, Elisha discovered that the walls were hung with huge pictures of snowy scenes. He didn't pay much attention until he noticed something moving in the pictures—snow! The snow in each picture was actually falling! Elisha shook his head and blinked his eyes. He must be seeing things. But after that, he noticed something else. The tree branches—They were moving too! He opened his eyes wider and stared harder. The tree branches were swaying in the wind, dislodging the snow resting on their branches. It fell gently and prettily to the ground just as it would outdoors.

Elisha rubbed his eyes. How could this be possible? These must not be pictures; they must be windows. Of course, that must be it! Quickly he ran over to look through the large bay windows. But what he saw outside didn't match the "pictures!" How confusing. How can it snow in a picture? What kind of house is this?

Just when he thought things couldn't get any weirder, he saw that the weather in them kept changing from sunny and clear to cloudy and windy with snow. "No way!" the boy breathed in disbelief. Determined to figure out this mystery, he reached out a finger to touch one, when a noise from not far away stopped him.

He saw nothing that could've made the sound, but he noticed two large leather chairs positioned to enjoy the fire as well as look out the large bay window. The nearest chair, with its back to him, looked large enough to curl up in, and, at just the thought of a nap, Elisha began to feel tired. He had just decided to go try one out, when he saw puffs of smoke rising above the chair's back. Something or someone must be sitting there! That would explain the noise, too. Oh, great, he began to fret. What else might he meet?

Summoning up a scrap of courage Elisha decided to peek around a wing of the chair. If what was in it was too scary, he could always run. He approached cautiously and as he looked, he found the contents of the chair quite surprising.

Chapter Twenty Five

Guardian of the Snowmen

Human or Snowman?

*E*lisha was facing another body, sort of like an aged man, seated in the chair dozing... but was it really an old man? The boy had already found he couldn't always trust his eyes, so he wanted to be careful, very careful.

Elisha continued to stare, for what he saw was a bit confusing. This person did not have ordinary human skin, but appeared more... snowy. Yes, he looked like a snowman, an old snowman, but also partly human. His hands, holding a pipe, were more human, but it was his face that was so different; it was more the face of a frosty, old human. (Had Elisha been older, he would have understood that the face had character, just as an old man's would, from many years of living.)

Could this be the Old Man Snow he'd heard the snowmen speak of? Surely, it must be. If so, he could tell him where to find Snowy. Perhaps he should wake him...

Just then, a familiar sounding, curt voice in the hall caused Elisha to look towards the door. There, he saw the strange rabbit who had helped him entering, standing tall on both hind legs. At least, he thought it was Jefferds. The boy was amused at the appearance of the rabbit, now wearing short knee pants and a velvety jacket.

The rabbit didn't smile or speak to Elisha; in fact, he didn't even seem to notice him. Instead he seemed to be all about seeing Old Man Snow, who now awakened and turned towards the visitor. The self-important rabbit began loudly announcing in almost one breath, "Yep, there he is! The boy! I told you he was coming. No stopping him, no, siree! Well, my work is done! Just give me a whistle, if there's anything else you need to know!"

It was indeed Jefferds, the Investigating Rabbit. Glad to see this friend he had been through so much with, Elisha opened his mouth to say hello, but the rabbit had already hopped away. He closed his mouth in disappointment. Of course, he acknowledged to himself, this was the usual Jefferds, barging in, making himself known as a carrier of important information and then directly vanishing before anyone could speak. It was almost as if he didn't want to get too involved with anybody.

The old snowman chuckled before looking at Elisha and stating the obvious. "That rabbit certainly needs to learn some manners."

Although Elisha agreed, he was already wondering what this old snowman would have to say to him, the trespasser. Old Man Snow spoke, however, in a warm, gentle voice wrapped in deep, understanding kindness. "Well, Boy, come on in and have a seat. You've had a long journey. Rabbit is right. You don't give up, do you?"

"Not much, I'm not a quitter..." Elisha began slowly but then the questions tumbled out, one after the other. "But may I ask...Are you Old Man Snow? Do you know where Snowy is? Is he okay?"

Laughter rumbled up from deep within the snowman. "Yes, yes, and yes, Elisha. That is who I am, and I can help you."

"How do you know my name?" Elisha asked.

"How do you know my name?" the snowman asked.

Elisha was embarrassed. He'd behaved as poorly as the rabbit had!

The old snowman laughed easily. "Oh, in Snow Land, no one is a stranger for very long. But, you know, you're really not supposed to be here."

"Why not? Somebody trying to hide something?" Elisha asked bluntly.

"We hide nothing here, Elisha. There's no shame, no fear of loss, and no guilt in Snowman Lodge, so why would we hide anything?"

the old snowman spoke casually, without a trace of apology or defensiveness. "Hidden things do have a way of being found anyway."

"Sorry," Elisha apologized. "I'm sorry I broke into your house."

"Trespassing, young man, does not happen here either. If you're here, in this land and in this house, it was surely allowed," he explained. "Besides, you did not force the door open, did you?"

"Well, no, I didn't. It just opened." Elisha thought about that a moment and then brightened considerably. "Really? Then you think I am supposed to be here? Cause Jefferds sure thinks I shouldn't be. And, well, it has felt like everything has tried to stop me from getting here. What kind of a land is this, anyway?" Elisha asked.

The old snowman laughed again easily. "Have a seat and I'll fill you in, Elisha. Please, feel free to take off your boots and warm your feet by the fire," he said.

"My feet are a little cold, but I don't understand. If it's hot enough to warm my feet, it would melt the snowmen, right?" Elisha asked.

"Oh, no, it's not that kind of warmth. All the snowmen and Wooly Snow, our dog, like it. The Home Fire gives them a cozy feeling. Try it," urged Old Man Snow, suppressing a smile. "How does it feel?"

Elisha, who had sat down on the floor, removed his boots and stuck his feet out towards the snow fire. He was astonished to find it amazingly warm on his still cold feet. "What? How can that be? It's warm! It's really warming my feet!"

"Yes, yes, of course. It's just what you needed."

"But, but how can that be? How... how could the snowmen stand here, by a fire this warm?" he asked.

"Because this is not the kind of fire like you know. A fire from your world would indeed be too hot for them. This Home Fire gives whatever the person standing beside it needs. As for you... well?" He grinned at the small boy on the floor.

"Me? Oh, it feels great. I didn't realize how cold my toes were!" Elisha enjoyed the heat as it traveled up his pant legs and warmed his chilled body. He hadn't realized how cold his fingers were until now, as he gratefully flexed and stretched them towards the fire.

"But, what if the snowmen and I stood here at the same time?"

"You would feel heat, but the snowmen would not. They would feel only a homey coziness that helps them to feel at home. As for you, this fire is total comfort. How does your face feel?"

The numbness and stinging in Elisha's face had now stopped. As he felt of his nose and cheeks, he found the blisters were gone and his skin was smooth again, healed of the frostbite he'd suffered. Lowering his hands from his face, he saw that the cuts on his hands were also healed. Although he was a little boy who didn't understand about healing of skin from cuts and frostbite, he was pretty sure this was a miracle. He smiled gratefully and turned back to the old snowman.

"We sure don't have anything like this where I'm from!" Elisha exclaimed in amazement. "I bet people would really like this."

The old snowman looked sad. "Yes, I know." He was quiet a moment before going on to something else.

"My boy, I've heard much about you. I don't know why, but an exception has been made, allowing you to be in this land. No human has ever been to Snow Land before, nor is it considered safe for boys," he explained.

"Yes, I found the danger or, it found me," agreed Elisha.

"Come, Elisha, have a seat," Old Man Snow said, pointing to the chair beside his.

Elisha dropped down into the deeply comfortable chair, beside the fire that did not burn but was bright, that was warm but not with normal heat. His feet now feeling wonderfully warm again, he sat up straight and alert in the chair, eager to hear the story of this place. He looked intently at the old snowman as he waited.

Old Man Snow took his time, first cleaning his pipe and lighting it with a cold match that ignited into a frosty flame. Elisha saw how the pipe rested comfortably in Snow's mouth, as the old snowman puffed without inhaling, causing small, snowy puffs to float out occasionally.

"Who were those snowmen that ran out of here?" Elisha finally asked, but Old Man Snow motioned for him to be quiet and listen.

"Later, later. For now, let's talk about where you are and how this place began."

Elisha sat quietly and dared to hope he would hear about Snowy.

The First "Real" Snowman

Old Man Snow began to speak in a soothing, storytelling kind of voice. "For as long as there have been snowfalls, children have loved to build snowmen. From the first snowflake that falls, children's eyes dance with excitement to build a snowman. Snowmen, and the building of them, make people happy. But there is always an unhappy ending, for the next thing you know, sadly they're... gone."

Old Man Snow's voice had faded to a sad whisper. He cleared his throat and spoke up again. "Once upon a snow... a boy named Zachary built a snowman. What happened to that snowman, changed things for snowmen forever. Would you like to hear what happened, Elisha?"

Elisha nodded eagerly. "Yes, and guess what? My middle name is Zachary."

Old Man Snow continued. "It's a good name. Well, this Zachary built what he felt was his most wonderful snowman ever. All his friends agreed that the snowman looked real enough to come to life any minute. And sometimes, as Zachary stared at his snowman, he thought he might! Zachary was so happy, he sang every time he was with his snowman."

"I know what that kind of happy feels like," said Elisha with a wistful smile.

"Yes," said Snow, "it was a happy time, even for the snowman. Everyone took delight in him, especially his smile."

"I love snowman smiles. They're so happy!"

"That's how snowman smiles are meant to make you feel, Elisha. Anyway, Zach spent every waking minute he could with his snowman until they got word a dear family member had died. They traveled by horse and wagon to the funeral in Ohio, a long, hard trip in winter. Oh, Zach did not want to leave, but he couldn't stay home alone.

"Unfortunately, while they were gone, some unusually warm weather came along, causing the snowman to melt rapidly. There was nothing the snowman could do to stop it as he stood helplessly and lost himself.

"After nearly a week, the family returned home. The horses had barely pulled to a stop, when Zach jumped out of the wagon. He could not reach his snowman fast enough. But the poor child found only a small mound of snow in a puddle where his snowman had stood.

"His face turned almost as white as the snowman's had been. Zachary cried his heart out, as he realized the snowman's time had ended alone."

"How awful!" sympathized Elisha.

"Yes, it was. That left the little boy brokenhearted. He clutched what pieces he found to his chest..." Old Man Snow's voice had faded into a hoarse whisper.

Elisha sat very still as large tears filled his eyes.

Old Man Snow saw how Elisha really empathized with the Zach in his story. Snow paused to calm himself by refreezing and renewing his pipe. As the old snowman struck a match, frosty sparks flew and then the match caught a frosty white flame. Holding the pipe to his mouth, he lit it and puffed gently, causing frosty puffs to float up once again.

"What's in your pipe, Snow? What do you smoke?" Elisha asked.

With a grin he answered, "Snowbacco. Pure. No nicotine. And it's not smoking—it's frosting. When a snowman frosts, it is pure and safe. Just to think that humans put real smoke in their lungs, makes us snowmen have a heat shudder!"

Elisha smiled at that. His mom had taught him the dangers of smoking and she would be glad to know this "frosting" was safe.

Now Old Man Snow was ready to take up the story again.

"Zach's friends quickly ran over to tell him how, only two days before, some of the snowman had still been standing. Zach began groaning, wishing they'd come home earlier. He was so upset he could not be comforted, not by his parents or anyone."

One lone tear rolled slowly down Elisha's cheek. "I know how he must've felt," he said.

"I know you do," Old Man Snow nodded kindly.

Elisha wiped his eye and sniffed a little, before raising his head again for the rest of the story.

Old Snow sent up a few more frosty puffs on his pipe before he continued. Elisha watched them rise up and make a frosty puff pattern on the ceiling. "Well, that night, after his parents had gone to bed, Zach sneaked back out into the yard. He stood over the puddle, crying till he could cry no more.

"Shortly after the boy left, there in the moonlight, the first transformation of a snowman began. A new body appeared and as the snowman gazed at himself in amazement, he was whisked away to Snow Land. The boy's love had given him a heart, making him the first snowman to become real and have a chance at Forever."

"Wow!" Elisha whispered in awe, "so that's how a snowman becomes real..." He looked up at the picture above the fireplace mantle. Suddenly another thought dawned on him. "That's... that's how Snowy got here... and, and I'm just like Zachary!"

Old Snow's eyes took on a faraway look as he sat quietly, thinking and puffing on his pipe. It was almost as if he were in another place. He finally put the pipe away, looked at Elisha and smiled kindly.

"In this land, Elisha, snowmen are only to play and be happy. That's all snowmen were ever meant to be."

Old Man Snow looked around, motioning towards the room as he asked, "Did you notice anything unusual about this room when you came in?"

"Yes. It's very... different," said Elisha, giving another look around the room.

"When the snowmen are here, the snowmen's Forever Hearts radiate Snowman Love into the room, warming and brightening it. That's what you felt when you came in."

"Wow! I felt Snowman Love!" Elisha treasured that to himself for a moment then pondered about how unusual this land was. "Did everything in Snow Land just... *happen*?" he finally asked.

"No, no," Old Man Snow chuckled. "Nothing miraculous such as this just happens. Good Kind King created Forever Snow Land... all because a boy loved his snowman with all his heart."

"Who gave this king that kind of power?"

Old Man Snow laughed. "That, Elisha, is a story for another time!"

"Oh," Elisha said. Sorry to be so bold, yet realizing the entire story had not yet been told, he ventured to ask one more question. "And what did Zachary's snowman do when he got here?"

"Out of gratitude for his new life, he began to serve the King."

"What? Like a slave?" Elisha asked.

"No, out of love."

"He couldn't go back to Zachary?"

"No." As Old Man Snow ended his story his eyes took on that faraway look again.

As the old snowman grew silent, Elisha noticed that there was something about Old Snow that was different from other snowmen, more than just his more humanlike appearance. His eyes and face carried a much more sober, serious look than any of the snowmen. In fact, it bordered on sadness, while the other snowmen always looked happy. Elisha didn't see why Snow should be unhappy; he certainly seemed to have an important place in the kingdom here.

"What should I call you?" asked Elisha when Snow looked back at him again.

"Oh, some call me Old Man Snow, some say Old Snow, and others just say Snow. I answer to them all. What would you like to call me?" he asked.

"Hmm. I think… I think I'll call you Old Snow."

"That's fine with me," the old snowman said, nodding.

"Well, Old Snow," Elisha began with a smile, trying out the name, "I was just wondering. What happens to the snowmen who aren't built with love?"

Old Man Snow's face suddenly appeared tired. "Oh. They never come here. They simply… disappear." The old snowman winced as he spoke the last word. He was quiet a moment in deep sadness before going on. "Some boys or girls don't care about their snowmen. They knock them down out of meanness or thoughtlessness." Old Snow's eyes seemed almost angry as he fired up a bit to declare, "Those are the snowmen that never have a chance to be real!"

"That's awful."

"Yes, selfish children never love their snowmen," Old Man Snow said sadly. "But Creation should be valued."

They were both quiet for a moment.

"And what happened to Zach's snowman?" Elisha asked curiously.

Old Snow looked away momentarily before answering. "He's still here. He's been around a long, long time," the old snow man said with a smile, before clearing his throat and proceeding on. "Now that you know your snowman is safe, you can return home."

He paused to send up another snowy puff from the pipe. Elisha watched the frosty "smoke" spiral up, form circles and float away. Old Snow leaned forward, looked Elisha in the eye and spoke firmly with emphasis, "He is safe here... *as long as we keep humans away.*"

As Elisha heard this, his face did not flinch or move. He knew he was being sent a message.

"Elisha, boy, if *humans ever* found out about this place, Snow Land, as it is, would be destroyed."

"But how?" Elisha asked, puzzled.

"Greedy men would snatch up the land and sell it. Snowmen would be put in cages like zoo animals. Oh, Elisha... The unhappiness of being caged would kill the snowmen. They only live forever if they're happy. There would be *no more Forever Snowmen.*"

"Oh, we can't let that happen!" Elisha said in alarm.

"I know," Snow went on. "As Guardian of the Snowmen, I can't allow that to happen. That's why this place must remain secret and why Builders may not come here to see their snowmen. You are a Builder, Elisha. You were allowed to come this far for some reason, but you may not see Snowy," said Old Man Snow.

Elisha thought a minute. "I would keep Snow Land a secret," he said, a determined look coming into his eyes, "but I came here to see Snowy, and I'm not leaving until I do. I just have to see him!"

Old Man Snow stood up, and his demeanor changed again. "You rest for your journey back, Elisha. It's just not possible." He went to a chest, withdrew an ultra-soft, downy blanket and laid it beside Elisha. "This will help you rest for your journey home." With that, Old Snow left the room.

A Missed Opportunity

Elisha took a deep breath and let out a sigh. Although he had no intention of giving up, once Old Man Snow mentioned rest, his body screamed for it. He watched the old snowman leave and resigned himself to an overdue nap. Totally exhausted, he curled up in the big, overstuffed wing chair, anticipating a delicious sleep. Not feeling he'd need the blanket, Elisha let it fall to the floor. As the warmth he needed from the fire spread to his body, he drifted off.

Not long after, he awoke with a start. For a moment, he did not recognize where he was. He tried to settle back down to sleep, but he kept waking, thinking of Snowy. Finally he got up and wandered over to the library of books. They all seemed to be books about snow. One in particular, a story based on the song of "Frosty, the Snowman," seemed to jump out at him. Although he knew the story from the song, he began to read.

Once finished, Elisha was almost sorry he'd read it. It had only made him feel his own loss more strongly. He'd never fully understood Frosty's ending, and he hoped very soon that at least his Snowy would "be back again someday."

Feeling too sad to sleep, he wandered over to the desk. Finding a paper and pencil he sat down and drew a map of Forever Snow Land so he would remember it always. Afterwards he folded the map carefully and put it into his jeans pocket.

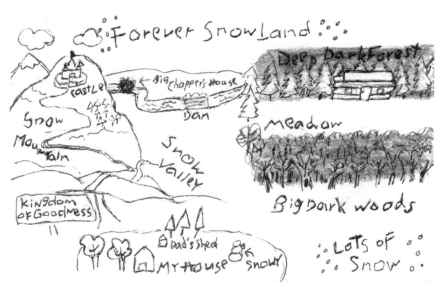

Elisha's Map of Forever Snow Land

Finally he fell asleep again, but dreams of chasing snowmen that were running away kept waking him. Try as he might, he could never catch them. The same dream kept happening over and over. There was always one in particular who would disappear just as he reached out, each time leaving him empty-handed. After that, a strange laughter would fill the air, as if something were mocking him.

Ah, poor Elisha. Had he just used the Blanket of Comfort which Old Man Snow had given him, he would have had a deep, renewing rest. Instead, his sleep was broken and fitful while the blanket lay in the floor.

Chapter Twenty Six

An Appointed Time

*T*here was no more waiting. As Guardian of the Snowmen, Old Man Snow needed some answers, and he knew exactly where to get them.

Leaving Elisha to a much needed sleep, Old Snow left the room. While he knew the Blanket of Comfort he'd given the boy wouldn't heal all wounds, as it covered him it would soothe the boy's spirit and allow him to rest.

Old Snow traveled down the hall and into his private quarters to prepare for his trip. He had but a short time in which to accomplish the journey. Normally he managed things from Snowman's Lodge, but he felt so keenly about this, a face-to-face encounter would be best, even though it entailed making a long trip. He had given to the older snowman instructions for the day on what to do with the younger snowmen. After certain goals were met, they could enjoy a party and some treats they'd previously prepared. That would keep them busy during his absence.

As he dressed for protection from the wind, Snow's thoughts centered on how to make this journey successful. He reached for the parka with a fur trimmed hood that would shelter his face and eyes, if needed. As he put it on, it reminded him fondly of a boy he had known long ago.

Snow finished snapping on the coat and picked up his gloves. He was the only snowman in this land with fingers and hands, although they didn't exactly match human hands. His boots, which looked like heavy leather, were actually made of a flexible, light-weight material to protect his legs and feet from wind erosion. Although cold doesn't hurt snowmen at all, blowing wind does.

Before he left the room he stopped to look into his ice mirror to see if he appeared ready to go, which was the only reason he ever used a mirror. While glancing quickly at his reflection, he suddenly remembered something important he needed to take and a silver whistle which the King had given him.

Removing one glove, he walked over to a massive bureau to withdraw some articles from a secret compartment in the top drawer. After picking them up, he carefully placed them in his deep pocket and put his gloves back on. There. Now he was ready to go.

He walked back to the study to look in on the boy, who seemed to be fast asleep. Old Man Snow smiled as he walked back down the long hallway and left the building. He didn't worry that the snowmen would disturb Elisha. They were never allowed into the study unless he was there. Snowmen rarely disobey and then only out of childish thoughtlessness.

Old Snow crossed the frozen meadow and easily found his way through Big Dark Woods. As he reached its edge, Ominous Owl hooted and he gave the soldier bird a friendly salute. "Well done, Owl," he commended, as he left Big Dark Woods.

Snow struck out on the shortest trail to Snow Mountain across the narrowest part of Snow Valley. Although he loved being Guardian of the Snowmen, it was freeing to occasionally get away and feel unencumbered by duty. Old Snow never tired of this trip, and it had been too long since he'd made this journey to see the King.

Intruding on his thoughts was the late arrival of his usual traveling companion, Echo. The small bird flew in and landed lightly on his shoulder.

"Well, hello, Echo. I began to think you wouldn't be making this trip," said Snow.

"Me, me-me? Not make this trip? You know I'm right beside you when I can be, be-be. I thought I'd never catch up with you though.

214

You left in such a hurry, and I had birdy things to tend to first," the chickadee explained. "Is this trip about the boy, boy-boy?"

"Yes, yes, it is," answered Snow. "I must see the King."

"I thought so, so-so," Echo chirped and sang a happy song as they traveled towards Snow Mountain.

"I met him," Echo chirped again.

"You did?"

"Yes and just in time, too. The Shadow appeared right after I did and overwhelmed the boy very quickly."

"Poor, unsuspecting child... I'm glad you were there. At least you knew what to do."

"Knowing what to do and getting someone else to do it are two different things, but he finally overcame the power of the Shadow. I was glad when that was over!"

They traveled on together for a bit longer before Echo spoke again. "You'll soon be out of Snow Valley and into the Kingdom of Goodness."

"Ah, yes, the Kingdom where no evil reigns," Snow mused as he answered the bird. As Old Snow walked, he meditated on the unusual land he was entering and the difference between Snow Valley and the Kingdom of Goodness. There was, he noted, a definite change in the atmosphere the closer he got to Snow Mountain, where the Kingdom of Goodness lay.

"I always feel something special about the Kingdom," said Echo. "What is it, Snow?"

Snow smiled as he spoke with pleasure. "It is the Goodness. The Kingdom's inhabitants live with good hearts and sunny attitudes, but most important of all, they do not allow darkness or evil to dwell there."

"How do they do that?" asked Echo.

"They have nothing to do with anything that isn't of Goodness or Peace."

"What might that be?"

"The enemies of Goodness? Evil of any kind. Enemies of Peace? Doubt, Worry, Fear, Fighting, Evil Speaking—That kind of thing. Then there's Evil Strangers that might come. That would be reported right away to Good Kind King. His Snow Angel Soldiers take care of Evil so it never has a chance in the Kingdom of Goodness!"

"Elisha sure could have used the soldiers' help! That poor boy has been through a lot," Echo observed.

"Since the King had Elisha fight those battles on his own," Snow replied, "they must have been tests to see Elisha's true heart and give him stronger faith and courage."

"But, the danger! What if he hadn't won?" Echo asked.

"The King would have saved him if he had seen he wasn't going to win."

Echo, sitting perched on Snow's shoulder, was quiet as he thought about that. "I like the way the King operates! It's always good, good-good!" Echo sang.

"And with your help, Elisha learned to use his faith to win over worry. Thank you, little friend," Old Snow smiled fondly at the wee, winged wonder in a black cap.

"No thanks to me. The King sent me," the bird tweeted happily as he prepared to leave.

"I know you can't go the rest of the way, Echo, but thanks for the company this far! Cardy will be meeting me soon," Snow said, referring to the bright red cardinal who accompanied him part ways up the mountain.

"Give my tweets to Cardy, dee-dee," the chickadee chirped cheerily as he flew away.

Having crossed Snow Valley, the snowman focused on his journey and quickly located Snow Mountain. Near the mountain top, hidden from view, was the dwelling place of Good Kind King. A fierce blizzard wall always brewed up at the base to discourage intruders upon the mountain, but since Snow was a welcome visitor, there would be no snowstorm.

Just then he heard his friend, Cardy, ahead. The bright red bird and Snow acknowledged each other with a nod. The cardinal was good company, leaving Old Snow to his thoughts when he needed quiet. Snow was eager to reach the mountain and the closer he got, the faster his pace became. In no time he arrived and began his climb. Rabbits and squirrels kept him company, playfully chasing one another as they crisscrossed his path.

Jefferds had not joined him as usual on this trip. Snow assumed he had too much investigating to do! Besides, Jefferds knew these rabbits would fill him in on whatever he missed out on. "Old Jefferds, what a character," Old Snow chuckled. He was a strange rabbit, but Snow was fond of him.

The Majesty of Peace

By early afternoon the Castle of Peace came into view on a large plateau near the top of Snow Mountain. "There it is!" Snow spoke aloud. He beamed with pleasure as he stopped to drink in its beauty. Snowy Owls, in the nearby trees of the virgin forest, called out to announce the coming visitor. White, fluffy clouds hanging in the azure blue sky created a perfect backdrop for the castle's grandeur. Just the sight of it filled Snow with a reassuring calm.

His peaceful gaze was interrupted by a magnificent pair of snow white horses galloping up at a fast pace in the nearby field. At about ten feet away, they skidded to a halt, sending a spray of snow into the air. Immediately they rose on their hind legs and pawed the air in warning, as if preparing to fight an intruder. There was no fighting today, however, for Old Snow pulled out his silver whistle. Upon hearing its musical sounds, they stood perfectly still. Old Man Snow blew once more and the stallions trotted over to him, where they waited patiently, nodding their heads, coats glistening and gleaming in the sunlight like pure snow.

"Well, hello, Blanco!" Snow affectionately greeted the first horse, who returned his hello with a neigh. He patted Blanco's handsome head and offered a carrot while the other horse whinnied and pawed the ground for attention. Old Snow laughed. "I did not forget you, Magnifico, my friend. Here's one for you, too." The horse eagerly accepted the treat and nibbled happily on it.

The only snowman to ever feel with his fingers, Old Snow reached out and gave each a final rub on their heads. Being used to feeling mostly cold, snowy things, he smiled. Their pure white coats felt soft as velvet.

"Well done, my friends!" he praised them. Having finished their treats, they returned to the field where they pranced and frolicked happily, satisfied they had guarded the path to the castle well.

Shortly after this, Old Man Snow was joined, as if from nowhere, by two lean, aged snowmen, like himself but equipped with powerful, snowy white wings. Their gold swords hung at their sides in gleaming golden sheaths. Settling into a comfortable walk beside him, they began to talk, like the old friends they were.

"Greetings, Rafaeo. It's been a long time," said Old Man Snow.

"Too long, Snow. We are glad to see you," Rafaeo responded warmly.

"How are things in Snow Valley?" asked the other winged snowman.

"Oh, all is well, Stefano, except for a surprise visit of which I'm sure the King is already aware."

"Yes, he knows that you're coming and awaits you with pleasure. He advised us to watch for you and to accompany you into the throne room," said Stefano.

Old Man Snow smiled as he thought of the kind-hearted King, who knew he would be coming before Old Snow himself knew and was already prepared for their meeting.

Snow and his two friends continued their walk to the Castle, which appeared shortly. Majestic and a pearly white, with architectural edges trimmed in pure gold, the Castle vibrated a pulsing, warm glow — inviting to friends but strangely frightening to strangers. The castle itself was surrounded by the Invincible Wall of Beauty. Twenty feet thick and made of massive Eternity Stone, it was loaded with blazing precious jewels, which added to the glowing effect of the castle.

A single large entrance gate commanded the front of the wall. To reach that the three snowmen crossed a long bridge spanning a large moat surrounding the castle. Wildly turbulent water with sharp spikes of floating ice filled the moat. Old Snow looked down at the fearsome water and barely breathed. "The King has protected the entrance well. No one could survive swimming that!" he said.

"Yes," said Rafaeo. "It's so frightening, no one has ever tried."

Just ahead, two gigantic white eagles with regal black markings flanked the gate, one on each side. Noting Old Snow's approach, the majestic but formidable birds raised their huge wings. Although Old Man snow had seen them before, still, he gasped at their size. With a twelve-foot wingspan each, they overlapped and effectively covered the entire gate. Their monstrous feet and powerful talons were ready to remove anyone foolish enough to try to enter.

With their keen eagle eyes, the birds watched the trio approaching. One look into their piercing eyes would cause any stranger to lose heart to go on. But as the three visitors were recognized, they gracefully lowered their giant wings to allow them to pass through. The movement of their weighty wings coming to a resting position created a strong wind blowing into the visitors' faces.

"Any closer and that wind would knock us over," Old Snow said with a laugh.

"You have no idea," Rafaeo said, looking serious. "Although it is not so strong this far away, any intruder daring to get closer would be flattened to the ground by its force. Then of course, the eagles' huge claws would easily finish them off."

Hidden Meanings

By now, they had crossed the bridge and reached a most unique gate. The carvings on its front meant a lot to kingdom dwellers who would stop to treasure the meaning of these symbols. On the other hand, any who thought of breaking in were discouraged by the gate's massive size.

"What an awesome door!" Old Snow said, quietly looking up. "Is there another entrance?"

Stefano answered. "No. That's why it's called One Way Gate of Meaning. It is the only way to get to the King. Only those truly seeking the king may enter easily."

The carefully carved pictures adorning the gate intrigued Snow. Although he did not completely understand the meanings, he deeply appreciated them. In the lower center a majestic lion lying with a lamb under a rainbow reflected the peace and unity of the Kingdom.

The majority of the gate was made of wood, but the rainbow itself was not. It was exquisitely fashioned from genuine, precious jewels. These gems, melted at a high temperature in some mysterious way, filled the rainbow's arches with their bright colors – ruby red, fire opal, yellow sapphire, purple amethyst, tanzanite blue, and emerald green. Light shining through from the other side only made the vivid colors more brilliant.

Visitors staring into these transparent arches often got lost in the depth of their beauty. A delight to the eye of any, they were even more so for Old Man Snow, who was used to seeing most things in white. As he saw the rainbow's sparkling colors reflecting onto the snowy whiteness of his body, he laughed in delight. "When I stand here, I'm a snowman of many colors!" he exclaimed.

"The King planned it that way," Rafaeo explained. "It tells everyone that he loves creatures in all colors, not just snowman white. The King loves and respects all equally and he expects all inhabitants in the Kingdom to do the same!"

Stefano spoke up. "The rainbow is also a reminder that in our darkest days, there's always Hope."

Snow smiled in appreciation as he held out his arms and continued to bask in the breathtaking colors shining on him. Finally his gaze returned to the gate's carvings. Intertwining grapevine, heavily laden with clusters of grapes, dressed the outside edges of the gate doors. A white dove adorned each corner, while at the top two doves held a banner of Peace. The bottom of the gate showed a glowing Cross, with a baby on one side, and a cave on the other.

As anyone in the kingdom would stand before this gate and think of the meanings of its carvings, the powerful Truths made each one feel strong and victorious. No worries or problems in their lives seemed too big to handle anymore.

Just when it seemed nothing could be more beautiful, something else would catch the eye. A magnificent sky scene commanded the entire top half of each door to the inner edges where the doors met. None the kingdom had ever figured out how the sunset was created on this gate, for the sunset colors did not appear to be painted, but real. Bright sunlight rays actually burst from behind clouds of glowing peaches and vibrant pinks in a majestic purple sky.

In the center of this sunset was the most important carving of all—Victorious King, riding forth on a white horse charging out of the clouds. This rider on the horse appeared mighty and victorious to all gazing upon him. Old Snow turned to his friends. "I've never asked, but, who is this rider? Is it supposed to be the King?"

"No, that is Good Kind King's son, the Prince of the Castle of Peace. It is said, and it is the truth, that one day he will return to Snow Valley. Many look forward to that day, for he will bring lasting Peace to Snow Valley and beyond. As it is now, only the Kingdom on Snow Mountain has such peace," answered Stefano. "It reminds us all that Good Kind King and his son the Prince of Peace will always be on our side."

"Why is the rider called Victorious King, if he is the Prince of Peace?" asked Snow.

"That is a mystery we will not understand until the Time of Forever Peace."

A loud voice brought Old Man Snow's attention back to his visit. It was Rafaeo commanding the gate, "In the name of Good Kind King, open to Servants of His Goodness!"

Instantly, in response to speaking the King's name, previously hidden pockets of gold and diamonds burst into sparkling splendor. The impressive, yet formidable gate swung open slowly and allowed their leisurely entrance. It closed in amazing silence behind them.

The gate was nearly forgotten as the most splendid Castle of Peace came into view. The castle stood serenely with flags waving in the wind, one on each corner and a larger one from the high center tower. The gentle, soothing sound of the flags flapping in the wind blended with the serenity and peace in the courtyard.

Old Snow was basking in the calm for a moment when, seemingly out of nowhere, a thunderous roar filled the courtyard! It rumbled and reverberated everywhere, rattling everyone in sight and bringing them to high alert. Another roar followed the first, then another and another, each more frightening than the first. Soldiers charged out from hidden places, flashing their swords, ready to defend the castle.

All peace seemed gone as two enormous lions leapt into view from opposite sides of the courtyard. These were no ordinary lions, as their unreal roars proved, but were guardians to the King. The very ground vibrated from their deafening warning, which continued to echo and re-echo in the courtyard.

Although Snow was aware this always happened, it still left him quite unsettled. Upon seeing the visitors, the ferocious lions had charged to protect the main entrance of the castle. There they took their positions, shaking their manes and showing monstrous, sharp teeth.

This time it was Stefano who spoke, holding out his hand as an added signal to reassure them. "Servants of His Goodness entering. At ease, Cats of Courage!"

Although the lions now recognized Stefano, they were still highly stimulated. They paced several times before they resumed their usual positions guarding the door. Trained only to guard (and attack, if need be), they were never as easily calmed as the stallions. With a last, single shake of their manes they gave up one more, quiet roar.

The three visitors laughed to themselves, finding it amusing how the lions, even after recognizing them, always gave one more warning, as if to have the last word.

"I'm not arguing with them," said Rafaeo.

"Me, either," laughed Old Man Snow.

"No disagreement from me," Stefano joined in, still shaken from the roars.

The trio walked quickly between the lions, hoping not to trigger another ferocious reaction. The lions merely shook their manes, bared their large teeth and gave a subdued roar as they passed by.

After passing through, they came to another door leading to the main entrance hall. Strangely, there was no doorknob or key. Above the door the instructions to enter were engraved simply as, "Faith," meaning that the door opens only if faith is present in the visitor's heart. None had ever entered without Faith. The door swung freely open for these visitors.

Reverent Preparation to See the King

After entering, the three friends stood quietly, drinking in the magnificent beauty in The Hall of Reflection. The hall reminded the visitor to not rush into the presence of the King, but rather to reflect first upon his great worthiness and their purpose in seeing him.

Old Snow lifted his eyes to the high, clear ceiling which not only revealed the blue sky and clouds but also allowed sunlight into the hall. The shadows of the moving clouds on the crystal floor simulated the peaceful movement of a quiet river. Diamonds in the floor sparkled in the sunlight, further giving the appearance of a gently rippling river. This twinkling movement somehow encouraged a mood in visitors to stop and reflect. During this time, visitors became filled with a calmness and peace beyond explanation.

Finally Old Snow looked at his two companions, questioning if they were ready. Both nodded in agreement and joined Snow in leaving the Hall of Reflection.

Old Snow stepped up his pace as he saw the welcoming Snow Servants ahead, lining each side and bowing as they passed by. The Head Snow Servant smiled and nodded, saying graciously, "A sincere welcome to the friends of the King."

Rafaeo answered, "Thank you, Dominic. Peace unto you. It is good to be here."

Now approaching the door to the Great Throne Room of Splendor, they saw a dozen soldiers in white uniforms, armed with gleaming swords, standing at attention on both sides of the hall. Two straight faced, helmeted soldiers stood with crossed swords over the actual door until the visitors approached. Upon recognizing the three, the soldiers lowered and sheathed their swords. The massive double doors, with the Royal Crown centered on each, swung slowly open.

Rafaeo and Stefano entered together first, bowing their heads as they walked forward. Old Man Snow automatically squinted his ice blue eyes tightly together as he stepped through the doorway. Normal sunshine never bothered the snowman, but this was much more blinding.

As the soldiers escorted them the sound of their shoes, clicking smartly on the floor, echoed throughout the Throne Room. Old Snow, walking with head bowed, looked at the floor of deepest blue granite, embedded with sparkling gold dust. Around them, the mirrored walls somehow reflected, not the physical appearance of any in the room, but only the Goodness of the King. Royal curtains, dazzling with diamonds, draped the front of the room from ceiling to floor, only adding to the brilliance of the room. It all combined to bring, not gaudiness, but a sense of grandeur and awe.

Draped directly behind the throne hung the Royal Curtains of spun gold, spangled with tiny diamonds. Old Snow felt something blowing within the room. Seeing the curtains gently waving, he realized it was the Breeze of Goodness flowing from the King. As the breeze reached the trio, each inhaled deeply of its refreshing purity.

Because of the brilliant light coming from the pure love and goodness within the King, he caused himself to be a blur to all. No one could bear to look upon him without this protective measure. The King's face appeared as pure Kindness, although, in reality, they did not truly see his features.

Rafaeo handed Old Snow a pair of dark glasses which he gratefully accepted. They allowed him to address the King in more comfort. These were not, however, sunglasses which darken, but were made of an invisible material, so that Old Snow's face could still be seen.

The three were then motioned by the king to approach the throne. With eagerness and respect they stepped forward with Old Man Snow in front.

Chapter Twenty Seven

Meeting the Munificent Monarch

*T*he King spoke in a voice reminiscent of the rushing sound of a waterfall, but one that was also deeply kind. "Welcome, Old Snow, my friend! Was your journey a pleasant one?"

Old Man Snow smiled. "Yes, very much so, as you know, oh, Good Kind King."

"I trust there were no evil happenings on the way. Did you have to use any of your weapons?" asked the King.

"No, I still have them," answered Snow, patting his pocket's contents, "but I've never had to use them. Why did you give them to me so long ago?"

"Because sometimes, Evil sneaks in when my people are not on guard. That happened once long ago in Snow Valley. All that area – the valley, meadow, woods and forest—they all used to be like Snow Mountain, filled with goodness, peace and joy."

"I can remember that time, Good Kind King," said Snow sadly.

"But some in Snow Valley became careless and did not use the Weapons I gave them," the King continued. "That's when Evil attacked and tried to take over. I sent my soldiers and reclaimed the Kingdom, but... There is always a chance of it happening again. That's why all must be on guard so carefully. A little allowed evil always leads to more."

"But that cannot happen here. Evil cannot stand up in your Goodness," observed Old Snow.

"True. Here in the Castle and on Snow Mountain, they are safe because I am here. But... you and the others must always be on guard. When you least expect it, is when Evil is likely to appear."

"I will remember that, King," promised Old Snow.

Shining, Secret Weapon of Power

"Good. Now, please take your Weapon out for review," the King requested.

Old Man Snow reached deep into his pocket and reverently withdrew the Weapon. The others in the Great Throne Room gasped in unison. A sense of awe filled the room as they all exclaimed, "Oh, the Book of His Goodness!"

An onlooker unfamiliar with the kingdom would have wondered how an ordinary looking, rectangular book could evoke such respect or be used to protect anyone from evil attacks. The residents of the Castle, always safe with the king, had no need of the Weapon, but they had heard of its power.

Old Man Snow then opened the Book and there within its covers lay a small, glowing, double-edged sword. He grasped the sword's handle and withdrew it from the Book. As he did, it flashed like a flame and became full sized! In salute, he raised it to the King and humbly bowed his head.

"Very well," smiled the King. "I see the Book is well worn, too, so I know its Words of Truth lie deep within you. Because of that, the Sword is shining, sharp and ready to fight off all attacks." The King leaned forward and spoke in earnest now. "That is good. No one using the Sword of my Words or My Name has ever been defeated by evil. Well done," praised the King, resting again on the throne. "You may put it away now."

"Thank you, oh, Good Kind King," said Snow. He lowered the Flaming Sword and returned it reverently to the Book, where it transformed to size.

"Remember, my friend, and I cannot stress this enough... it is not by just *knowing* my words, but by *using* my words, that your Sword remains sharp. Do you understand?"

"Yes, King, I do."

The King relaxed and smiled. "Now, share with me, please, what brings you here," he urged.

The Boy

"It's about the boy in Forever Snow Land," stated Old Snow.

The King was stirred with affection as he reflected on the boy's life so far. "Ah, yes... Elisha," he murmured with a smile. "What do you think of him?"

"He seems to be a fine boy," Snow answered.

"You think he's quite obsessed with the snowman he built, don't you?" probed the King.

"Uh, yes, he is. He has battled his way through many dangers and has now found the Snowman Lodge. He says he will not leave until he finds Snowy. Then he wants to take him home," said Snow.

"Yes. Reminds me of another boy, don't you think?" asked the King.

Old Snow shifted uncomfortably. Although it definitely stirred his memory of someone else, he did not answer.

"Do you think he's obsessed with his snowman?"

"Obsessed? Well, all he seems to live for right now is getting his snowman back, so I suppose so," Snow answered cautiously.

"Do you think his 'obsession' with his snowman is wrong?" asked the King.

"Wrong? Why... I... uh..." Snow did not know what to say.

"It certainly seems to be a love that cannot let go, does it not?"

"Only you know, oh, King," shrugged Old Snow, not knowing what to think about it. "But you have kept this land hidden from humans up to now, so why has this boy been allowed to come here?"

"Why, indeed?" the King mused, with eyes that softened as he spoke. When the King rose, all in the room bowed down. He walked in flowing movements and, as he did, the light that surrounded him moved with him. All were deeply affected by the simple movement of his Goodness. He paused and turned back to Snow.

"Why would I change the laws of Snow Land for him?" The King smiled fondly. "In short, I was so moved by this boy's deep love that I wanted to help him through his suffering. He thinks this is all about his snowman, and it partly is, but it is about so much more."

The King's face took on a very serious look. "His love will now face the supreme test. If he chooses well, he will have peace about his snowman, but if not... it will be very sad," the Good King said. He took a few steps away as he continued on.

"This is not the only loss the child will have in his life. For in life, loss comes to all. But choosing to let go of what you love is different than feeling something has been taken away from you." The King drew nearer and stopped to look straight at Old Snow with eyes that seemed to pierce right through him. He spoke very slowly and distinctly to the snowman. "The way he handles this will affect how he will take other losses in life. Do you see?"

"I think so," said Old Snow, once again shifting uncomfortably.

"Another boy many, many years ago also experienced great sadness when his snowman melted." The King paused to look at Old Snow's face and, although he saw a flicker of response in Snow's eyes, Old Snow dropped his head, remaining silent.

The King went on. "My Snow Angels brought the boy's snowman here, the first snowman to ever come to Forever Snow Land. That first snowman has lived here sadly, not happily."

The King paused and looked for any reaction to his story. There seemed to be none. "You do know about that, don't you old friend?" the King prodded gently.

Old Man Snow seemed even older as he stood silently. "That long ago boy eventually got over his pain... but the snowman never did!" the King said speaking the last very pointedly as he looked intently at Old Snow. The King waited for him to speak, but as he did not, the King sadly and slowly sighed.

"So, Old Snow, what is your concern today about Elisha?" the King asked, returning to the business at hand.

"Well," Old Snow began, first clearing his throat as he hesitated before asking his question. "Elisha insists on getting his snowman back. As you know, no snowman has ever gone back to his Builder. As Guardian of the Snowmen, what am I to do?"

"You will know, when the time comes, what to do and say. I will guide you as it happens," instructed the King.

"I know you are as wise as you are good, Kind King, but shouldn't I know ahead of time, so I can prepare what to say and do?" asked Old Snow, quite concerned about how to handle this.

"No," said the King. "When you lean on me alone, there is no doubt that I am guiding you. There is only one test you must use— All you do or say must always agree with the Book of Goodness."

"I just thought if I could practice—" Snow began to explain.

"You are already familiar with my words. They will return to you as needed," he said closing the subject.

Old Snow considered carefully all the King had said and then spoke. "I know your way is best, oh, King. I will trust you to guide me what to do at the time."

Good Kind King beamed with pleasure at the words of his servant snowman. "You will not fail, and... you do know that you may make requests of me, for yourself or anything, do you not?" he asked.

The old snowman answered in reverence, "Yes, most certainly, King."

The King had given every chance to Old Snow to speak up for himself, but he had not. The Monarch sighed and with effort added, "You may go now, old friend."

Old Snow wiped a tear, touched that the King had called him friend. All three visitors bowed and backed out from the throne before turning to exit together.

"Go in peace, Old Snow!" called the King.

Turning back to him, Snow smiled a half smile again. "How can I not? Your Goodness and Wisdom go with me!" He turned to the door again and left the Great Throne Room of Splendor, removing the protective glasses as the door closed behind him.

He and his friends had just begun to share their thoughts about the visit when, after only a few steps down the hall, the doors opened again and they all heard a thunderous voice that reverberated within them, saying, "**Return at once!**"

The booming order left the three shaking. Rafaeo and Stefano both said, "Stop!"

"The King wants you back immediately!" said Rafaeo with urgency and they all returned quickly to the Throne Room.

A Reckoning with the King!

As they walked back, Old Snow was terribly confused. He couldn't imagine what could possibly be wrong. He put the protective glasses back on and, approaching the throne with a clear heart, he knelt without fear. As he humbly remained bowed again before his King, he wondered why he was called back.

"Rise," said the King ever so quietly.

Old Man Snow rose slowly to his feet and looked up at the King's face in bewilderment.

"Do you know why I have called you back, Snow?" asked the King somewhat sternly.

"No, I have no idea at all," answered Old Snow.

"You have no fear?" asked the King, already knowing the answer.

"No fear. I just don't understand," said Snow simply.

The King, who knew that, smiled slightly. "You have no fear, because your heart is clear of wrongdoing. My obedient servants can come before me in confidence about anything. You came here today for a good reason, for the boy. But... there's one thing you have not asked and that has stirred my righteous anger."

Old Snow was even more confused. In his mind, he quickly reviewed their conversation but couldn't see what he'd left out.

"I'm sorry, King. I do not know what I forgot."

"You did not forget," the king corrected.

"Then... what?" asked the now thoroughly perplexed snowman.

"You did not forget, because you never intended to ask anything for yourself, only for the boy. And yet, you have a great need." The King sighed again. "You have not received what you have not asked for. That is my only disappointment with you over these years."

"I am sorry I have disappointed you, King," Snow said contritely.

The King seemed irritated. "Your repentance is pleasing, but your lack of asking has deprived me of the joy of giving to you." His voice rose louder and he stood as he declared, "I am the Munificent Monarch, King of Goodness, and I can stand it no longer!"

All others in the Throne Room fell to their knees in fear, knowing the King's power and fearing what might happen..

"I-I-I... I don't understand, oh, King."

"As you know, letting go of the old life with your Builder is a requirement to live here. *You never did let go!* I broke my rule by letting you stay. As a result, you have not lived happily as the others have. This is true, is it not?" the King scolded.

Old Snow nodded slowly, with his head still down, half in sadness, half in shame.

"And now! Now you have felt Elisha's and Snowy's pain so much, it renewed your own. In spite of all that, your only thought has been how to help them. That, in itself, is good, but—"

The King paused and shook his head, somewhat amazed.

"For all these years, I have waited for you to come to me for yourself," the King explained, "but you have not. As Guardian of the Snowmen, you've watched their playfulness, put up with their silliness and not begrudged them their own Snowflake Laughter—which you, yourself, have never experienced!

You have used wisdom to help others, but not for yourself." The King appeared very upset. "I... will... wait... no longer!" he declared angrily. He motioned to Snow, who came forward obediently.

"Come closer, into my presence," bid the King.

Old Snow had never even been this close, much less closer, so he hesitated. But seeing the warm smile of this gracious monarch, he stepped forward respectfully. After doing so, he stood quietly, still not sure what was going on, except he began to feel comfort as of the Home Fire, as if he were basking in a warmth flowing to him from Good Kind King.

Finally, as Snow's concerns melted away in the monarch's warmth, the King spoke firmly.

"This sad Forever Life you've lived must end now!"

Old Snow wondered if this meant his life was over. Quickly, he surrendered to that thought. If the King ended his life right now, he would still be grateful. He knew he had already lived like this longer than he deserved. He trembled slightly, not knowing what was going to happen, but Snow trusted the King.

"Come to me, closer. Do not be afraid," the King commanded gently. "You must trust me now, completely, with what I'm about to do. Do you?"

Overwhelmed, Old Snow nodded yes and waited humbly, with bowed head. He was ready, for whatever the King chose to do to him. If he melted into nothingness, then so be it! He stood listening, not only with his ears, but deep within himself. It was the way in which to take in all the King was about to say.

"Receive my blessing now, Snow Friend," said the King with great pleasure.

A blessing? That surprised Snow to hear 'blessing,' when he had displeased the King. Even so, somehow, Old Man Snow knew what his proper response should be. "I gratefully receive from your hand, oh, King, whatever you see fit."

Next, the King of Goodness rested his hand above Old Snow's head and commanded, "Old Snow, it is time. Release the pain. Let Peace reign and Joy abound!"

Snow would have been amazed if he could have seen what happened next.

The Transformation from Old to New

Immediately a light appeared, first as a twinkling flash, then as a steady glow of light surrounding Snow's head. Snow drew in a quick breath as he felt something occurring, not only in his memory but deep inside. He felt old pains loosening.

Next, he jumped slightly. "Oh, my!" Snow exclaimed. It was as if a fountain were springing up and bubbling within him. Old Man Snow had never felt anything like this before. It was refreshing, renewing... it felt like—new life coming into him!

Suddenly, a chorus of "Ahhh!" filled the room as it lit up with thousands of lights shooting out from the crown of the king and surrounding Old Snow. This glorious Lighting of the Room always happened when the King's Goodness was active. Snow started to open his eyes but quickly closed them again.

Old Snow looked down at his own body. Although he saw nothing unusual, something unusual was taking place. It was as if his entire being had been dipped in warm, blazing love. Even though he had no idea what that would feel like, he somehow knew it was like a liquid soaking into his whole body. His painful loss left his heart. In its place, a joy grew so big within him, it seemed as if it would spill over and flood the whole room.

"Think about your Builder," the King instructed. Old Snow obediently thought of his long-ago Builder. Why, he could think of his Builder no longer with pain, but with great pleasure! He looked at the King in surprise. The King smiled, deeply pleased.

Gradually Old Snow settled into a peace within himself. He felt so new inside! To be rid of pain and sadness after so long overwhelmed him. Real tears of gratitude began running from his eyes and spilling onto his chest. Falling to his knees, he wept out of sheer happiness. No one had ever seen Old Snow in such a state.

The snowman thought all was done, but it was not. All movement and talk in the room had stopped as they waited for what was still to come. The usually reserved old snowman rose to his feet and began twirling and dancing around the room. No one, not even Rafaeo or Stefano, had ever seen Old Man Snow behave so joyously. But Old Snow had never felt free like this before.

This completed change in Old Man Snow caused the King to begin to laugh deeply—a resonant, resounding laugh that rolled up and bellowed out, stirring the whole room to join in, including the delighted snowman. As the room finally quieted, all present heard Snow still laughing and recognized that the laughter was part of his healing.

Oh, my, thought Old Snow as the laughs tumbled out, a King who comforts, heals, and fills to overflowing, too!

"Yes," the King said aloud, answering Snow's thoughts. "This is how you were meant to be. I did not create my servants to be miserable!"

Anyone looking on might have thought that at this point it was all finished, but he would have been wrong. Everyone in the room suddenly grew silent as they watched Old Man Snow's continuing transformation. Something was happening now that none had ever witnessed before; though long delayed—the final transformation of a Forever Snowman!

Old Snow's very own Forever Smile stretched across his face!

Everyone in the room began whispering and pointing. The whispering soon changed to loud talking, followed by shouts and appreciative laughter, as if they'd witnessed a birth. Finally the whole room turned to the King and began clapping in praise for what he had done.

The King held up a hand to quiet them all and motioned to them to continue watching. First Old Man Snow gave a little guffaw, then a short laugh, followed by the largest rolling belly laugh any had ever heard. In fact, had he been a normal snowman under normal circumstances, it would have been called Hail Laughter. The whole room cheered at such a wonderful happening. Old Snow laughed until he could laugh no more. Old Man Snow was becoming what he was always meant to be – happy. Finally all laughs subsided and he quieted, but his long-awaited Forever Smile remained.

Good Kind King looked at him, pleased with Old Snow's now completed transformation.

"Now, you can truly go in peace and joy!" With these words the King happily dismissed his old servant friend, but Old Man Snow made no move to leave.

"Is there something else, my friend?" asked the King.

"Yes. I just wondered... what happened to my Builder?" Snow asked shyly.

The King threw back his head and laughed. The fact that Snow finally asked something he needed to know for himself confirmed the work was done. The King was pleased.

"Your Builder had quite a good, long life. He told many stories about you to his children."

Old Snow smiled.

"But it was not until he had his own children that he built snowmen again. None ever had a place in his heart as you did. As you know, you have outlived him, but the same spirit that was in him, was in his children and his great, great grandchildren. Your Builder, Zachary Winters, had a great heart, and so does his great, great, great grandson, Elisha Zachary Winters.

Old Man Snow's head jerked up to look at the King, utterly astounded at what he had heard. "You mean, *this* Elisha...?"

"Yes, of course that's what I mean," said the King. "Now you know why you felt such urgency concerning this boy."

Old Man Snow smiled a smile that could have lit up the castle itself. "One more thing, oh, King."

"Yes?" said the King, quite pleased Snow was finally asking him things.

Old Snow thought for a moment. "I was the only unhappy snowman ever to stay in Snow Land. Normally snowmen who can't adjust, melt away in their unhappiness. Why did you allow me to survive and stay? Why didn't I melt away and cease to be?"

"Because, my dear old friend, you were the very first snowman here. That made you special. Over the years, you changed into more than a snowman, into one with unique human qualities and feelings, which equipped you to be Guardian of my Snowmen.

"Go, now! As a true Forever Snowman with your own Forever Smile and heart, you have a new life ahead of you," said the King.

As Snow left with a new bounce in his step, Good Kind King actually began dancing himself. No one thought any less of him; indeed, it endeared his servants to him even more, that he cared so much for all of them. This was a King who often danced in joy over his servants' lives.

A symphony of music swelled up out of nowhere, filling the room and spilling out of the castle, its strains floating far into the kingdom and beyond. Everyone in the kingdom, including the animals, looked towards the castle deeply pleased. Ah, they knew — Another good thing had happened in the Kingdom of Goodness, because of Good Kind King. He, their most Munificent Monarch, never holds back; he overflows in giving good things.

The changed snowman left the castle feeling more like New Man Snow than Old Man Snow. As he left the castle, he paused to tell his friends, Rafaeo and Stefano, goodbye.

"Well, Old Snow, you received a lot more than you expected today," Rafaeo chuckled.

"And we never knew, old friend," Stefano said sympathetically, "that anything was wrong."

"How could I complain, when the King allowed me to remain in Snow Land against his own rules? It was amazing that he dealt so graciously with me," acknowledged Old Snow with gratitude.

Although Snowmen and Snow Angels do not hug, their eyes told of their deep respect and affection for each other. Rafaeo and his fellow snow angel, Stefano, both held the Guardian in great regard.

"May Peace and the Goodness of the King always be with you," said Rafaeo.

"Thank you," said Old Man Snow. "May Peace be with you, also! Until next time..." With a farewell salute he turned and began his journey home, grateful to be free in his heart and anxious to meet again with a special young man.

Chapter Twenty Eight

Joyful Journey Home

*O*ld Snow's trip was swift and with renewed purpose. With the King's blessing, Snow now felt confident to do his part. Briefly he wondered what would happen. Could the boy change from the determined, stubborn spirit that had brought him this far, to a willingness to let go? That would be difficult for a young child, but since Elisha came from his great, great, great grandfather Zachary, Snow decided he must have the right stuff within him.

During his journey home Snow noticed that everything around him seemed more beautiful. "Is it possible, Mr. Sky, that you are even bluer than before?" he called out. His heart felt bursting with joy as he bent to scratch behind the ears of several squirrels and rabbits.

"Are you as happy as I am?" he asked the chipmunks scampering at his feet. In answer the chipmunks ran under the curve of the squirrels' tails, scampered and did a few flips just for the fun of it. The rabbits, picking up on his joy, began hopping and bouncing like pogo sticks.

"I can do that, too!" Snow shouted out in glee. He began to do something he'd never done before—skip down the trail and even kick his heels together. Suddenly, a hearty laugh rang out and he found— it was his own! His very own Snowflake Laughter flooded the air, along with a symphony by sparrows, bluebirds, finches, chickadees, and cardinals. They joined in singing and dipping down into the trail of snowflakes. Old Man Snow felt more like New Man Snow than ever. He was in fact, a new snowman.

Cardy, perched in a nearby tree, sat cocking his head back and forth as he watched, trying to figure out the change in Old Snow. The red bird finally concluded that it wasn't as important to understand it, as it was to enter into the happy occasion, so he flew down to join in on the fun.

"Welcome, Cardy!" Snow said, still laughing. "I'm happy to hear your song."

The bright red cardinal puffed up to sing and then flew circles around him, spreading his own cheerful notes.

Snow's journey home became a parade of celebration. The nearby forest trees swayed in rhythm, while the breeze carried the jubilant notes into the far parts of the kingdom. As the joyful sounds reached them, the valley and forest dwellers began smiling and humming their own happy songs. Good Kind King caught sound of the happy symphony and joyfully danced some more.

Snow's new Forever Smile felt good and stretched even wider as he thought of Elisha. "Just to think that the boy I was appointed to help is my very own Builder, Zachary's, great, great, great grandson! What an honor," he said aloud, finally at peace and filled with gratitude.

He bid goodbye to the parade of animals as he left the mountain area and wound his way through the valley. By the time the shadows fell, the happy snowman had passed through the woods and crossed the meadow into the forest sheltering the Snowman Lodge. Entering and going straight to his room, he quickly put his things away, touching the Book with respect as he laid it in the drawer.

He had no further dread of talking with the boy and headed directly to the study.

Chapter Twenty Nine

Stirring the Fire of Unselfish Devotion

*W*hen Snow entered the room, the fireplace was cozy with the perfect warmth for the boy; of course to Old Snow, it just felt comfortably cold. He stirred the Comfort Embers with the poker and watched the Home Fire roar up briefly, before settling down.

His dear Wooly Snow, stretching before the fire, took a deep sigh and continued his nap. Old Snow shook his head in amusement. You give this dog a fire, and he sleeps all the time. Perhaps the Home Fire gives Wooly Snow a little too much comfort, he chuckled.

Old Snow turned to the boy and saw that Elisha was rousing from his sleep. Old Snow sat down and waited quietly.

"Have I been asleep long?" asked Elisha when he awoke and saw Old Man Snow.

"I imagine just long enough to refresh you, right?" Snow answered.

"Sort of…." The still tired boy hesitated. "Actually, I kind of had a hard time resting."

Snow looked puzzled. Elisha's hair was all disheveled from his restless attempt to sleep and he looked a bit haggard. "You didn't rest well?" he asked, puzzled, but then seeing the blanket in the floor, he had a thought. "You did use the blanket I gave you, right?" he asked.

"No, I wasn't cold after the Home Fire warmed me up. I just kept having bad dreams and waking up," Elisha explained.

"Oh, I see. Had you used it, you would've found the Blanket of Comfort is a special cover that soothes you to rest."

"Oh, sorry," said Elisha, feeling foolish.

"No apology needed. It was only your loss, and you're not the first to experience that. I trust you got a little sleep?" he asked.

"Some," admitted Elisha. Now he looked more intently at Old Man Snow. Something about him had changed. "Snow, you look different."

"Yes, I suppose I am," he murmured with a smile.

Elisha drew his head back and stared. He couldn't put his finger on it, but something was definitely different. Suddenly it hit him.

"I know! It's your smile! You look so much... happier!"

"I am, Elisha," Old Snow said, smiling. "And I want you to be happier, too. Are you ready to finish our talk?"

"Yes, but I feel the same. I can't be happy without my Snowy. I really, really want him back," the boy almost moaned.

"Yes, I know. I do understand how you feel." Snow walked over to the window and looked out for a minute, before turning back to the boy.

"I watched another boy once, a Builder, who didn't make the needed break. Seeing the boy in pain hurt his snowman so much that he became crippled."

"Huh? Crippled? What do you mean?"

"Just like a crippled person can't walk well, the snowman's emotions didn't work well anymore. When a snowman can't let go of his builder, he can't move on to be happy. See?"

"Sor-r-rta," said Elisha, still looking puzzled.

"Seeing you again after coming here would confuse Snowy and your leaving would break his heart. A broken heart is the worst thing to happen to a snowman." Snow paused before continuing. "Only one has been able to stay and survive, but he has not been happy."

Old Man Snow's thoughts drifted a moment. Finally he roused himself to end his case. The old snowman spoke gently, but firmly. "So, it's kinder to just go home and not see him."

No! Elisha couldn't accept that. His brain raced, in a panic to find a more convincing argument to keep his snow buddy. Suddenly his face lit up and he spoke excitedly.

"He's unhappy because he wants to be with me, right? So I'll just take him back home, and he'll be happy again!" Elisha was satisfied that this argument settled it. Now Old Snow would surely see the wisdom of not trying to squeeze Snowy in where he didn't fit.

Old Man Snow looked deliberately into his face and stated simply, "You're not hearing me, Elisha. It won't work."

Elisha's excitement over his idea drained from his face at Snow's answer.

"Snowmen were made for fun and to be loved. They thrive on that. Everything is perfect for that to happen here."

"And when I get him home, we will have fun and I will love him!" countered Elisha.

"But, in your world, you will not always be a boy. You will grow up and be busy with other things. His heart would break and that would be the end of him."

"But I won't! I won't stop loving him, ever! I'll always love Snowy!" Elisha cried out.

Old Man Snow looked quietly at the boy.

"I'm so sorry, Elisha. Snowy can never, ever go back." As he spoke he put a hand on the boy's shoulder to comfort him and, strangely enough, Elisha immediately quieted and was almost ready to accept Old Snow's words of wisdom.

"Why wasn't Snowy hanging out with those other snowmen in here?" asked Elisha.

Old Man Snow hesitated. "Your Snowy can't enjoy himself until he lets go of his old life with you. Those other snowmen have been here awhile so they can laugh and play. By the way, did you notice the way they behave and talk is still quite simple?"

"Yes! They even seemed kinda, kinda..." Elisha searched for the right word.

"Silly?" laughed Old Man Snow.

"Well, yes," said Elisha grinning.

"They are," he agreed with a chuckle. "They're so simple and childish, more like babies in grown-up bodies. That's why they must be protected."

"Is that your job? To protect them?"

"Yes, I protect and teach them here at Snowman Lodge. Some older ones, like Frosty, help me. After new snowmen mature, they act a little older, but can never be totally on their own."

"Why not?"

"Because they're so sweet and simple, they can't think complicated things out or care for themselves. They can only have fun."

"Oh." Elisha had been watching Old Snow, and now he spoke carefully. "You're not like the others. You seem more like a human than a snowman."

Old Snow smiled. "You recognize that. The other snowmen do not. That part of me that can think and make decisions is why I am guardian of these silly, carefree snowmen."

"And why do they call you Old Man Snow instead of Old Snowman?"

"Old, because I am old. Man, because I am a human-like guardian, who watches over them. Snow, because I am still a snowman and understand them as only a snowman can. Put that together, I'm Old Man Snow."

Now Elisha better understood exactly who he was talking to. Old Snow is the one he must convince to let him see Snowy! Somehow he had to make him understand.

Old Snow returned to the subject more important to him now.

"I do hope now you understand why you can't see Snowy again. His heart would break when you left, which means..." Old Man Snow paused, thought for a long moment, and then shook his head furiously declaring, "... he would simply melt away."

"Melt away? That's horrible! Who would do that to snowmen? Who would destroy my Snowy?" Elisha cried out in panic.

"No, no, they are not destroyed *by* someone. Any longtime suffering causes a meltdown. Melting away is much kinder than suffering. Remember, snowmen can only survive if they are happy."

"But, you don't understand. He will be happy with me!" Then Elisha rushed on, bursting out defiantly, with rising anger, "He's *my*

242

snowman. I made him, I named him and I'm taking him home!" Suddenly Elisha's emotions flashed to a resentful anger and, unlike his normal self, he blurted out an accusation that even he didn't believe. "You just want to keep him for yourself!"

Elisha saw that his hasty words brought pain to the aged snowman's face, making him look even older. The boy, shaking from anger, took a long, deep breath. His heart softened and now he spoke more respectfully. "I'm sorry. I mean, since he is mine, I should be able to take him home. I'll always take care of him... really, I will."

"Oh? How could you keep him from melting in the heat?" Old Snow asked, trying one more time to reason with Elisha.

"I could... umm, let me think...." Elisha grasped for ideas. "Uh... I know!" His young face lit up with excitement as he explained, "My uncle has a grocery store with a huge, walk-in freezer room. I could keep him there during the summer. It's freezing cold, so Snowy wouldn't melt!"

"And you think he would be happy? Locked up in a freezer? Instead of being free, here?"

The boy's face fell. "No, but, but..." stammered Elisha, "I'll find a way...."

"Ask yourself something, Elisha. Do you love yourself or Frosty more?"

"I..." Elisha stopped. He knew the answer down deep but wasn't ready to say it.

Old Man Snow walked over to the fireplace. "Look at this fire. Looks dead, doesn't it?" He picked up the poker and stirred the fire that wasn't a fire. "It can look dead, until you take the poker and stir it up." As he poked around in the embers that looked dead, they began to flame again.

After laying the poker back down, he turned around slowly and looked at the boy with his compassionate, ice blue eyes. "I'm going to give you the poker to stir up what's inside you, and it is this..." He began speaking slowly, emphasizing each word. "Elisha, your love *made* him, but now that he has become real... he is *not yours anymore*. He belongs here."

Elisha was stunned by the power of the words, "not yours anymore." They felt like a slap in his face. He didn't know if he could bear such a thought, and yet, the words echoed over and over in his mind... "not yours anymore... not yours... *not yours!*"

At first it hurt so badly, he couldn't think about what it meant. Gradually, as the meaning of the words began to sink in, tears ran in skinny trickles down his cheeks. Each trickle said, "Not yours... He belongs here." Truth flooded his mind and heart, poured out his eyes and ran down his cheeks. Elisha knew he had to make a decision.

Finally Old Man Snow spoke gently. He touched the boy on the shoulder and let his hand rest on him. This, he knew, was Elisha's final test. "You alone must decide—to *own* Snowy, knowing his life will end, or to let him go and live without you. Is what's best for him more important than... what you want?"

Elisha was somewhat stunned by that equation. His tears stopped. All he'd been able to think of was, "I want Snowy." He felt so torn: choose what's best for himself... or Snowy... himself or Snowy.... Oh, why couldn't it be both! He felt like he was on a teeter-totter that wouldn't stop. The pressure was giving him a headache! The poor child put both hands to his head and held it. He felt he must decide something or it might explode.

Old Man Snow watched as the boy wrestled with his decision. At last Elisha looked helplessly at Old Snow. Elisha knew the right thing to do and say, but found it too hard. Large, unshed tears filled his eyes.

Snow cleared his throat with finality and walked over to a beautiful, treasured wooden chest with specially hand carved snowflakes on it. Lifting the lid triggered a music box, which sent out soft, soothing tones into the room. Amazingly, the music could be seen as well as heard. The notes floating over to Elisha were in the form of gentle snowflakes that settled on him, but he did not see them through his tear filled eyes. Neither did he know that, as they landed, the flakes melted. The flakes did not fight their melting but gladly accepted their purpose, soaking a gentle peace into the boy.

Old Snow removed a heavenly comforter and handed it to Elisha. "Here, Elisha. I think you're ready for this Blanket of Comfort. Use it this time. It's the best I can do for you. The decision can wait until you're rested. I'll return later." Old Snow remembered how the Home Fire had healed the boy's frostbite; now a deeper healing was needed.

Elisha looked at the thickest, fluffiest blanket he'd ever seen, the same one he'd rejected earlier. As soon as he held it, he was overwhelmed with its heavenly touch. "Oh!" he cried out softly as he rubbed it on his cheek. Incredibly soft and light as air, the comforter had absolutely no weight.

As he pulled it to himself he snuggled into an amazing comfort like he'd never experienced before. A flood of healing tears flowed, replacing the ones of hurt and frustration. When all tears ceased, it was because the boy's pain had stopped. With the blanket comforting him like a mother's love, Elisha drifted off effortlessly this time and fell into a deep sleep.

Old Man Snow shook his head sympathetically as he left the room. He, more than anyone, knew that joy could come out of pain, if it was handled right. He wanted so much for the boy to have the healing he felt. As the door closed behind him, he was sure it would work out all right. This boy, a descendant of his own Builder, Zachary, would do the right thing.

Back in his room, Old Snow was grateful to the King for helping him. What a benevolent King. He'd helped Zachary with the same love and wisdom he showed those in his kingdom.

Chapter Thirty

Discovered! Love's Reward

*T*he shadowy room lay still and quiet as Elisha slept deeply, gaining strength for the journey home. His chest rose and fell gently as he breathed in easy and regular rhythm. His dark blonde eyelashes, though curly, lay long on his cheeks as he rested from all his arduous adventures.

A fireplace mantle clock, carved just like the Snowman Lodge, gave out its rhythmic tick-tock sound until a snowball hand struck the hour, causing a door to open. A cheerful snowman slid out of the Lodge clock, filled the area with tiny snowflakes of laughter and disappeared as the door closed again. Once again, all was quiet except the ticking of the clock.

Elisha slept so soundly he did not hear the door open nor did he know that someone had quietly entered the room and now stood staring at him in the dark. The boy began to slowly awaken with a lazy stretch when suddenly he sensed he was not alone. Quickly he opened his eyes to see something staring intently at him. Totally startled, he cried out loudly in surprise, "Ahhh!"

Whatever the curious creature was, it too was startled and tried to run away. Unfortunately, it was not used to moving very fast.

"No, wait!" called out Elisha after he composed himself. "Don't go! I didn't mean to scare you. You just surprised me. I'm trying to find someone. Please, come back and help me. Please?"

The being stopped in the middle of the darkened room and stood motionless with his back to the boy.

"Do you know where Snowy is?" Elisha asked breathlessly. He didn't know why, but as he stood up, he felt himself trembling. He looked and waited expectantly for this creature to turn around. Could whatever this was help him?

Slowly, cautiously, the being turned around and their eyes met. Elisha found himself looking at a snowman, but not just any snowman... it was his very own snowman wearing his dad's plaid scarf!

"Snowy! Snowy, you're here!" he exclaimed, almost too shocked to believe he'd finally found him.

Now Snowy looked even more startled than Elisha had. The snowman stared in amazement for a moment before a smile lit up his face. Seeing that Snowy was glad to see him, Elisha ran joyfully to his dear snowman, grabbed and hugged him. As he held on he didn't even mind the coldness of Snowy's body.

Impulsively Elisha grabbed Snowy's hands and began to laugh and dance joyously around him. As for Snowy, he grinned a shy, black-button smile and moved awkwardly in place as Elisha circled around him. Suddenly Elisha stopped dancing. Something was different. He looked down at the snowman's hands he held in his own.

"Wait a minute... I gave you stick arms and hands, but look! You have real arms and hands of snow, but... how?"

He gazed at Snowy's face hoping for an answer. But Snowy gave a simple Snowman Shrug. He didn't know; he was just glad to be here.

"Oh, you're right. It doesn't matter. You have what I wanted for you in the first place. I'm just so glad to see you!"

Snowy grinned and nodded. Elisha grabbed his hands and began dancing again. Although Snowy's dance was more of a shuffalong, (shuffle along) it was a happy one.

After a few minutes, the two sat down. Elisha had been so busy celebrating their reunion, he realized they had not talked yet. He was eager to finally, for the first time ever, be able to talk with Snowy!

"Snowy, my forever friend, I've finally found you!"

Snowy stared at him and then raised his eyebrows in a questioning way.

Elisha laughed. "Oh, okay. *I* didn't exactly find you—*you* found me!"

Snowy grinned shyly.

"I've missed you so much! Are you okay?" asked Elisha, a bit of concern tempering his excitement.

Snowy simply nodded and smiled his crooked grin.

Snowy was not talking; why? Elisha began to think about what Old Man Snow had said about new snowmen being like babies. Did that mean he had to learn to talk? He began to worry whether he'd be able to talk with Snowy at all! To have talked to so many animals in this land and even heard other snowmen speaking, but be unable to talk to Snowy, would be so disappointing.

Snowy

After a moment Snowy pointed to Elisha and then put out both hands with a questioning look, raising high the inner eye edges of his little stick eyebrows in concern. Elisha smiled. He saw his snowman cared about him, too. "Yes, my friend. I'm okay, now that I'm with you!"

Pleased but embarrassed, Snowy bashfully dropped his head.

"Oh, don't be embarrassed, Snowy. You're great! You're the best ever!"

If snowmen could beam, then Snowy surely did. They had both made the connection that is only made heart to heart. Each felt reassured for the moment that there was nothing to worry about.

Snowy's smile began to stretch and Elisha's stretched right back! Although Snowy had nothing to say in words, pure joy and happiness radiated from his face. A few times, Elisha thought he saw a tear, but he wasn't sure. However, there was no mistaking his smile. Those silly snowmen who said he didn't have a smile yet! Well, thought Elisha with pleasure, he's smiling now.

Chapter Thirty One

How "Real" Snowmen Party

Snowman Shake, Shuffle and Sniggles

Snowy and Elisha were really bonding in friendship when they were abruptly interrupted by boisterous, happy sounds. Before Elisha knew what was happening, other snowmen began piling in the door. They each pointed at Elisha and Snowy, saying, "Snowy Boy, sno' happy!"

Elisha and Snowy watched in surprise as the snowmen began to party by breaking out into the Snow Shake Dance. First, the snowmen formed a circle and raised their arms high, shaking their hands as they lowered them again, like snowflakes falling. As they danced faster and faster, (which does not get too fast for snowmen), the snowmen laughed heartily, causing the snowflakes in their laughter to do the same dance!

Soon a line formed for the Snowman Shuffle, with each snowman holding on to the generous waist of the one in front. Feet sliding three steps forward, two steps back, then sideways, they chanted, "Who does the Shuffle? Snowmen, snowmen! Snowmen sh-shuffle, do the Snowman Shuffle!"

"Why, they've got rhythm!" Elisha exclaimed.

"Snow rhythm!" called out one of the snowmen who heard him.

These sweet snowmen had come to celebrate the reunion of snowman and Builder, something they themselves had never experienced. The generous, pure nature of a snowman is never jealous, so each was happy for Snowy and fondly remembered his own Builder.

As Elisha and Snowy watched, the air in the room filled with waves and billows of Snowflake Laughter from happy snowmen dancing around the room. The flakes drifting their way brought a touch of giggles out of Elisha, yet he noticed it didn't seem to affect Snowy. How very strange—Elisha realized that Snowy was the only snowman in the room not dancing and laughing.

"Snowy, wouldn't you like to join the others and have fun?"

Snowy looked at Elisha like that was a strange thing to ask. He then shook his head no and continued to watch. Elisha felt a twinge of sadness that Snowy was left out, especially, if it was because he had not adjusted.

Elisha turned back to the snowmen and listened to their talk here and there. They sounded quite simple and childlike, as Old Man Snow had said. Except for a few more mature ones, these had to be new snowmen.

Sno'quaintances

After a time, Elisha rose to his feet to call out loudly, "Hey, guys! I've never met live, talking snowmen before! Won't you please tell me your names?"

Silence filled the room when they heard him speak, as all the snowmen immediately became shy with such pointed attention.

"Please?" he asked again, noticing their hesitancy.

Each one looked at the other one, but no one answered.

"I would be so happy to know you better," Elisha added. He looked at the largest and oldest, the more traditional looking one with a tall, black top hat. "How about you? Could you tell me everyone's names?"

The snowman raised himself up taller, stood a little straighter and nodded, yes. "I," he began, with a tip of his hat, "am Frosty."

"Frosty! Frosty, the Snowman?"

Frosty nodded modestly.

"Really? The one all the kids sing about?"

Frosty

Frosty nodded his head, slightly embarrassed.

"Why, you're famous!" said Elisha excitedly. "I even read Old Snow's book about you!"

"S'no true. That's me," he answered, now more pleased than embarrassed.

"Glad to meet you, Frosty!" Elisha said, shaking his hand. "And the others...?"

Frosty looked at the group and picked them out one by one.

"The tall, skinny one is Icicle. Most everything about Icicle is skinny, except his thinking. He is our serious thinker," added Frosty.

Elisha, excited to finally get to know the snowmen, stepped forward to shake his hand and say, "Hello, Icicle. I love your long stocking hat!"

Icicle nodded his head, replying very seriously, "S'my thinking hat."

"Oh, I see," Elisha answered smiling. He looked next at a very large snowman. "And who is this big guy over here?"

Frosty answered, "Oh, this is Blust'ry—blustery like a windy day, talks up a storm. Weather Warning... Hang on to your hat when he talks or he'll blow it off! Can't help it, he's sno full of cold air, it rushes out in strong gusts."

Icicle

251

Frosty chuckled and shook his head as he added, "Our Blust'ry sure loves to talk."

"Hi, Blust'ry. Anytime you want to talk, I'll listen," said Elisha enthusiastically.

Blust'ry removed the icicle from between his button teeth to speak. The others stepped back a little.

"Sno glad, meet sn'u. Sn'u… first human, first boy," Blust'ry said. A strong burst of frosty wind poured out as he spoke, rushing towards Elisha and the others.

Blust'ry

Elisha's eyebrows raised up in surprise as Blust'ry's forceful breath blew by him, immediately frosting and freezing his eyebrows. His hat flew off his head, but the alert boy caught it just in time, although the force of wind made him lose his balance.

Blust'ry began laughing heartily at what he'd done, which sent forth even more of his blustery breath.

"Sno no! Here we go!" they all cried. Elisha became tickled watching as all the snowmen ended up standing crooked, from the force of air bending them back. As the wind died down, they all

252

grabbed for something solid, bracing themselves against the next burst of his stormy breath.

Elisha rubbed the frost off his eyebrows and began laughing. "Wow, Blust'ry! You just about blew me away!"

Blust'ry, holding his big belly, just laughed again in response, sending another blast of frosty wind. This time Frosty grabbed onto Elisha to brace against its mighty force. Finally, after the laughing stopped, the rush of cold air died down and everyone could stand again. Before Blust'ry could blow again, Frosty quickly moved on.

"Elisha, may I properly introduce you to the next snowman? Elisha, this is Prop Brrr. Prop Brrr, this is Elisha." Frosty whispered on the side to Elisha, "He is always sno proper about manners and all."

"So glad to meet you, Mr. Prop Brrr," said Elisha, politely shaking hands.

"S'my *(I am)* honored to meet you, Mr. Elisha," answered Prop Brrr.

Prop Brrr

Frosty continued. "We call him Brrr. He will always do the right thing. If we're not sure, just ask Brrr."

All the snowmen chanted a couple times, "If you're not sure, just ask Brrr!"

"Yeah, he s'nows everything!" called out one.

"Or, *thinks* he does," teased the jokester snowman, with everyone joining in, including Brrr.

Elisha really liked Brrr's fat belly covered with nice, round burrs from the burdock weed and arranged in a burry nice design. He was the only one with such a burr belly.

Brrr agreed about knowing what's proper by nodding his nice round head, also covered with burrs, giving him the appearance of curly hair. Elisha noticed his nose was a fat chunk of parsnip and his eyes were coal, with coal mouth pieces for a friendly, proper smile. He sported a distinguished looking scarf, along with a nice set of furry ear muffs and matching mittens.

Brrr, who had always longed for a proper top hat like Frosty's, one that he could tip politely, appeared a little embarrassed. He shook Elisha's hand and apologized. "Sno sorry, s'no hat. S'not proper."

"It's okay, Brrr. I don't need a hat-tip. Ear muffs are cool," reassured Elisha.

Brrr stood taller and lifted his head. "Thank you, s'no much."

"You're welcome, sir," answered Elisha.

Meanwhile Frosty had been motioning strongly for someone else to come forward. A big, fluffy snowman stepped out of the corner reluctantly but then stopped.

A couple of the others encouraged him with a gentle shove.

"Come on, sn'okay," said Frosty, beckoning him to come closer.

The fluffy snowman was unsure of who Frosty meant. He looked around behind him and saw no one. Turning back around he then questioned Frosty, "Me? Me, come?"

"Yes, of course, sn'u, Fluffy," Frosty chuckled.

The big snowman seemed quite bashful and hesitant to join the group. He took a few unsure steps, then stopped.

"Come, Fluffy. Please come meet Elisha," Frosty encouraged.

Fluffy

Looking around to see the others encouraging him also, the timid snowman finally reached the circle of snowmen. With eyes cast down and a snowy blush to his face, he stood with hands clasped behind his back, smiling shyly.

"This is Fluffy, made from mounds of fluffy snow, which gave him a fluffy body. He's also a bit fluffy in thought. You see," Frosty explained with a wink and a chuckle, "his sweet snow brain gets easily flustered. When that happens, he becomes a little lighter in the head than usual."

"That's why," added Icicle, "Old Snow gave him that name. I might add, however, that although his brain is fluffy, his snowman's heart is very solid."

"S'no right!" said the other snowmen, nodding in agreement.

Fluffy twisted and turned in discomfort with the attention, but continued to smile, holding his head down modestly into a very fluffy scarf around his neck. Except for a puffier tummy than the others, he had a normal snowman's body. Eyebrows made of twisted, frayed pieces of material gave him expressive, fluffy brows above shiny black button eyes. One dark, continuous piece of pink roping formed his mouth below a cute, round, frosty pink pincushion for a nose.

Elisha reached out to shake his hand, prompting Fluffy to do the same. When Fluffy reached out, however, the weight of his fat belly tipped him forward. Both arms flew up as he pitched forward, landing on his puffy belly, whereupon he bounced up and down like a beach ball a few times before stopping.

"Snoh, dear! Snoh, dear!" cried the poor, flustered snowman as he stopped bouncing but could not get up off his belly.

"Snoh, no! Fluffy Man down! Snoh, no!" the others cried out in dismay. They all rushed to help him up, but one by one they all fell, too, except Frosty and two others.

"Here we go again!" said Elisha with a laugh.

After they were all standing again, they reached out to help poor, awkward Fluffy stand up. Fluffy, finally standing, found his balance and apologized to the others. "Sno sorry my fall. Sno sorry!"

As Elisha looked kindly at the snowman, Fluffy suddenly seemed familiar to him. "It's okay, but... haven't we met before? Aren't you the one in the meadow who tried to... scare me?"

"Snoh-h-h-h! My sorry," moaned the snowman pitifully, shedding a few icy tears and hiding his face behind his hands, as before, in the meadow. After a moment, half embarrassed and afraid, he peeked out and asked, "Boy sorry, too?"

Elisha, feeling sympathy for the timid snowman, reassured him, "It's all right, Fluffy. I'm sorry if I scared you that day. I think we can be great friends now, though, don't you?"

Fluffy gave a shy grin but then nodded yes so hard he became a bit dizzy, which made his brain fluffier in thought. Little puffs swirled out of his head until he quieted himself down.

Elisha turned to Frosty, saying quietly, "I thought his name was Chilly Man."

"Yes, it was when you met him. Hadn't gotten his new Forever name yet. Old Snow decided he's more fluffy than chilly."

Fluffy stood awkwardly, giving a little wave and looking bashfully down again, as he smiled and nodded yes.

When Frosty moved on to the next snowman, he announced, "And he-e-ere is Quirk Flurry!"

Elisha was surprised by Quirk's unusual, quirky appearance. The short, somewhat disjointed looking snowman was made up of a strange assortment of parts. Not so plump as the others, he was trim, with a rusty, upside-down oil tin for a hat. An assortment of differently sized pebbles and small rocks crookedly lined his mouth. Pop bottle caps, smashed into crescent moon shapes for eyes, gave him an impish but happy looking appearance. With two short, chunky corn cobs for ears, and a fat, bright blue bottle cap for a nose, he was certainly the most interesting looking one of all.

Quirk

Frosty noticed Elisha's puzzled look at the disheveled appearance of this hastily made man and laughed. "Yes, this is Quirk Flurry, thrown together in a hurry, but... he has it all together now! He's either all hurry or no hurry at all, with s'no in-between. With Quirk, s'nu get what sn'u get, but he'll always hurry up to be your friend!"

"I love you, Quirk!" exclaimed Elisha in delight. "I like your different look."

"Different, he is," agreed Frosty. "The family who made him was so poor, they had s'no money for toys, so they made the kids a snowman. Using whatever was handy for his parts gave him a quirky, or, unusual personality, so they named him Quirk. His builders found him quite irresistible, which we do, too." Frosty half covered his mouth, speaking only to Elisha, "S'nu have to look out for Quirk, though. He was built out of love and so much fun, he's quite a jokester. Always ready for fun!"

"I'm glad to meet you, Quirk," said Elisha. The boy was ready to shake hands, but hesitated upon seeing Quirk's hands. Poor snowman, he thought, as he saw they were made of old mechanical parts fastened together. Tenderhearted Elisha wondered if they hurt. The hands had been loosely tied to arms made from broken broom handles.

"Glad to meet you," said Quirk with a mischievous grin. He stuck out his hand for a shake. Just as Elisha's hand touched Quirk's, it fell off into the floor with a loud clunk.

Elisha let out a sharp gasp and jumped back, fearing he'd broken off the poor snowman's hand. "Oh, no!" he immediately panicked, beginning to apologize. "Oh, Quirk! I'm so sorry, let me help..." but all the snowmen burst out laughing, which left Elisha very confused.

As for Quirk, he doubled over laughing. His hair, made from little rolls of springs, bounced up and down from shaking his head as he laughed.

"See what I mean?" said Frosty also chuckling as he bent to pick up the hand for Quirk to reattach.

Just as Frosty was ready to pick it up, however, Quirk gave a pull on an invisible string, causing the hand to fly back up to his arm where it re-attached itself. That sent Quirk into another naughty scream of laughter. He had pulled two tricks in a row.

This caught Frosty by surprise, but being a good sport, he joined in on the laughing also. Finally he spoke to Elisha. "That jokester Quirk! You never know what he's going to do, especially when he meets someone new. Likes to shock, you snow. That's our Quirk Flurry!"

Elisha was so relieved that he had not really broken the snowman's disjointed hand off. "Oh, man! Am I ever glad you can pull yourself back together," he said joining in on the laugh.

"Behave now, Quirk," warned Frosty with good humor.

"S'never gonna happen!" cackled Icicle.

That set off all the snowmen to laughing again and agreeing, "Sno true! Quirk, good? S'never gonna happen! Ha, ha, ho!"

"Quirk may be a prankster, but he's always ready to help others," said Frosty.

Quirk straightened up to explain his jest. "And I was just trying to *give you a hand!*"

"You sure did that!" said Elisha laughing.

Breathing a happy sigh, Elisha realized how good it felt to be around these laughing snowmen! He remembered a verse saying that laughter is good medicine. He sure did feel better than when he was afraid or worrying! His smile faded, though, when his eyes fell on Snowy.

The snowman stood forlornly apart from the others, waiting politely out of the drift of Snowflake Laughter. Elisha wondered why Snowy was not a part of this; surely it would be good for him. Then, he remembered that Old Snow had said Snowy wasn't taking part in things yet. Once again Elisha felt sad and a twinge of guilt shot through him—was it his fault Snowy wasn't taking part in the fun?

When all had quieted down, Frosty resumed his introductions. "And the last sno'quaintance is..."

Elisha interrupted. "A, what? Umm, excuse me, Frosty. What is a sno'quaintance?"

"Oh, that's just the new snowmen you meet... Sno'quaintances," Frosty explained.

Now Elisha understood.

"The last sno'quaintance is our easy-going Slush," said Frosty, motioning to a tall, lank, back-woodsy looking snowman with pieces of bark for eyes, a long, strangely curved pinecone nose piece, and a crooked mouth of twigs, giving the appearance of a smile with missing teeth. Tightly twisted grapevine semicircles formed his ears, rounding out his woodsy look.

Slush

The woodsy snowman, leaning easily against a tall cabinet, wore a long burlap vest which hung loosely down. With a broken down straw hat shoved up on his forehead above his eyes, he looked as if he were sizing Elisha up. Finally, his smile warmed and widened, as he straightened up and reached out a stick hand and arm.

"Sno glad to meet y'all, Elisha," greeted Slush in a deep Southern drawl and with a wink. (Elisha wondered how in the world you wink with a hard eye made of bark, but he did.)

"Hi, Slush," said Elisha, shaking the snowman's hand quite carefully, making sure nothing fell apart.

Seeing Elisha's nervousness, Slush called to the jokester, ""Hey, Quirk! Y'all has him worried!"

Quirk began to squeal in delight causing everyone to burst into good natured laughter. In a few moments Quirk quieted down and nodded, acknowledging the honor.

Frosty continued the introduction. "Slush came from the deep woods of a Tennessee mountain. He can find his way around anywhere, so he's our guide on trips. He is what he is, anywhere and everywhere. Smart, too. Can't fool that one."

"Yeah, not like me," Elisha said, rolling his eyes at how easily he fell for the hand trick.

"We've all been tricked by these two. Quirk and Slush together, equal laughs all day long! And we snowmen love to laugh, don't we, men?" asked Frosty turning to the others.

"Yeah, we sno cryin' over split snow shakes!" said Fluffy, laughing like crazy.

The snowmen immediately laughed at Fluffy's mispronounced word. " 'Split' snow shakes? Ha, ha, ho!"

"Spilt, Fluffy, not split. It's *spilt* snow shakes," Prop Brrr corrected as kindly as possible.

"Least my sno cryin' over 'em," said Fluffy, still laughing. Fluffy shook so hard as he laughed, he stirred up his fluffiness. He stopped and thought a second. "What were we laughing about?"

That set off a series of the highly contagious Snowflake Sniggles, which Elisha had to join in on. It seemed that, even if remarks they made weren't that funny, their contagious sniggles made you giggle, whether you wanted to or not.

"What were we laughin' at? Ho, ho! Split snow shakes," said Slush. As he bent over laughing, he began to lose his balance. "Whoah, I'm falling! Hurry, Quirk, can you give me a hand?" cried out the wobbling snowman.

"Sure," said Quirk, "anything for a friend!" First slipping off his hand again, he threw it to Slush, all the while screaming with laughter.

Slush simply fell to the floor in stitches. The whole room roared, and Elisha, himself, laughed again until he was in tears.

Now, as the more mature snowman, Frosty noticed the room was practically vibrating with their loud, boisterous laughing. He nervously gave them a warning. "All right, men, settle down! Especially you, Quirk Flurry, or we'll be into Hail Laughter and that would make a terrible mess in here. Old Man Snow would not be happy!"

As soon as Frosty mentioned Old Man Snow, the men dropped their heads and quieted down to just a snicker here and there. In a short time, however, they looked at each other and, one by one, burst out again. They did keep it from turning into Hail Laughter, but soon they were partying again as only silly snowmen can... all except for Snowy, who remained sitting off to the side, somewhat bewildered.

Chapter Thirty Two

Snow Eats and Sno Manners

"Time for Snow Eats!" Quirk announced.

"Yeah, y'all come!" hollered Slush as he banged an ice triangle with an icicle, getting the snowmen's attention. All the snowmen stopped whatever they were doing and immediately scurried toward the ice table.

"Wow! They must really be hungry," said Elisha. "Look at 'em go!"

Frosty gave a gleeful chuckle. "That's the fastest you'll ever see snowmen move. We call it a Sno-go and it's always for treats. We snowmen don't get hungry. It's just a snowthing we enjoy. Come, join us," Frosty said inviting Elisha along.

Elisha followed, wondering what kind of party treats snowmen would enjoy. There, on the far side of the room, sat a long ice table, heavily laden with all kinds of frosty treats that Slush and Quirk had brought in from the Ice House.

As they approached the table, Fluffy was just reaching out for a frosted snowball, ice drooling in anticipation of its yummy goodness. "Mmm, s'my favorite!"

"Snoh, no, no! Not proper," scolded Brrr quickly. "Guests, first!"

Scared and hurt, the tender hearted Fluffy jerked his hand back immediately and held it close to his face.

"S'nokay, Fluff. Sno harm done," Frosty reassured the fearful snowman with a pat on his snowy back. Fluffy smiled a bashful smile and stepped aside to wait his turn politely. Then Frosty turned back to Elisha. "You're our guest. Please, try some."

Elisha looked at the table. Seeing nothing he recognized, he whispered, "Uh, sorry, Frosty, but I don't know what any of this is."

"Slushes, flurries, snow shakes and snow eats," Frosty explained.

"Snow eats?"

"All kinds of frosty treats. Each snowman prepared his favorite and they've been stored in the Ice House, waiting for a party," Frosty said. "Snowmen love their snow eats."

Slush, who overheard him, spoke up in his southern drawl. "Well, boy, ya'll will have to try my famous mountain drink, Slush's Slushy. Bet you can't say that three times."

Immediately all the snowmen began trying to say the tongue twister and Slush was right. No one could say it clearly—"Slush's slushy, Shush's sushy, Sh-sh-shushy." When Elisha tried, it was even more mixed up, which gave everyone the Sniggles.

"Y'all can't say it, but ya can shorely drink it!" Slush declared, handing Elisha a tall cup made of white birch bark with an exceptionally handsome handle. A reed straw stood in the cup with a bright, red berry on the end of it.

"Looks yummy!" said Elisha, accepting it eagerly. But when he raised the beverage to his mouth, he coughed, jerking his head back in surprise.

Slush warned, "Y'all should be careful where ya stick yer nose. Y'all might get more than ya bargained for!" Then he squealed with laughter.

Tiny bubbles popping up out of the drink had tickled Elisha's nose and taken his breath. Embarrassed, he looked around to see if anyone noticed. No one but Slush had, so he was ready to try again.

"You should've told me that first," said Elisha.

"Aw, but that wouldn't have been as much fun!" Slush answered with a tee-hee.

"True," Elisha agreed with a big grin. "Do you mind if I ask what's in it?"

"Yep, I do. It's my see-cret recip-ee. Never give it out. That's why it's Slush's Slushy. But... I reckon I can tell y'all." Slush bent over to him and whispered ever so carefully into Elisha's ear, "It's birch and licorice drink, half frozen, then stirred and broken up."

"But what makes it bubbly?" Elisha asked, thinking it reminded him of the bubbly in ginger ale.

"Snoh, yeah, the bubblies... Well, that's my real see-cret. Don't give that to anybody. It's a lot of work but worth it," he added proudly. "Snowmen like a little tickle." The other snowmen took a sip of their slushies and giggled. "See?" he said with a laugh. "Now, your turn. Y'all can use the straw if ya don't like the bubblies." Slush watched and waited anxiously for Elisha to taste it and give a verdict.

Elisha did not use the straw, but held his breath to take a tiny sip of the slushy. He swallowed, smiled, and then took another slurp or two. "Mmm, good, Slush!" he declared, immediately covering his mouth as he burped loudly. " Scuse me! Pretty powerful, too!"

"I snow!" Slush agreed. He tipped up his own cup, chugging down most of the slushy. He ended with a pleasurably loud burp which got everyone's attention.

"Snoh, no! Slush, slow burping again," warned Icicle.

"Watch out for burp balls!" added Quirk, exaggerating his disdain before laughing.

Immediately following Slush's burp, a little frozen ball rolled out, dropped to the floor and began bouncing around. The snowmen squealed as they hopped to dodge it.

"Burping! Really, Slush!" Prop Brrr scolded. "We have a guest."

Slush, paying no mind to Brrr, burped again, even slower and louder. " 'Scu-u-use me, but where I'm from, that means, sno-o-o good!"

Slush continued to drink his carbonated slushy and burp, with burp balls rumbling out one after another. (Now these unusual balls do not just bounce a few times and stop; no, they continue to bounce until someone catches them or they melt. And slow snowmen are not good at catching them.)

The frozen bouncing balls rolled over towards Fluffy, who immediately took off running as if a disaster was coming after him. Fluffy slid into Icicle and down the two of them went. The distressed Fluffy cried out, "Slush bad! Burp balls bad!" To the others, it was just a big game. They were continuously hopping up and down, trying to avoid stepping on the ever bouncing burp balls.

Meanwhile Slush continued 'slushing' and burping. "Two at a time means, it's very good!" he explained, burping out two even bigger balls without shame. Afterwards, he stood with a foolish grin on his face. The others snickered and sniggled, until Brrr looked reprovingly at them. After Icicle and Quirk had captured the last ball and all was finally quiet, Brrr turned to Slush.

"Really, Slush! You just steam me! Where are your manners? Were you built in a pond?" Brrr scolded.

"S'no, but I've skated over a few!" Slush responded goofily, pausing to show off some of his best skating poses. Upon noting Brrr's peeved look, he added, "Aw, come on, Brrr. Ya know, sn'u love me."

Brrr looked a bit sharply at him and declared in a huff, "I certainly don't know why, as uncouth as you are!" With that Brrr took Slush's remaining drink away.

Just then, Frosty spoke up. "Elisha, try one of my Snow Angel Cakes for a heavenly chill!" As Elisha reached for one, he was stopped by Quirk.

"No, no, wait! Try this!" he urged eagerly, picking up a tall, see-through cup. "My creamy, smooth Meadow Shake made from spiced deer milk. It's the best tasting snow shake in Snow Valley," Quirk bragged proudly.

Elisha began to accept the snow shake in his other hand when Blust'ry's offer came blowing out.. His fiercely strong announcement blew the muffs off Burr's ears. "Oh, but my flurry is like a flavor blizzard in your mouth! I freeze blasted it myself. Here!" Blustry insisted as he shoved his flurry at Elisha.

"Snoh, here," said Icicle, "try one of my N'icicle stirrers with it. Sn'u can dip and stir!" He proudly held out a long icicle, shaped like a spoon on one end.

As they all crowded round, begging him to try their treats, shoving them at him all at once, Elisha began looking very distressed. Soon his arms and hands were so full, you could barely see his face.

Quirk spoke up quickly, "Wait, wait! Taste my heavenly Hail Balls—"

"Sno sorry," interrupted Fluffy, "but please, try Fluff Drops. 'Sno good!"

Elisha looked in confusion from one to the other, not knowing what to do. He certainly didn't want to hurt their feelings.

A booming voice suddenly stopped all their requests. Brrr had had enough. "Shameful men of snow! Listen to you, only thinking of yourselves. And look! Look what you've done to our guest!" he scolded as he glared at them and pointed at Elisha.

The snowmen saw that Elisha stood politely with arms full of their treats, looking very overwhelmed and stressed. One by one they stepped back and stood with shamed faces. They had meant no harm; they had just gotten carried away, each overly excited for Elisha to try their recipes.

But it was too late to be sorry. Suddenly Brrr began burring loudly, which meant he was very upset.

"Uh-oh!" the snowmen began panicking.

The burring grew louder and suddenly three or four burrs popped off Brrr's head. All the snowmen were frozen to their spots. Now that he had their attention, Prop Brrr began instructing in his most proper voice. "Brrrr! Snowmen, take turns! Brrr... Show your best manners!"

Slush began cackling in mischief. "Sure, I'll show my manners, as soon as I find 'em. Any of y'all seen my manners?"

"I think snu left 'em in the snow," giggled Fluffy quietly.

"Yep, yep," said Icicle. "We have sno manners (*no manners*) cuz we left 'em in the snow!"

Soon everyone was arguing over whether they had sno manners (*no manners at all*) or if they did have snow manners—true snowmen manners.

Elisha's head bobbed back and forth as he looked from one to the other. He felt totally "snowed" by all the confusing snow talk. As Slush continued to burp and Quirk made silly jokes, the room grew louder and louder. Snowmen Sniggles turned into hearty Snowflake Laughter.

"Snowmen, find your manners now, this instant, s'no matter where you left them! Excuse these silly snowmen, Elisha," Prop Brrr alternately scolded and apologized. The embarrassed snowman was quickly drowned out by all the joking and belly laughs.

The proper snowman was quite ashamed of them, but as their Snowflake Laughter surrounded him, even he couldn't stay serious. He first began laughing a little, then a lot, then so hard, he popped off a few belly burrs, which embarrassed him but tickled the snowmen even more!

"Really. It's okay," Elisha assured him, even as the snowmen shouted, "Brrr popping burrs again! Sno funny!" Then a few rolled in the floor with laughter.

"Snoh, my! I really try to teach them manners, but... but... it's hopeless," moaned Prop Brrr. He rubbed his burry head in frustration before breaking helplessly into laughter again as he reattached his fallen burrs.

Elisha smiled and just shook his head at them. He loved their delightful silliness.

They all enjoyed the treats while Elisha sampled a little of everything. He decided the stuff wasn't too bad, although it would never sell among humans. These were definitely treats only snowmen could fully appreciate.

The jolly snowmen continued to party and dance around the room while Elisha rejoined Snowy, who sat alone in a far corner of the room.

"Snowy, why don't you join in with the others?" Elisha asked as he sat down with him.

Snowy just shrugged, pointing first to Elisha then himself.

"I think I understand. You're more comfortable with me, right?"

Snowy nodded yes. That made Elisha feel good, and bad, at the same time.

Chapter Thirty Three

Busted and Bumfuzzled!

A sudden loud, "Bang!" snapped everyone's attention toward the door as it slammed hard against the wall. In the doorway stood Old Man Snow, glaring icily at the men with his ice blue eyes. The snowmen froze in mid-motion, knowing they were busted. They had been caught in a room they did not have permission to be in. They were bumfuzzled, because they didn't know what to do or what would happen. Never before had they disobeyed.

Old Man Snow was angry but also sad because he understood. More than anyone, he knew that snowmen do not think before they act; they simply get caught up in the excitement. However, their not obeying could put them in danger, like when their Hail Laughter caused an avalanche. It was up to him as guardian to discipline them.

"Disobedient men, leave!" Old Man Snow finally ordered in a booming voice. There was no mistaking they were in big trouble.

In a flash, every snowman but Snowy scrambled for the door, knocking each other down. In a heap, each one rose, helping each other up and then motioning politely for the other to go first. "Sn'u, go," one said. "No, sn'u go first," said the other. "No, sn'u first," they argued politely on and on.

Old Man Snow raised his voice somewhat to help speed the pitifully comical exodus of ten snowmen who couldn't seem to get it together enough to get out. "Men! Out, now!"

Finally all had gone except Fluffy and so all attention turned on him. This caused Fluffy's level of fluffiness to rise. Poor Fluffy, the most bumfuzzled and flustered of all!

After much clumsy struggling and stumbling, Fluffy finally stood—but it was as if his fluffiness had frozen him to the spot. He kept saying, "Sno sorry!" as he turned to leave, but his feet didn't go anywhere. This made Elisha want to laugh, but he did not dare hurt the tender snowman's feelings.

Old Snow, trying not to give in to the laugh rising within him, gruffly cleared his voice instead, "A-hem!"

Poor Fluffy quieted and stared helplessly at him.

"Fluffy, just go. Please?" Old Snow said simply.

The flustered, fluffy snowman nodded and answered, "Fluffy go now. Sno sorry. S'no more mad? Sno sorry," Fluffy kept repeating, still standing there.

"It's okay, Fluffy Man. Just go," Old Snow repeated, in a calmer, more compassionate voice.

The awkward snowman seemed relieved and grinned, finally making a true exit with one last, "Sno sorry!" They heard him going down the hall, still apologizing.

Elisha shook his head sympathetically. Why, they can't even make a serious exit when they're busted, he thought. As his mom would say, they're too bumfuzzled. Poor, silly snowmen!

Old Snow then turned to Snowy who still stood there, not in defiance, but in need. The snowman helplessly held his hands out, as if pleading for time. Old Man Snow understood. His voice softened somewhat as he turned to Elisha to deliver his final decision with quiet authority.

"This is it, Elisha. I trust you've made your decision. There will be no further extension of your visit. Snowy has everything he needs here. You really must go, now." He spoke with finality and looked very meaningfully at Elisha with those ice blue eyes that seemed to go to the very heart of his soul.

Chapter Thirty Four

When Hearts Speak Louder
Than Words

The Final Test—
When does love become real,
when it is first birthed or when it is put to the test?

*E*lisha thought hard. "There is one more thing I need to ask," he ventured.

"Yes?" asked Old Man Snow.

"Well… it's just… How did I find my way to Snow Land in the first place?" Elisha asked.

Old Man Snow thought for a moment before speaking. "Elisha, Love found the way. It was *your love* that caused the King to open a portal to allow you in, out of *his* love. Your love will *show you how to leave and close the door back again.* Pure, unselfish love can do hard, impossible things."

Old Man Snow had Elisha sit back down and he began sharing the story of his own journey to see the King and most all that had happened. He did not go into detail about who his Builder was, however, only his story of what the King had done for him in restoring his joy. Elisha took in every word, listening with his heart as well as his ears. It was a lot for a young boy to process.

Snowy listened also, with limited understanding, mostly with his heart.

When the story was finished, Elisha partially understood that Old Man Snow had also suffered and been in the same pain he wanted to spare Snowy.

"So... it's been a long time since you came here?" Elisha asked.

"Yes. Many, many long years."

"And it's only now that you have stopped hurting?"

Old Snow nodded yes. "Thanks to the King."

Elisha thought sadly of all the years of joy Old Man Snow had lost. His eyes traveled to Snowy. Now he really understood why Snowy did not have his smile or laughter yet. Yes, whether Snowy would melt away or live forever, depended on what he decided. This was a great responsibility. If Snowy truly had to stay here... Elisha knew his being here was making it harder on his snowman.

"So, you're saying... There's no way we can stay together... " His voice trailed off.

Old Snow knew the King waited to see if Elisha would do the right thing... Show real love for Snowy by not hanging on. Letting go would be the final test of Elisha's love.

Elisha knew he was ready. His heart swelled with more love for Snowy than he ever knew possible... His heart of love grew larger than his pain. As he walked over and touched Snowy's arm, Snowy felt cold and yet strangely warm to his touch. Elisha hoped it was not too late to get through to his snowman.

"Snowy, now I know..." Elisha took a deep breath, "...this is your home. Your place with me was *never meant to be forever.* It was only for a time."

Elisha looked Snowy straight in the eyes.

"When you left, I missed you so much, all I wanted was to have you back."

Snowy dropped his head and an icy tear escaped his eye.

"I know. You felt it, too," the boy said quietly. Snowy nodded and the icy tear fell to the floor. When Elisha saw that, his voice became more animated, and so Snowy lifted his eyes again to look at him. "But Snowy! My heart has truly changed. All that I went through...

leaving home, almost freezing to death, being buried alive, being scared… none of that matters now! You know why?

"Because now I know that Snow Land is the best place for you, and if you're happy, then I am, too. No matter how far apart we are, you'll always be my very special, best snowman of all!"

When Elisha had first begun talking, Snowy's head hung low, but as Elisha began expressing his feelings, Snowy's whole countenance changed, and he lifted his head higher.

Then Snowy did something that would be forever etched in Elisha's mind and heart. Snowy put one hand on his own heart and reached out his other hand to cover Elisha's heart.

Without uttering a word, Snowy had spoken volumes to him!

Elisha turned to Old Man Snow. "He feels the same as I do about him!"

"Yes, there are times, Elisha, when hearts speak louder than words," stated Old Snow, also touched by Snowy's love for Elisha.

Snowman and boy smiled at each other, each pleased their hearts had spoken.

"Snowy, you may walk Elisha back to his home," instructed Old Man Snow. "By then you'll be able to say your goodbyes. I understand how you both feel."

Understanding slowly spread across Elisha's face. "You *do*, don't you, Snow?" The light came into Elisha's eyes and in amazement he stammered, "Y-y-you… are you… Zach's snowman?" Elisha asked.

"Zach made many snowmen," said Old Man Snow, evading the question.

"But…" Elisha continued, "but I bet you were the first, right? You were the first Zach built, the first to come to Forever Snow Land?"

Old Man Snow smiled kindly and left the room. He knew Snowy and Elisha would both do the right thing, because each had real heart. That's what those who truly love each other do—what is best for the other.

On the other side of the doorway, Old Snow turned and stuck his head back into the room for a moment. "I'll send someone to walk you back here, Snowy Boy, after you take Elisha home," Old Man Snow said.

Elisha's eyes lit up as he asked, "Is that Snowy's new name—Snowy Boy?"

An even wider smile spread across the Old Man's face as he nodded yes and answered, "It will be, if you do the right thing."

The old snowman left the room recalling with great satisfaction how Snowy's face was changing. If Elisha could truly carry this through till the last goodbye, Snowy would shortly have his own Forever Snowman Smile, a new name, and a new life. He had confidence Good Kind King's plan was coming together and all would be well.

Chapter Thirty Five

A Laughing Snowflakes Goodbye

Snowy Times to Treasure

It was nearing sunset when Elisha and Snowy left the Snowman Lodge and began slowly walking back. Very quickly the shadows fell and a bright moon rose in the sky. With its light reflecting from the snow, it still seemed as if it were day. Giant snowflakes drifted down, floating and sparkling in the moonlight. Snowflake feet brushed and tickled Elisha's face and bounced off Snowy's cheeks bringing silly giggles and hearty belly laughs out of both of them.

Elisha knew things would come to an end soon, so he savored every moment. For a bit they did silly things, like seeing who caught the biggest snowflake in his mouth. Elisha always lost, because, unlike Snowy, snowflakes melted on his warm tongue before they could compare. "No fair!" Elisha would cry out each time. Snowy just shrugged in response. They laughed at that until Elisha's belly hurt.

Together they measured to see who had the largest belly. Once again, Snowy won. Elisha had known what the outcome would be, but he wanted Snowy to win.

Elisha started to suggest they see who could smile the longest, then he smacked his forehead as he realized that, with Snowy's snowman smile, Snowy would win that one, too. That tickled his snowy friend so much, that he fell on the ground laughing.

"You know, I'd win a foot race for sure, but I won't do that to you," Elisha said.

Suddenly Snowy took off running or attempting to run. The dare was on! Elisha laughed and decided if Snowy wanted to race, he'd give him a handicap.

"Okay, Snowy," Elisha called after him. "We'll race to the biggest oak tree around the bend, but I'm going to count to 100 before I take off. 1, 2, 3, 4... " Elisha counted as Snowy ambled his way down the path. After counting to one hundred, Elisha chuckled and began running slowly to give Snowy a better chance. "You better look out!" he teased. "This race is mine!"

Without trying, Elisha was indeed closing the gap. He couldn't believe how hard Snowy was trying, and yet the snowman kept stopping to look at Elisha, which slowed him down more. As soon as he would see Elisha gaining, he'd look alarmed and take off again as fast as he could, which was far from fast.

"Ha, ha!" Elisha laughed. "If you keep stopping, you'll never win, Snowy!"

Little did he know, Snowy had a plan. Snowy rounded the bend first. Right there, the path went downhill the last twenty feet to the oak tree. As Snowy topped the hill, the snowman plopped down, gave a hard shove and began sliding down the hill, picking up speed as he went.

Running far behind, Elisha panicked when he could not see his snowman. Snowy had literally dropped out of sight. Frightened that he might have fallen and gotten hurt, Elisha frantically raced to reach the top of the hill to see what happened. "Snowy! Snowy, are you all right?" he yelled as he ran, but Snowy didn't answer. Elisha hoped his idea of racing hadn't caused harm to come to the snowman! The boy speeded up to reach the top of the hill where he stopped to look. Suddenly he found himself laughing in relief.

"You trickster, you!" Elisha yelled, for there was Snowy, sliding down the hill on his bottom and coasting easily to the finish line. Just as Elisha caught up with him, Snowy slid to a stop at the tree, raising both arms in victory.

Elisha came to a stop and laughed. The simple snowman had tricked him.

"You sneaky snowman! You are so cold! I can't believe you faked me out and won! But you did it, fair and square." Elisha grabbed Snowy's arm declaring, "The winner—by a snowman slide!"

As he looked at Snowy, Elisha stopped laughing and stepped back, totally taken by surprise at what he saw. The victorious snowman was doubled over with snowflakes billowing out of his mouth. Elisha was the first and only human to ever see a snowman experiencing his first Snowflake Laughter.

The laughing snowflakes flooded over onto Elisha. Thrilled to see his snowman finally happy, he threw back his head and let out his own carefree laugh. The air was filled with such happiness and joy, the birds above joined in with their own happy songs.

As the Snowflake Laughter faded away, snowman and boy rested before continuing on their way. They soon crossed over a little bridge and spied a small frozen pond nearby.

"Hey, look, Snowy! How about we go ice skating?"

He looked at Snowy and Snowy looked at him. In a burst the snowman took off in wild abandon sliding down the bank, bottoms up. Elisha quickly followed, but bottoms down.

They tried skating on the ice for fun, but that didn't last long. Having snowy feet made it too slippery for Snowy. Rather than continually fall and struggle to get back up, he finally just stayed down, sliding easily on his snowy bottom and playfully doing a few donut spins.

Elisha thoroughly enjoyed seeing Snowy have so much fun. He marveled as the snowman's silly laugh tinkled out leaving a trail of laughing snowflakes everywhere behind him. As he watched the snowman, Elisha felt contented, realizing that, this is how Snowy was meant to be and would always be, laughing and having fun.

Soon, both knew it was time to get going again. They continued on, enjoying an enchanting walk through the wintery wonderland of Snow Valley. Elisha noticed the still quietness amidst all the snow. He would always remember the beauty of Snow Land.

Just after they passed Snow Mountain, Elisha heard a chorus of voices calling his name. He turned and looked around, wondering what could be happening now. He strained his eyes; was he seeing things, or was that a line of animals coming down a nearby hill?

"Elisha, wait!" one called.

"Yes, wait. You didn't say goodbye!" said another.

Forever Friends

As he looked, he was pleasantly surprised to see that, yes, it was indeed a trail of animals. As they drew closer he realized it was all who'd befriended him in Snow Land: a row of the thirty-one rabbit cousins with Uncle Peter; the whole beaver crew, led by Big Slap, Big Chopper, and Benjy; Yowler, Rack, Ominous Owl, Minute Mouse, Sly, Spunky and Serena. Elisha's entire face beamed as he ran toward them.

"My friends, my friends!" he exclaimed in joy as he reached them at last.

"We came to say goodbye, Elisha," said the littlest rabbit cousin with a shy little smile.

"We consider that important, here in Snow Land," Mouse squeaked chidingly.

"Aw, I consider it important, too, Minute. I'm so glad to see all of you. Oh, but... I won't see you anymore, will I?" he asked sadly.

They all hung their heads down, genuinely sorry this would be the last time. It was Uncle Peter who cleared his throat to answer, "No, your purpose for being here has been accomplished. Now is the time for our final goodbyes, I'm afraid."

"Well, thank you all, not just for coming, but for all your help. I'll remember each one of you always," said Elisha.

"And don't forget your Snow Land Lessons, boy," said Big Chopper.

"Lessons?" asked Elisha.

"Yes, like... things-s are not always what they s-seem... deceit can make things-s look better than they are," he said, whistling through his teeth for emphasis.

"And... " Big Slap stepped up to add with a jovial twinkle in his eye, "it never hurts-s-s to know some friends-s with good choppers-s!"

Elisha laughed heartily. "That is true! And I had a whole brigade of friends!" he added, to which all the beavers gave a hearty cheer.

Next, Owl landed silently and stepped forward to hoot with a dramatic flourish of one wing, "Be prepared and carry your sword, but remember, you release your weapon's power!" added Owl.

Just then the boy saw a masked face grinning at him. "Rack!" he exclaimed. "You helped save me from the Grumble Weeds. Thank you for chopping me out."

"My pleasure, but it was your believing in good that saved you," the raccoon said modestly. "Always remember, Grumble seeds will sprout into something worse than what you're grumbling about," said Rack.

"I know!" agreed Elisha. "It's just not worth it to complain."

"That's what I say," said Yowler, speaking up shyly. "Besides, you make a racquet no one wants to hear." Elisha thanked the strange cat and actually felt an affection for him.

"I've got one, I've got one!" piped up the littlest cousin. Running up to him and landing with a hop, his little whiskered face began frowning as he stopped. "Now, what was it? Let me think, let me think," he said hopping in a circle and tapping his forehead to stir up his memory. He suddenly stopped and brightened.

"Oh, yes!" he said, greatly relieved to remember in time. "Jefferds said to tell you to always forgive... uh... make time to share your favorite tea, and umm... what was the other? Oh, yes! Stay out of trouble." He paused to think again. "And... he still thinks you should've been born a rabbit! Why, I'll never know," he ended with a giggle and wiggle of his cottontail.

Elisha laughed. "Oh, I know what he means. He thinks that's the only way I can stay out of trouble. But... why didn't Jefferds come himself?"

"Oh," said Uncle Peter, "he had some things to do."

"Oh," said Elisha rather disappointed. "Well, at least he sent a message. I wish I could have seen him just one more time."

"Well, he did say something about wanting to miss all the drama of a goodbye," said the littlest rabbit cousin.

"Now, that sounds like Jefferds!" Elisha said with a smile and a nod.

Minute Mouse scurried up to him to get his attention. "Do you remember my lesson?"

He grinned. "Of course, I do. It's not size that's important!"

"Yes," she affirmed with an impish grin. "I proved that. But also... only Faith unlocks the door in dark places!"

"How could I ever forget that?" Elisha agreed.

The very handsome Sly Fox stepped forward, his beautiful red fur swaying as he walked. "And Elisha, will you remember to ponder before starting off on your next venture?" he asked.

"I sure will, Sly. Thanks for talking me into it," Elisha answered. "That was not just any old pond!"

"Ah, such a clever boy," Sly said with a satisfied smile.

The littlest cousin had put his ear to the ground and was listening. "Oh!" he said, jumping up suddenly. "We have to go! Old Man Snow just sent word to get back to Snow Valley and he's sending someone to walk Snowy Boy home."

With that the whole row of ears waved goodbye and with the wiggles of thirty cottontails, they all followed Uncle Peter and the littlest cousin.

"Goodbye, little cottontail friends!" Elisha called as their white tufts bobbed out of sight. Next the beavers saluted their farewells and followed after the rabbits. As the line stretched out, Elisha watched, waving until they were out of sight, before turning to Owl and Mouse.

"You've both been real friends. You risked everything for me, Owl," Elisha said warmly.

Owl's large eyes blinked kindly at Elisha. "You learned well, Elisha. You showed real courage, fought hard and persevered through every obstacle."

"Even a Mr. O smack down," Elisha said with a snicker. The owl's luminous eyes twinkled as they remembered their first meeting. Then Elisha became serious to add, "Oh, and Owl, your flight to rescue me? Thanks. I know it was hard on you," Elisha said.

Owl's large eyes blinked again and softened. "It was my honor. I have a feeling that you would do as much for me."

Elisha smiled. "Uh, the flying part might be a challenge," he said with a grin.

"That's why you have friends with wings," responded Owl with a wink.

279

From overhead Elisha heard a distinct whistle. He looked up to see Hawkeye soaring while Spotter, the falcon, made a lightning fast dive for show. Everyone cheered and clapped as the two raptors performed a few aerial stunts, then swooped down with a salute and flew away.

"Wow!" Elisha breathed in appreciation. "What a show!"

Owl stepped aside to let Minute have another word with him. She stood sadly and quietly at first with her head down. Finally she lifted up her head. The poor mouse had something to say but hiccupped every time she tried to speak.

"I was going to ask how your hiccups are doing. I guess I got my answer," said Elisha. After making several attempts to speak but ending only in spasms of hiccups, Elisha reached down, stretched out his open hand and she stepped onto his palm. He lifted her up to his face and spoke softly. "Thank you, Mouse, for staying with me in the dark."

Minute tried to answer, but she hiccupped again as she blushed.

"It's all right, I understand. Sometimes true friends don't need words anyway," said Elisha. He affectionately touched her nose and added, "I'll never forget you, Minute."

Finally Minute's hiccups were gone and she spoke in her squeaky voice, "When I came to help, I never expected I'd find a friend in the dark!"

"Well, let me tell you, being in the dark without faith was scary, so it sure helped to have a friend with fur," then he added, "and a tail!"

Minute responded with a squeaky giggle then she became serious. "With faith and friends, you'll always win the battle."

Owl gave a gentle hoot. It was time to go. As Elisha lowered her to the ground, she slipped down, ran up Owl's wing and jumped onto his back. Fully recovered, Owl gave a final wing salute before launching into the air and soaring silently away.

Elisha waved back with a tear in his eye. He would miss them, he thought as he watched them begin the journey back to Big Dark Woods.

Elisha hadn't noticed Spunky and his mother had stayed behind waiting quietly. Unable to be still any longer, Spunky ran up to him. "Well, for snow sakes, don't forget me!" he piped up, impatiently tapping his hoof, then giggling, bouncing and flipping his white tail around before Elisha came up to him.

"Oh, I could never forget my spunkiest friend of all!" the boy said as the young deer came closer. "It's like you have springs in your legs."

"Nope! Just my own bouncy legs. I'll remember you, too, even if you do have a bald face and only two legs! But maybe next time I see you, you'll have all four legs and a little fur," he said, before beginning to frolic back and forth on the path again.

"He has a lot to learn," Serena said in her silky smooth voice.

Spinning around to look behind him, Elisha was pleasantly surprised to see the mother deer waiting quietly. Serena reminded him in her calm voice, "Family and friends on the journey make the go worth going, Elisha. Value them." Elisha reached out and gave her a gentle hug.

Spunky, who had been watching the other animals getting farther away, ran back up to them, prancing with increasing restlessness. "Come on, Mom! We're missing the parade!" he said urgently.

"Have patience, Son," she said. She turned again to Elisha. "Always make time for the important things in life—like parades!" she said and left, calling to her son to wait.

"Goodbye!" Elisha called after them. "I'll work on those other two legs, Spunky!"

Spunky looked back to proudly announce the obvious, "I'm ahead. I already got four!" and he kicked his hind legs into the air with a laugh.

As he watched mother and son bound away, Elisha relished seeing their white tails bouncing with every leap. Just as they disappeared from sight, he came face to face with his tiny friend, Echo. The black-and-white bird circled a moment in the air. Elisha held out his hand to give the chickadee a place to land.

"Echo! I didn't expect a Chickadee Goodbye!"

The small bird cocked his black-capped head to one side and looked at him with shiny black eyes. "You don't suppose, pose-pose I'd leave without a bye, bye-bye?" he asked.

"Not you! I'm glad you came, Echo. We had a scary time together, didn't we?"

"A little too scary, I'd say," said Echo.

"Aw, you weren't *worried*, were you?" Elisha teased.

"Not singing my happy song," he said, chirping a few more notes. "Remember, Faith and Worry don't sing the same song! Goodbye, bye-bye."

Elisha called goodbye, watching wistfully as the bird flew away.

Beginning of the End

The boy sighed in satisfaction and turned back to the best friend of all. Snowy had waited quietly through all the goodbyes and now they began walking leisurely towards home again, Snowflake Laughter trailing behind them as they walked. Too soon, they reached the field near Elisha's back yard. Elisha stopped to look around.

"This is where I met Jefferds," he said to Snowy. He half expected to see the rabbit pop out somewhere, but it was just the two of them to say goodbye. Elisha knew he would miss that ornery rabbit. "You will tell Jefferds I said good bye, right? And that I'm sorry I was so much trouble? Well, not too sorry, I guess. I got what I wanted, didn't I?"

Snowy patted his own heart, as if to say, "Me, too!"

"But I guess you shouldn't tell Jefferds that last part. It might set him off again about boys!" Elisha said trying to look serious, but then they both burst out laughing.

Snowy's Snowflake Laughter danced out and settled on them, setting them off into more laughter. As the flakes melted, the laughter died down and they both became quiet again, dreading their final moment together.

Snowy stopped walking. He looked reluctantly back towards Snow Land, then at Elisha.

"You have to go now, don't you... Snowy Boy?" Elisha said softly, in a husky voice, aware this was finally the end.

Snowy's head hung down to his chest, barely nodding.

Elisha remembered what Old Man Snow had said and knew he must fight away the sadness for his snowman's sake. Taking a deep breath he raised his voice, speaking cheerfully and confidently.

"I'm glad to know you're going to have a great life, Snowy, with lots of friends, laughing and playing. Just remember to keep your Hail Laughter off the mountain! No more avalanches, right?"

Laughing Snowflakes tumbled out of Snowy's mouth as he agreed. Then, Elisha asked seriously, "No more worrying about each other, right?"

Heart to Heart

Snowy smiled sheepishly, turning side to side like a little kid. Elisha's heart filled beyond capacity with love for his friend. Feeling a tear start in his eye, Elisha searched for something positive to say. "Just think, Snowy. No more melt-downs, ever."

Snowy nodded slowly, then began acting strangely as if... as if he wanted to say something! Elisha waited as Snowy struggled to speak, but nothing came out. Finally, however, he managed some halting sounds. " Sn... sn... sn..." Unable to say any real words, the snowman stopped and shook his head in frustration.

Elisha remembered Old Man Snow explaining a snowman's first words would be like a baby beginning to talk. He thought Snowy must be stuck on "snow," like a baby gets stuck on "da-da" for his first word (and, of course, a snowman's first word would likely be snow).

"It's okay, Snowy... just relax. You can do it," Elisha encouraged.

Snowy started over, pointing first to Elisha saying, "S-sn-sn-nu," then he patted his own heart as he continued, "m-mm-me... fr-r-r... fr-rv, fr-v-v..." Snowy stopped and seemed quite exasperated.

Elisha so wanted to help his snowman. "It's okay, Snowy. Your heart has spoken. I understand." Elisha took Snowy's hand in both of his and clasped it. "I think you're saying, 'You and me, Forever Friends' – and we are!"

Snowy nodded, smiling his biggest. Both felt satisfied they had spoken, heart to heart. With a goodbye wave, Snowy began walking away, but after a short distance the snowman hesitated and turned back to him.

"Remember, stay strong!" Elisha encouraged, raising a fist and pumping his arm.

As Snowy saw that, he looked down at his own arm, lifted it into the air and flexed as if he, too, were making a strong arm and fist.

Elisha called, "Yes, strong! And Snowy Boy, you will always be the best!"

Hearing that, the once forlorn looking snowman stood taller and straighter. Even Snowy's smile had stretched wider. Wait a minute! It wasn't just wider; it was different. Snowy had his own Forever Snowman Smile! Just like Old Man Snow, Snowy had adjusted at last. Elisha gave a grateful sigh of relief as Snowy Boy walked home towards his Forever life.

Still watching from a distance, Elisha noticed when someone joined Snowy, hopping alongside him, motioning and talking every breath. It was his rabbit friend!

"Mr. Jefferds, Mr. Jefferds!" Elisha yelled and waved excitedly, but the rabbit was talking so much he never heard him.

Snowy, however, did hear and stopped, pointing towards Elisha. Turning toward the boy Mr. Jefferds gave a brief wave, still talking as they started on their way again.

"Goodbye, Mr. Jefferds," Elisha called after them, somewhat disappointed, but then he snickered to himself, saying, "I'm sure Jefferds is giving you lots of snowman advice, Snowy, even though he has never been a snowman himself! At least he'll keep you company."

As he continued to watch them, the rabbit fell to the ground, rolling around and laughing. What a surprise. "Well, I guess Snowy is good for you, too, Jefferds!" Elisha said. "And who knows, maybe even I loosened you up a bit, you crazy rabbit!"

By now the laughing snowflakes had reached Elisha. As they drifted by, he smiled happily. He felt at peace about things and turned towards home, but after walking a brief distance, he was surprised when everything around him suddenly changed.

One minute, he was in snow and the next instant, sloshing through standing water in his own back yard. Quickly his boots and pants became soaked. Without even knowing it, he had walked through the portal into his own yard, leaving Forever Snow Land behind.

Seeing the flood reminded him of the day he lost Snowy. Just as he felt a momentary twinge of sadness, a single, stray, laughing snowflake floated by. Elisha knew that the Snowflake Laughter was a reminder that, since Snowy was "real" now, he would always be happy.

"It's okay. Snowy's in a good place!" he declared confidently.

As for Elisha, his journey was over and, right in front of him stood his own house. It sat snug and warm as he'd left it, filled with love he could always count on. For a moment he paused. Once, when he was still obsessed with Snowy, he might've stayed in Snow Land with him, but that would never happen now. His love for his mom and dad swelled up and washed over him. Hey, he liked being Elisha Zachary Winters!

As he went toward the house, he wondered about many things. He had gotten so caught up in persevering through the adventures he'd had, he hadn't taken time to think about how incredible it all was. No one would ever believe him. In truth, he, himself, could hardly believe it. How was it all even possible?

He turned to look back in the direction he'd just come from. There, behind the pines he could clearly see old Joe McPheeny's farm and the other farms beyond with no sign of Snow Land or Snow Mountain... It was as if they had never existed at all.

Chapter Thirty Six

A Heart Goes Home

*B*efore opening the back door, Elisha wondered what he'd find waiting on the other side. He hoped it wouldn't be frantic parents looking for a missing son. With relief he met only the quietness of the night and the familiar sounds of home—the furnace humming, the steady tick-tock of the kitchen clock, sounds he'd heard every winter of his life, sounds that comforted him. Home meant many things to him, mostly feelings... Love, warmth, safety, coziness. And of course, Mom, Dad, and Mollie. He gave a happy sigh.

Now to take off his dripping wet things and squishy boots! In the warmth of the mud room, the wet clothing felt yucky. There was so much snow still caked on his coat from Snow Land. He should've shaken it out, but he was too tired. Since his pant legs were soaked from walking through the water out back, he dutifully hung them up. He hoped they'd dry by morning. If tomorrow was Saturday, he'd be playing outside with Tim. Ugh! He couldn't stand the gross feeling of his feet inside his soggy socks another minute! Sitting down, he peeled them off, squeezing them out in the utility sink before hanging them up to dry.

As he headed upstairs all he could think of was crawling into a warm, dry bed, but as he tiptoed past his parents' door, he wondered what night this was. Elisha knew he'd left at night and was returning in the night. It couldn't be the same night, could it? Too much time had passed in Forever Snow Land for him to have been gone only one night, but then... if it's Forever there, who knows how time in Forever would count, compared to here? His wonderings came to a stop as the lingering fragrance of his mom's vanilla candle filled his nostrils. Elisha was glad to be home.

Upstairs, he opened his bedroom door as quietly as possible so as not to disturb Mollie. There she was, lying right by his bedside, just as he'd left her. He was amazed she had not awakened to greet him. She barely opened one eye, sighed, and went back to sleep. It was as if she was in a near coma or something! Hmmm. Could the King have whammied her with a deep sleep so she wouldn't bark and awaken his parents while he was gone?

All at once, Elisha felt extremely tired; all the why's didn't seem as important as getting in bed. And oh, did his cozy flannels ever feel good! Barely able to lift his legs, he crawled into bed and flopped down exhausted, his head hitting his soft, downy pillow with a gentle whoosh. Pulling the covers up to his chin, he snuggled into the cozy warmness and, with a sigh he settled down and drifted off to sleep.

Not long after, silvery moonlight danced at the window and into the room as once again snow swirled madly outside. The temperature dropped rapidly, and the watery yard quickly glazed over and froze. While Elisha slept, an outline of something appeared outside the window briefly and then disappeared into the distance, surrounded by tiny snowy tornadoes, whirling and leaving behind a luminous layer of still, white, moonlit snow.

Chapter Thirty Seven

Reality Dawns

*W*elcoming rays of sun stretched all the way to Elisha's bed, lighting the edge of the covers hanging down. A dormant fly, nestled on the cold window ledge, stirred in the warming of the sun and buzzed in its half awakened state.

Elisha's eyes fluttered open lazily. As he stretched, luxuriating in the comfort of his own bed, he could hear the off and on buzzing of the fly and the songs of the winter birds outside. He knew his mom and dad were nearby. Home. This is belonging. Home and family.

As Elisha stretched again, he felt the chilly air then snuggled back into his covers. As his thoughts began to focus, he began wondering at what had happened. Wait. What *had* happened?

Here he was, lying in bed just as he did every other morning, but what about last night, his adventures and seeing Snowy?

"Elisha," his mom called from downstairs, "better get breakfast and chores over. Tim will be here later."

"Okay, Mom," he answered. His young spirit drooped as he realized... This is Saturday morning. There's no way all that stuff could've happened in one night. It must have been a dream. But then, that means... I didn't really see Snowy... or did I?

Elisha was so confused. He sat up and looked for Mollie. She must have already gone downstairs.

It's just as well, he thought. He needed time to review all the things about last night... Talking animals and snowmen, wild adventures and escapes from danger with the help of beavers and rabbits! It all seemed unbelievable and pretty crazy now.

Sadness overwhelmed him with the cruel logic forced on him by the bright light of morning. It seemed he was right back where he was after Snowy melted... just feeling empty and hurt.

Elisha finally lifted his head and gazed blankly toward the window, not really focusing on anything. Who would want to? All you could see was a flooded yard with no sign of a snowman. Eventually, though, he wandered to the window and gave a real look outside.

"What!" he exclaimed, shocked at the change he saw. Severely dropping temperatures had frozen the flooded yard into an ice rink. Over that a layer of light, fluffy snow, recreated the former grandeur of winter. Still, for all its beauty, without Snowy it seemed so desolate.

Just then something colorful and out of place caught his eye. What it was, he wasn't sure, but he could see a piece of something stuck on the lower outside edge of the window. Curious to see what it was, he swung the window wide open.

There, indeed, a piece of colorful, crumpled material lay with its tip gently flapping in the wind. Elisha reached out to retrieve it and examine it up close. As he did, his mouth dropped open in amazement. It was his dad's old plaid scarf—Snowy's!

The sight of the scarf bombarded his logic that had convinced him Forever Snow Land and his adventures there had been a dream. Although he swallowed hard and tried to stay calm, the boy began pacing the floor excitedly, holding tightly to the scarf.

Think carefully, Elisha, he told himself. He recalled how Snowy was still wearing it when he melted, and how there had mysteriously been no trace of it in the remaining puddle of the snowman. The next time he remembered seeing it was last night in his dream. Snowy was wearing it when they said goodbye... And now, here it was in his hands!

As he sat, pondering what all this meant, hardly daring to believe such wild adventures had been real, he looked outside again. An exclamation of amazement escaped him, "No way!"

There, in the snow on the small roof below his window and down below, reaching all the way across the back yard, he saw *large trailing tracks with smaller rabbit tracks* alongside them, both coming and going!

Elisha's heart began beating faster. Something had come to his window overnight and left Snowy's scarf. Why, those tracks could belong to none other than Snowy and Jefferds.

At first he was stunned in amazement, but then a huge smile spread across his face as he realized—his adventures had not been a dream after all!

"Snowy, my Snowy!" He danced around the room holding the scarf close to his face. "And Jefferds, you must have cared after all, since you came, too!"

But, how? How could they have come into his world? It suddenly occurred to him that the same King that had allowed him to enter Snow Land must have allowed Snowy to come to his window last night, leaving proof that his adventure had really happened. Good Kind King had chosen something that would erase away all doubts – his friends' footprints and Snowy's scarf!

Elisha sat down on the window seat with overwhelming relief. The ache deep inside him was gone. Thankfulness welled up within him as he paused to thank his Heavenly Father, so good and so kind. Then he stopped to think about that. Good Kind King in Snow Land was sort of... sort of like his good, kind Father in Heaven!

Soon his thoughts returned to the scarf, for it began feeling soggy in his hands. Elisha decided to take it to the mud room to dry by the heater, but when he stood up to leave, something dropped from the crumpled scarf onto the floor. It rolled a bit before coming to a stop. Elisha had no idea what it could be.

Quickly he picked it up; it felt a little hard. Upon examining it, he saw that it was crudely made, roundish and a bit crumbly with orange flecks in it. Its smell was appealing and so he took a small nibble. Why, it was a small carrot cookie! He took a larger nibble. Yep, though not like his mom's, that's what it was.

But wrapped in Snowy's scarf? What did that mean? Was the cookie from Snowy? No, surely not, he thought, remembering the treats at the snowman party. They were nothing like this; they were all frosty and snowy. But who else could have left him a carrot cookie? The only one with Snowy was... Jefferds? He shook his head as he thought about it. That's silly. Where would a rabbit get a cookie?

Oh, well. He took another bite. It was pretty good. The only thing... it made him wish he had a cup of hot chocolate to go with it.

Epilogue

The Rest of Elisha's Story

Tying Together Stray Snowflakes (Loose Ends)

Later that morning, Elisha's friend Tim came over to play. Elisha was a little quieter than usual, but he and Tim had a good time. He liked feeling like a normal kid again, at least for awhile. Sometime this weekend he'd call his other best friend, Kaylynn, but what would he say? Maybe, sorry? Would he ever be able to tell her what had happened?

After Tim left, Elisha had a lot to think about. He felt peaceful about Snowy's new life, but he spent the rest of the day full of wonderings: Should he tell his parents any of this? Would they even believe him? Why had this happened to him out of all the other children whose snowmen had melted? What about this kingdom no one else knew about? Why couldn't life here be like life in Snow Land? Questions ran on and on in his mind. Even if he told his parents, how could they help him? Elisha didn't even know if he could explain any of it to them.

After supper he decided to speak up. "Dad, Mom. Could I talk to you about something?"

"Of course, son, what is it?" his dad said, giving him full attention.

"You have been a little quiet today, Elisha. What's on your mind?" asked his mom, coming to sit down.

"Well... it's about... about..." Elisha began tentatively and then sighed. "Mom, I don't know where to start. It's about Snowy, but not exactly." How could he possibly begin to tell them what had happened?

With a smile Beth patted his hand. "Just start, Elisha, wherever. It'll eventually all come out. We're listening."

"Well, I guess you've noticed I haven't been as sad lately," he ventured. "About Snowy, I mean."

"Yes, we have and we're so glad you're feeling better," said his dad.

"Well... it's cause something unusual happened. I mean, *really* unusual... something I'm not sure you'll understand. It started a week ago and ended last night, I think."

He looked at his mom, then at his dad waiting quietly with encouraging looks and smiles. Taking a deep breath, he continued. "I went to a kingdom last night and looked for Snowy, and... and I found him."

"Oh! You had a dream then?" asked Beth.

"Well," Elisha began, hesitating slightly, "I thought it was a dream, but it was very real." After that he barely took a breath as everything tumbled out rapidly. "First I entered Forever Snow Land where the snowmen laugh funny, I was chased by monsters – even though they really weren't, and I got locked up by an evil old man." He saw his mom's concerned face and added, "Don't worry though, an owl, mouse and the beavers saved me!"

He saw his parents sitting with their mouths hanging slightly open in surprise, so he hurried on. "Then there was Old Man Snow and the new snowmen, and best of all, Snowy found me! We talked and he walked me back home." Thinking that should cover it, he looked anxiously at his parents. Now that he'd said it out loud, he thought it all sounded ridiculous.

"Is that *all* that happened?" laughed his mom.

"Well, I did leave out about the avalanche, caused by the snowmen laughing so... hard..." he finished lamely, feeling rather foolish after seeing the look on his parents' faces.

"An avalanche! That would be a big thing to leave out," Mom said with a chuckle.

His dad began to laugh, but as he saw Elisha's seriousness, he said respectfully, "That was quite a dream!"

"Yeah... a dream. It does seem like a crazy dream, doesn't it?" Elisha muttered, half to himself.

"Oh, I've had some crazier dreams than that," his mom said quietly, not wanting Elisha to feel they were putting him down.

Elisha laughed a little uncomfortably. Maybe he should just let them think it was a dream.

"Did you, uh, need to talk about this?" his mom asked.

"Well, I do have some questions, but..." Elisha paused, wondering how much to share.

"Go ahead and ask, Elisha. Dreams often sound crazy. Don't worry about how it sounds," she said.

"Ask away!" encouraged his dad cheerfully.

Living Forever

Elisha took another deep breath. "In my, uh... 'dream,' I found out that after snowmen melt, they live forever. But just the ones with a heart!"

"Oh?" asked his mom, "and how does a snowman get a heart?"

"Just by being loved. But, Mom, Dad, what about when we die? We live forever, too, right??"

"Yes, our bodies die but our souls live on forever," his dad answered.

"And, we go to Heaven, right?"

"If our hearts are right with God, yes," answered his dad.

"And do we get a new body like Snowy?" asked Elisha.

"Yes, a new forever body, and the older I get, the more I'm looking forward to that," his dad said with a laugh.

"Snowy's in a perfect place now, kinda like a Snowman Heaven," Elisha said, thinking out loud.

His mom and dad looked at each other. "How do you know that?" his dad asked.

"Oh, cause I saw him in Forever Snow Land, where everything's perfect for snowmen. They'll never melt or be unhappy again. It wasn't perfect for me, but it is for snowmen."

Heaven on Earth?

Elisha thought a few seconds before going on. "Dad, why do we have to wait for Heaven for things to be perfect? Why can't it be perfect now?"

"Why can't earth be like heaven? Well, that's like asking, why can't Detroit be Paris? They're two different places. And two different times... earth is for now, but Heaven is later, in Forever. Do you see what I mean?" he asked.

"Yeah, I guess. But I sure wish Heaven was here now," said Elisha.

"It is hard to wait for something so wonderful, but Heaven is our reward when this life is over," explained his dad.

"So... we get a reward for going through all the bad stuff?" asked Elisha.

"Yes, the best reward," said his dad.

"I think we should just skip the bad stuff and have a forever life now," Elisha said. "It would be a lot easier on everybody!"

"Elisha, I don't understand all of God's plan, but, actually, believe it or not, a little hard stuff helps us to be stronger."

"Well, with all I've been through, I should be Iron Man!" Elisha said.

"I'm so sorry things have been so tough, Elisha," said his mom.

"But when things are always easy," his dad said, "that's when many people start thinking they don't need God. On the other hand, during hard times, many turn to a God bigger than their problems. But God doesn't allow bad stuff because He wants us to suffer."

"He doesn't?"

"No, He wants His people strong. He lets everyone choose how to live. In hard times, we who choose our faith, get stronger. He blesses our faith and heals our hurt," his dad explained.

Our Blanket of Comfort

"Heals our hurt?" Elisha drew in a quick breath of excitement. "That's it, Dad! That's why the King opened the door for me to go to Forever Snow Land. I was hurting so bad, he wanted me to feel better about Snowy!"

"And this King helped you feel better, Elisha?" asked his mom.

"So much better, Mom. That's the way the King is," said Elisha.

"Well," explained Mom, "I don't know about *that* king, but I do know King Jesus. He cares so much that, after He left, He sent us a Comforter, remember?"

"Yes," added Dad, "the Holy Spirit. When we allow Him, He comforts our spirits."

The wheels in Elisha's head started spinning. "That sounds like the *Blanket of Comfort* Old Man Snow gave me!"

"Well, yes, I suppose you could say the Holy Spirit is like our blanket of comfort. He is called The Comforter. He heals the things deep inside us, if we let Him," his dad said.

Elisha's eyes opened wide as he began to understand more. "I didn't use it until Old Snow explained it to me. When I wrapped up in it, I felt so much better. So... Good Kind King helped me." Elisha's brows turned into a frown as he tried to understand. "But why me? Out of all the little boys in the world, why me?"

"I can't answer that, Elisha, because I didn't have that experience. But I do know many times my Heavenly Father does things I don't deserve... just because! Because He loves me. And now that I think about it... I did pray and ask God to do whatever would help you through your pain."

"Yes, we both prayed that God would heal your heart," said his mom.

Elisha smiled at his parents. The look in their eyes told him that this was true.

Protection, Direction, and Power

Soon Elisha was thinking again. "So when we go through hard stuff, He always helps us?"

"If we let Him. Sometimes the hard stuff is because we didn't follow His directions," explained his dad.

"Directions, like in the Bible?"

"That's right, Elisha," said Mom. "At the hardest parts of my life, it was always faith in His words that got me through them. Some just can't seem to believe in a God who loves them if things aren't going perfect. Then when things are going well, they think they don't need Him. Others don't even try to use their faith."

"I had to have faith to get through lots of things in Snow Land!" said Elisha.

"Me too, Elisha. Many times He has shown me which way to go in my life because I trusted Him."

"I didn't know which way to go when I was looking for Snowy," Elisha said. "I walked so far and got so cold I would've frozen to death if it hadn't been for that investigating rabbit."

"A rabbit!" exclaimed his mom, a bit amazed at this sudden twist in the conversation.

"Yeah, that's what I thought, too, Mom. A crazy talking rabbit! He says boys are just trouble. But he did help me, even though he didn't want to! The first time, I just about froze to death, so he took me home and warmed me up. The next time, he saved me from the avalanche, even though we got buried alive and chewed out by Uncle Peter." Elisha laughed as he remembered, "Ha! Never thought I'd meet Peter Cottontail or Frosty the Snowman, either!"

Beth slightly raised her eyebrows and David looked just as puzzled, but Elisha didn't notice as he was deep in thought. "You know what? The King must have sent Jefferds to save me both times."

"Jefferds?" asked his mom.

"The rabbit," said Elisha, as if everyone should know that.

"Oh, yes, of course," said Beth, although very confused.

His dad spoke up. "Well, you know, God often helps us in surprising ways, so... I suppose He could use a rabbit, too," he reasoned.

"Even a rude, know-it-all rabbit?" laughed Elisha.

"I imagine so! Was he really rude?"

"He was way, way rude and impatient, too! But he did have a good heart," said Elisha, fondly remembering his rabbit friend with a smile.

"I'd like to meet this Jefferds. Sounds like he's not the normal cute and furry little rabbit," said his dad.

"Oh, trust me, Dad, he's not! You can't meet him though. People aren't allowed in Snow Land," Elisha said, as if explaining to a child. Seeing his dad's curious look at him, he added, "Yeah, I know, I was there, but I was, umm... what's that word?"

"An exception?" asked his dad.

"Yeah, that's it. I was an exception," Elisha said.

"That, you are. You're a very exceptional young man," his dad teased.

"There you go with your puns again, David," Beth said with an eye roll. David just gave a good-natured shrug and a grin.

Real Love

"Dad, there was something else. Snowy could only stay in Snow Land *if he let go of his past*, but... that was the part with me in it! I wasn't bad for Snowy, was I?"

"No, what he had with you wasn't bad. Maybe it was just time for a change. Changes are pretty hard to accept sometimes," his dad said.

"Snowy couldn't be a part of Snow Land until I quit hanging onto him. So... I gave him up, and that's when he really changed. He got his Forever smile and a Forever life."

His mom was realizing how deeply Elisha had been affected by all this. "Sounds like you showed what real love is, Elisha—doing the right thing, even though it had to be the hardest thing you ever did," said Beth.

"Elisha, we're so proud of you. It's like you've grown ten years older overnight," his dad said, patting him on the back.

"Yep, it was crazy, Dad. To find Snowy, I had to hang on and not give up," said Elisha, talking like a wise old man, "but then *after* I found him, I had to *let go*! That was very hard..."

"Well, I imagine so. But when things are hardest, that's when we trust the One Who knows best," said Beth quietly.

"And never give up, right, Dad? Just like I didn't give up on finding Snowy?" asked Elisha.

"Right. Love never gives up or quits, just like you and your Snowy," said David.

Elisha smiled. "And like God! He doesn't give up on us, does He?" asked Elisha.

"He doesn't, not even when we make wrong choices," answered his dad. "And when things don't go our way, we don't give up. We trust and have faith God will work it out."

"You mean... like when my snowman melted? Iri says to always have faith, no matter what!"

"Iri?" asked his dad.

"Yeah, Iri, short for a name I can't say. She was the snowflake who helped me find my Faith. Echo helped, too!" Elisha smiled as he stopped to remember his friends. He didn't see the shocked look on his parents' faces. "I really got in a mess when I worried or complained. Words have power, so I learned to say words of Faith instead. Our faith is in God, isn't it, Dad?"

David shook his head, finding it hard to believe what he was hearing. He didn't understand these crazy things Elisha was saying, but whatever had happened had sure helped his son's faith.

"Faith, huh? By the way, how'd you get so smart?" he teased, tousling Elisha's curly blonde hair.

"Same way as you, Dad. God made us that way, of course!" Elisha answered.

"He sure did, but... if you want to see *perfect*," he said, nodding towards Beth with a wink to Elisha, "you'll have to look at your mom!"

"Oh, David!" said Beth blushing. "None of us will see perfect until we get to heaven!"

"And I'm going there!" cheered Elisha, raising his fist high up in the air.

Mollie, who had been sitting at their feet at the table, spoke up, "Woof! Woof!"

"Mollie says, me, too!" laughed Elisha.

"Me, three," joked David.

"I make four!" Beth chimed in happily, not wanting to be left out.

"Four, plus God, equals—in-fin-i-ty!" Elisha sang dramatically.

"Whoa! Infinity! Listen to our mathematician, here," teased his dad.

Mollie gave four more barks. "That's right, four, Mollie, but don't demonstrate infinity!" warned David. "Barking forever would not be good!"

They all agreed, laughing once again. Each of them loved being a part of the Winters family fun, especially Elisha Zachary Winters.

The First Zachary

Then Elisha remembered something else. "Hey, Dad, by the way, didn't I have another grandfather, a long time ago... named Zachary?"

"Let's see. You must mean... way back, there was a Zachary James Winters."

"Yeah, that's the one! Dad, were there any family stories about his being sad, like me, when his snowman melted?"

"Hmmm," said his dad, crossing his arms and putting one hand up to cup his chin. "I think I remember my dad, Zachary, the one you're named after, telling about his great, great grandfather having that problem, much like what happened to you."

"I thought so," said Elisha.

"Oh? How did you know about that? I don't remember ever talking about it. In fact, I'd almost forgotten it myself."

"Oh, I kinda figured it out from something Old Man Snow told me about," Elisha answered.

His dad and mom looked questioningly at each other, but said nothing.

"But that long ago Zachary – Did he stay sad for always?" Elisha asked.

"Well, if I remember the story correctly, it took him a long, long time, but yes, he finally did get over it," answered his dad.

"Oh, good."

"Why do you ask, son?"

"Oh, I'd like to know more about my grandpas I was named after."

"Hey, David," said his mom, "didn't your dad find an old diary, where someone in the family wrote about that? I'll bet he still has it."

"That's right, honey. Would you like us to look that up sometime, Elisha?"

"Oh, yes, I would!" he cried. His eyes shone bright with the thought of reading something Old Man Snow's Builder, his own great, great, great grandfather had written.

David glanced out the window. "Oh, look," he said, "it's snowing again."

"Whoa!" said Elisha, running to the window. All three of them squeezed together with Elisha standing in front to watch the falling snow.

"It's so beautiful—our favorite time of year!" Beth said softly as they watched. The large fluffy flakes falling to the ground were quickly creating a blanket of snow.

"This could be a good, deep snow!" said David excitedly.

Soaked in Reality?

"And oh, I just remembered!" Beth said as she went quickly to the back porch. "There is something I wanted to ask you about, Elisha." She pulled a scarf out of a cabinet drawer and walked back in, holding it up. "I found this hanging in the mudroom this morning. Did you want to keep it?"

"Yeah, Mom, that's Snowy's. I'll keep it, but just for old times' sake, because I don't need it to remember Snowy. He's in my heart," said Elisha, smiling as his thoughts returned fondly to Snowy.

"I thought so," said Beth, smiling and handing it to him. "I did notice, though, there were a lot of crumbs on the scarf. Have you been hoarding cookies in it or something?" she teased.

"Yeah, sorta," Elisha said. In a hurry to not have to explain that cookie, he turned and called to Mollie who was waiting, more than ready to take off with him. "Come on, girl, let's go play!"

Immediately, Mollie sprang into action, running back and forth before turning to wait for Elisha.

David put his arm around Beth as they watched the two pals run off to play in the family room. "Beth, I feel like we've been tying up some loose ends tonight for our son."

"Yes, David, and you know, it's so great to see Elisha happy again after such a rough time," said Beth.

David smiled with contentment. "I agree, honey. For a while there, after his snowman melted, I was pretty concerned."

"I know, me, too! Even more so when his teacher called about him last night," said Beth. "At least he's okay now."

"And he felt like playing again this morning."

"Oh, David, I forgot! I wanted to ask Elisha about his soaked snowsuit I found hanging in the mudroom this morning. I mean, the pants, gloves, boots, *even a black bird feather* in his coat pocket... everything was just soaking wet!"

"What's so unusual about that?" asked David.

"Well, honey, the last time he wore them was yesterday. They should have been dry by now, after hanging by the heat register all night. But instead, they were sopping wet!"

"Did you forget he played with Tim this morning?"

"But I found them soaked early this morning *before* they played out! That's why he wore his old snow pants to play with Tim." Pausing to think a second, she added, "I know this snowsuit was dry by bedtime last night, so why was it soaked first thing this morning?"

"Well, that is strange, but we can just ask him later."

"I suppose," she agreed. "And oh, you should see the cute map I found in his jeans pocket. It said 'Forever Snow Land' on it... Wait. Wasn't that the name of the place he went to in his dream?"

"Why, yes, I believe that is what he called it," said David. "I'd like to see it."

"Yeah. Pretty good drawing for a kid. Almost as if he'd been there..."

***

Outside the Winters house, swirls of snow enveloped the pine trees briefly then danced across the fields. As carefree laughter echoed in the distance, the same watching Eyes that had planned and overseen everything smiled with great pleasure.

Elisha never did forget his best friend, Snowy. In later years he built many more snowmen, and when they melted away, it was okay, for he knew it wasn't really the end. He knew that...

Somewhere …

in that place where well-loved snowmen play and make silly jokes amid snowflakes…

there's a snowman who is special, who has a heart beating,

because of love.

The best snowmen really do have a heart in

The End.

Forever Snowman with Heart

Appendix

Snowmen Language

*A*fter arriving in Snow Land for their Forever Life, new snowmen must learn how to speak. They talk and act very childishly for a long time. Although more mature, older snowmen's language is still hard to understand because of so many of the same-sounding words.

These guides are to help the reader understand the meaning of "snow" words:

1. Words ending with a long "o" are often pronounced "snow".

   Word: Meaning:
   "Sno" -   *so, no, or snow*
   "snoh" - *oh*
   "snow"-   *know (Note-Sometimes "snow" just means snow)*

2. "Snu" *(pronounced 'snoo')* is often used for "you" (but not before another "snow" word). Two words beginning with "sn-" (as in snu and snow) would not be used together, since it would be too hard to say one after the other.
   Eg. Snowmen wouldn't say "Snu snow?" meaning, "You know?" Instead, he would probably say, *"Snu know"* or *"Ya snow."*

3. New snowmen (like Fluffy) say, "my" instead of "I."
   Eg. *"My go," for "I go."*

4. Slush, being from the mountains, says "Y'all", meaning, "You all." It can mean one, or many, depending on who he is talking to.

Wintry Acknowledgments

*T*he joy of WINTERTIDE 2015-16 came to me from these professionals with busy work schedules, who read and endorsed this book:

Kevin Elmore, MA Psychotherapist, Pine Rest Christian Mental Health Services, (Grand Rapids, MI)

Paul Palpant, retired Elementary Principal at Lenawee Christian School, (Adrian, MI)

Cathy Jenkins, Certified Massage Therapist, Christian Mission Board Member (Adrian, MI).

Thank you for being my SNOW ANGELS by giving generously of your time to write such gracious endorsements. I SN'OWE you a lot.

HAIL to New York's SNOW KING of editing, Janet Spencer King, for your expertise, counsel and edit. After nine months of labor in editing, we finally gave "birth" to this SNOWMAN book with heart. Although I did not ICE SKATE through the deleting process, in time I really did learn. For not FREEZING out on me, through the many bizarre COLD SNAPS of computer problems, I thank you, Janet.

In a DEEP FREEZE over finding a cover designer, Janet suggested Lisa Hainline, who captured my vision perfectly. Lisa, your excellent rough drafts made it difficult to decide until I saw "the one." Thanks for giving this book the perfect "face" and praying over your work. You are the best.

As blinding BLIZZARDS covered my path to publishing, each time proved to be a blessing in disguise. A total WHITEOUT, however, panicked me when the only copy of my working manuscript disappeared from my computer. Edward Pokryfsky at Melron Electronics (Tecumseh, MI) dug me out of a FROZEN state several times to get me moving again. Thank you and God bless you, Ed, for your many SNOW RESCUES.

Happy SNOWFLAKE thanks to Brad and Courtney of Image Gallery (Adrian, MI) who burned my pencil illustrations to a disc. Honest enough to tell me I could do it myself, I preferred to have the pros do it.

Sparkling and GLISTENING "SNOW" thanks to my project representative, Jennifer Kasper, for her kind help and to Xulon Press for publishing The Best Snowmen Have A Heart.

A GLACIER of appreciation follows to special friends, who all proved to be my "cup of hot chocolate" on a COLD WINTER day:

To Cathy Jenkins, who read and critiqued nearly every version of my manuscript, I slide an ICEBERG of gratitude. Your wise input on my BLACK ICE days was a SNOWBANK of immeasurable support. Sharing my vision that no one should be SNOWBOUND by hurts or FROZEN without God's love and goodness, you prayed over and believed strongly in this manuscript's purpose and message. Faithful friend, I shall always be indebted to you.

Brad Weekley, who walked me through DEEP SNOWDRIFTS of computer issues, always ended every episode cheerfully with, "There you go, kiddo." He persisted when we were both "SNOWED" by strange technological glitches. Bountiful SNOWDRIFTS of blessings to Brad, and to Shirley Weekly, as well, for friendship and Shirley's initially "volunteering" Brad's help (as wives are wont to do).

Kathy Elmore, my "butterflies and rainbows" friend, listened to my trials, prayed and believed in my vision for this book. For your child-like faith even on darkest days, I offer a FROSTED SILVER BELL of thanks. (We will always ring the "Bell of Truth.")

I send fond SNOWTHANKS to Rev. Edmund Burkey (very influential on me as a young woman,) and to his gracious wife, Jean. So many times Jean's words of complimentary encouragement to write have returned to me over the years. Now 96, Rev. Burkey's kindness, (like my father's), his teasing and mischievous remarks still make me smile. In loving remembrance of both, (My dear Rev. Burkey joined Jean in Heaven before I published this book) I offer a bouquet of SNOWY WHITE Eidelweiss flowers (as Eidelweiss was Jean's last request of music for me to play for her).

Neither SLEET, HAIL nor SNOW could distract me from my treasured family, *many of whom were lovingly woven into this story:*

There's "s'no" way to adequately thank my real life SNOWMAN HERO and husband, Larry Sneed. You saved me from an AVALANCHE of duties, enabling me to write and edit, as well as be a caregiver to my mom. When my publishing path seemed COLD and FROZEN, your SNOW FORT of support cheered me on. Thanks for ever trying to turn this bumpy TOBOGGAN RIDE into a more pleasant SLEIGH RIDE.

I would be remiss not to mention my mother Helen's ICE CASTLE of strong love and support for me, even through her illnesses. Sadly she, who requested the first copy of this book, did not live to see this through to completion. I remember her laughing at the cocky, know-it-all Jefferds character, even when she felt miserable. An ever-loving SNOW QUEEN of a mom, who always wanted to help make things better, she often threw a SNOWBALL of silly fun into difficult days. *(The humorous parts of this story are reminiscent of my mother's spunk and sense of humor.)*

A SNOW SCULPTURE of tribute to my father, the King of Kindness my whole life; I truly loved, admired and respected him with my whole heart. His gentle, easy, and loving manner made it easy to believe in a Heavenly Father. By example, he taught me **Kindness** *(as reflected in Good Kind King in the book.)*

My caring parents always modeled Love, Goodness and Compassion to others. *(Perhaps that's why their **virtues** are such strong components of this book.)* I was blessed with parents who provided the kind of home every child should have. Because of the warmth Helen and James D. Vance passed on to me, I am who I am, and I shall never have a COLD, FROZEN heart.

A "Harley" ICE SCULPTURE goes to my one and only "favorite brother," Jim Vance. Always keeping me humble, Jim makes me laugh, teases, and gets away with things no one else can. Little did you know that our talks gave me needed respite, warming and cheering me during CHILLY days of this writing. You're so special to me. *(Your no-nonsense, common sense, often mischievous manner, layering over a kind, tender side, were somewhat reflected in my favorite character, Jefferds.)*

JACK FROST himself could not withstand my daughter Christy's sunshine on my FROSTBITTEN days as an author. Love you, Little Stinky. Thanks for listening. Her husband Howard Crick's thoughtfulness often surprised, gladdened and restored my spirit. His polite, sincere "thank you's" for everything, awoke me to the importance of verbalizing gratitude—everytime. Laughter you both supplied were and are my good medicine. *(Both gratitude and laughter play strong parts in this novel.)*

Also bringing delight to me like FRESH FALLEN SNOW, are my son, Nick Sneed, who has tugged on my heartstrings since my first sight of him, and my SNOW CRYSTAL, grand daughter Kaylynn, *(the basis for Elisha's friend in this story)* who is lively, bright and sparkling like a crystal. *(Kaylynn, may you always have Faith and beauty inside, as well as out, like Iridescence, the Snowflake.)* Nick's maturity and selflessness as a father are much like *Elisha's devotion and love on point in this story.* I always stopped writing for your heartwarming visits.

A SNOW MOUNTAIN of praise goes to grandson Zachary Waters, for being, "you." Your whole life, you have been so wonderfully loving, kind, and considerate. *If my main character, Elisha, seems too good to be true, one need only look at Zach, my inspiration for him.* Oh, that every child could have the love that has been poured into you. You are proof that love brings great rewards. My only grand child for twenty-four years, Zach and his thoughtful and sweet wife, Kaylie, (first nurse in the family) have given to me my first great grandchild, Zoey Waters. I look forward to many memorable, SNOW-DELIGHTFUL moments with her.

The caring, laughter, and joy from all of you have centered me during the WINTER SQUALLS of this intense writing period. If I searched the FRIGID North Pole and the Continent of Antarctica, I couldn't find adequate POLAR thanks for any of you, any more than I can thank a God who loved me enough to entrust this message and vision to me.

Note: *Great nephews, Gavin, Austin and Colton Ekle and great nieces, Alexis, Mya, Sydney, and Chloe Vance—although minor characters in the story, are definitely major in my heart.*

About the Author

*H*aving had a lifelong love of writing, (short stories, poems and plays) Frances Sneed wrote her first novel, *The Best Snowmen Have A Heart*, following a twenty year career working with at risk children in Tecumseh, Michigan.

The year 2016 also marked twenty-four years as pianist/choir director for Sunday morning services at Maurice Spear Campus, a youth detention and treatment facility in Adrian, Michigan. She considers it her favorite ministry.

Born in Elizabethton, Tennessee but living most of her life in southeast Michigan, Frances' own love of snow and snowmen led her to choose a snowy setting and subject for this story with many parallels to the Christian life. A strong believer that laughter, loving, forgiving, and guarding our thought life are essential to healthy living, these were incorporated into her writing.

Married to Larry Sneed since 1967, they have a daughter, Christy Crick, a son, Nicholas Sneed, and two grandchildren, Kaylynn Sneed and Zachary Waters. A great grand daughter, Zoey Waters was born in December of 2016. In addition to serving on the Christian Mission Board and at her church as a council member and pianist, she also prepares weekly music for the Campus Choir. Frances' personal life is full and very busy, as well, with family, writing, and rose gardening. *In spite of the busyness of life, she knows in her heart, her Lord must come first. It is with His guidance and daily presence that she finds life filled with joy, blessings and His goodness, even in the midst of hardships.*

CPSIA information can be obtained
at www.ICGtesting.com
Printed in the USA
FFOW02n1212280717
38273FF